CW00521719

ON SEAS OF REAPERS

BENJAMIN REES

To Jenny,

Hope you enjoy the Adventure!

Ben

On Seas of Reapers

Copyright © Benjamin Rees, 2023
Cover Design by Benjamin Rees
Edited by Atlanta Revill
All Rights Reserved

No Parts of this book may be used or reproduced in any manner whatsoever without written permission except in the case of brief quotations embodied in critical articles or reviews. This book is a work of fiction. Names, characters, businesses, organisations, places, events and incidents are either the product of the author's imagination or are used fictitiously. Any resemblance to actual persons, living or dead, events, or locations is entirely coincidental.

Hardback ISBN: 978-1-7384092-0-4

Trade Paperback ISBN: 978-1-7384092-1-1

E-book ISBN: 978-1-7384092-2-8

For the people closest to my heart – may they forever dwell there

ON SEAS OF REAPERS

Act 1:
A Swirling Squall

1

In a sea far to the west, a pale moon straddles a darkening ocean, casting a dim radiance across the pitch of night. Water glistens in parts, adding to the silence and whispering winds. At times like this, all men should be wary of what lies harbouring within their hearts as all desires and wanting can be plagued by whispers. Nevertheless, the winds on this night blow cold and make men's stomachs churn.

On the edge of night, a ship departs an island under ghostly sails. Inside, nestled away within the depths of his cabin, sits a tall, bald man, his head imprisoned between his enormous, calloused hands; his thoughts sent sailing upon miles of crashing seas and swirling headaches. He isn't alone, however. The noises his crew make as they dance amongst him are almost deafening as they fling themselves across the room. Shaking their booze filled tankards, their jaunting, rattling against warping floorboards; rancid, ugly faces, appearing and disappearing within shadows and flickers of blood-red candlelight. He wanted to cut half of them down just for being near him, and it took every fibre of his being to restrain himself as their laughter bit at him. And so, Atlas Vain: Pirate Captain, raised his head, scratching at his short black beard, barely seen as it tried to escape through the small jail-like gaps between his fingers. A crystal-amulet swung about his neck. Shaped as a crescent moon, it's two dagger-like edges ebbed as if it were the sea, waning as one colour bled into the next. Like his thoughts, it too longed for release as it began to rest against his olive skin, glimmering with a faint indigo light. It wasn't the only thing lurking in the darkened maelstrom of the captain's mind; from those platonic shades a creature peered at him with the sharp yellow eyes of a snake. Laughing. Taunting. Reaching from within a menacing twilight as it scoured the dark. It was a cursed, foul-some creature, with spikes for teeth and scales for skin. It refused to die, and it stalked his dreams.

Atlas heard some of the men snarl at him from across the table as he tried to focus on the map that laid in front of him in the stead of a dinner-plate:

"Oi! Captain, when are we getting paid!"

Alas, that was just the problem! They had no money, no treasure, and at best a fearful crew, dragged to their island hideaway by the whites of their knuckles. He required a solution as the amulet swung impatiently. Gritting his teeth, the captain was about to utter a response when the faint light illuminating from the amulet, began to grow brighter, causing the crew to murmur in confusion amongst themselves. The browned, burned scroll before him began shifting and altering the symbols that lay upon its surface, scattered with red ink, as if scribed with blood.

At last! He thought, his eyes widening in bewilderment. He had missed the last window of opportunity, barely a month before when he had acquired the map – secretly wondering if what that lecherous Troll had told him had been true – that the map would only awaken with the light of the month's first crescent moon. But now a wave of excitement washed over him, and Atlas could feel himself begin to itch, gazing at the unveiling wonder. Slowly, the map revealed several pictures from its brunt and dusty exterior as each layer peeled away. For three weeks they had waited, unsure they had even found the right island. He had had to guess at their present location from a fleeting and disappearing glance - something the crew did not take kindly to, given the treasure had become another one of his obsessions.

The island on the map was shaped akin to a shattered bottle; a broken, crumbling podium was also visible, flanked by a circular stone door with runes carved deep within. Cold moonlight simmered in silver abundance through the high windowpanes as they rocked along the bay of the island and out to sea, making the room seem murky and as though dancing ghosts lay within, fluttering like wisps. As this was taking place, a member of the crew shouted yet again from the mid-section of the long dining table positioned in the very centre of the cabin. The candlelight highlighted the man who had called out as he stood, wiping a smear of chicken grease from his lips. He was a rat-faced weasel with bulging arms and a temper.

"Hey, Captain!" He shouted with zeal. "I *said* when are we 'gonna' get paid? The articles say -"

Atlas lifted his head ever so slightly, causing the man to hesitate before continuing his speech – though he had turned a few shades paler as the captain gazed across tattooed-covered arms. Atlas knew what the articles said. He wrote them: 'May every man earn his fair and justly earned reward'. As a policy, he had made sure every man sailing under him had learnt his tale; there would be no pandering as to who was in charge in Atlas' mind. The group of men assembled with him in his cabin had failed to learn this. Presently however, Atlas found himself ever engrossed in the drawings of the map as the pain in his head continued, and suddenly, the black mark pulsed. It was a vile thing that clung to the back of his neck, writhing as if it had been a freshly inflicted wound. The pirate growled in frustration, gritting his teeth yet again. He'd almost forgotten about the mark. Dormant for the better part of a week, it was a parting gift from his inevitable foe, the one with the eyes of a snake.

Still, the weasel-faced pirate continued to speak, boasting to the others, who listened intently. Atlas still paid them no mind. In anger, the pirate approached the dais at the foot of the captain's throne-like chair at the head of the table.

"Are you listening?" The pirate spat.

He was now next to Atlas, bent down so close to the captain's ear that he made sure he could hear every breath of pestilence, a knife to his throat to make sure of his intent.

"Some of us have had enough!"

The noise around them grew louder, as some of the other pirates concurred. A splitting pain then flew across the captain's crown and his heartbeat began to rise, the black mark making its presence known yet again. He knew he needed to hurry, and his eyes seemingly closed for that of a moment. Even with a chilled blade pressed against his skin, and pain swirling in his head, Atlas' only real concern was that of his goal – he could see those yellow eyes staring back at him from shrouded darkness. Cold crooked teeth, crimson stains spattering the tips, a monstrous cackling bellow...Only one Giant left now.

"I heard you." The captain groaned - he had tried to ignore the vagrant.

Only one giant left...One Giant in the entire world...

"Then I suggest you -" The pirate retorted, but he was too late.

Atlas too, had had enough. In a swift movement, he pushed the blade free from his neck, letting his precious map drift to the floor as his fingers enveloped the cold iron. The cut had stung for a brief second as he pulled the knife from the fiend, but that was of no real concern as he just as quickly unleashed his own upon the traitor's throat. In a single, furious slash, Atlas' arm was soaked in blood and the weasel slumped over, whimpering as the light dwindled from his eyes. Grasping at his wound, he'd looked perplexed, but could he really have counted on anything less? Every gruesome battle the captain had ever faced was illustrated on his own chest, scrawled in black ink wherever his own hand and a mirror could reach. He glanced up and down his bloody arm and torso, wearing nothing but a darkly cloaked sleeveless jacket, rolled up trousers and his effects.

Atlas smirked as he bent down to pick up the map, being careful to keep it away from the fresh blood pooling beside it. That was one wretched dissident dealt with he thought, as he returned his ruby-pommelled blade to its sheath. As he stood to place the map upon the table, once again, he grew tired, his head throbbing. He had purposely invited those stirring up trouble to his cabin – he couldn't be so direct as to go to his quartermaster, as it would've inevitably drawn in more flies and Atlas did not have the time to swat them all away. Instead, he'd wine them, dine them, fatten them up, and eventually quell the unrest lurking amongst his web before more spiders came – so much for restraining himself. He watched their faces, gaunt jaws tightening as if they were stuck, ashen faces now felled silent.

'Captain's done it again' some of them spoke afterward, as the party simmered to a whisper; glaring, ghostly visages gazed back with distraught countenance, quickly drinking up their ale or grog – whichever they deemed more palatable, fearful of death.

"What're we to do now?" One whispered.

"Has he gone completely insane at last?" They spoke, seeing that the captain had begun to nurse his headache with wine.

"Brother?" A voice abruptly asked from the shadows.

As if on cue, the door to the cabin creaked open, and the pirate captain looked to where the voice had come from.

"Silence, the lot of you!" He shouted, causing the backdrop of whispers to draw eerily quiet. "Be done with your mutterings, Ye dogs!"

"Oh? You're always so harsh on them."

At the other end of the room, Atlas' brother stepped out of the long shadows. He was smaller than his sibling – much closer to five feet than the six of Atlas. With short, shaved black hair and smooth elegant features. He strove into the large cabin they both shared. Unlike his brother, he was clean-shaven, but still had the same bright, piercing blue eyes, making them both dreadfully frightening to whomever they opposed.

"Orion." Atlas grumbled, swallowing the last of his drink. "For fuck's sake, what do you want? You know better than to disturb me."

Orion drew closer to the flickering torchlight.

"As if you weren't disturbed enough." He smirked, motioning to the freshly dispatched sailor sprawled across his brother's feet, still faintly twitching and labouring for breath.

Atlas gave Orion a weak smile as he realised the fatal strike had caused the man to pass out. The band of pirates that sat around the long table grew restless as they spoke.

"Looks like you left one alive." Mocked Orion. "That's not like you, brother. I would have never been so careless if not on purpose - you're getting sloppy. Want me to take care of your mess?"

"No!" Snapped Atlas, quickly interjecting.

He once again swiped his hand across his forehead and groaned, leaving a red smear along his brow. The wine wasn't working. There was only one singular cure for his headaches and his precious supply was dwindling.

"I can handle it." He said after a while. "Is she awake?"

"Yes." his brother smiled. "And it appears the information we bought was correct as well – Gill spotted a Navy ship along their supply route."

A jackal-toothed grin crawled across the pirate captain's face. He had had enough of the waiting, of the running. Everything was finally coming together. The muttering about the room began once more from those that did not value their lives.

"Kaine!" They began to whisper across the table. "He's coming for us, but he's not the only one!"

Atlas gave them a bloodcurdling glare, he wanted to punish them for mentioning that name, but he kept uncharacteristically silent when the giant was mentioned. The only reason he'd spared their rotting lives was because Orion was present and hadn't heard what they said, moreover, he was about to teach the rest of them a lesson they would not soon forget. He would have to keep his secret regarding the monster for a little while longer though.

On his right-hand side, sat a tiny bowl of dark, black powder with purple flecks speckled throughout. Whoever controlled a supply of this illusive powder, seemingly controlled destiny itself - if only for a small time. Without hesitation, Atlas snatched the bowl in one hand, and proceeded to greedily suck the powder up through his nostrils. Feeling every speck course within, he tossed the little bowl back over his head. The ceramic smashed against the window, its broken shards clattering down joining that of countless others in a mass-grave-like pile. With Atlas clenching his knuckles, a crackle shot across the room, extinguishing the wavering candles in one fell swoop. Black storm clouds gathered outside the tall window, amercing the pale crescent moon; the only light remaining being the sparks of violet that appeared in Atlas' palm and the indigo radiating from within the amulet.

"Good." Atlas muttered.

In the distance, thunder rumbled on the horizon and the sea roared as if it were ripped in two. Staggering from the table, a few of his pirates clambered for the cabin door in a panicked rush. Without leaving his throne, Atlas reached down, taking hold of the weasel he had felled earlier in one solid grasp. He knew exactly how to set an example. The dying man coughed as Atlas rose to drag him across the table, scattering food and goblets in his wake.

Outside, upon the mammoth deck of his vessel, the remainder of Atlas' skeleton crew had gathered. There were forty in total, still substantially large by all accounts. Every single one was scarred, battered, and bruised. He'd had Orion round up all that he needed from their island base, with the remaining one hundred and sixty of their party staying there. Atlas only cared for the handful. Almost a quarter of them he knew were mutinous, but his next act would put an end to that. Atlas gazed up to the black sky, the dying man's hair still in his vice-like grip. Rain poured down as he pulled the man along the sodden deck. The weasel had lost every ounce of his strength, now only pawing at his wound, dribbling a slimy trail from the cabin. They were just two miles outside the mainland, approaching the cusp of the Navy's trade route; the winds were blowing cold, and Atlas could feel the ripe sea air swell within him.

Tightening his grip, Atlas ordered for the chains securing the hold to be cut. The crew gave him a worried look as two large brutes, Taylor and Brent, came forward with hefty battle-axes and struck at the chains with all their weighted might.

"Are you sure, captain?" Someone from the clumped group asked nervously. "She's up, and not been fed!"

Atlas gazed down at the man he was holding, as the chains broke apart with a metallic, almost thunderous scraping across the deck. Both axemen were breathing heavily as they stole a fearful glance into the black pit below. A roar shook the ship, but it was not the roar of thunder from above that most expected. It caused the skeleton crew to look to the gate of the hold, a devious amber eye starring up at them. Atlas laughed.

"Hello, my darling!" He called, the amber eye moving to rest upon him. "How are you feeling today?"

The beast erupted once again in reply, making flashes of light race across the sky in frantic arcs. Orion then appeared behind him.

"Dinner and a show, eh?" He said to his brother.

Atlas gazed back at his sibling for just a moment, moving to address the crew and holding the dying man in front of him for all to see.

"Some of you, it seems, have doubted me. Have I not always provided for you as if you were my own?"

The crew murmured and nodded in response.

"Have we not seen together treasure and gold so abundant that it has filled the halls of this very ship? I offer you power, gentlemen, power to change the very world – to hunt the last of giant-kind with me, instead of cowering like dogs! The great storm is upon us..."

It was then that the black mark on the back of his neck pulsed yet again, and out of the corner of his eye, Atlas saw his brother rub his own bandaged hand. Some of the crew did the same, Atlas knew he needed to draw their attention away before their true trials began.

"So let this be a lesson to all that doubt and cower!"

The pirate captain then let his fingers loose, dropping the traitor into the hold far below. The lifeless man fell into the dark pit. He did not scream as he did not have time, subsequently swallowed by the roaring of the beast held within. A moment passed and none of the crew dared questioned the captain as they stood there on the semi-rotting wooden deck.

"Anyone else?" Asked Orion.

No one uttered a word.

"Excellent! Now make way, we sail as my brother commands!"

However, Atlas was already returning to the cabin, eager to plan his next steps as his brother gave chase.

"So?" Asked Orion, his arm stretched across the frame of the doorway as he caught up to him. "When are you going to talk to me?"

Atlas grunted.

"Now is not the time, little brother."

"Then when is?" Orion held up his bandaged hand, pulling down the stained fabric to show a weeping black mark of his own.

"We all have these, and I do not know how. Everyone else seems to remember, so why is it I cannot? What aren't you telling me? Everyone is so afraid that they dare not murmur a single word!"

Atlas was about to reply, when a crew member called out from the gargantuan rigging, that a ship had been sighted. Atlas smiled maniacally, turning from his brother, and rushing to the wheelhouse where he sat astride another massive throne-like chair. His guests had finally arrived and again, he smiled. Cracking both his hands as he sat in his chair, violet sparks flew once more from the edge of his fingers and ascended to the dark sky above.

With the crew confirming that the speck far ahead of them was the ship they wanted, Atlas began to brew the perfect storm to welcome them. He looked to the map, it being fastened safely to his belt, and then to the amulet; he could have sworn he'd heard a slight whisper escape from it, if it hadn't have been for the relentless rain and swirling winds.

Only a few pieces now remained to the puzzle he sought. The Navy had what he wanted, and he was going to take it.

2

The Inspectre sailed towards the nearest port-town from the west, bobbing up and down upon the early morning waves against a backdrop of misty, muted skies. So far, not a single thing had gone wrong on their long journey. The captain sighed to himself as he gazed through his bronzed and crooked spyglass.

"Who is out there, I wonder?" He whispered, feeding his own paranoia as he clung to the side-rail to which his deckchair had been propped.

His face was as cold and grey as the weather, looking out onto the dark waters as he scanned the horizon. Gusts of icy torment flew across his nape, and he shuddered at its chilling bite, hoping it would be the last of the foul weather that had followed them for the better part of an hour as they arose from the strange gloom of dawn. Nevertheless, he set the spyglass down to pervade the crew, looking upon them with worry. It was all too silent.

Posed next to him was a bear of a man; Theodore Rockwell boasted an enormous brown beard that hung down to the midpoint of his neck, and as the first officer to the crew, donned a Navy uniform all in white. The blue trim adorning the edges of his cloak ruffled in the wind.

"You thinking about Adira again, Captain?" Rockwell asked, his hawk-like eyes piercing the captain with a contrasting comforting, warm glow.

The captain gripped the side-rail tightly, turning behind him to look at his second – had the man realised he'd gone too far?

The day had an ominous air to it, but to talk of monsters! Captain Robbinson grimaced to himself: Mermaids were arguably the worst of all the creatures scouring the dark sea, dragging people to their depths, never to return. Adira was a monster such as this, having almost killed him with a single kiss many years ago at the edge of a waterfall. Joining the Navy soon after, he'd never been able to love another since. He imagined her luminous dark hair and beauty shifting within the deep recesses, it troubled him almost as much as the current darkness itself. There were no sea monsters lurking now thankfully - he hadn't seen any at least, but that was always the case with creatures, and his eyesight wasn't as good as it once was.

They were all afraid of sea monsters.

"Even those ghastly Troll creatures haven't dared to put in an appearance, you know?" He retorted with a wry smile after a moment, changing the subject.

Rockwell had just as much history with the Trolls as Robbinson had with the mermaids and again, the captain shuddered at the thought as the first officer glared at him. Trolls were bad news. Vast, snarling creatures, that usually made themselves known under the blanket of night. They stole away children, sailors, pirates, and wealthy folk; pretty much anyone or anything that took their fancy. Then Robbinson wondered as his old brain ticked away 'Would they come to this region of the sea for what his crew carried?' The captain wasn't quite sure, and he hoped above all, to see a tall shining light over the horizon, but there was nothing, and the sails rippled on in ghostly silence.

They'd been commissioned by the North Sea Trading Company to deliver perishables and supplies to an island on the very edge of the Leon Archipelago, a place dangerously near the infamous central sea: The Devil's Doorstep. Robbinson hated that place. For the last fifteen years it had been a haven for creatures and outlaws of all kinds, ruled by five separate pirate crews whose captains were known collectively as The Demon Five.

Regardless, Robbinson left as soon as he got his orders – better that than to lose his job. He had more sense than to question the Company. If he had learnt one thing from all his years in the Navy, it was to never challenge the higher-ups. He breathed deeply in and out a few times to calm his nerves and sighed. Hopefully it would soon be over. Suddenly, it started to rain.

"I'll need a report." He said as he watched the navigator of the crew creep nervously along the dampening deck, aghast as others worked around him, his blonde hair twisting in the wind.

"We're still down a sailor thanks to that recruit – you realise no one has even seen him! Ill the entire time!"

"Ship's doctor has, sir." Rockwell grumbled, jibbing the captain for his earlier remark.

Robbinson was not impressed, his mood had been tainted by all the talk of sea monsters, Trolls, and horrid weather.

"Just see to it will you." He barked, trying to push the thought of monsters from his mind – he was getting far too old for this.

"Your will, Sir." Rockwell saluted and went about his work, heading to the hold to check on the cargo, somewhat annoyed the captain had decided to bring up the Trolls.

The subject was too heavy for him to bear, swearing under his breath so no one could hear. Eventually, he decided to call a few of the rookies lounging around the deck to check on the ship's doctor and his patient.

"Captain?" A young man asked.

"What is it, Mister Fryedai?" Groaned the captain, still irritated something was amiss, turning towards the ship's navigator.

"Well Sir, because of the wind, we should reach our destination a lot sooner than we thought." Fryedai stuttered.

Captain Robbinson flashed a look at Fryedai, giving him a wrinkly grin. Finally, there was some good news, and he looked back to the helmsman staffing the wheel, having to twist his fat neck to see. It seemed nothing was going to happen after all.

"Can you keep us on the straight and narrow, Mister Rivers?" He asked.

"I should be able to, Captain. Although these waves have become a bit choppy, I see no reason why Mister Fryedai should be wrong." Said the helmsman, his concentration growing as he spun his charge with more vigour.

Robbinson breathed a heavy sigh of relief.

"Good, I'm going up to the nest to take a look at the island." He muttered, slowly getting up from his chair.

"I've not been to Ale town before, I'd like to know what all the fuss is about."

Walking towards the mast, the captain saw the early morning sky had begun to grow darker from the earlier timid grey. Squinting his old eyes to see, he realised he had forgotten his spyglass. 'Odd?' He thought. Never had he once seen a sky turn to darkest night as he had then. It was as if the gods had struck the inkwell asunder, and suddenly, he was flung headfirst into the decking as an unexpected wave struck against the starboard side. Thunder bellowed overhead. Above, clouds spewed forth violet shards of lightning, making the already maddening wind groan further with rage. Sails flailed, tearing themselves apart in places, as onyx waves grew violent, hurtling the ship along rising crescents.

The captain looked up, astounded as he rubbed his head. 'What on all the seas was going on?' He thought. 'What bizarre weather was this?'

"Squall!" He heard the helmsman shout, though it seemed muffled and distorted.

One by one blurs of men in white began to unpack safety ropes from under the deck cannons, tying down their lines to whatever they could. In the sea around them, Robbinson glimpsed frequent flashes hurtling into the seabed, as he turned his head in a daze. The shards were striking either side of the ship. The captain looked back to the wheelhouse to see Rivers jostling as he tried to avoid the strikes. It was too late, however, as *The Inspectre* turned to avoid the darkening storm. Robbinson was amazed to see that not only had the storm appeared out of nowhere, but it also encompassed the entirety of the island, forming a terrifying wall.

Suddenly, a wave arched over them – a tremendous roar as its herald – drenching the captain head to toe in seawater. He made his way over to a cannon and unboxed a line for himself from underneath the housing. He fumbled as he tied the line around his waist, crawling back to the mast, where he was knocked over by yet another wave.

His mind raced as the onslaught continued.

Damn it all! He thought, gasping as water spewed uncontrollably from his mouth. He spied Rockwell continuing to bark orders as he emerged from the hold. Once he had crawled his way over, the Navy captain quickly grabbed his arm and pushed the man to one side, forcing him against the very heart of the ship, where his voice struggled to be carried over the deafening squall.

"Rockwell, you're the first officer; what is going on?"

"We have to lower the anchor!" The man shouted, his voice cutting through the wind more clearly.

Robbinson froze. They were besieged on all sides by thick, black clouds with nowhere to go. There was a tremendous surging screech and he turned to look over his shoulder. Just a little further beyond from where they sat, there was another bright flash, and a wave of water bounded directly towards them. They were done for, death approached.

* * *

Some minutes before, down below within the bowels of the ship, Ann stirred under the covers, pulling the coarse blanket over her head as far as she could. She hated being confined; the blanket itched, scratching irritatingly as it had done for weeks on end. She never did like getting up. The porthole window above her bed swung ajar, letting in the cold morning breeze and a spittle of rain – being located on the port side of the vessel, beneath the forecastle and aside the galley. Ann had caught the old captain groaning many times as gulls shrieked across the skies. 'Lucky him', she began to think as she wiped her brow. He got to go outside, breathe the air, and all she ever did was hide away in her cramped, stuffy cabin.

She thought about her reasons for doing this - joining the Navy, and, as she began to twist and turn, she had to admit that the lumpy bed was still far more pleasant than what she had been used to. Still, a safe place to sleep wasn't all bad. Ann remembered the songs her mother would sing to her as a child, before she tucked her away in a bed that was once her own: Tales of creatures, monsters and humanity, of gods, spirits and fairy-folk. None of those memories mattered now, they couldn't, Ann had a job to do. Besides, the creatures in the stories had never scared her anyway. She looked out of her window at the dark, ominous weather. Some of the cold rain had splashed upwards, lapping against the ship to form a pool on her window ledge, giving the grey water an icy reflection. A sudden feeling of uneasiness washed over her, dragging the pit of her stomach down. Was that thunder she heard, rolling in the distance and across the waves? The captain had mentioned that monsters would take men often enough, but the truth was, Ann had only ever met one monster in her life, and *he* was all too human. If monsters were out there, upon the dark horizon, then what form would they take? All her jumbled thoughts seemed meaningless as the doctor waddled over. She felt an abrupt tear come to her eye, but wiped it away before he could ever notice, using the ribbon she kept tied to her wrist.

She had to get out of bed now, the long voyage and confinement were forcing her to. Time wouldn't wait for her, not with so much at stake. They had to be at the island and soon!

"No, no!" The doctor insisted as she moved, looking around and behind his shoulder, a hurried urgency about him.

"You must stay down."

He had blonde hair, crooked glasses, and wore a regular white Navy cloak with blue trim around the cuffs.

"Why must I?" She whined, tired of being confined to the dusty and overbearing cabin.

She'd had enough of being kept away.

"You know I feel fine, right?"

After being stuck in the cabin for weeks, books were littered across the doctor's desk, almost toppling over from the high mountains of pages that were compiled in them. From what he'd said, he had been researching strange occurrences of creatures near and around his home island, always having a crazed look in his eye whenever it was mentioned.

"You know the reason." He said, looking to the door nervously, not wanting to be overheard.

Even though Ann wasn't satisfied with his reply, she played along, giving him a half-smile, trying her best to hide her disappointment. How much longer would she have to wait then? Everything she held dear was depending on her getting to that island! It was the reason she had joined the ship. It bit at her that the doctor couldn't afford her some simple privileges without the threat of him bring reprimanded by his superiors. He was about to say something, but was interrupted by a furious thumping on the door.

'Shit!' Ann thought. Had she been found out? She had agreed with Doctor Rudolf that he would tell the captain that *she* was in fact a *he*, and that she had contracted a rare illness. Since then, not once had anybody come to the door. Frightened, they both looked over with panicked eyes.

Doctor Rudolf quickly pressed his finger to his lips and told her to stay hidden. It worried her that now everything she risked would be for nothing. Joining the Navy had been a mistake for her, a silly, stupid mistake! Once again, she adjusted her covers, only this time pulling a gun from her side and pressing it to the sheets. Everyone had their price, and it was only thanks to Doctor Rudolf and his greed that Ann had managed to get this far, paying him off to keep quiet. She believed she wasn't a terrible person, but she had connections. Connections to people who would want her dead. Suspecting the North Sea Trading Company of commissioning the journey from the whispers she'd heard through her cabin window, Ann knew the captain was trying to keep something secret, and she endeavoured to know what exactly that secret was.

As the doctor slowly opened the door, he peered through the entranceway, shuffling his feet. Ann had learnt through the many weeks that Doctor Rudolf was nervous in almost any (if not possibly all) situations not pertaining to his own medical study, or personal experience. In fact, it was in one of these situations where the two had met. Ann had found the doctor in a port-side gambling den along the coast of an island where the Navy crew had been based. Hearing him bragging they were soon to depart, she had decided to enter the game, thus saving him from well-deserved financial ruin and a gang of eyeballing thugs, who would have surely taken everything he had. However presently, three men in Navy uniforms adorned with red trim were stood in the doorway.

"Bloody bullshit, that's what it is." Scoffed one of them.

"Why does he have to make us do it?" The sailor complained as Ann peeked from under the covers.

He had large, muscular arms crossed about his chest, with dark skin and a vertical scar spanning the surface of his right eye.

"Keep it together, Luke." Another said, looking worried and placing a hand on the man's shoulder.

The one-eyed man looked back at the sailor, who was so like himself. Ann guessed they could have been brothers from their voices alone. Still, her head swarmed with thoughts. She had always been curious, and she knew the men wanted to know what was going on. Inwardly, she cursed herself from underneath the sheets, being so reckless as to choose a Navy ship.

"Is he going to be alright? Rockwell and the captain want a report." Luke grunted, pointing to the mass of tangled sheets that Ann was buried under.

The ship slowly started to tilt. The man wanted to come in...

"Yes, err, the sickness is a widespread cold from my home island, he will be well in a few days, with rest." Doctor Rudolf replied.

That was a lie, Ann smiled to herself, he almost sounded convincing. The men weren't so sure though. They barged into the room. 'Perfect!' Ann thought, time seemingly slowing down at the prospect of her dreams being dashed against the rocks. Why had she come up with the idea to be sick when she played that card game! Now she'd never get the chance to see the island she knew she had to reach. She had to think and quick. Holding the weight of the flintlock in her hand, she pressed the barrel of the gun lightly against the covers; the bright candles projecting the thick shadow of a reaching, looming hand across the room, her pistol clicking as she cranked the safety back. Her finger inched on the trigger, feeling cold against the tiny piece of metal. It was all she needed to take a life. Ann thought to herself, pausing only for a moment... would she? No... she was better than that, better than the people from her past, and better than those moving against her. Letting out her best fake cough, she relaxed her shoulders against the mattress and took a shaky breath as the shadows withdrew.

"You see, Bosun?" The doctor interrupted.

Ann heard them sigh.

"Come on, we've the cargo to check on again." A second later, they were gone, the door slamming shut behind them.

Ann breathed a long and heavy breath. Though it did make her wonder: What was it that was locked away within the bowels of the ship that made them want a report? It wasn't her business, but Ann wanted to figure out then and there what cargo they were guarding. As soon as the unwanted guests retreated, she flung from her confinement, racing to put on the boots that lay at the end of the bed.

"And what do you think you are doing? We haven't reached the island yet."

The look of annoyance spreading across the doctor's face was plain, however, Ann didn't care.

She wanted to get off the ship and find what she was looking for before it was too late. Shattering the peaceful lolling of the sea, a crack of thunder struck thrice, dividing the sky into jagged shards of violet. Ann raced to the window, that unmistakable feeling in her stomach gnawing at her once more.

The ship was now rocking wildly, crashing headlong into walls of towering water.

"We must be nearby." Ann said as she went back to stuffing her legs into the long boots.

She hoped they were, but before the doctor could even question her, the word 'Squall!' was echoed from somewhere above them and they were both thrown towards the doorway.

They landed on the floor that had begun to seep with foaming, lapping seawater, emerging from underneath the cabin door. Gazing up wearily and slightly dazed, Ann shook her red tendrils out of her face to try and focus herself, finding that the window on the other side of the room had started to crack.

Her heart stopped.

Thump went the waves again against the side of the ship, with thunder and lightning flashing all around. She knew she had to move, but Ann's eyes were drawn to the spectacle of the glass window, growing like a spider's web; soon the ocean's icy grip would have another entrance point. 'This was no normal storm,' Ann thought. Outside, a mass of swirling greys and shades of navy, broken up by purples and violets and sparks of fire fought a battle across the sky. The only solid thing that could be made out below the chaos was a slither of white. Within the cabin, the wisps of wind escaping through the webbed glass wailed like howling beasts, poised to attack. It was as if something was trying to sink them. Ann looked again, through the shattering glass, at the line of white she had seen just to make sure it had been real.

It was a beach!

They were going to hit a beach, a beach they couldn't see! Then, from above, came the tinniest murmur against the storm, a bell sounded out of the crow's nest in warning; a rushed clatter, resembling the sound of a kennel master calling his charges for their last meal.

"I need to get out of here." Ann muttered.

She quickly pulled on her jacket and reached for her gun, now fallen to the floor, and as drenched in seawater as she was. Suddenly, the spider-glass gave way, and, out of the corner of her eye, Ann spied something else, as pressure from the attacking waves forced shards of glass to fly by her face, a single shard slicing just above her cheekbone. Something darker, larger than the waves that bombarded them, drew close, and strangely, the chaos ceased.

A drifting silence passed over everything, and Ann offered a hand to help Doctor Rudolf, lifting him to his feet. There, bobbing up and down on the waves, with lanterns cast high aloft, something moved. Through the gaping hole that had been left, a ship emerged out of the cover of night, appearing as if from within the mist.

'Pirates!' thought Ann, as she worriedly glanced at the doctor. This distraction would only put her back further if she did not get away. Nevertheless, Ann grabbed the Doctor's hand, opened the door, and ran.

"Where are we going?" The doctor screeched.

"Out of here!" Ann replied.

That last wave had flooded them, and she knew she had to somehow make it to the cargo hold at the end of the hallway before the entirety of the ship was underwater – that was where she knew the Navy kept their smaller ships. Something seemed off to Ann, she had spent too long lying about in the doctor's cabin not to notice otherwise and she tried to piece the events together in her mind: the sudden squall with unnatural storms and raging lightning, the appearance of pirates when none had been sighted for weeks!

She realised then that they were being targeted, as water rose to just below her knees. The Navy had something the pirates wanted, and she betted on her life that it had something to do with The Company. She'd only glimpsed the pirate ship, but from her quick inspection she could see it was a massive creature, a brute, shrouded in shadow – at least twice the size of *The Inspectre* and able to ram it in two; its bow, decorated with the bones and skulls of long dead creatures. The most distinguishing feature of the gargantuan colossus was, however, its pitch black, sails.

They raced to the door guarding the cargo hold. A massive, solid metal slab of wall that was littered with locks and moving mechanisms, giving it the impression of a giant living safe.

"What the fuck is this?" Ann questioned as they reached it. She watched the mechanisms move and twist in bewilderment, first clockwise and then back again in a counter direction.

The Doctor looked at her blankly.

"...The hold?" He retorted.

Ann rolled her eyes as the water level continue to rise. She had to do something, and quick.

"Yes, I know that." She gawked, bringing one of her pistols out of her jacket and aiming it at the door.

"No! Don't do that!" The doctor shouted, but it was too late, as he tried to move in front of her. Ann gently squeezed the trigger.

She didn't know what the doctor was going to achieve by telling her not to do it, but it was only thanks to the rising water that the explosion from the barrel of the gun wasn't heard, the bullet quickly pinging across the metal before settling somewhere in the freezing water.

Ann turned to him and scowled as she reloaded.

"Then what were you going to suggest?" She asked.

They were both soaked to the bone and quickly growing tired from the plunging temperatures. Still, the safe continued to twist and turn, its mechanisms were ever moving, and Ann had no conceivable idea as to how they were going to get through, unless Doctor Rudolf knew the combination?

"You know how to open it, don't you?" She said at last, a complacent smile coming to her face.

"Maybe." He mumbled.

"I've heard Rockwell and the captain talking about it, but it seemed silly to me that they placed guards on it in the first place. Who needs to guard an impenetrable safe if it's supposedly unbreakable?"

"But you can crack it, right?" Ann urged, now growing impatient as she started to shiver.

Whatever was kept within the hold must have been incredibly valuable – but now the guards had gone away to help with whatever was happening on the deck above, and there was no need to guard what would be kept secret by the shadows of the sea.

"Yes, I know the combination." He spoke simply.

Ann breathed a sigh of relief. Above, shouting could be heard as the pirates drew closer, a sure sign the squall had died and weirdly the water began to recede. Hurriedly, the doctor approached the door and began to turn the small wheel at the bottom right of the safe, in four quick turns counterclockwise and five to the right. Ann watched as the hold door began to tick and jeer, then suddenly came a dull crack.

"It's open."

The doctor sighed with relief, and quickly they both fled inside, closing the door behind them.

Inside the hold, it was dark and damp. Walls and walls of barrels were stacked high amongst themselves, all pale and brown. Ann had no idea as to what the pirates would want with them. From the looks of the barrels, the ship was only carrying food for the island. There was nothing else to see, the room was too enveloped in darkness. The shouting on the deck fluttered down to them in a soft echo.

"So, how am I going to get out of here again? I thought there would be boats, I don't see any." Ann asked.

The doctor hurried to move one of the barrels but hesitated as he set the container down.

"The rest of what you promised?" he raised an eyebrow as he spoke, a grim countenance across his visage; pale and ghastly.

"What's the point if there's pirates coming? They'll bleed you dry for coin, besides, I paid for your greed."

The doctor looked irritated and gritted his teeth. Had he always planned on doing this, she wondered?

"Pirates were not privy to the conditions!"

"You work for the Navy, Doctor. Pirates are always privy to the conditions." She retorted.

The man growled, and immediately Ann pulled a pistol on him. The air grew tense.

"Get me out of here, and I won't come looking for you… if you survive."

She didn't want to shoot him, but she would if it ultimately came to it, despite how much he had helped – some things were just too valuable to risk. He unexpectedly lunged at her, and Ann fired off a shot into his arm. The doctor yowled in pain, a bead of sweat drizzling down his oily exterior. He shouldn't have tried to jump her.

"So, we have an accord?" She asked, and again the doctor nodded, he was out of breath, gritting his teeth and red-faced.

The shouts from above were getting louder. Ann lowered the gun, climbed inside the barrel, but she was still hesitant to trust him.

"There's still food in here." She complained, holding up what looked like an apple in the dusky light of the hold.

"You want pirates to find you?" The doctor spat.

"No -" Ann said, however as soon as she did, the lid was shut, and everything went dark.

A feeling of weightlessness passed first, then several heavy bangs as her stomach jumped in response. She could hear rushing water pound against the barrel and after a few moments the lid was abruptly forced free as she was tossed from side to side. Looking back, she found the fog around *The Inspectre* had cleared, letting in precious orange sunlight. Ann had been rolled through the small part of the cargo hold that allowed for the disposal of waste. Now she swayed at the mercy of the waves as a rising shadow was cast over her once floating prison.

It was the horrifying mainsail of the pirate ship that she saw, trembling against the wind as the sea drifted her away. The image of two skulls; one atop the other, a bleeding heart at its centre, eclipsing a field of black. It was not the image of a heart that a child would draw, but of an actual pulsing, beating heart, flanked by two spears lapsing over one-another, like clashing swords.

She heard someone on *The Inspectre* curse. She was still close enough to the ship to hear their shouts as the waves rocked her.

"What is it, Captain?" Another shouted.

"Not what – who. They work for one of the Five! Kaine, The Devourer!" The captain called out, his voice dripping with despair.

It was the last time Ann saw or heard from them as she was carried away, floating away in her lonely little barrel.

She got what she wanted, a way to the island. She looked towards the slim section of white beach that could still be seen, brushing off the splash of salty water from her brow. A ring of black storm clouds still hovered, and she hoped that her plan would work. Into the squall, she thought. Into the eye of the storm. If she was ever going to succeed, Ann knew she would have to face what dwelled at its dark centre.

3

Atlas and Orion rowed along at their own leisure, towards the waiting ship that appeared to sit dead upon the darkening water. The waves were calm now, forced into submission by Atlas, who had used the powder he had inhaled to make the waters recede around the Navy vessel and set in a thick fog. The amulet about his neck was luminescent in the mist and the winds were silently still; only the rhythm of their oars provided any song at all as Atlas motioned to his brother to begin the next part of their plan. Orion hoisted a glowing scarlet lantern above his head, lit with a blood-red candle.

"Hey, Atlas?" Orion called as he swung the lantern. "How about a song, eh?"

"We agreed you were meant to be silent!" Atlas sneered, continuing to row across the space between the two ships.

The Navy had been lured far enough inland to see the glimmer of beach that existed off the southern coast of the island, ebbing into bay that led out to open sea.

"Alright! Here I go then -"

"No!" The pirate captain snapped.

His brother always did this sort of thing when he was annoyed or wanted something from him. He would sing and sing until eventually, Atlas would give in from the sheer travesty of his brother's voice, and, in this case, Atlas figured that Orion wanted a continuation to the conversation they had back on the ship. Nevertheless, the Navy had already seen *The Ymir's Extinction*, as it came to shadow over them – after all, he was a "*Noble pirate*" and came to offer the stranded Navy his aid.

"Row, row, row your boat, gently down the stream,

If you kill a Navy-guy, make em scream ya name!"

"Orion?" He grunted, looking his brother dead in the eyes, he had even dropped the oars for a moment, letting them drift in the water.

His patience was wearing thinner by each line. He had waited a lifetime – they both had, and he could hear Kaine's deep laugh cackle in the recesses of his mind.

"Row, row, row your boat, gently down the stream,

If you kill a Navy-guy, make em scream ya name!"

"Orion!"

"Row, row, row your boat, gently down the stream,

If you kill a Navy-guy, make em scream ya name!"

"Orion!" He boomed.

Atlas' eyes closed for a moment, trying to block out his frustration, regret immediately washing over him as he saw the giant's face staring straight back at him, grimacing as the black mark pulsed.

'What will you do now, bug?' He remembered the giant asking, his voice echoing through blood-soaked teeth, his bright snake-like eyes peering into Atlas' soul with a searing yellow heat.

Kaine's face had been covered by shadows in that cavern, and Atlas only remembered the most horrifying details. Above him, the giant had dangled Orion by his scaled, pointed fingertips.

"Perhaps, I should swallow him whole?" The giant mused, tilting back his head as his dark mass shifted.

Atlas had responded in a rage, hacking at the giant's feet with his father's war-axe tight in-hand, but the scales were too thick to penetrate. His crew had crawled for days to make their way into the giant's cavern lair, hoping to steal from the behemoth and kill him in his sleep, but it had gone all so terribly wrong, and his brother had been captured trying to fell the creature. Atlas' horror had been insurmountable in that moment as he stood clutching the pommel to the axe – they should have died. Only the chilling intervention of another - a raven with emerald eyes - had saved them. It had swooped down from the cracks in the rocks above, perching malignantly on the beast's ear, spreading whispers. At this, the giant cackled, making the volcanic lair shake and rumble.

"It appears you have been marked by another, bug!" The giant laughed.

"Am I the first one you came after? Was that the reason you followed my banner? How easily I could crush you. You do not have the power!"

And he swatted the bird away with his spare hand, causing it to vanish in a wisp of shadows.

"But…" Kaine added, letting a dangling Orion down onto a scorched rock beside him.

His brother was still breathing, but the breaths were short and shallow, and Atlas' heart almost leapt from his chest as the heat in the vast opening began to swell.

"I like to play with my food." Said the giant.

"So, it is up to her to catch you, before my pets do… What is it you and your band say: May every man earn his fair and justly earned reward?"

Kaine's smile faded then, and with another deep cackling laugh, he breathed a blanket of black dust out from between his chapped lips. It quickly enveloped the space, spreading out to everyone that the brothers fought beside. Atlas felt the spray seep into his lungs, and he stumbled back from where he held the axe. He felt something inch and convulse on the back of his neck, a burning pain that would not cease. Never in all his life had he experienced such pain as he did in that moment. As the pirate dropped to his knees, he drew a sword from his belt, using the murky edge to try and strike the giant. A reflection caught his eye as he swung the blade, and, upon the back of his neck, Atlas found a pulsing black mark.

"Yes, brother?" Orion asked, ripping Atlas from his thoughts, the singing continuing in a hum as his sibling waved the lantern in frantic arcs above their heads.

The memory faded and Atlas' face strained. So many years had passed since then. They had run from fight to fight, place to place, killing as they went. He thought about the rumours he'd heard - that Kaine had gone back to his slumber when they fled the cavern. Atlas had left their father's axe behind, unable to free it from within the beast's iron scales. The giant had no idea about the war Atlas had inflicted on his kin in the years since. There had been so many bumps along the way for Atlas to uncover, so many riddles swirling in his head. It was only by chance when they raided a temple some months ago that they had found the clues they needed - the map and the amulet. Presently, the pirate captain could feel the veins begin to pop from his forehead and his olive complexion turn to a crimson hew as his brother continued with his tune.

"I love you dearly." He glared, "-but will you stop singing that infernal song!"

Orion paused.

"They'll be able to hear us." Atlas added softly, lowering his own voice as his brother looked over his shoulder to the ship.

"Then you better tell me about the mark?" Demanded Orion. "Or the Navy will start firing."

Cannon fire was the last thing they needed, and Atlas continued to row till the keel of their boat tapped against that of the Navy ship's.

"Orion, I -" Atlas began, rubbing his neck. His headaches had gone for the time being due to the powder in his system, but the pain from Kaine's mark still subsisted.

"Row, row, row your boat!" Orion started.

"I said I will, Orion, that should be enough!" He seethed. "Just let us see to this first. Now, douse the light, they'll have seen enough through the fog I left." Atlas sniggered, as he stood, and they met each other's steely gaze.

"Fine." His brother smiled, and did as his older sibling bade, throwing the lantern into the sea, watching as the red light was swallowed beneath its depths.

The Navy took no chances when it came to dealing with pirates. Atlas was glad he had managed to barter an accord with the Hoarder-King at the temple for information, knowing for sure as he climbed the ladder that there would be a musket pressed against his head when he reached the top.

"Stop!" An obvious Navy rookie called out. "I don't wanna kill you, so come up real slow-like."

Sure enough, Atlas donned a wicked grin. He stepped up on to the deck without a word, immediately feeling the heat of more guns upon him.

"Head up!" Another shouted.

Atlas raised his head.

"Oh great! You're him!" The rookie croaked as his gun rattled up and down, eyes widening in horror.

More guns locked onto Atlas, clicking back their safety.

"Don't just stand there, shoot!" A man with a long beard commanded.

Before anyone could fire, Atlas stretched open his arms and a show of crackling violet lightning began to appear, dousing him in a vale of power. With a crack of his knuckles, a torrent of lightning spewed forth from Atlas' fingertips, arching over everything in a blinding, sweeping, wave. It travelled across the ship in a flash, doing exactly what he wanted: finding everyone on-board and making the sailors fall to the floor with a thud. Behind him, Orion stepped up on to the deck, brushing himself off. He had another disappointed look on his face, like he had just missed out on the fun.

"Why didn't I get shocked?" He quizzed. "You always find it funny when I land on my arse."

"That's because it *is* funny." Atlas replied with a chuckle, allowing himself a rare moment of brotherly bonding. "And the power goes where I tell it to. That's why you didn't land on your arse."

"Huh, I see." said Orion. "Well, guess I should start killing some guys then before the crew boards. Shame, I sort of like it when they try to kill me first."

"No!" Atlas commanded, holding out his arm towards his brother.

His palm was shuddering with lightning, it wouldn't kill him, but at least he could see him land on his back.

"Why in all the hells not?" Orion complained, starting to put the blade he held back in its sheath.

"The Hoarder-King." Atlas said as he began to wander the deck, looking for the entrance to the hold and skipping over bodies.

Orion cocked an eyebrow at that.

"Lazarus wants them as a part of the accordance you made without me, doesn't he?"

Atlas nodded slowly.

"That and other things. In exchange, he'll offer up information on the second piece of the treasure."

"Fuck! That's why you didn't let me kill him at the temple! He said something to you to worm his way out of dying." Swore Orion. "You can never trust a Troll, especially if it's one of their kings, Atlas! You're meant to be the smart brother! We still don't know which one the old boss sent after us when we parted."

Atlas rolled his eyes.

"Ugh! Well, I did punch him in his horned and slimy face after I stole the map, if that makes you any happier?"

"It doesn't. What did that foul thing utter?"

"He knew of the prophecy, little brother - but all will become clear soon, I promise."

"It better." Orion grumbled, crossing his arms as Atlas continued to search the top deck. "You should really tell the three of us your plans. I'm tired of running from Trolls. What exactly does that pig want anyway?"

Atlas lifted one of the bodies of the knocked-out Navy, dragging them to the side for his crew to collect.

"Diamonds to rebuild his kingdom, men to do it and a pretty girl on his fat arm. He has lived long enough under Kaine's grasp, Orion. He wishes to be freed, and we, as the saviours of this world, shall bring him justice. He even told us where this island was right before it vanished from the map and today's moon confirmed it! Far before the moon's crescent light revealed the riddle."

"There's a riddle on the map now?" His younger sibling asked, as if nothing surprised him anymore.

"Oh yes, written in Runic verse, the one that father taught us." Atlas explained, letting the body fall limp to the floor and rubbing his beard.

"All quite real and trustworthy for now. The slime delivered on his word. In return he wants the bodies, the islanders will do, but the Navy, he can barter for."

Orion smiled.

"I see, so that's why we raided the Company too, to get the correct codes to trick the navy out? But we're going to kill them after we're done, right? After all, we already have what we want."

Atlas could see the sparkle of mischief in his brother's eyes as he said the words and he couldn't help but feel a swell of pride.

"Of course we are, little brother! We're pirates. Alliances never hold." And with that, Atlas went about the ship, scouring for his quarry.

* * *

"Did you find it?" Orion asked as his brother returned from wandering the ship.

"Indeed."

"You should be happy then. You can sustain your dirty habit for a little while longer." He joked from above the stairs of the wheelhouse.

He had taken to sharpening his cutlass, *Blood-drip*, with happy strikes from the side of the ship as he watched the ocean, embedding chips and notches in the woodwork. To Atlas, the use of the powder wasn't a habit, it was an addiction. He craved it... needed it... to feel power flow through his veins. It was the most natural thing he had apparently ever felt, he had told his brother, and he did it all so he could crush his enemies.

"Come, help me with this."

Orion sighed as he slipped the blade away once again. 'More nonsense,' the pirate thought. He wondered what their father would have thought of it all as he descended to the lower deck. A former raider turned farmer; their father had been a brute, raising his sons to be strong and hardy with utter ruthlessness, though Orion had been much different to begin with. As a boy he had only gone along with his brother's wild adventures and plans out of love and now it had become so ingrained in his lifestyle that he found he somewhat enjoyed it. He craved power too, deep down, but he was not driven by revenge and prophecy as his brother was – Orion had taken to piracy for wealth and the sheer joy of doing whatever he wanted. Still, his brother's revenge had become legendary. When they had raided Lazarus's temple, the Hoarder-King ambushed them and the Troll had demanded that their accumulated wealth be given over to him, in exchange for the stolen map and amulet. Atlas had seemed to recognise their value immediately, whereas he could not. His brother's usual calm and calculated exterior was overcome by awe, wrath, and a pure, unfaltering rage.

He had not been present for the words between the two, Orion knew from his brother's mutterings afterwards that he had seen the drawings he had once spoken of in a book from their childhood come to life, to which his eyes widened extravagantly as he gazed upon the newly acquired beautiful crystal he now possessed. At once, on their return to *The Ymir*, Atlas had shut Orion out of their cabin, muttering over and over "A child born of Devil's blood will bring giants to their knees..."

The meeting with Lazarus had happened moments after the last crescent moon, and Orion remembered saying to the only other two friends the brothers had, Gillian and Silvers, as they waited outside the cabin, that tensions would begin to run high from that point on; they would have to follow Atlas on his quest, to prevent his own self-destruction. They had all nodded in agreement, swearing a pact. The rest of the crew would just have to believe their captain had gone down the whirlpool.

Presently, at the very bottom of the Navy ship, along a narrow hallway, Orion saw Atlas standing in front of a strange metal door as he combed his long fingers through his shaggy black beard once more, pondering his thoughts.

"Is that a fucking safe?" The younger Vain asked him, as they waded through the flooded passage.

He pointed his sword directly at it as the light of his brother's amulet gleamed off the surface.

"How are we meant to get inside a fucking safe? Only Company ships are meant to have those, did Lazarus happen to mention that, too?"

Atlas gritted his teeth, sneering at the metal as if it were taunting him with disfigured aspersions and shapes.

"No, little brother, the troll neglected to mention it would be this confined. Fetch Gillian, tell him to bring Taylor and Brent. I want this door ripped in twain!"

"I'll get right on it, Atlas." A voice said suddenly, out of thin air, from behind the pirate captain.

Orion flinched slightly, turning around as he scanned the wrecked hallway.

"Hells! I hate it when he does that!" The vice-captain complained.

Atlas grumbled as he continued to stare at the mechanical door to the hold.

"It annoys me how he has that ability permanently also."

"Wish I could turn invisible."

"I sometimes wish you would." Retorted Atlas. "Now why don't you show yourself, Gillian?"

Suddenly, a pirate dressed in a black leather long-coat appeared. He had spiked salmon-coloured hair and wore a plain white shirt with ragged brown shorts and sandals. An overly large mechanical serrated blade was strapped to his back. A sly grin grew on his face as he came to wrap his arms over Atlas and embrace him from behind.

"I suppose you're both wondering why I'm not on *The Extinction*?" He spoke slowly, moving to kiss Atlas' neck, purposefully avoiding the black mark.

"You were meant to be on look out!" Said Orion angrily.

Gill smiled, stopping to look at the Vice-captain and how his blue eyes blazed with fury whenever he was near.

"Well, as first mate can I not take my privileges? And I was. I sat alongside you in the rowboat. Couldn't allow the captain to get hurt after all."

"How thoughtful of you, but don't get clever." Sneered the younger brother, placing his hand on the hilt of his sword.

"Gillian, the door, the twins, if you please. I want this ship salvaged and cleaned too." Atlas snapped.

He was growing impatient of the constant bickering between his brother and his closet friend, and the huge metal door in front of them only provided yet another obstacle for them to overcome – he would what he wanted, and he would have it now. Atlas could already feel the power starting to wane, energy oozing out of his body slowly. In the back of his head, gnaws and aches returned to wreak havoc upon his mind. Suddenly, with a single kiss placed upon his inked neck, he realised Gill had disappeared again.

"Is he gone?" Asked Orion.

"For now." Said Atlas as he rubbed the invisible mark the first mate had left upon his tattoos.

Ten minutes later, the brothers heard their own ship docking with the incapacitated Navy vessel, and two twinned brutes came lumbering through the tightly designed hallway. Panels supported by the overhead beams were torn asunder as they raced, the smoothly finished flooring being crushed to splinters where they stepped. Nothing was going to stop them from tearing apart everything in their path, and both Atlas and Orion quickly dived out of the way as their underlings set to work, smashing and clawing at the door.

Atlas laughed to himself as he got to his feet and Orion looked at him in surprise as he brushed himself off. Gill had gone overboard yet again! At the door to the hold, the two creatures were banging and snorting, tearing it apart as they continually pounded it with their massive fists. One had dark brown fur covering its body, with massive pink ears and claws escaping from its fingers; the other was silver and white, standing upright on two hind legs as it began to rip chunks of metal to one side.

"What did he do to them? I've never seen this type before!" Gasped Orion.

Slowly the creatures started to tire, and the brothers saw a dark hole had formed where the mechanism to the safe had once sat. They could now climb through, and the pirate captain started to feel himself tingle in anticipation.

"After all I've taught you about Ash, brother, I'm surprised. The power it gives us can only be taken from the natural world around us." Said Atlas. "Gillian must have taken the last morsels from our cabin; it shouldn't last long."

Abruptly, the growling and snorting from the beasts ceased as they began to shrivel in size, eventually looking up at the brothers with a hazy countenance, their bodies reverting to what they once were.

Orion looked at the two men in confusion and horror as Atlas stepped into the dimly lit hold. It dawned on him from his brother's words, that somehow, somewhere, out across a wide and raging sea, those creatures he had just witnessed had existed. And why not? If Mermaids, Trolls, and Giants were real? Still, that did not shake the horror from his mind.

Now inside, Atlas found rows of stacked brown barrels upon shelving and walls, but oddly, just slightly into the doorway was a Navy officer and for a moment he was puzzled. The man, Atlas assumed, had been knocked unconscious by his lightning attack, and as he bent over, the pirate looked at the man's palm, which had been badly burned. Atlas could only guess that the man had touched the door when the lightning was carried about the ship, but it still did not answer why he was there in the hold and not with everybody else?

"What's the matter now?" Asked Orion, seeing his brother in deep thought.

"Nothing." The captain replied as he rubbed his beard and began to walk the room. "This one wasn't armed, meaning he wasn't a guard. Judging by the slanted position of these barrels over here, it seems that he moved some of them…Aha, found you!"

Atlas found himself staring at ten red-coloured barrels hidden behind a wall of brown that had been obscured by the dim light. Immediately, he placed his hands on the top of one of the barrels, gripping the sides, and bringing it to the centre of the room. Proceeding to apply pressure to the lid, he shattered the piece of wood in an instant, throwing what remained to the side. Eyeing it with awe; as if it was his new-born babe, Atlas trailed a hand through the smooth black powder within, sifting it through his fingertips and feeling the grains fall lightly between his rough skin.

"Is that one of the ones we wanted?" Asked Orion.

Atlas lifted his hand up, letting the Ash pour from his palm. He watched it trickle back into the barrel, sniffing the air, as if to sample its potency.

"It is."

"So, what's the difference between that and the one you snorted this morning?"

Atlas huffed, placing his hands once again on the sides of the barrel.

"The difference is, dear brother, that the one I snorted this morning, as you so eloquently put it, was a much rarer Ash; it takes great skill to bottle a storm."

Orion looked confused, yet again, by what his brother had said, and Atlas groaned in frustration.

"Seidr, brother! Magic to you. There are people in this world that use the Old-Arts. They grind a thing down to its core elements so that the power can be borrowed. It is a rare thing indeed, in a world full of rarities, and that is why the power must be taken. Besides, this batch is untreated, which means it will be even more deadly. Now, help me move this."

On the count of three, the brothers lifted the barrel, carrying it up to the top deck. The fog caused by the storm had lifted, leaving behind a bright, glaring sun. A small fragment of their crew had joined them now; it was looking to be quite a special day.

"Everything went alright then?" His first mate asked after a while.

Now that everything had been cleared, Atlas was resting against the mast as he watched Orion direct the last of the barrels to their own ship – a prize to show the crew they were making progress, and that the Navy could be stripped bare.

"Everything went fine. It was just that idiot. Have this ship trawled to the harbour, Gillian. We can laden it with our gifts for the Hoarder-King. We must make it seem to that slime-bag that we intend to honour our accord, and make sure the crew is put to work." Atlas ordered, directing a giant finger towards Orion.

"You, okay?" The first mate asked.

"He's his old self sometimes." The captain continued with a distant voice about him. "And constantly yapping at my back, but then I see the vacant look that he gets, like he has just forgotten everything you told him. I can't help but think that we did that to him because of what happened – I may be ruthless, but I still love my brother."

Gill smiled.

"You're doing your best to protect him. He's just a little crazy after what happened is all." Gillian said reassuringly.

Atlas shook his head, grunting as he felt the torment of his headaches return. Was the plan really going to work? It had been years!

In the blink of an eye, a black raven landed on the stern of the ship, letting out an ear-splitting cry. Atlas turned to see the glimmer of a smirk arise from its beak, and in-between those lips of crooked scorn, beneath a twinkling ruby-stare, rested a freshly plucked lily, the colour of palest snow.

The pirate backed away. The eyes… a deep blood red. Did his thoughts betray him? Out of all the things he hated and feared, those ravens, and whom the black birds might bring were the worst. The giants had earned his scorn, but nothing held his fear as those birds did; they only brought decay.

"I better be."

He shuddered as the bird cackled behind its fear-mongering gaze.

"Otherwise, we're all dead."

The black bird flew towards Atlas, dropping the lily down by his feet and flying away towards the rising sun in a chorus of squarks.

Obsessions and whispers, they were a funny thing. Atlas knew the prophecy had to be completed.

4

Why was it always carrots? Jackson thought, quivering at the sight, a stream of slurry running down the path of cobbles as a dim glow radiated from the tavern. Tom patted him on the back. They were the only two that had ventured outside the pub. Though the chilling wind had slithered down his spine and cooled his shoulders, Jackson still got the feeling that he'd continue to heave, and he wiped his chin with the edge of his sleeve. The brothers had gone for the night, skulking away in the shadows from the moonlight. Acting on this, a small group of them had decided to sneakily open the local pub, as the pirates that were left behind partied at the top of the hill – either they ignored the light coming from the little shack below or were too drunk to care.

"Time for another drink, me thinks!" The old man laughed.

Tom was always good like that, though the old man did have his oddities. During many nights as the evenings wore on, Jackson's drinking partner would begin to say strange things. 'Say, Jackson? You ever explore the undergrowth of the jungle?' He would wonder in a drunken slur, or 'Did you know that there's a secret on this island-' he would begin, but usually never get the chance to finish before they both passed out.

Jackson lifted his head, sitting back against the window-frame of the tavern as the outside air made him dizzy. Out towards the coast, he watched as the palm trees rustled in the wind below the twinkling stars – not since before the pirates had arrived had it been this peaceful, yet all he could really think about was his life and his past mistakes. He closed his eyes and sighed.

'I hope it was worth it. I just... I just can't see you anymore.' She had said, staring at him plainly, not an ounce of regret lingering in those beautiful eyes of hers, as the fated words slipped loose.

Jackson had wondered after all these months if anything she had said had been real or truthful? And yet, it had broken his heart. What tugged at him more was the guilt. His wife was gone, and he had used Arie to get over her! He could have never imagined falling for her, or hurting her as he did, no matter how unintentional it may have been.

"I hope it was worth it." He mumbled to himself, mulling the words over in his mouth.

Weeks ago, a hooded man had come to the island. Shrouded in a cloak, he sped along the streets of the town, traversing through the alleyways and the shadows so he would not be seen, all so he could come rapturing upon the house of Arie's father. They'd been in bed at the time, and Jackson had snook across the marble-laced landing to see who it was at the dead of night. The drunk still remembered the commanding voice and the slight glimpse he had caught of the stranger against the orange candlelight, as both he and Arabella lent over the landing rail to get a better look.

From what they could see, the stranger had a tuft of silver hair escaping from under the hood that concealed his eyes. As he shook hands with Arabella's father, a grey bandage could be seen wrapped around his left hand. The man seemed sure of his purpose. Arabella had looked at him with interest before the two of them had crept back along the hallway. For weeks since the pirates had arrived the visitor had apparently come to the house again and again, with each visit being longer and more mysterious.

Was this the stranger's doing? He certainly thought so. Hells! Why had he been so stupid?

Tom then returned, interrupting his thoughts with two tall drinks in hand. Drinking was the only other way Jackson knew how to deal with situations he couldn't control. It gave him a sense of freedom that he couldn't obtain otherwise; always feeling bound to this island, his home.

"Curse the stars!" He groaned, shaking his head in preparation for the next round. "Do you ever think I'll get my luck back?"

Tom frowned as he swayed towards the table, the golden liquid he was carrying jumping slightly from its iron casket.

"Not if you curse the heavens above us, you won't! Whispering brings about the wrath of the gods. The Old Ones must stay in their slumber."

Jackson sneered at that, almost mocking it with a drunken laugh.

"You do say some shit, Tom, you know that?"

"It's only shit if you don't believe it."

"Then where are these gods now, eh?" He taunted. "All the children's books say otherwise."

Tom passed him a tankard of ale and sat down as another cold wind blew. He had one of his serious looks about him now and gripped Jackson's arm to the table with all the force he had.

"Sleeping, hidden... Their power held in pieces across many lands."

Jackson knew this was nonsense! Folklore! Nevertheless, as he looked into the old man's eyes, all he found was crippling fear.

"Listen to me, Jackson! Treasures of great power do exist, even if you don't believe them. You've travelled, years ago.

You know that monsters roam the seas, that some stories are true."

Jackson raised his eyebrow in concession at that. He had fought down many beasts on his way across the waves but had disregarded all the tales of whence they came, passing it all off as some freak selection of nature and the merciless world they lived in.

"The only monsters I saw on my travels were man. There's nothing to suggest there's treasure on this island, everybody already knows that -"

"Then why are they still here, eh?" Tom interrupted, taking a gulp of his own drink and glancing up the hill. "But you make an excellent point, best move on to something else before somebody hears. You mentioned something about luck?"

Suddenly the winds began to stir.

"Is everything okay with you and Arabella?" Tom asked after a moment. "Didn't see her in there?"

Jackson ignored the question as he tried to hold back his emotions. It was well known on the island that the pirates now used Arabella's house as their base of operations, and because of that, the entirety of the island had become his own personal living nightmare.

"Looks like there's a storm coming." He said, wiping his hand over his eyes.

Tom raised an eyebrow as he looked out onto the dark bay and turbulent coastline.

"Oh? So, there is."

The tavern rested on the middle hill in the centre of town. It was surrounded by buildings, steam vents, and jungle, with a twisting cobbled road leading all the way down to the south beach, where the swash had begun to foam.

"How long do you give us?" Tom croaked.

Jackson took his drink, downing it all in but three gulps and wandered out into the middle of the road. Windows began to shake as the winds rasped and roared against them. Thunder cracked and the heavens opened, soaking both men to the bone in a sudden downpour. The storm had come to finish them all off and the air made him feel uneasy. The drunk swayed as he tried to steady himself, rocking from side to side on the balls of his feet. He went to take a swig of ale but found none and threw the empty tankard to the ground. In a haze, pressing a finger to his lips, Jackson turned and spoke to the island's attacker as the night's drinks caught up with him. A dark wave of water tore up the beach and along the road.

"Why are you so loud and why the hells did she break up with me?" He yelled.

Tom said something in return as he struggled to get over to him from his seat, but Jackson could barely make out the blurred movement of his lips as he turned once again, collapsing to the floor.

Now the old man had to think; the eye of the storm was metres away as winds rampaged across the island and he needed to do something to get his friend to safety, but what could he do? The two of them were the only ones stupid enough to be out in a storm such as this, and he knew the alcohol had ripped him of his strength to lift the drunk. Certainly, he couldn't get them both inside before the storm outran them and he turned in disbelief to find that the door to the tavern had been barred shut.

"Bastards!" He bellowed.

Then, out of nowhere, someone tapped him on the shoulder, and Tom turned to see a young girl with vibrant crimson hair billowing in the wind.

"Need a hand?" She shouted above the squall.

She too was soaked, looking only a little worse for wear than Jackson. The girl must have been no more than eighteen or nineteen and had a curious expression on her face. Tom gazed at her in confoundment. Given the island's latest mishaps over the last month, he was wary of trusting any stranger, however, the man didn't have the time to say no as the dark storm drew ever closer.

* * *

Jackson awoke hours later, groaning as if something foul burrowed deep within his head. He remembered the drinks, things dragging through to the early hours of the morning. The storm! He thought suddenly, touching his head only to discover himself laying in a bed that was not his own. Looking at his surroundings with half opened eyes, Jackson let out another groan. It had happened again.

Presently, the sweet-nutty scent of bread toasting on an open fire filled his nose, and he immediately sat up. Above Jackson, sunlight seeped in through the window. It looked like they'd just about made it through the storm, but only barely. Everything in the house was a wreck, most things seemed unusable. Jackson now knew where he was.

"Morning, it's good to see you're alive Mark." A voice called out to him.

Jackson turned in bed to see his old friend, James Nelson, standing by a stove and grinning at him from across the room. Nelson was one of Ale Town's professional cooks and had known Jackson since they were both boys.

"Ugh! What the fuck am I doing in your bed, Nelly?" Grumbled Jackson as he began to climb out of the covers, grateful he was still fully clothed.

Shaking his head, he walked over to the kitchen where James handed him a bowl of freshly cooked stew.

"You got drunk again. Old Tom had to pull you out of a storm."

"Tom did that?" Jackson asked in surprise.

"He's stronger than he looks." Replied Nelson.

The stew smelled delicious and of sweet onions. Jackson always told his friend his cooking was terrible, and to begin with, he had been right, it tasted like rotten boar, but now he desperately hurried to dunk a chunk of bread into the warm broth.

"Thanks." He grumbled again.

"What's wrong? Bad hangover? You never thank me." Nelson quipped, beginning to tuck into his own bowl.

"Just the usual." He said, stirring the thick liquid with his spoon.

He knew where Nelson was trying to lead the conversation.

"I see, I just never see you anymore, not since -"

He closed his eyes before taking another bite. The truth was, Jackson didn't want to be around anyone any more, especially those who knew his wife, and he knew the cook wouldn't stop nagging him until he did something to explain himself. He began to say he didn't know how to thank him for letting him seek shelter from the storm, he supposed he'd better get that part over with before Nelson started to ask questions.

"Ha-ha, what are you thanking me for? I'm not the one who dragged you across my floor." Nelson laughed.

Jackson looked at him, confused. He remembered collapsing on Tom, but it all went dark after that. He tried to think back, but nothing came.

"Then who should I thank?" He asked with a mouthful of stew. "Come to think of it, where is Tom? I remember something about Arie being there too, did she help bring me in?"

Nelson laughed again, this time giggling so much he had to move the rest of his stew to the stove.

"Man, you must have had a lot to drink last night. Arabella broke up with you. You were whining about it in your sleep. But no, it wasn't her who helped you." He sniggered. "*I*, on the other hand, just let you crash here for the night. I have enough problems trying to deal with pirates at the restaurant."

"They're still here?"

Nelson nodded.

Pirates aside, Jackson was still puzzled. If Arie didn't help him, then who did?

"How's the stew?" The cook asked abruptly.

"Bad as always, like rotten hog." He replied as he finished the bowl. "Speaking of which, where's the porkchop?"

Nelson grinned.

"That's beef stew, hard to get with the pirates reserving the supply – alcohol has dimmed your senses. Whole island's going to the dogs I tell you. If Molly were here, she would -"

"Anyway... who helped you and Tom bring me in from the storm?" Jackson interrupted, putting his bowl down on a side table.

Nelson grinned again, walking his friend over to the door, placing a hand on his back.

"I didn't catch the name, but she's still here in town, hiding away somewhere so the pirates won't find her."

"*She*?" Jackson gawked.

"Yup, working for the Navy if you can believe it. Left just before you woke, wanted to ask you something about your work as well."

"Really?"

"Yeah, said she was trying to get some supplies from town. I don't know if she'll get them or not. The brothers were seen coming back to shore once the squall passed."

Nelson opened the door for his friend.

"Oh, and Mark, if you see her, don't forget to thank her."

"I'll try." Jackson smiled, unsure if he would or not, not even knowing what the girl looked like.

His mind was hazy at the best of times, remembering events that happened years ago in vivid detail, yet sometimes struggling to remember what had happened the previous day.

"Besides, I need to get a drink since you're shoving me out already."

With that, he patted his friend on the back. As he did, Nelson looked up and down the street.

"Be careful." He whispered. "They guard the mayor's house on North Hill like a fortress!"

"You think they finally found something?"

Jackson had grown to hate the pirates since they'd started their raids. All they ever did was search the town for that rumoured treasure they didn't even know a thing about. *He* had never seen anything, and yet his friends would not shut up about it - Tom had said weird things too. Couldn't they understand he just wanted a calm life, free of trouble. Jackson questioned what they would even find in a town such as this, once famous for its Ale and now gone to ruin? It seemed that his friend had learnt more from working in the kitchens.

"Maybe?" Nelson said. "They've been digging since they arrived, but you've never wanted much to do with anybody and that's why they've left you pretty much alone."

Nelson was still very fearful of the pirates, they forced him to cook day and night, rousing his staff as if they were cattle.

"Clive saw them dragging a Navy ship into port. Promise me you'll stay away from this. Just a day more and they'll be gone."

Nelson looked only partially optimistic. Jackson could see the fear in his friend's eyes. The pirates had stayed for weeks now, it was no coincidence with their battered ship and search for plunder – not to mention the appearance of the girl from the Navy – that only now things had begun to move. Nelson didn't say a thing more, closing the door as Jackson walked on. He knew they couldn't be overheard.

Looking up at the sky, he saw the sun was shining, no clouds in sight, a warm rung of heat filtering down from the heavens. Despite all the rage and destruction of storms, Jackson admired how beautiful the skies would look afterwards. It was as if the air was someone's canvas and the artist had used the storm as a brushstroke to wipe the surface clean. As he looked about the town, however, Jackson found that the main road down to his beach hut home on the south shore had yet to be cleared. Bits of driftwood, flotsam and jetsam, hovered above a grim swash of grey storm water, which he had little desire to wade through with his head as it was. The drunk groaned, he supposed he would have to take the blasted train!

* * *

After trekking through the station, Jackson was just glad to get to his compartment before the iron monstrosity departed under a cloud of steam. A few glaring pirates who lined the aisle of the car had confronted him when he got on, and Jackson wondered what they could possibly be up to that would warrant so much attention. Either way, he had shown them his ticket and they had let him be with a begrudged snarl, the air ripe with tension. Were people seriously considering that this rumoured treasure actually existed? Tom had been certain of it, so much so that he believed himself it's protector. Jackson began to doubt his reasoning. He hadn't seen his friend since last night, and nobody, not even Nelson, had known where he could be found.

Eventually, Jackson reached his seat, slumping down lifelessly, collapsing on the soft leather interior of the passenger car and closing his eyes. Then - as it did whenever he attempted to drift into the almost endless void - the image of Molly came into view; her radiant smile was as warm as a summer's day; her eyes sparkled with life, and she laughed as they sat together on the edge of the beach-tide with water lapping between their feet. Jackson tried to push her from his mind, but ultimately found he couldn't. He never could, even after so many years.

'Jackson? Do you love me?' Her voice echoed in his mind. He was torn inside whenever she appeared. He had made many mistakes, mistakes that he could not take back or ever change.

An announcement blared out of the overhead speaker. It crackled with a buzz and a pop, making Jackson scrunch his eyes in annoyance. Molly faded away, drifting like the waters they sat upon, leaving Jackson to sit on the beach-edge, alone. A small tear fell from the corner of his eye at the memory. He just wanted to go home and get a drink. He heard the other passengers on the train start to complain and moan and the pirates sniggered with laughter as they walked by after the driver announced their usual trip to South-station would be extended.

Typical, he thought. He disliked the way the island had quickly accepted the train. He still hadn't got a handle on those new mechanical carts the ports used when transporting goods, and he slowly felt himself starting to become irrelevant in this new industrial age. Soon, the man with no one to belong to would have nowhere to belong, and since the brothers arrived, no one wanted to be near the island. More and more people wanted contracts further out to sea. Jackson couldn't do this as he kept his routes close to the shorelines of the surrounding archipelago. He couldn't run the risk of coming across the Company's path again further out to sea, and he couldn't deal with the pain those memories caused.

All of a sudden, two pirates walked past where he was sitting. Both had oozing black marks that clung to the backs of their necks, and they itched and scratched at them as they walked the isle. Jackson noted the wide mischievous grins that were spread across their faces as they muttered amongst themselves. What were they up to? He wondered, as he thought about what Nelson had said to him. The drunk couldn't catch all the conversation, but what he did hear piqued his curiosity. As much as he wanted to be left alone, he found he couldn't be at peace so long as the pirates swarmed the island; they were drinking up too much of his precious booze and he needed that to deal with the memories.

"Are you sure that's what the Vice-Cap'n said?" The one wearing the crew's signature torn leather jacket whispered.

He was clearly shocked by what was being said and the other one sighed in response. This one had the Jolly Roger tattooed on the side of his arm. He was a thinly built man, with scars littered across his face down to his neck, making him look much like a child's patchwork doll.

"Yes, I'm sure!" He spat. "So, when old fatty gets here, don't give the game up. Orion's orders also come from his brother, and you know how Atlas gets when things aren't followed through."

He then made a cutting motion with his thumb across the belly of his neck. Jackson already knew this pirate from the sound of his voice, the Boatswain: Patchwork Jake. Jake had trashed his home, stolen at least half of his contracts whilst he and Tom had been out drinking – the pirate even had the audacity to leave a note!

As they made their way down the car, the pirates spoke quietly amongst themselves. It all seemed somewhat mysterious. Then Another person appeared from the end of the car. He was a fat, slightly greying, man, who's skin tone resembled the colour of used straw; as he closed the conjoining car door behind him, he carried about him a rich stuck-up demeanour. It was Mayor Johnson, realised the drunk! Being evermore curious as to what Arie's father was doing, Jackson got up out of his seat and followed them down the car, seating himself just out of view. If he could learn something here that would help finally force the brothers of the island, Jackson could get back to his life without anyone else interrupting.

"Do you have it? Have you brought me what your brother promised?" The fat man whispered.

More disproving grunts came from the two pirates as they sat down next to another man, who twirled a cutlass haphazardly in his hand as he watched the outside world from a window.

"Yeah, I got it. Quit your worrying, we always deliver. I trust everything is in order for the rally?" The pirate said, as Jackson heard him toss a sack over.

It sounded like coins or even jewels?

Jackson peered through the tiny gaps in the seating to get a better look. Though he couldn't see his face from the position he sat, he knew who he was. He wore a light shale green shirt with a pistol was tied around his waist by a red piece of fabric. The vice-captain of the invading pirates: Orion Vain.

"I personally think this is too much, little bird." Continued Orion. "Even Jake here agrees with me."

Jake sniggered.

"May every man earn his fair and justly earned reward."

"But my brother decides how much we pay you, so I have to go with what he says. All you did was make one lousy cable call to the Navy. We will ask more of you in the future, and I think you know what we mean." Orion spoke, his voice growing louder with every word.

"Thank you, thank you." The mayor uttered quickly, almost grovelling as he tore the bag open to inspect its contents.

Still, Jackson saw very little.

"Tell your brother he has my gratitude, and if there is anything he needs, I am willing to keep up our arrangement."

As if on cue, Jackson heard a sword being drawn across the metal of the train compartment, and the unmistakable sound of a whimpered gulp.

"Just you remember, Mister Johnson, that as long as we're on this island, we control you. Me and my brother can take anything you have – including your life, and that lovely daughter of yours. What is her name again, Jake? Atlas always forgets. He just keeps calling her girl. Gill and Silvers have a thing for her."

"Arabella, I think, boss." Chuckled Jake.

"Yes!" Sang Orion, all the while continuing to scrape his blade down the side of the compartment, honing its edge.

"That's it! Arabella. What a lovely name you gave your daughter, Rupert. It would be a shame if one of them had to pay her a visit. So, you'd better make sure this goes smoothly. Atlas wants the saboteur uncovered at the rally; the menace has been halting our progress and the crowds should draw him out."

Jackson had to stop himself from getting involved. He still cared for people despite how much he liked his isolation, and Arabella had been there for him in a way that Nelson and Tom could not. He could almost hear Mayor Johnson grit his teeth.

"The deal was that you left her and her friends out of your little game! She's not meant to know any of this, she is innocent!" There was a peculiar bite to his voice.

Orion laughed, with Patchwork Jake joining in as the train pulled further from the station. Jackson heard Orion put away his sword.

"But for how long, Mayor? For how long?"

The mayor just sat there, not knowing quite what to say as the pirates taunted him. Jackson had had enough. He lifted his head up slightly over the seats to see what was going on - luckily, the pirates were too busy laughing to notice and unexpectedly, the mayor spoke back.

"I would say the same about you as well, Orion." He croaked. "How long do you and your brother expect to run from him with that black mark on your hand? What was it that lackey just said? May every man earn his fair and justly earned reward?"

Orion's eyes filled with rage as he looked down at his hand, then back to the mayor as the gooey black mark oozed and writhed. The pirate sprang from his seat, slapping the old man, forcing him back.

"You know, I have no memory of how I got this." Spat Orion, reaching for his cutlass again, raising it to the mayor's neck.

A pinprick of blood slid down the glint of the sword, and the pirate twisted the hilt in his grip. The mayor shook his head, whimpering as glimmering jewels and golden coins spilled onto the floor. The pirate smirked, his blue eyes seeming to glow as he held the man, frozen in fear.

"But I can't be killing you just yet. You have an event to get prepared for, you need to be seen after all."

The mayor breathed a sigh of relief, a bead of sweat slid down his greasy exterior. Orion scowled, his gaze veering across the compartment as he held the fat man in place. Jackson ducked back down to his seat. It was a miracle that none of them had seen him.

"Let us retire to somewhere more private." the Vice-Captain said, and Jackson breathed a sigh of relief too as the four men ventured further up the train; the mayor led by the tip of a sword.

* * *

Finally, after an hour of travel, Jackson returned to his hut on the south-beach. He had not followed the mayor and the pirates, deciding that it was all too much trouble. No sword fights on trains for him thank you very much, he thought to himself. He was either still too drunk from the night before, or just too hungover to care. Although, he had to admit, Nelson had been right. Something was going on. Jackson just had to keep his head down and stay away. Still, his thoughts nagged at him as he trudged along the beach, the waves licking at his sodden shoes and the gulls crying out into the air. Why were the pirates hosting a rally? They had never done so before. Had they really found something on the island when everyone else could not? He'd had a lifetime of racing through the jungle's groves, flirting with the razored rocks of the coast, and running up and down the back alleyways. Once again, Jackson reiterated to himself that he had never found anything. He had been all over the island as a child with Nelson and Molly. In their infancy, the three of them had played games of hide and seek wherever they could, racing across the town, causing mischief and terror, but those were different times, now long gone. As he looked up from trudging along the sand, Jackson watched as the front door to his hut swung open in the warm beach wind. Odd, he thought, the storm gales must have blown the latch.

He took a few more steps closer, and suddenly, heard rummaging coming from within. Was someone trying to steal from him? He swore if those damned pirates took anything they would have thunder to pay! He had too much to think about at the moment; the pirates; the girl that had saved him; and now it appeared he even had to worry about Arie again. It was too much. His temple still ached slightly from the amount of booze the night before, and his throat was still sore. Hells! He thought, did he hate hangovers.

A crash came from the hut, and he ran swiftly and softly across the sand to find out what was going on. However, little did Jackson notice that on the roof of his hut was another visitor, one that was black with emerald eyes. The raven watched leeringly and closely. Unbeknownst to the human below, it was not the gulls that had cried out that morning but instead the black bird, and her work was done. The drunk knew he didn't have any items of value that a thief would want, just some old sea charts. His eyes widened as he slowly realised a couple of those charts were of hidden coves, canyons, and back-water trade lines - immensely valuable to the right person.

Thus, Jackson drew his sword and held his pistol tightly in his grasp. Reaching the old rickety door and peeking through one of its holes, he raised his rapier above his head, just in case the thief came running out. Looking through the hole, he saw that everything was mainly still intact and untouched. Although, to his surprise, sat on the bed was a beautiful red-headed girl. So, the thief wasn't a man at all, as he initially expected. He took a step back. On closer inspection, the girl had a red ribbon tied around her wrist, seeming to be in her late teens. Jackson panicked as she began searching underneath his bed, where he kept his most treasured items.

"My, my." She muttered to herself. "What do we have here? What have you been hiding, Mister Jackson?"

No, no, no, the drunk thought, as the girl picked up a vial of a dark red and blue coloured powder, holding it to the light above her head for a closer inspection.

Shit! The Ash. It was a stench that no one could avoid; sought by monsters, pirates, and others all the same. Jackson had kept some of his own, just in case the worst came to it, but he hated to look at the accursed vial. He wondered though, how she knew his name? Was he spoken of that often? Nevertheless, as he crept backwards to recount his position, Jackson stepped on one of the loose panels of decking that littered the outside of his hut, and, hearing it groan, grimaced. The raven above cackled. Unfortunately, the sound distracted the girl. She looked up and Jackson saw her glistening green eyes dart towards him through the cracks of the door. It was at this point that the bird took flight, soaring into the sky so it could watch from above the heavens.

"I don't take kindly to uninvited guests." He blurted out without thinking. "Especially ones who rummage through my things!"

His right index finger lay resting on the trigger of his pistol while his left hand still gripped his sword tightly. Jackson did not trust this girl. He didn't trust thieves, nor pirates, nor any creature of-the-like, but surely with her looks, the girl could have gotten anything she desired without having to lift a finger. Then something she said threw him:

"Of course you don't, why would you, but I assure you, I didn't come to this island for that." She said, calling to him from inside the hut.

Jackson smirked. What a person says, and what a person does are two entirely different things.

"Your friend Nelson said you used to do trading deals with the N.S.T.C?" She asked.

Jackson froze.

"Wait, what? What do you know about the company?" He urged, trying to wrap his head around things.

"Lots of things, but let's save that for another time, hm?" She hummed.

The door swung open, and the girl smiled at him, waving the vial in front of her.

"As I told your friend, if you're wondering how I got here, it's a long story."

Jackson was astonished. Was this the girl Nelson spoke of? The one that had helped him out of the storm and was now stood inside the doorway of his hut?

"Don't worry, I won't bite." The redhead added, noticing that he kept his distance and that both sword and pistol were held. She then tied a sliver bandanna across her forehead, covering the top of her red locks, waving to him as she walked into the centre of the room. The irony slowly struck him, that the thief that had broken in was inviting him into his own home. Still, Jackson decided to take the risk because of the vial. He watched in growing anticipation as her hips lustrously swayed from one side to the other in tense silence, her heeled black leather boots making a clacking sound as they met the wooden floorboards. Jackson was almost willing her not to do anything, the frail glass tube poised above her. Then the girl turned her head, perking her lips.

"You're still not going to back down, are you?" She asked sweetly.

Even if she did help him, no one stole from him and got away with it.

"I like that about you, Mark Jackson. A strong mind and heart do a lot for a person in this world, even if they can't survive it."

She trailed off and muttered something inaudible under her breath, shaking the vial of powder above her head, making the navigator cringe.

"This stuff's illegal to the public, you know. Well, unless you have a permit, which I'm guessing you don't. I wonder what type this is?" Her eyes widened with childish wonder.

Jackson didn't breathe a single word as he held his sword and gun. At the bottom of the glass, the powder hid something, something that the drunk did not want anyone to see.

"I know! Why don't I try it?" The girl exclaimed in excitement. "This Ash isn't like the specky elemental type, so it must be one of the others – Is it treated?"

Jackson cringed. He didn't need that kind of power let loose upon the town. The people had just been through a storm that had almost ripped them apart, and, with the pirates still around, there would be nothing left for hope to cling to. He wasn't going to let anybody get hurt by that power. He'd seen it countless times before. Therefore, placing the gun to the girl's forehead, he stepped nearer. He wasn't afraid to do it, to pull the trigger. However, throughout all of this, the girl's expression remained unchanged, and she continued to smile infectiously as she toyed with the vial, even with a gun to her head.

"Fine. If that's how you want to thank me for saving your life...but with this, you could beat those nasty, nasty pirates." Said the girl, her playful expression suddenly vanished, and she dropped the vial on the floor, causing it to smash into several tiny pieces, throwing him completely off-guard. The Ash spread across the wooden slats of the hut like wildfire, he looked down and before Jackson even noticed, he was staring down the barrel of not one, but two pistols.

Shit! Where had those come from? Jackson gripped his sword, trembling, his mind jumped to and fro going through a marathon of possibilities – perhaps he could get away somehow? All they both had to do was pull the trigger, but could he really do it? To kill this girl in cold blood, someone who had helped him. Stabbing her was no different, if not more personal. Fuck! He needed that drink. Jackson's eyes shot to the left, then to the right, and upon the covers of his bed, he saw a ruffled and up-turned black leather jacket, matching that of the girl's high-heeled boots.

"So, what do we do now?" He asked, making her giggle. The girl moved closer, close enough that he could feel her steady, shallow breathing.

"Well first, you're going drop the rapier. Don't think I've forgotten you're still holding it. I may be young, but I'm not an idiot," she said coyly. It was almost a whisper as he felt her breathe against the skin of his lobe seductively.

Silence fell.

"No?" Questioned the girl into his ear after a moment.

"No." Jackson replied, and suddenly a shooting pain pricked him, causing him to drop both his weapons.

"Ugh! You're sick!" Jackson exclaimed, clutching his ear as the teenager backed off, giggling from the love-bite. "You said you wouldn't bite!"

"I lied." The girl was still grasping both her pistols, and Jackson wondered - Was this all a game to her? If so, then she was no better than the pirates that plagued the town.

"What kind of person are you? What are you here for, if not to steal and lie to me!" He shouted.

"I'm the best kind of person, Jackson. I'm me."

The girl then lowered her head and looked down to where the vial had broken; her eyes glinted as she caught something in the pile below and bent down to get a closer look.

"Huh?" A smirk appeared on her face. "And to answer your question - I'm here for you." The girl began as she searched through the pile of red and blue powder. The drunk, however, had other ideas as he saw his moment. The girl had somewhat ignored him as her fingers brushed against the corner of an old black and white photo Jackson had kept hidden in the vial. She lifted it from the accursed powder, a quizzical look on her face.

"I had to make sure you weren't with -" she started, but Jackson pushed her over before she could finish what she was saying, and the redhead rolled to the floor.

"The maps." He said, believing the girl had hidden the charts. "Where are they?"

He had scanned the room upside down when he had entered. The lids to his trunks had been flung open and reams of paper hung from the sides as they lapped over one another. The girl, looking up in a daze, threw back simply, that she had no idea where his charts and maps were and that she had only looked under the bed, as the light from the beach had caused the vial of Ash to glimmer from its box. Jackson saw that the girl's guns lay in front of her, and he kicked them away so that they landed in the soft embrace of the sand outside.

"I don't believe you." He spoke. "I don't trust you."

"Even if I'm against The Company?" Pondered the girl.

Jackson stepped back for a moment, hesitating as the girl brushed herself off, holding the photo she had discovered in her hand. Why would she continue to mention the traders if she did truly seek his maps? The Company would just take them if they desired - they knew better than the pirates. He thought back to the moment in the photo. He'd been happy then, taken three years prior on the docks of the island. It was before he'd set out on that fateful day when it had all gone wrong, when he had worked for the dreaded North Sea Trading Company.

"Who's the person in the picture with you?" The girl asked, pointing out him and another.

Jackson didn't want to reply, it was too painful, and he remained silent. Then something surprised him, something he didn't expect; the girl handed him the photo back.

"You don't need to explain it." She whispered. "I've seen that look before. I only came here to ask you a question."

Jackson was astounded. She had broken into his house, held a gun to his head, and she did all this just to ask him a question? She certainly had some explaining to do.

"Well, I -" He began to say as the girl smiled.

"Excellent!" She chimed. "Come on!"

In a moment, the girl flew out the door and wound her way down to the long pathway that led to town.

"Wait!" He called after her, as he spun on his heels. "Didn't you want to ask me something?"

The girl continued to run, the warm sea wind from the shore blowing in her scarlet tendrils.

"Yes, but we're friends now, after all!" She grinned as she raced across the sand, stopping for just a moment to reply before running into the town again.

What? He thought, still astonished. Friends? A person such as him rarely had friends that he wanted to be around, and Jackson only had the small handful. How could he have been friends with this girl when she had just tried to kill him moments before?

"Friends don't try to bite other people's ears off!" He yelled after her.

"I was just playing!" She quipped back, laughing as she did.

He saw that she began to walk up the pathway, leaving him no choice but to follow. The island was swarming with pirates and even if just one of them saw her, things could get very bad indeed.

He rushed back over to the pile of Ash, scooping what he could into the small money-pouch he kept. He couldn't risk it being found by anyone, he had to keep it a secret. The pirates, in all likelihood, would steal it, use it for themselves, and they would kill the girl if they found her. Despite what had just transpired, Jackson found his sense of honour and loyalty nagging at him, as he scooped the remainder of the deadly powder into the bag. He didn't care for the girl, but she had saved his life, and what Nelson had said to him earlier that morning spoke to his over-caring nature when it came to the promises he made to his friends. Damn him for promising the cook he would look after the girl in some small way, and adding to that he still hadn't thanked her. Jackson then rushed out the door, as steady as his hungover legs could carry him.

"Who are you?" He asked her as he dragged his feet across the sand, trying to keep up.

The waves were swishing gently across the shore, and he could hear the midday gulls calling as the wind blew. The girl stood at the very top of the wood-chipped path, waiting for him as she neared the entrance to the town. She turned around with her arms by her side and called down the beach.

"The name's Ann, but we can talk all about that and how you're going to repay me over a drink!"

5

'*Looty and Booty*' was the only bar open in the whole town thanks to the storm. And, as Ann found out, it just so happened to be Jackson's favourite place to drink. Since the pirates had arrived, the old dive had apparently seen better days. The wooden porch on the outside of the loose rickety shack groaned and creaked like flimsy piano keys, and the murky stained windows reflected a dusty, gloomy light.

A charming place to have a round Ann thought, and so out the way. She hoped those looking to pry wouldn't interrupt.

The air upon entering was deadly quiet, so thin and frail, Ann could have sworn she could cut through it with the delicate touch of a fingernail. Like the outside of the bar, the floorboards creaked as Ann tiptoed across them. Her high-heeled boots clicked against the wood, and a damp, musty smell came seeping out of every crack and orifice, like rats racing from a sinking ship.

"Well." She began, underneath her breath as she syphoned in the putrid smells and tastes. "What's up with this ugly bunch?"

Jackson, who was standing next to her, turned his head and gave her a dry smile. Everyone was staring at her; the room full of strange, drunken, snarling faces, eyeing her clothing with disgust. Ann stared back at them with equal repulse.

"They're old and broken, like most of the things that wash up here." Jackson explained, quietly.

Ann ignored his slyness and turned her back to him, folding her arms. This was not what she had expected things to be like. Weren't navigators meant to be friendly and help people out when they asked for it? Jackson seemed to be the complete opposite.

She noted however, that he was right. All the patrons were made up of almost entirely older men. Most had grey-white hair and were injured with body parts missing. One whistled at her sharply. When Ann glanced to see who it was, she saw that the man had an eye missing, along with most of his teeth. She decided to turn back around and inched closer to Jackson. Despite the confidence and bravado that she had shown earlier, Ann still did not like that all the eyes were on her when she entered the room. It hearkened back to a time she would rather forget and made her feel unnerved and alone.

"Don't mind them." Jackson whispered in her ear, perking her confidence.

His tone had a layer of sarcasm, and Ann supposed that was fair considering how they had just met.

"They just probably hate what you're wearing. You are dressed like a pirate after all, and by the way, I still don't trust you, you have to earn that."

Jackson then waved at the man with one eye, and the man nodded back and returned to his business.

Ann hated that Jackson didn't trust her. She had told him she didn't steal anything, which was true, and it made her wonder why they just couldn't be friends, as it was all water underneath the metaphorical bridge. After all, Ann had saved him from that storm.

"And why would that be a problem?" She huffed, flicking back her hair, trying to disguise her disappointment,

"We're not exactly welcoming of strangers." The drunk mumbled.

"So, they have a thing against pirates?" She prodded, this time a bit quieter so only Jackson could hear.

He nodded then waved his hand over to the barkeep. The bartender eyed Jackson with a venomous scowl, scrunching up her face as though she'd just sucked on the world's sourest lemon. She was mildly good looking in Ann's opinion, dressed in a frilly white chemise with an apron fitted around her waist.

"Now there's no need to be like that, Arie." Jackson began, as he sat down in front of her. "Ann's just a stranger. I hardly know her or trust her for that matter." He continued.

"I'm right here." Ann mused.

Arabella folded her arms, apparently not satisfied with Jackson's excuse, after she poured out two drinks, placing them in front of her ex.

"There you go." She grumbled.

Ann got the feeling that many things were left unsaid between the two of them simply by the fire in the barmaid's eyes, and she was pleased not to be partied to it. Ann had her own set of problems to worry about, and time was of the essence.

Jackson then reached forward to grab the ales, but Arabella snatched them away.

"What in all the hells?" He grunted.

"Are you going to pay this time?" She asked.

"Yeah, after I'm done." He muttered, as he tried to reach for his drinks yet again.

"No, now!" Arie demanded.

All of *Looty and Booty* turned to look at him in bemusement. The drunk only sighed.

"Alright, how many Threds?" He asked, reaching deep into his pocket.

"Fifty."

"What! Fifty Threds, are you serious?"

"Pay up Mark!"

Eventually, Jackson paid her the fifty Threds, however, with all the arguments over drinks, Ann saw that he had forgotten what he had also placed there, and Arabella was glaring too. Jackson looked in horror at the blue smear that was left about his fingers, and he scurried to wipe his hand before any others could discover his almost deathly folly. Arie raised an eyebrow as he grabbed the drinks from her and tossed over the dusty coin. If the pirates knew he had such a thing, they would surely come after him and the barmaid quickly brushed the metal into her apron.

"Why is it that prices are so high here?" Ann asked, wanting to know more about the pirates and to change the conversation.

Looking around the room, she could see the misery that had built up about the town. As she and Jackson had walked up from the beach, she'd discovered that the majority of the people were sick, poor, and hungry, whilst the pirates were fruitful in their fat and lazy ways. She had to do something to help.

"The Vains control pretty much everything here." Said Arabella.

Jackson huffed in annoyance as he finished his drink in one glorious, yet horrifying gulp, and both girls paused to look at him.

"What?" He asked.

"You're making a scene." Hissed Arie.

The look on her face had turned from annoyance to that of concern. Jackson waved her off.

"You know what. I've had enough with everyone being that bald-headed freak's dogs, why is everyone so afraid of him anyway?" He burst out in anguish as he slammed the container down.

Everyone was still looking at him, seeming more frightened than before at just the mention of the pirate's image. Suddenly, there was a crash from the doors, and all in the tavern turned to look as a man in a pirate's jacket stormed in. Surrounded by lackeys; a wisp of smoke ascended from a pipe held between his lips, and he sang to himself, his gruff voice reaching to all the corners of the dank and dusty room:

"Ahoy - Ahoy, Ahoy! Ahoy!

Many years ago: I was a boy, I set to sea,

To seek a path 'o'glory n' build a' wealth unseen.

For I sailed for Ragnar, on promises of gold!

But taken by the Devil' s lust, he fell and left us cold.

Now that famous pirate was a brute, a hefty lad,

We followed him across the sand, to treasure 'o' so glad,

But when the Devil came, she smiled n'took his clammy hand.

The gold was ours within the earth and crimson wet the sand,

For what we do to traitors, we will show but never tell –

For old Ragnar, he paid the price and knew it 'o' so well,

For now, we're bloody rich, as flush as fucking kings and queens!

For if you cross us, we'll slit your throat and throw you to the Sea."

"Ugh! Silvers!" Jackson spat as he recognised the pirate's signature silver hair. "What's he doing here?"

"Jackson, don't! He's here for the rally." Cried Arie as the pirate made his way over to them.

Jackson glared at her.

"Why are you defending him?" He poked, but the barmaid just waved him away.

"Hey, is someone going to tell me who he is?" Whispered Ann, as the barmaid went to see to the pirates.

"Silvers Kent, the quartermaster working under Atlas. His captain's a complete and utter psychopath, an addict!" He began as he snarled at the man who had summoned Arabella.

The pirates were mocking people as they passed by, kicking over tables and sending drinks flying into the air.

"He and his brother are on the island looking for something, some kind of treasure, they've been here a month now and they've done nothing but ruin our lives."

Ann thought for a second about what her newfound friend was saying. So *they* were the pirates who attacked her ship! To her, the answer was simple, they were just lowly thugs.

"And the treasure?" She asked. "What of that?"

Jackson groaned yet again, appearing fed up at the mere mention of it.

"No idea."

Jackson then looked back over the counter, rubbing his ear. Arabella was serving Silvers at the far end of the bar, and the drunk had a concerned and annoyed look to his face, but before Ann could get up to confront the pirate, Jackson leaned in close so he could whisper in her ear.

"Look, I don't exactly trust you yet, but Arie was right. This isn't the time."

Ann turned to look at him, her newfound horror apparent.

"Then why do you tolerate this? The pirates?" She asked. "Clearly you care for the people in your life! You've got to believe in something. Stand up for yourself!"

It was then that she saw Jackson grind his teeth.

"Because the mayor's in on it as well, and he's Arie's father." He whispered coldly, looking over to Silvers. "But don't tell Arie. Kent used a power on her. I don't know what it was, but I don't want her to get hurt - she has moments where she's not herself, like she's forgotten who she is, and someone's placed the words there. The pirates promised her dad a cut, and they have no intention of keeping that if they did. They're a bunch of liars, the lot of them. It's not real."

"So, he's a user too?" Ann confirmed, as she watched Silvers lean in to kiss Arabella on the neck, and nevertheless, the barmaid slapped him back.

Jackson nodded. There was a small kindling spark in his eyes, and Ann hoped to ignite those smouldering flames into a roaring fire. If she ever had any hope of doing what she intended to, Jackson just had to believe in her... and himself. Whatever power Silvers was using, it seemed to Ann like he hadn't seen that he was being watched. His men laughed at him as he reeled. Kent sneered at the barmaid with a growl, as he rubbed the greyed bandage around his hand, telling her she would regret what she had done, and with that, he stormed out of the tavern as fast as he came in. Arabella stood there for a time, watching the swinging entrance of the tavern doors. It seemed the danger had passed.

Ann breathed a sigh of relief as she returned to her conversation. Now more than ever, she had to convince

Jackson that he could trust her. She had to convince him that something about her was real enough to believe in. She'd seen it in his hut, that the drunk had already lost a fragment of himself.

"You know… myths, legends, every tale under the sun can be proved real with some evidence." She mused optimistically. "And not all pirates break their word."

She looked at Jackson curiously as he watched the barmaid. Clearly Arabella could handle herself. Ann twirled her ruby hair around her fingers in thought. Jackson sounded like he knew their betrayal was a certainty.

"I've been on the receiving end of people's lies before." He grumbled, clenching his fist around his drink, and tapping his ear, which Ann noted, was still a little pink.

"I don't trust pirates, I don't trust those pigs at the N.S.T.C, and at the moment, I don't trust you."

"Why?" Ann asked, still pondering his reasons. "I trust you, plus I happen to agree with you about the Company. However, some pirates can be reasoned with."

Jackson smirked at this. At least they found something they both had in common.

"And how would you know, Navy-girl? Are you a pirate?" He laughed.

"We are being bled dry of everything. Silvers marched in here just so he could prove how powerful he is!"

"I just know, okay." She replied, answering him with a smile.

Jackson ignored her and continued ranting, giving Ann the opportunity to sit back and watch.

"Gold, food, water, booze – why'd they have to take the booze?" He complained. "These pirates are causing all types of problems for the town without any regard for who gets in their way, and his quartermaster had just shown that."

"He sounds…terrifying." Ann wobbled her voice mockingly as Jackson continued. She was not afraid of someone who was just a simple thief, there were far more dangerous people in the world than Atlas Vain.

"You have no idea." Whined the drunk, forgetting that Ann had said she was from the Navy.

"Anyway, about that question I wanted to ask you." She abruptly began. "Would you be open to taking me on as a customer?"

She edged her way closer to the drunk and curled her hair in-between her fingers as she did, making sure that her shining emerald eyes met the sullen depths of his brown.

"That would depend on where you wanted to go, I don't come cheap. The pirates have scared away everyone else." He muttered, tapping his drink.

"Please, I need to see a friend!"

"Yes, where though?"

"Black Ridge."

Jackson's eyes widened, causing Ann's smile to fade as he stood up, reached over the bar, and grabbed the pitcher Arabella kept for spares. Was this girl crazy! His mind screamed.

"Please." Ann begged. "I'll pay you double your normal rate or whatever it is, just take me!"

Jackson, spooked by her request, handed over fifty more Threds to Arabella as she returned to their end of the bar, still gazing somewhat fearfully over at the tavern entrance.

"I'm not going to that infernal place ever again." He snapped, taking the now filled pitcher from the barmaid. "Never, do you hear me!"

He seemed absolutely terrified at the prospect of going to that place and Ann wanted to know why. She had heard whispers that Jackson had been to Black Ridge once before, and that he had sailed its dark and deathly creeks and crags.

"What's your friend doing in a place like that, anyway?"

Ann was about to answer when Arie interrupted.

"What's going on?" She asked, her attention suddenly snapping back to the present.

"Nothing. Are you alright?"

Jackson was still as pale as a winter flower, rubbing his eyes as he shook his head.

"Yes, Mark. I'm fine. I am intrigued though. I've not seen you this frightened in years. I don't know where in the world she wants you to take her, but you need the money to pay off your tab."

Jackson groaned once more and took a gulp of the pitcher to try and return his sunned island complexion.

"I said I'll pay when I've got the money." He mumbled as he wiped his mouth.

"And when will that be exactly?" Arabella asked with a glare, mopping up the escaped drops of alcohol from the drunk's drink.

Ann opened her mouth to chime in, when all of a sudden, the centre-parted doors swung open yet again, and Nelson came walking through carrying a large wooden crate.

"Lunchtime." He grinned, and the barmaid grumbled, cursing under her breath as she went to collect something.

Moments later, with several bottles of ale, Arabella returned, putting them in the crate that Nelson had set between Jackson and Ann. Jackson, having finished his drink, reached into the crate, and grabbed one of the bottles.

"Hey, that's not for you!" The barmaid seethed.

It was too late however, and Jackson was greeted by a surprising squealing and hollering sound as he pulled the drink free.

"You pesky, little blighter!" He swore, covering his hand as he put the bottle down on the counter.

Inside the crate, Ann could see two pinkish ears point out from behind the slats, with a small snout grumbling as if to say 'Oi, you! Bugger off!'

"Who's that?" Ann asked, looking at the small pig that greeted her with jangling bottles of alcohol.

Nelson was about to reply, when Jackson opened his mouth. Clearly, those last two drinks had gone to his head.

"This little bacon butty!" Jackson growled. "Is my old nemesis, Napoleon. Nelly keeps him as a pet to show-boat his restaurant."

"Restaurant?" Ann wondered aloud.

Napoleon squealed yet another greeting as Arie petted his head. The piglet, in obvious delight, was all too willing to snuggle up to her hand. Much like a kitten to a ball of wool.

"Nelly runs a crappy restaurant in town." Jackson continued, somewhat drunkenly. "They say it's the best, but if you ask me, it's a load of rubbish. Anyway, those pirates have been forcing Nelly to cook for them and invade his place every day. Arie just so happens to supply the booze."

"I'm sorry about that, by the way." Arabella said to Nelson. "My dad still won't budge."

"It's fine." Nelson responded. "I see you two have met then?"

Ann nodded as she noted a tinge of fear in his voice as he spoke about the pirates, and she felt frustrated that she couldn't do anything to assist someone who had helped her survive the night.

"Are you still wearing that bracelet I had Jackson give you, Arie?" The cook asked the barmaid suddenly. Arabella glared at Jackson as he taunted Napoleon with avid stares.

"Yes." She said, showing him the red ribbon around her wrist.

"Good." Said Nelson as he loaded up. "Don't take it off, okay?"

Arabella was unsure why, but she agreed to his request nonetheless, as Jackson also looked at him in a confused manner. For as long as they had been friends, the drunk affirmed that there were still some things about the cook that he just did not understand. Nelson then said his goodbyes and sorrowfully made his way back to the door, where another gruelling cover awaited him.

"Could you guys look after Napoleon for me while I'm gone?" He asked, looking back at the piglet who was now sprawled across the counter.

"Yeah, sure thing!" Arabella agreed, stroking Napoleon. "The little pork chop will be no problem."

Jackson let out a sloppy chuckle.

"Especially if he's between two pieces of bread." He snorted, causing Arie to bend round the bar and slap him.

"Ow! What was that for?" He moaned, rubbing his head.

"You know full well."

Then, just as Nelson departed, a thought crossed Ann's mind. If Jackson wouldn't help her get to Black Ridge because he didn't trust her, then perhaps getting the help of someone he did and ridding the town of the pirates would change his mind? In fact, Ann figured that Nelson was the perfect person for this.

"Is he always like that?" Ann asked Jackson and Arabella curiously.

Having only known Nelson for just half a day, she now wanted to know more about the mysterious cook, to which the barmaid responded.

"Aha!" Nodding her head and tearing her eyes to Jackson. "Molly, Nelson's sister, was like that too. Very adventurous."

"I like that." Smiled Ann. "Is she around?"

"No!" Jackson erupted suddenly after taking another swig of his drink. "Will you just stop asking questions already!"

Ann now saw the concerned look on Arabella's face as she ordered the drunk to go to another table, having made too much of a mess at the bar. Ann could feel the entire weight of all the eyes in the tavern on them as Jackson begrudgingly did what he was told whilst Arie cleared up; mouthing the words 'Lost at sea' to Ann before she continued their conversation.

"Just do us all a favour and take him with you." She urged, pointing to Jackson as he went, then rubbing Napoleon's belly yet again. "The whole town is fed up with him, he needs to do his job and take people where they want to go."

Ann smiled at that, wondering if Molly was the woman she had seen with Jackson in the photograph, and upon further reflection, she realised that she and Nelson looked remarkably similar.

"He's one of the best navigators around, he'll get you anywhere." The barmaid added, and Ann knew she was right.

She desperately needed that ride if she was going to make it in time, still, she couldn't help that dire and in-conquerable feeling of wanting to help the people around her. Wondering what had happened to Molly and what she was going to do about it if she was ever going to help Jackson.

"That's why I'm here." she said solemnly. "Somebody told me that Jackson was the best, and I need the best, so I can go get my friend."

"Where are they?" Arabella asked, once again petting Napoleon, who squeaked with happiness.

Ann was reluctant to tell her having just seen Jackson's reaction, however, she decided that Arie might actually help her in bringing the drunk around, so decided to whisper it into her ear as she leaned over the bar.

"Black Ridge Prison." Ann uttered, causing the blonde woman to go rigid in pure shock; Napoleon too, squawked in horror.

"Why in the entire world would you want to risk getting into that place? It's an impenetrable fortress, so they say, and even more dangerous once you're inside. The most infamous pirates and criminals in the archipelago are kept in that pit."

"So?" quirked Ann. "The only problem I'll have is getting in."

"I hardly think they let people in for visiting hours." Arabella half-joked.

Ann smirked brightly with a wild look in her eye as she began to curl her hair between her fingers once more. She was about to say something else when Jackson returned from the stalls. He drunkenly pushed himself against the counter, scooping Napoleon up in his arms.

"I'm borrowing this." He said, as the piglet squirmed in his grasp, and he walked out the door.

"Hey!" Arabella exclaimed, but Jackson just waved her away as she had done to him.

Ann too was about to leave, getting up and grabbing her jacket to follow the drunk, however, Arabella stopped her.

"If you're going after him-" She started. "He'll know. Jackson may be a drunk, but he's not stupid, well unless he's had Snake. You'll have to wait."

"And do what?" Ann sighed, raising her arms to motion around the tavern in dismay.

She didn't know the town particularly well, and she didn't want to be stared at by the weird old men any longer than she already had.

"Why don't we play a game?" The barmaid suggested. "I'm not doing much. Jackson is the only one who even remotely tries to pay off his tab, the others downright refuse. It's like getting blood from a stone."

Ann thought for a second. She really didn't have the time to be playing games. However, if she couldn't follow Jackson, she might as well do something to pass the time.

"What did you have in mind?" She asked.

"How about Scourge?"

"Scourge?"

"What! You've never played Scourge?" Exclaimed Arabella, raising an eyebrow.

She shrugged in response.

"No, I've been... away for a while." Ann trailed off.

Arabella bent down behind the bar and brought out what seemed to be a sizeable, circular chess board. The barmaid then produced a small box and opened it up. Inside was a large worn stack of illustrated cards, the edges torn and curling. A black and red coloured die appeared alongside them; it's shaved features were that of the previous item, shortly followed by a dozen wooden pieces that Arabella had compiled into one small hand.

"This is going to be fun." The barmaid grinned, handing half of her palmful of pieces to Ann.

Arabella then set her own pieces out in front of her. Ann found the barmaid had gifted her three ships: a galleon, a frigate, and a sluice. The ships were all different sizes and were coloured contrastingly to the ones that Arie had on the other side of the board, which were stained in a marvellous bone white. Ann's own ships were dyed a deep onyx. She had no idea what she was doing or even how to play this supposed board game. Arabella dealt out the cards, six each.

"Okay, here's how it goes. We each have three ships; the aim of the game is to move across the board and sink the other player's ships. There can be four players at a time and each player must always have six cards in their hand. Once the hand has been dealt, each player takes three cards from the spare pile and places them face-down. You're not allowed to look at those cards."

"Okay." Ann nodded, growing more and more confident as the rules were relayed to her.

"You roll the die to move and can only move one ship each turn. The amount you roll is the amount you can move, and all of the ships can move in any direction across the board. When you want to attack an enemy ship, you have to be in range. All ships can fire forward, back, left, and right, but cannot attack diagonally, and each ship has a different range of attack. Galleons have a range of three spaces, frigates two, and sluices one. Are you with me so far?"

Ann nodded slowly, hoping that what Arabella was saying would stick in her head.

"When attacking a ship, you choose to turn over one of your face-down cards; the number on there is your attack number. Then, with the cards we have in our hands, we play a game of liar and turn a card on the spare pile to play on. The cards you say you play have to be equal, one number above or one below the value of the last card on the pile. The first one to be caught lying by the other wins the battle, and a new hand is dealt with the recycled cards."

"What happens if the person is telling the truth?" Asked Ann.

Arabella smiled.

"Then the person who called liar loses. If the defending player wins, they can either move their ship or can turn over one of their cards, inflicting the damage on the attacker if they are in range. Once a turned over card has been used it has to go back to the pile, and another card has to be selected. Each ship has a different health rating; galleons have forty health, frigates have thirty, and sluices have thirteen, and that's the rules."

"Wow, is it as complicated as it sounds?" Ann gawped.

"Nah." Arie chuckled, waving her hand. "It's straightforward once you start playing; it's just strategy and knowing how to tell a lie."

She gulped.

"What's the matter?" Asked the barmaid, curiously.

"Nothing." She muttered, taking three cards from the spares pile.

"Good, then let's play. The person that rolls highest goes first."

She passed Ann the die. Ann shook the small red and black cube in her palm, cupping her other hand over the top before throwing it out on to the large circular board.

Could she really beat Arabella at this game? She had lied to Jackson earlier in the hut, but that had been a very different situation and one where it benefited her in working towards her goal. The pirates on this island couldn't discover she had said she was from the Navy. With all the commotion going on around them, she knew they would hunt her down if necessary. However, this game was dangerous – it was created to uncover lies and reward those who got away with it. The die rolled and rolled over the black and white spaces, eventually coming to a stop at the other end of the board. Ann held her breath.

It was a five – a high number. Was it good enough? Arabella would have trouble beating it. The barmaid picked up the die and tossed it around in her hand before eventually rolling it back towards Ann.

A two.

Ann had the first move. She hovered her hand above the die and thought about the move she would make. The sluice had less health than all the other ships; would it have been easier to move that ship first, so she could place the others in a better position? Admittedly, that was more preferable than just side by side, and she could use it to get closer. Perhaps Arabella wouldn't notice when she started to reposition other pieces? She smiled, deciding to move the sluice. Ann picked up the die again, flicking a lock of hair over her shoulder in the process.

Another five.

Yes! She moved the sluice forward. It was almost halfway across the board now, almost within touching distance of the white enemy ships.

Now it was Arabella's turn.

The barmaid picked up the die and rolled a six, the best number she could possibly hope for. As soon as she saw the black blotches of the die, she placed her fingers on the galleon, steering the keel of the ship through ivory waves and beyond.

Great, Ann thought as she frowned at the board. Now her sluice was in range of the ship's cannons and would easily be blown from the would-have-been water of their roaring exchange.

Arie was smiling. Ann watched in painful anticipation and astonishment as she turned her middle card to reveal a queen. She gritted her teeth. If Arabella won the game of liar, the sluice would only have one health point remaining.

Nervously, Ann slid a card from the spare pile. Her hand was shaking, jittering up and down at a furious pace, the card almost escaping from her grasp. Why was she so afraid of a simple game? Of course, she already knew the answer. The distrust she had seen so far in this place boarded on the obscene, and, whether she had been Navy, pirate, or otherwise, it made no difference – she would have been treated with mutual distaste. Apart from Nelson and now Arie, not one person had given her a warm welcome. She placed her card down so that she and Arabella could see the number: it was an eight.

Both girls scanned their hands. Ann held a seven, a four, an Ace, a King, a Jack and a nine, and she looked at the mayor's daughter with a delicate slyness.

"You know, it was good of you to pull him out of that storm – nine." Said the barmaid, putting down her card with a confident bluster. Ann knew Arabella was good at this, but she had to be better.

"I was only trying to help. Nine also." Ann nonchalantly replied, doing the same.

The barmaid's face was not giving anything away and Ann knew it was going to be difficult for her to win.

"Ten." Said Arabella, quickly exacting her next move.

"A Jack!" Boasted Ann, quickly putting the card down and looking back to her deck.

If she made it look like she was lying when she wasn't, the blonde might call her bluff.

"Queen?" Asked the barmaid, slightly extending out the 'E' as she put down the card.

Quickly Ann slid in her king and announced her intension.

"I'll always try to help someone if they need it."

"Liar!" Called Arabella and Ann grinned as she turned over the card to show what lay on top.

"Damn it," the barmaid cursed, seeing the turned over card.

Ann decided to take her health points; now she only had seventeen left on her galleon. Quickly, with the decks reshuffled and changed, both players had fresh cards. Ann rolled the die for her next turn. It was a four. However, because of the galleon's three space range, she knew she could just about reach for an attack if she moved it near the sluice, so she picked the piece up and positioned it four diagonal places across the board. Ann now had to choose which card to turn over, and she picked the card to her left-hand side. The card turned out to be a Jack, meaning eleven attack points were up for grabs. This time, Ann saw Arie pulling the top card. A three.

Ann gazed down at her new hand, damning them. Only high cards.

"Two." Arabella said.

"A three." Ann lied.

Her nerves hadn't gone completely, but she was worried she might soon catch on.

"Four." Chimed the barmaid, putting the card on the pile just as quickly and as fast as Ann had.

The redhead looked at the blonde, hoping to see any signs of hesitation in her expression. The entire thing was beginning to feel very tense. If Arabella had figured out her lies it would all be over.

"So, what did your friend do?" She asked casually.

"Four also." Ann spoke quickly, flicking her next card down.

Her heart began to beat faster and faster, and Ann could barely contain it from leaping in one clear bound from out of her slim frame and onto the field of play.

"What do you mean?" She asked.

"And another four."

"Well, why are they rotting in a place like Black Ridge, they must have done something to get thrown in there?" Arabella said accusatorily.

Ann's jaw tightened. She had no idea how she managed to keep her composure and took in a breath before answering. Arabella was an extremely skilled liar, and much better than herself in this given situation, but those sapphire eyes continued to stare at her in some form of twisted jest from across the bar, and Ann felt as though she couldn't take any more. She gripped the card tightly, slightly bending it in her palm.

"Five!" Yelled Ann, slamming it down, causing the counter to shake, anger washing over her.

"And she didn't do anything, all she was guilty of was being put in the wrong place!"

"Liar!" Called the barmaid.

Ann gritted her teeth once more, turning over her hand to show she had placed a depraved seven.

"Ha, I knew it!" Arabella smirked.

The barmaid turned over her own face-down card, revealing a king. She was lying all along.

"I choose to attack your Sluice, and skin it."

Then, before Ann could even protest, Arabella took the piece off the board and it flew headlong into the box, crashing like the fictional waves that swept across the entirety of the board.

Time passed, the two of them kept playing and talking and eventually, Arabella won the game with Ann's poor naval tactics not serving her particularly well. Ann then looked up at the clock atop the bar, and she was surprised and shocked by how fast the time had gone. It had felt as though she'd been playing that dreaded game for an eternity.

"Shit! I've got to get after Jackson. Thanks for the game."

Ann flew from her seat, grabbing what remained of her unattached attire and abandoned the bar.

"Oh? Bye then." The barmaid laughed as she waved her goodbye, instructing her to look after the drunk.

Truthfully, Ann was just happy to get away from Arie's probing questions. She rushed out of the swaying doors, breathing a long sigh of relief. That was a close call.

Outside, the sun was baking hot. The town was swarming with people and pirates. It was drastically different from when she had first entered the tavern with Jackson, as hundreds of footprints and tracks lined the roads and trails to and from the jungle. Taken a-back by the numbers, Ann was sure that being caught with, or following the drunk, was the fastest way to get herself recognised, realising she had immensely down-played the powerful position the pirates were in. How in all the world was she going to follow Jackson now?

Ann had to think on her feet. Taking in to account the growling, shouting pirates, she decided she didn't want to get herself killed just yet. Ahead of her, the road was filled with gloom and dust, made humid by the swelling heat. A crowd of people appeared as powdery silhouettes, making their way up the hill in the direction that Jackson was heading. So, being as cat-like and stealthy as she could, Ann huddled herself within her black leather jacket - it being similar to what the invaders wore - and crept into a passing crowd that was being funnelled along the main causeway. She smiled to herself as she remembered what Jackson had said earlier in the tavern. As the group pushed and stumbled amongst themselves, no one seemed to notice that she was any different from any other pirate milling around the island. Her person-like camouflage was herded along, almost like cattle, as they made their way further into town and eventually up the hill.

She wondered where they were going? The pirates were out in force, allowing her first real sight of what she was dealing with, and she was beginning to feel like she had made a fatal mistake. Everyone looked nervous and on edge as the pirates grunted and snarled, lashing their whips and guns only to incite terror. She still hadn't spotted Jackson, and Ann hoped he was okay. Being drunk and carrying a pig; he was sure to be picked from among the throngs. However, the same question nagged at Ann. Where had all these people come from? Scores of bodies were ragged and dirty, covered in dark, black soot and bound in chains as they clanked along next to storm-laden debris. The pirates undoubtedly had a leash over the town, and it seemed to be getting tighter by the second. Banners draped in lilac and red hung across buildings and balconies, and Ann spied that the jolly roger fluttered at the centre of the stage. Fanfare followed, as more people started to arrive.

The silver-haired pirate from earlier, Silvers Kent, stepped into the centre of the stage. Flanking him were two massively built men, each the size of a small house. The brawny brutes carried a podium and several chairs with them; presumably for Silvers, and what Ann could only assume was the rest of the pirate hierarchy. The air fell deadly silent.

Up on the stage, Ann spied a man that looked eerily similar to Arabella's description of her father. He was stood next to a pirate with salmon-pink hair and seemed to be sweating profusely; dabbing his face with a handkerchief as the pirate whispered in his ear. Ann hated the fact that they were forcefully taking advantage of the people they had overrun. She caught a slight smirk and snigger from Silvers. The way his eyes glinted, and laugh cackled with the crack of whips caused by the sight of people crammed into the marketplace - it made

Ann sick. It was just like when she was younger. She had to make sure that no one who didn't deserve it ever got hurt again. She was a different kind of person to these pirates. She believed herself to be anyway.

A sudden murmur spread across the imprisoned crowd as the pirate quartermaster launched into his speech. Ann could have sworn she saw some of those within nod in agreement, seeing the mark of the pirate group through small gaps in the crowd.

"People of Ale Town!" Silvers bellowed, his voice carrying itself across the distance of the town's market space.

"Hear me and rejoice! May every man receive his fair and just reward. For your salvation is at hand!"

The pirates in the crowd began to roar in approval. Soon after, Ann heard the squealing of a frightened animal not far ahead from where she stood, as well as the harrowing laughter of more pirates as they jostled someone from side to side: Jackson and Napoleon!

"Great!" Ann muttered sarcastically under her breath.

She ducked further out the way as more people brushed against her; she didn't have the time for this. She needed to get away from the rally and move more freely without anyone noticing. She had to gain Jackson's trust, but, in the confined space she found herself, it would be too risky to reach for her guns and stop his attackers. Ann's attention turned to the stage, her fingers tapping against the outline of the firearms beneath her jacket. To take their leaders on would gain too much attention, she thought; all the while Silvers continued his speech, smiling maniacally to those in chains below.

"Our captain has decreed that we are almost ready to leave you in peace. The item we are looking for is close at hand, and we are here to convey a most profound message to you all."

"Has quite a way with words, doesn't he?" Somebody in the crowd said next to her.

She was pondering what kind of treasure the pirates were after and almost jumped out of her skin as her ears met the soft voice. Ann turned to see who it was, taking her eyes off Jackson and Napoleon for moment, only to find a small old man standing next to her.

"Tom!" She remarked in surprise, recognising the old man from the previous night.

He was wearing a large trench coat, similar to that of Jackson's, although his pockets bulged like he was smuggling something. The man purposefully tried to keep his head down. Ann couldn't blame him. The pirates continued to laugh as they started picking people out from the group, one by one. Ann wondered what they were doing, as they worked their way inward. Those they had picked out were forced onto the stage by gunpoint. In the distance, Napoleon's screeching could still be heard, echoing through the crowd causing Ann to clench her fists, her nails digging into her palms.

"What are we going to do?" She asked Tom, her mind filled with worry.

Jackson was her only way of getting where she wanted to go, and now that she was here on the island surrounded by a horde of enemies, the dread of not knowing what to do was beginning to set in. Up until now, she had no idea about the numbers she faced. On the navy ship, it seemed as though the pirates were one small group, and she had dismissively brushed away Jackson's claims when he had warned her. Once again, she felt herself becoming confined, helpless to do anything as she had been for all those days locked in the Doctor's cabin. Ann knew, deep down in the depths of her memory, that the journey to the island was not the first time she had felt this way.

The sound of panicked squeals dissipated as Jackson bolted up the hillside, Napoleon clutched underneath his arm. Ann caught glimpses of their tiny figures through the throngs of people, till eventually the pirates ordering people to the stage were metres away. Those around her began to push and shout against their captors. Tom grabbed her hand.

"Listen to me!" He pleaded to her, as the pirates came for them. "We're going to go up there and I'm going to put an end to this madness. The treasure they seek, they cannot have it, you understand? Darkness must not arise to cleanse this world. It whispers to you, warps the mind!"

Ann's heart thumped against her chest as shots rang into the air and a pathway emerged from the crowd parting. Tom still clasped her hand as the pirates seized them. At least Jackson and Napoleon had gotten away. Ann spun to see the face of Silvers Kent on the podium. A smoking gun fizzled upwards from the shots he had fired; seeing the wild look in his eyes, Ann didn't want to imagine what would happen if she and Tom were brought on stage.

"That's enough!" The quartermaster roared. "The captain has informed me that since daylight, one of you among us has taken up arms against our glorious endeavour. You have plagued our path with traps, torture and death and we will stand for this no longer. This so-called guardian will pay."

Ann felt damned. With no possible avenue in which she could escape unnoticed, she cursed herself for the mess she had dragged herself into. Still clinging to her hand tightly, there was a worried look in Tom's eyes; they welled with sadness and pride. With the pirates only steps away, Ann found herself being tugged along by the old man.

"It's you, isn't it? You're the one they're after!"

"Atlas wants them battered and bruised, broken for the mine – I can't let them hurt any more people. I can't let them find it." Replied Tom, forcing the two of them along through the hordes of people.

It was too late, the two of them ran into a line of chained prisoners as the pirates from the stage barrelled after them in rampant fury. Behind the line of prisoners was another group masked within the crowd. A gun shot rang out from the podium and the line of condemned men in front of them surged forward towards Tom and Ann as they were pushed by the pirates hidden within. The fleeing pair were thrown to their backs as they fell to the ground and landed with an almighty clatter against the cobbles of the market square. It had all been planned.

"And you have a plan, right?" Ann hissed to the man.

The sound of chains rattling above, along with the bruise from where she had landed, ignited a dull ache in Ann's chest.

"So says the girl who appeared as if from nowhere at the edge of a storm." He retorted.

Silvers Kent had raised the crowd to a fever pitch and everyone around them converged, whether they were forced to or not. Ann clambered for an idea as to how they would escape, but couldn't find one. They were surrounded and there was no way out; no gaps they could run through, no chains they could dive or leap over or under. The pirates were bound to catch them. Ann thought again about her friend in prison. Would she ever see her again or reach her in time? Her heart sank at the precedent. Glaring at her were snarling and ferocious faces. Tom too found it hard to believe the pirates would ever leave peacefully after this. They were ruthless and had set up all this to stop him from protecting the tunnels they had found underneath the jungle. That was where the treasure sat, lost within the twists and turns of darkest earth and stone. Every moment he waited; Atlas drew closer to it. Without him in the way, Tom knew they would surely find it.

He gripped Ann's arm tightly.

"Can I trust you?" He asked, as the pirates bore down upon them.

Ann nodded. His worn and wrinkled face was grey with dread, and Ann felt his hand turn cold as the pirates finally reached them, hoisting them up and holding them in a vice-like grip. The brutes that had once been on the stage next to the podium now wrapped their arms around them and forced them to walk through the crowds to where Silvers stood, grinning from ear to ear.

As they went, the lines of the weathered prisoners, draped in black rags stained by earth and mud, glared at them. Some others were fresher faced. The red marks newly borne on their bodies showed the unmistakable signs of skin rubbed raw by iron constraints. These faces she knew little of but knew all the same that they had sailed with her to the island. Their once pure white Navy cloaks now stained a murky grey with dirt and hardship. Rebellion against their captors was still ripe on their faces – they hadn't lost all their fight at least. They had not yet been broken as the island had been, and Ann felt a swell of hope rise within her that at least not all was lost. However, as she passed them, her head dipped, her scarlet hair acting as curtains against their prying eyes. If the pirates knew she had escaped The Inspectre, she'd be done for.

"Bring them here!" Silvers commanded, and both Tom and Ann were forced to the stage; the crowd turning to that of a murmur.

"Old man!" Cried the pirate with the salmon-pink hair, sitting forward in his chair. "We've been thwarted all this time by one old man, and a girl?"

Tom spat at the floor as they mentioned his name and the brutish pirate restraining him forced him down by crippling his knee. He yowled in pain.

"People of Ale Town!" Kent announced once again, this time raising a pistol across the stage. "This is not a farewell party; this is not an announcement. We have gathered you here today to be witness to this man's execution. His fate was predetermined as soon as he set arms against us and woe befall those who think to do the like! All who side against us will feel Atlas' might!"

Silvers then steadied his hand as he waited for the impact of his speech to settle upon the crowd. His voice reverberating from the podium, his finger resting on the gilded metal that had sowed death to so many. The air was strangely silent, despite the cold wind that blustered through the market.

Tom whispered something to Ann as the pirate brought him up in line with Kent's vicious eyes. She couldn't make out what he was saying.

"What?" She hissed back, unsure of what he meant as her own brute tightened the grip around her arms.

Silvers was about to pull the trigger. It would be over for both of them if something did not happen, and soon! Ann felt her heartbeat quicken once again.

"Wait!" The pink-haired pirate urged from his seat and leapt up with a joyous smile upon his face as he produced a saw-like blade from the sheath on his back.

Silvers rolled his eyes.

"Ugh! You always do this, Gillian. Always wanting to get into Atlas' good books, well guess what, I can kill people just as well as you can, you know. Just as well as the captain and Orion!" He bickered.

Gillian giggled in childish delight as Silvers glared at him.

"No, you can't." He taunted, lifting the heavy blade on his shoulder across the stage. "All you're good for is using people and you know it."

"Wait, are they arguing over who's going to kill us?" Said Ann aloud in amazement.

She shuffled from side to side, trying to break free of the captor that held her in place. The brute that restrained her lifted one of his massive hands, loosening the grip slightly as he scratched his head in thought.

"Yeah." He laughed, as if it were an inside joke between friends.

The first mate drew painstakingly nearer at an ever-quickening pace.

"This always happens. Really unprofessional of them. Rest assured; they both take real pride in their work."

"I'll be sure to fill out a card." Mocked Ann.

Suddenly, Gillian disappeared before her widening eyes. She panicked; this one was a user too, she realised. Before her, Ann saw that nothing was there and yet the creaking of the pirates' steps could be heard across the stage. The crowd, still dreadfully silent, watched the two hostages in anticipation, as even the pirates who had foiled Ann's escape remained uncharacteristically mute.

Next to her, held captive by her side, Tom suddenly let out a pained and heavy gasp. Crimson liquid cascaded from his mouth followed by a waterfall like gushing from his side. His eyes widened as the pirate reappeared in front of him, holding the hilt of the bloody dagger he had raised from his belt.

"May every man earn his fair and justly earned reward. This is your last chance, old man!" The pirate sang. "Tell us of the jungle tunnels and you may yet survive a moment longer, though unlikely it may be."

Ann tried to reach for him as he looked up to her; a tear falling from her cheek as she realised what he had asked of her moments before. The brute that held her remained firm, and again, she felt helpless to do anything. With what courage he had left, Tom spat at the pink-haired man, spattering his shoes with droplets of blood, before setting his face with an almost ghoulish, bloodstained grin. With that, the pirate raised his mighty serrated blade, the gears slowly starting to grind. Ahead of her, Ann could see Silvers laughing; her memory serving her that despite the good intentions she held dear, some men were inherently evil. Jackson had been right after all. There was no thought or regard for what these pirates; these marauders did. They were only in search of their prize. All the consequences of the world be dammed. Ann knew she had to do something fast - if she wanted to get out of this still breathing.

The girl steeled herself with thoughts of what would happen to her friend should she die, and so, with a long, drawn-out sigh, she brought her head down in preparation for her next act.

She knew she would surely die, but she would not surrender to that cold embrace so easily. A strong heart and a strong mind did a lot for a person in this world, and Ann was no exception to that rule.

She noted that the brute holding her had loosened his grip ever so slightly. It took only a second for the following events to unfold as Ann smashed the back of her skull against the pirate's chin in a reversed headbutt, sending him toppling from the stage in surprise. Immediately after this, her hand fell to her jacket, where she grasped her gun, raising it into in the air. Ann closed her eyes tight. Her thumb pressed against the small catch at the top of the pistol; a tiny silver switch that changed the ammunition setting from that of normal rounds to one of the special alterations that had been gifted to her when she had received the weapon. She didn't want to do this, moreover, it was definitely going to gain her the notoriety that she did not need, but having little choice in the matter, Ann gently squeezed the trigger towards those seated on the stage as the other brute dived to tackle her. She had tried to be better by running away at first, and yet, it was her own fault for venturing into the crowd. Much like how it had been when she boarded the Navy ship. Now it was too late, the choice had been made. The brute dived towards her, and a ruby coloured mist rocketed westward from the barrel and squealed with a fiery burst into the pirates. Ann dived sideways to avoid the brute as the steam vents and pipework above the stage exploded into a display of fire, encapsulating the street in an infernal blockade.

Flames swept across the stage moments after, the wooden planks crackling, the curtains of lilac dissolving in the acid-smoke, and the pirate jolly roger smouldering into cinders as the fire grew ever higher. The chaos scattered the pirates that were sitting on the stage, separating her and Tom from their attackers. They could do nothing but lay on the floor; their anguished faces glaring at her with malice and venom as they mouthed orders to their underlings.

Ann could barely hear what was being said. Everything was a blur as she attempted to climb to her feet, watching around her as the pirates rushed to usher their captives back from whence they came. It was a horrible sight to witness through her eyes. Knowing she was the one that had pulled the trigger, the smoke filling her lungs – it was a heavy burden to bear, and yet, she had not hesitated to do it for the sake of her friends. She thought back to when she had made the threat to Doctor Rudolf before he had cast her away. Would she have really done that back then if push had come to shove, just as it had done moments before? She shuddered at the thought as more tears crept down her face, unnoticed until now. The smudges of singed people barrelled around before them. They had to run now. They had to run before the rest of the pirates got to them and claimed this cursed treasure they spoke of. Unlike Jackson, Ann believed wholeheartedly that it was just as much real as it was dangerous - knowing that it had already caused so much pain just at the prospect of retrieving it. Below her, something burned upon the stage. Either an arm or a leg was caught by the flames, melting and searing skin from supple flesh, emitting a sickening smell. The pirates continued to push them onwards. Ann hated fire. She hated the flames she had caused from the barrel of her Ash-filled gun. She knew it would consume all in its wake, sweeping like a scythe of death across the land.

Next to her, Tom began to wheeze and cough, blood pooling at his feet as he uttered a few words under his breath. Again, Ann had no idea what he had said as the flames around them multiplied. In a dazed motion, she hoisted herself upright so that she could help the man to his feet, staggering a little as she wrapped her arms around him and pulled him up. Out of the corner of her eye, the girl noted that an odd few figures in grey-white coats had slipped like fleeing shadows away from the throngs; the scraps of black iron in crumpled heaps upon the uneven ground. She wished she could have helped more to free them but was stopped by the consequences of her own creation. However, there was still one more deadly thing that Ann had forgotten to deal with, as she worked to move Tom from the stage. Looming over them, betwixt a thinly veiled curtain of crimson and orange flame, was the brute that had tried to tackle her. He was burned and charred almost beyond recognition and he screeched at Ann to drop both Tom and her weapon.

She attempted to steady her breathing, though making sure not to breathe too deeply as they were besieged by the wall of flames. This always ended up happening to her, she thought, her eyes glaring at the snarling, bloody pirate. All the death and destruction that constantly swirled around her as if it were a raging torrent - it never seemed to end. What was the good in always seeing the best in everything if she could never do anything good herself? Ann told herself that at least she would have to try.

With a determined smile upon her face, Ann turned to the menacing heap behind the smouldering and dying wall and mustered all her strength, making sure to hold on to Tom as tight as she could.

"Bye big guy, see you later." She quipped as she dived off the stage.

She told herself that she wasn't going to let Tom die here and began to run in the direction that Jackson had gone.

6

It was a just after twelve when Ann finally dragged Tom away. She hid herself and Tom down a secluded alleyway, as pirate goons scoured the town in search of them. It had been two hours since the incident at the rally and they had flitted from place to place as Ann tried to make sense of Tom's inconsistent mutterings. He seemed to speak of what the pirate's ultimate plan was and how it all fitted together. She was trying to come up with some sort of plan before more people got hurt. Jackson in particular, as she still needed him to take her to Black Ridge.

Ann knew in the back of her mind that the pirates couldn't possibly have found what they were looking for yet, recalling how the old man had said that Atlas only wanted the townspeople bruised, which therefore implied they were still needed. The only question left was for what purpose? Arabella had been no help. Kent himself had announced in his speech that the treasure was close at hand. Jackson too had mentioned something about the mayor, and the pirate Gillian had hinted towards the island's jungle with dire intrigue.

"Great job, Ann." She mumbled to herself as she sculked in the shadows of the alleyway, pacing about the looming entrance that opened up before the hill. She peered at the special chambers of her pistols and how the different coloured powders sat in their canisters; the bullets all bundled tightly into a magazine that fitted seamlessly into the butt of the gun as she gripped it with a resolute hand. "You just had to make a spectacle of yourself, didn't you? Just had to use some of the gift that was left."

Just a short walk from their shadowy and dank reprieve, at the bottom of the hill and making his way towards Nelson's restaurant, was Jackson. They had finally caught up to him! He was swaying slightly from side to side, none the wiser that she had been in pursuit. Clearly, he hadn't quite sobered up yet, and Ann thought it best to keep her distance as he cradled a squealing Napoleon in his arms. That piglet could ruin everything with its crying if she was to get too close. Already, pirates scattered the lower-hill in search of her; they didn't know who she was, but sure enough word would have gotten out that there was an unknown girl on the loose.

"Are you going to be okay?" She queried to a pale and weakening Tom, whom she had sat slumped against the brick wall. He took a sip from his hip flask.

"What was your plan, to just let them kill you?" Ann seethed.

A sullen face winced back at her, and the old man coughed before answering; his breath having a peculiar odour of summer berries.

"The door that safeguards this world requires many things before it can be opened, that's what the last guardian told me. If I died with the password never passing from my lips, then the pirates would never reach it, but fear not, I'll be fine and I'll never speak a word to those scum." He rasped out, rubbing the bandaged and bloody wound that his invisible foe had inflicted. "Just need to get some rest."

"But you've been stabbed!" Exclaimed Ann.

Tom looked down.

"That I have, never stopped me before though -"

"Hells! You need a fucking healer, a doctor. There must be one on the island that the pirates haven't enslaved?"

The old man fell silent as he bit his lip and Ann got the feeling she had touched on something controversial that he wasn't quite open to telling her.

"Tom!" She almost screamed in fear, quickly shushing herself for fear of drawing even more unwanted attention to the two of them.

He was growing paler by the second and Ann knew that Jackson would not forgive her if she allowed one of his closest friends to die.

"Nelson." The old man coughed. "Nelson has Alchemic blood – he could heal me with the correct instruction."

Ann's eyes widened and she bent down to grip the guardian's hand.

"Alchemy? You mean he practices Seidr! Proper Seidr, like The Guild can do? I thought only one in a million existed, and even then, practitioners have to be trained since birth."

Tom forced a pained smile as he adjusted his seating position against the cold and jagged brickwork.

"For one who knows so little of the world around you, you sure seem to know a lot." He wheezed slightly, and Ann squeezed his hand.

"I know how rare it is."

"Then you also know why everyone wants to use the powder they create?" He gestured towards her pistols. "What a miraculous inve1ntion! I have never seen the like to apply Ash to a projectile as it's ignited from the barrel – How did you come across it?"

"It was a gift." She said flatly, looking down to the floor.

Ann didn't know what to say as she felt her heart pang. Looking into the man's tired eyes, she felt a deep lulling within her chest that had been the same one, if not similar to, what she had felt this morning when the storm had hit, and again when she had uncovered the vial at Jackson's hut. It was one of sorrow and terror, from a memory long ago. However, before she could answer any further, a cart came barrelling past her, speeding through the dark alleyway. From a glance, the driver was no pirate from what Ann could tell. No mark of any kind seemed to identify that, the cart being used to carry supplies and materials, as the back of the wagon was stacked high and to the brim.

"Stay here." She ordered the guardian.

Thus, the old man grumbled that he would have nowhere else to go at this present time and continued to make himself somewhat comfortable against the wall. Perhaps there was something there that could be used to help her treat him? With this thought, she ran into the piercing daylight, making sure to stay behind the rumbling vehicle's frame to avoid detection.

Maybe this way she could watch over Jackson unseen, hiding her figure underneath the brown shaded tarps as she passed him by. As Ann drew closer, she reached for the back end of the cart as it jostled along the hill-side road and up towards the restaurant, further beyond that being the mayor's mansion at North-hill, where the pirates kept their base. In the distance, Ann could make out that it was a large building, though blurred by mist, and had a windmill rotating from the middle and highest tower of its structure. Panting and almost breathless, her hand was mere inches away from the wagon. Suddenly, the cart jeered upwards as it sped over an up-turned cobble, Ann barely having any time to react. The movement was so swift and so abrupt that she almost tripped on the stone as it neared, managing to catapult herself headlong into the back latch of the shaded cart, using the cobble as a steppingstone to gain the elevation she needed.

Now exhausted, she slipped as she clung to the back of the wagon by the tips of her fingers, using all the strength she currently could. In her mind, she thanked herself that she had spent so much time on the city streets growing up, but still it was not enough, and she fell, her hands still clasping the mechanical mechanism that was attached to the underside of the rattling cart. She was now bent over backwards against the rushing cobblestoned street as it flew by her. Ann gripped the connecting iron bar and began to shuffle herself along the underside, but this wasn't exactly the way she had imagined her life going when she had sworn to herself many weeks ago to remain inconspicuous. As soon as she had stepped foot on the island, it had all gone from bad to much dastardly worse by each encounter. Nevertheless, she wound her way along the rumbling underside swiftly, to avoid unwanted eyes. The rushing wind made a tangle of her low hanging hair and eventually Ann pulled herself into the back of the cart, lifting over the tarp and collapsing with a gasp as it rattled up the hill.

In sweet relief, Ann closed her eyes as she lay there. She had done it. All around her, barrels rattled and shook, and Ann turned, seeing they were coloured in a deep burgundy. Markings covered the caskets, as well as a proactive layer of wool.

"Shit!" She cursed, remembering that terrible moment from her childhood.

The choking, acrid smoke still clung to her as it had done that day; a charred reminder, never to be forgotten. She didn't move a muscle. She didn't dare a breath. These barrels were the very kind used by the N.S.T.C for untreated Ash, and although she had not had the same reaction with Jackson's vial, the sense of fear remained the same. These barrels were untreated and another matter entirely as she felt a tear stream down her cheek. Her father had been using barrels like these before that fateful incident occurred.

He was a clever man, her father, a genius in some regard. He discovered that violent movements or flares would cause any elemental type to have a diverse reaction. Ash could explode, implode, combust. The outcome was never the same, but working with the material under moonlight was best if it was to be treated. The dark nights and soothing silver moon seemed to have a calming effect on the sleeping animosity. Ann never knew why; her father had never explained. Looking at her wrist, to the ribbon tied tightly around her skin, she thought back to what Jackson had said about the crew she had abandoned. The Vains had lured them here deliberately, attacked them deliberately. It was all planned!

So, the Navy was carrying untreated Ash! Now the safe in the cargo hold and the guards on the ship made sense! It was to prevent damage from storm and sea. Although now the pirates had full control of it and the island, and that meant no one was safe.

Slowly avoiding the barrels, Ann crawled on her stomach towards the end of the tarp and slipped out the back. The cart was almost at the restaurant, but it would be going further beyond that towards the manor house - towards Atlas and his madmen. No pirates were near her, she had slipped by the checkpoint unseen and their eyes were all on Jackson as he wandered up the hill behind her.

Again, why did they leave him alone? Jackson didn't trust anyone, he kept everything hidden. Even from his closest friends. He hated the pirates as much as anyone and had fought with her over the apparent threat of his maps when they had met, pushing her to the ground.

Then it hit her! If the pirates were telling the truth at the rally, then what was their next destination after they were done with Ale town? They would need somewhere else to go. They would need Jackson's maps to sail into the only safe haven for pirates in the world... The Devil's Doorstep.

Ann now only hoped for enough time to do what was right. She had to find Nelson so that he could see to Tom. Seeing to Tom meant he could finally tell her about the treasure; where it lay, so she could beat the pirates to it and stop Atlas Vain, before it was too late. With that amount of Ash, they could do anything. It made her fearful of what this fabled treasure they searched for actually was. If she could do that, she could secure Jackson's help, and with it, save her friend from a fate most horrid. But most of all, the thing that had happened in her past to her father and her family – Ann wouldn't allow that to happen again, not even if it took her last breath.

7

Jackson swayed from side to side, clasping a squirming Napoleon under one arm. He had the most abominable headache that he'd ever had the misfortune of having, wincing as he stood before the doors of the Trafalgar. He'd needed the drinks after the events of the morning; the storm, Nelson, old Tom, followed by the mayor and his jewels - and after all that, there was Ann. He supposed he would have to figure out that problem when the time came to it.

"O' Molly." He whispered to himself, staring at his warped reflection in the clouded glass of the restaurant doors.

"What am I to do about this mess? I just want them gone, but what's that going to cost me in the end?"

He took one look at his friend's restaurant, sucking in a sharp breath. Shadows wandered along inside, beyond the smoky glass; rabble-rousing pirates swore and drank and swore again, banging their swords and knives on the tables, shouting obnoxiously to the kitchen and back to bring more food. They oppressed and ruled as they pleased, and Jackson hated it.

"Well, Pork-chop. Here we go." He mumbled, looking down at the wide-eyed Napoleon.

The rosy piglet gazed sweetly up at him, completely oblivious to everything around him. Jackson decided that Napoleon simply wanted to go home to his owner, thus giving him an excuse to barge in there unannounced and confront the mayor about his dealings with the treacherous Vains.

He breathed in once more, shaking his head. To confront the brothers all on his own was just suicide, and he knew he was far from inebriated enough to bolster that amount of courage. Perhaps it was the pure optimistic energy of that girl, Ann, rubbing off on him? Perhaps there was something else urging him on. Jackson gripped the doorhandle and with one great push, entered the bustling restaurant. Immediately, the laughing and shrieking from the pirates assaulted his ears, as he stepped over the threshold. His nostrils were overcome by the delicious aroma of spices and roasting meats. These pirates really did have it good, didn't they, he thought.

As the door slammed shut behind him, Jackson was greeted by a crowd of rowdy pirates on the first-floor balcony.

"Oi, drunk!" They called. "Go home, nobody wants you here!"

Jackson couldn't have cared less about what they said, no matter how true it was, and raising his free arm towards them, produced a finger. Napoleon let out a snort in support.

"Good pig." He praised his snuffling companion.

He knew what he'd come here to do. It only concerned him and the mayor. If he could get the old fool to stand up for himself, stop taking money from the brothers and bring the town together, then perhaps it would ruin the pirates' plans and they would scarper back from whence they came. However, just as he neared the tables, Jackson noticed something: every single one of the enemy groups was covered in bandages; burnt, dark patches covering their bodies, bulging boils and blisters appearing from within the gaps. What luck! Had somebody finally taken a stand against the brothers?

"Bloody girl!" Jackson heard one of the pirates' underlings groan.

A girl? Jackson thought, smiling to himself as he stumbled further into the building. He only knew one girl on the entire island that was crazy enough, nay, bold enough to take on the invaders like this. One of the pirates on the balcony above him grumbled, seeming to have taken offence to Jackson's gesture.

A brutish man, wearing large pale green slacks with red braces had a gash of burnt flesh running down his right cheek. He hadn't bothered to wear a top to conceal his boulder like belly. Despite his gruesome appearance, the thing standing out most about this man was that his fists were the size of an ape's, moreover, he had the body hair to match. Gripping the banister of the balcony tightly, the brute's primal hands squeezed until the wood shattered into splinters.

"Are you going to let him disrespect you like that, Brent?" The pirates' smaller, weedier companion jested.

The remnants of the pirate crew above roared and jeered in response, and again, Jackson recognised the voice. The scarred face of Patchwork Jake, the Boatswain, stood beside the mighty assailant.

"No!" Brent roared.

The gargantuan thug jumped down from the balcony, meeting the ground with a tremendous thud. He landed just behind Jackson, causing a small crater to form in the floor. The monster was twice the size of an average man. Jackson thought himself frail and insignificant by comparison. The other pirates cheered in response, chanting his name over and over.

Unfortunately, Jackson took little notice of the snarling monster behind him and continued to make his way toward the central table where, he noted, a young white-haired man was dining with the mayor. Napoleon squealed and squealed, and eventually Jackson had to let him down. He watched as the piglet ran towards the kitchen.

"Good, I need a bacon sandwich." Jackson mocked, calling after the swine: "Just make sure to dip yourself in the red stuff first, not that horrid brown muck your master likes."

Jackson paused then, noticing the thumping, war-like atmosphere the pirates had drummed into the very building.

"Forget the sandwich, you fight me!" Brent snarled, pressing a sizeable podgy finger against Jackson's back, causing the drunk to stumble forward.

Jackson sighed.

"And I bet you like brown as well, don't you?" Said Jackson. Suddenly he spun around, turning his attention towards Brent. He was a little bit unbalanced from all the booze, but the drunk could probably still put up a good fight and he had just about had enough of how the pirates had pushed everyone around the last few weeks. Taking a massive glance at Brent's face, the colour abruptly drained from him. The brute had one of the ugliest Jackson had ever seen; round and swollen. He had a little button nose and most of his teeth stuck out like jagged white tusks, like the sort the drunk had seen on long-dead animals in the old picture-books of his childhood. He looked as if he could rip someone in two, perhaps even in three.

"Well, aren't you a pretty boy." The drunk remarked, patting Brent on the side of his mammoth chops.

His fingers brushed against the burnt flesh that resided there, causing the brute to groan.

"But I just have to see someone else first." Jackson continued. "Then I'll be right with you."

And with that, he pointed a finger in the direction of the mayor. Brent had other ideas, and raised his massive arms high above his head, clenched his fists tightly.

"You'll fight me now!" He screamed, immediately bringing down his arms to where Jackson lay waiting.

The brute shook the floor, sending ripples throughout the building. Jackson barely had enough time to roll away before the ape attacked again and again in desperate desire to crush him. Brent's arms swiped across Jackson's body, knocking him left to right before eventually throwing the drunk on a table.

"Is that all you got?" Jackson taunted, as he picked up a random pirate's drink from the table, gulping it all down in less than a second.

He was still laid flat on his back, but the alcohol helped deal with the tremendous pain he was now feeling in his jaw. Blood poured from his nose like a freshly popped keg and he wiped his hand across his face, smearing it across his cheek without realising. The big guy, thinking he had won, paraded around the restaurant with his arms held high in the air; a massive grin plastered across his face.

Not so fast, Jackson thought. When Brent's head was turned, the drunk leapt off the table and ran straight for the pirate's back. It took the pirate by surprise, and the man did not know what to do apart from violently shake, so that he could throw the navigator off. Jackson though, held steady, managing to grab one of the monster's monolithic shoulders as he drew his sword.

Holding it against the air as he flailed, and, with one quick motion, Jackson sliced into the brute's arm, making him scream in horrendous torment. The navigator knew the moment was now and pressed down further. Blood spurted into the air. With another loud thud, the monster's arm dropped to the floor. Jackson breathed a sigh of relief. Brent's face paled to a deathly-white. The brute desperately tried to cover the wound with his remaining giant hand.

No use. Jackson knew he had won and put up his rapier. He could now go talk to the mayor, whom, sat at his table, silverware shaking in his hands, a look of absolute terror across his face. Silvers Kent was glaring at him as he ate his dinner but didn't seem too concerned by the drunk. How embarrassing for him to witness that, thought Jackson. He was certain he wanted him dead.

When he was almost upon them, Brent called out to the quartermaster sitting in the centre of the room.

"Can I use it, Mister Kent?" Wailed Brent.

Silvers, whose eyes seemed void of emotion, suddenly lit up as he looked at the henchman in wondrous excitement. It was as if he loved watching his own men beg. Then, reaching into his pocket, he produced a small money pouch similar to Jackson's. Silvers tossed the bag towards the brute. Unfortunately, for Jackson, Brent was already greedily ingesting whatever it was before he turned around, sprinkling a pink powder into his mouth.

"Fuck!" Jackson swore alarmingly.

Silvers had given the pirate Ash, and Jackson had no idea what type it was! Quickly, he produced his pistol, and without hesitation, fired off a quick flick of a shot at Brent. The bullet flew out of its chamber and rocketed towards the brute, who then collapsed on the floor with a crash, the impact kicking dust up into the air as the bullet found his skull. Finally, it was over.

"Mayor Johnson?" The drunk called out, still somewhat fizzled over by his encounter with the ape-like giant. "It's me, Jackson. I'm friends with your daughter."

Rupert Johnson dipped his head as Silvers glared at him.

"You know him?" Silvers hissed in the mayor's ear, having not seen Jackson before – though the drunk knew the quartermaster all too well.

The pirate was vaguely aware of a drifter that always hung around Arabella Johnson; clinging to her as a lost puppy would, but up until this rude interruption, he had not been too concerned as to who it was.

Still, Rupert Johnson shook his head, denying the fact.

Silvers had a thick red scar, a burn mark, circling his neck, and he stroked it gently as he watched the fat man tremble, swooping over him like a hawk.

"Huh, that's funny because I could have sworn he just said that he was friends with your daughter?"

The mayor gulped and tried to look away from the pirate's harrowing stare.

"Now, I'll ask you again." He spoke, this time putting down his knife and fork and placing a hand on the mayor's shoulder.

White energy seeped from his hand, and gradually the mayor's eyes became the purest white, the same as the pirate's own hair and eyes.

"Do you know that man?" Asked Silvers Kent again, this time in a much more relaxed tone.

The mayor nodded slowly and reluctantly, as if all the willpower had been drained from him. Silvers donned a crooked smile, drawing his gaze upon the fallen Brent.

"Excellent. Brent, finish him off." He commanded.

In amazement, Jackson pivoted to find that the brute's limb had begun to grow back. What kind of Ash had Silvers given him that could make a severed limb grow back? He was meant to be dead! Jackson watched in horror as Brent's body began to convulse and shake. He thought he even saw something sliver glinting under his skin. Brent's hair grew longer and lighter, resembling the colour of bone; his muscles became larger, more defined, his face started to ooze and pulse and grow and stretch. Even his feet began to look like giant hands.

"Double fuck!" Jackson cursed again, finally realising what type of Ash Silvers had given his subordinate. The realisation was made much more frightening, as now stood the very menacing body of a giant, white-furred gorilla.

Jackson turned to run.

A huff of warm and putrid breath sprang forth from the creature's slobbering mouth and landed on the back of Jackson's neck with a wet and disgusting slap, slivering down slowly to his shoulder blades. Brent roared loudly, pounding his arms on his bare white chest, preparing for his triumphant return to the fight. Most of the pirates in the room now climbed out of their chairs and ran out the back of the building. They were smart enough to know that things were about to get messy, and they didn't want to be around when that happened.

"Brent's gonna kill him!" They chanted and sniggered with glee.

Jackson woefully agreed. Brent's attacks were monstrous; he slammed down his fists one after the other in an ape-like rage, smashing several tables and throwing what remained at the drunk. Trying to avoid the shards, Jackson once again drew his rapier and raised it towards the animal. The ape swiped first, swung left and then again to the right, trying to maul Jackson, but the drunk batted him away with the edge of his blade and proceeded to press his counter. One slash after the other, Jackson landed hit after hit, the gorilla crying out in painful torment. Eventually, the ape fell to the floor in a heap with small cuts littering his chest and arms. If he'd been an ordinary person, Brent would have fallen with the first blow.

"Dirty ape, that's what you get for liking brown." Spat Jackson, wiping his blade against the gorilla's fur and slotting it back into its sheath.

In the background, he could hear a slow continuous clapping mocking him. He looked up warily to see Silvers applauding him with his signature crooked grin. What was with this man, Jackson thought. Did he actually enjoy all this mayhem?

Silvers continued slowly clapping as he observed Jackson, closely watching all the drunk's movements. Up until recently, their group had been under the protection of one of the five, and Silvers wanted to know how the crew would react to a challenge. The quartermaster had never seen anyone openly defy their pirate group before, and the day had now brought not only one but two attempts. Atlas would not be pleased. Curiously, the telephone in the centre of the table began to ring and Silvers moved to pick it up. Clearly, it was important; no one ever bothered him if it wasn't.

8

Atlas Vain sat in the mayor's hall, resting against his thick wicker chair, holding his head in his hands once again, as the amulet glowed beneath. O' did his head throb and ache as if it had been besieged by a thousand storms and a dozen treacherous, thundering winds!

The puzzling piece of paper before him alluded his mind, and he cursed to himself that woe was the task that he must accomplish, ought all else be doomed if he failed to see its completion. Every inch and detail of the dreaded cartography slithered away from him in ragged, distorted, blood-red blurs, shifting from one place to another. Everything achieved thus far on their journey had been a trial! This map, this single piece of parchment had caused so much misery in the previous weeks that he would rather see it burn than have the contents betray him. Had the Hoarder-King told him the truth? He would rather destroy everything, have the world burn at his feet, than have it betray him. The prophecy, it was all encompassing, however he knew the map was too valuable to part with.

He sat at the head of a large dining table in low candlelight — a faint red-glow in an otherwise dark room. He watched as non-existent figures twisted into shadows. Atlas wondered what manner of creatures had yet again come to taunt his sanity. What ghosts from the past had come to haunt his vision. At his front was the ever-present old, tattered, circular map. It was as thin as a bride's veil, its delicate movable sections twisting and turning to show a variety of different things. Atlas could even make out the graining of the table-wood as he gently stroked and caressed the corners of his torment, melding it with cold indigo light. How wondrous this ancient map had been to survive the ages without a fragment unscathed. But now he faced one of the many riddles scattered around the map, the letters blurred and jumbled by his vexed eyes and always moving in constant disarray.

He needed more Ash!

Atlas now pushed the cross-sections and faded lines delicately with the edge of one of his long bony fingers. The shifting words and drawings conveyed in the Runic-language still gave little meaning to the twisted tale it wrought, though the ghostly parchment had revealed the Troll king's word had rung true. They had indeed made the correct landfall, but the riddle – only some of it made sense. Atlas read aloud the faded scripture in Runic-tongue as best he could, echoing to the taunting and shadowy apparitions that floated hither and there:

"Combine the pieces in order, you must,

To save or raze, a choice that will turn some to dust,

For the dragon's keep, you must prevail; Otherwise, you are doomed to fail."

Some things were clear, and some things were not. The treasure, or indeed treasure pieces, needed to be found for him to fulfil his destiny, that much was clear. For the moment, they only sought the first piece, however, Atlas already knew where the second piece resided, he had known that from the start and that was the reason why he had chosen to align himself with Lazarus. It was the third piece that was lost to the passages of time; the precise whereabouts of this first piece as well also alluded him, but Atlas knew they were close, with this last bit of Ash they could do it. The treasure made up some kind of weapon he discovered, the first mentioning of which he had seen in an ancient book long ago. It spoke of a prophecy just as old – the prophecy. It was a myth to begin with, he had thought. A legend only mentioned in the wild fantasies and tests of children's' tales. However, these things were ever rarely false.

As he brushed over the thin sheet once more, he found the map now revealed something different: the podium and broken-shaped bottle from before had vanished and the first piece of the treasure was marked with a solitary numeral, showing a small, peculiar little item with gold chain mail. From the looks of things, someone, or something, had apparently gone to great lengths to make these pieces hard to find.

Who had created such a thing? He sighed, warily rereading the second part of the curious puzzle, evermore plagued by the writhing headaches and twisting words.

"However, tricky to find they are to this day,

As Traps and dangers lie in the way,

With an inhuman power, you must use in haste,

I stress only that you use once, or death will come, and for art thou chase,

For I know not thou where the fingers lay, only in the underground, I know they stay."

"Blast it! Why haven't those idiots found anything yet!" Atlas screamed, overcome by the taunting rage and the monotony budding from within. He turned his gaze over his shoulder, shadowy forms flouting adrift from the candlelight and troubling his every thought. Atlas clenched his teeth in bitter rage.

"We've been here a month, and yet nothing! Crew member after crew member dig beneath the earth with the help of those rotting townspeople and we're still nowhere all the same! I need that treasure, now!"

He slammed his fists down on the table in frustration. How long was it going to be until Kaine's dogs finally figured out where they were and followed their tracks? If that demon knew

Atlas and his brother had stolen the map and amulet, he would have surely sent an army of a thousand trolls and demonic hounds. It was true that he had been one of those creatures in the past, but it was all for a purpose. Atlas was by far the puppy of that brood that were called to heel by that monster, but even a puppy had bite. There were worse things to fear than he when it came to things crawling from out of Kaine's reaches.

The door to the hall creaked open.

"What is it?" Groaned Atlas, as his first mate strolled cautiously into his black domain, shutting the door behind him.

The pirate captain was too tired from the sheer amount of overexertion his problems caused. Adjacent to him, ever at his side, was the usual bowl of Ash, and it was hastily consumed as the first mate drew closer.

"I've just come from surveying the town after the rally." He explained, fumbling to find a chair in the creeping black void. Atlas turned to look at him longingly.

"And?" The pirate captain asked. "Did you catch him?"

"Everything seems to have calmed somewhat, no reason for you to worry. We'll get him soon, Atlas. Perhaps you should get some sleep, eh?" The first mate suggested.

"I refuse!" Atlas spat in bitter spite, rising from his chair.

He could not waste time on sleep. Kaine, the last of his ilk, had to be destroyed.

"Why?" Asked Gill, moving to place his arms around Atlas.

"Let me sing to you, my captain." He whispered softly. "Let my voice soothe you. Let me carry you away and whisk you over a thousand lands."

Then, in the corner of the room, against the dwindling edges of the dying candlelight, did an ebony winged raven appear. It perched and cried upon the buttress of an open window. The room fell cold, as if winter's frost had been upon them, and so too did Atlas' face. The pirate captain shot the black-winged creature a fearful look and the bird replied with a glance of its own; beady emerald eyes shone brightly against a crystal sea-blue, before a smile grew upon its curved and slanted beak. Then, with another crow, did the creature take flight, and just as suddenly as it appeared, it was gone. Had they been discovered already?

"Atlas?" The first mate asked again as if for a second time.

Atlas stared at him blankly, lost in memories.

- "I don't need sleep." He murmured.

"Yes, you do." Gill urged, putting up his hands.

Atlas continued to glare into the empty room and at the shadowy figures that floated above it.

"Have the visions come yet?" He asked, pointing to the bowl.

Atlas ignored him.

"Just get some sleep." The pink-haired pirate spoke softly to him once more, despite the captain's anger. "What are friends for when you have power, right?"

"I said I do not need sleep!" Roared Atlas, slamming his fist down on the table.

He then grabbed Gillian by the wrist with all his strength and threw him from the room. With a slam of the door, the chamber and hall fell silent, and Atlas was left completely alone with only the map and amulet to keep him company. Dreams never came well to Atlas. They were always a reminder of the harsh reality he lived in. They replayed his past, his fears, his mistakes and made him question his own future. Most importantly, the dreams reminded him of her, and what happened on that fateful day. He needed the Ash not only for its power, but for the onset of visions as well. The more a person used the substance, the more visions they received before falling into a sleeping sickness. Sickness always followed Ash-use, it was the way the Alchemists punished those not properly trained in their art and consequently, for great power. The greater the amount, the more vivid realism existed in the dream and the longer a person would walk its depths in the abyss. In all his years, Atlas had never been able to find an Alchemist of his own. He knew some worked for the Lords and the N.S.T.C; most for The Guild, being a separate entity from the government, who recruited through a network of spies. Finally, there were those who were renegades; private practitioners who did not agree with the current status quo and lived in hidden isolation.

All of a sudden, a familiar bedtime melody his mother used to sing resurfaced in his memory, and Atlas realised it was Gillian, singing to him from outside the chamber door as he began to hum the sweet song.

"Come to me, prince-ling,

Let your dreams sprout wings,

Slumber softly, slumber soundly, may your dreams come true,

I will find you; I will keep you; I will hold you warm, Trust me, dear prince-ling, Mothers do know best.

So, slumber softly, slumber soundly, climb the highest peak,

I will find you; I will catch you, only if you fall,

Dream on, dear prince-ling, and sleep, forever more."

"I said begone!" He roared once again. "I do not need sleep."

And yet, Gillian Mayers continued to sing; the darkness finally and gently washing over Atlas as his eyes closed and he collapsed upon the table. The pirate was thrust away to places unknown, drifting like the ever-changing sea.

Atlas was slowly sailing away, and it started the way all his dreams did, with him staffing the wheel of his ship on a familiar sea.

A grey wind seemed to be pushing them to a yet unknown land and the massive sails rippled and soared as Atlas raced towards landfall. *The Ymirs' Extinction*, or as the crew liked to call her, just *The Extinction*, rode upon the crest of a high wave, almost sixty feet in length. Atlas shouted his orders and they worked to turn the enormous beast into the prevailing wind. The pirate captain had no doubt they could handle it; his ship was big enough to fell and carry a dreaded giant, a simple wave would not stop them. No doubt this was a simple wave, for where they were sailing was the treacherous, Devil's Doorstep.

Atlas then began to think about the giants yet again. What was he going to do about the one that remained? The Lords of the World Republic did not care about what happened to the giant race in their high-walled parliamentary citadel. To them, those monsters were just a sore on the land that needed to be prized away. They were happy to let pirates do it, and for them to take the blame. They could start a purge then, say it was divine retribution and the government could act as if they had saved the world. In actuality, it would be Atlas! He didn't mind these claims, of course. He had long made peace with the fact that he was never going to get the credit for what he had started – that honour lay with another. However, what he was going to get credit for was how he was going to finish it; better he go out after achieving something great than nothing at all.

I would rather destroy everything, have the world burn at my heels than I would it betray me! He thought to himself.

Out of nowhere, as if from a haze, a reaching hand appeared from the waves and outstretched its gapping arm towards *The Extinction*. Atlas gazed at the ghoul's monstrous fingernails as they swooped towards him. They were rotten and black, eroded by the sea, and clung to wet torn pieces of slimy seaweed. Atlas dived out of the way, crashing on the foredeck. He looked up and saw rocks clinging to the skin of the beast as it tried to claw at him. Its eyes roared with fire and glowed a blood red; its head, bound in an iron helmet with teeth bared against a metal grill. Atlas could see the yellow stain inside the giant's mouth, he knew if this were real, he would have ordered his men to fire the harpoons and make ready to bring the beast down.

"I am the master of my own dreams!" Atlas roared.

The giant bellowed in laughter at the pirate captain's pathetic retort.

"We were peaceful, once." It called, pointing a finger at the pirate, and rattling off a cold metallic voice.

"That was before you caused the unnecessary deaths of so many! Our blood is on your hands, and the hands of your family, bald one. Let me show you what you have wrought!"

The grey one lifted his hand from over the ship and pressed it down on the sea, unleashing a tremendous downpour upon *The Extinction*.

"Drown in your own thoughts and dreams, mad one. This is what awaits those who abuse the power of Ash! The great storm will come to cleanse you all. The prophecy must be fulfilled!" The giant screeched, then vanished in the blink of an eye.

Atlas traced his mind back and forth, thinking about the giant that had just emerged and vanished out the sea. The great storm? A cleansing? How was it possible? With his crew and the help of others, Atlas had managed to kill almost all the giants! Yes, something was coming – he was the rising wave that chased Kaine and he would herald a great storm that would wipe the monster away. The giant was right; he had his own prophecy to fulfil.

Suddenly, images of raging fires and thunderous lightning storms began to fill Atlas' vision. Overgrown fields of wasteland icecaps ran over crashing waves and a deafening buzzing sound filled his head. This happened every time Atlas closed his eyes, the sickness had come, and each time it got worse. This must be the giant's doing, he thought. Yet, deep down, he knew it was the Ash playing tricks on his mind like it had done with the shadows in the mayor's hall. He had to remain in control; if he let the power overcome him, he would turn to dust.

Atlas breathed in and out, trying to climb back on the wheel to regain control of *The Extinction*; the pirate captain had to think of the things that made his life worth living, things that he could control, that would make the visions cease.

His brother!

Atlas had to keep Orion safe, it was imperative that he did not let Kaine get to him. He kept thinking about this repeatedly. Orion himself did not know why they were running from their former overlord, but Atlas did. It was knowledge he would soon have to share with his younger sibling. The only thing his brother did know, was that they were looking for the three treasure pieces hidden on their stolen map, and that it had enormous power, enough to kill the last of the giants. Though that mark, the black mark on his neck. The black mark was a sticking point; Kaine could find them with that. He and his trolls had a way of finding people through the pestilent mark they bestowed.

Gradually, the rolling thunder and the crackle of lightning began to subside, the fires in the skies began to simmer away into nothingness and return to a field of black. Only the solidified icefields remained, and soon, they too began to crack and melt thanks to the power of the sea. Atlas realised *The Extinction* had wandered to an unknown shore, a long-forgotten island.

"Land ho!" He called and they gently drifted toward the beach before stopping dead in the water, exhausted from their voyage.

Atlas took a spyglass from next to the wheel and gazed out at where they had landed. The land seemed barren and desolate, yet there was something strangely familiar about where they had fallen. In the distance, the pirate saw a small stone hut; it looked worn, broken down and abandoned and had begun to crumble away. Atlas went as far as to say it looked as if it had been attacked.

"Set out!" He ordered. "And where in the world is Orion and those other two?" He added, wondering where his most essential crewmembers had gone.

"Never mind." Atlas grumbled, betraying his order and gripping one of the ropes at the side of the gangplank. "I'll go without them, it's their fault if they miss out on killing that giant, it's around here somewhere."

A crew member next to him nodded and began pulling on the rope. Because of *The Extinction's* enormous size, it was safer to lower a boat than to jump straight on to the beach. When they reached the bottom, Atlas planted his feet on the warm, hot sand and felt the earth move between his feet. It was roasting, and he could feel himself start to sweat; yet he felt oddly at home. He couldn't quite place his finger on it, but he could have sworn he had been to this island once before. The only problem was that he did not know when.

The pirate captain started to walk towards the dilapidated building, gradually surveying the scene. Again, nothing was around the area apart from the hut and the vast dry dessert that surrounded it. He looked back from where he had come, even his ship had disappeared. The sun was almost melting him, with little hope of getting any reprieve. Atlas was beginning to feel like he was back on his home island. For days on end when he was a child, Atlas would play and roll in the sand with Orion and then fight with either Gill or Silvers to decide who built the best sandcastle. There were, of course, greener, cooler parts to his home and Atlas remembered his father telling him never to go to those parts. However, as he walked towards the small structure, no greenery of the kind could be found; by all accounts, the place where he landed was desolate.

After trudging across slippery sands, Atlas finally reached the old house. The scene was much more surreal up close. The roof was torn open and letting in cascading beams of sunlight, the brickwork was littered with cracks and slits for all manner of insects to crawl through, and the front door was battered and broken, as if something tremendously large had forced its way through and turned what remained into sharp wooden spikes.

Atlas pushed open the door cautiously. It creaked and moaned a dreadful, lowly shriek that sent shivers down his spine. It was as if Atlas was stuck in a never-ending cycle of torment. A crowing could be heard from above, and the pirate captain jumped back, just as a raven swooped down and landed on the stonework. Atlas hated hose things, always spying.

Inside, Atlas recognised something; at the very back of the one singular room was a long, smoothly polished chest that was coloured in a deep chestnut brown. He knew at once what it was, as both he and his brother had used it to hide everything from their childhood adventures. Atlas rushed over to it in an instant and as he bent down on the floor, he ran his large hands over the smoothly finished top.

"There you are." He whispered against the rusted and decaying red lock. Perhaps the old memories would release him of some of the madness plaguing his mind.

"Damn it, damn it, damn it, curse you!" He roared, unable to find the key.

He had to get it open. Atlas had to see if everything was still there. In his frustration, he began slamming his arms on the ground, his face had turned red raw, and his beard ran slick with sweat. What Atlas was unaware of, was that his dream had swallowed him whole. Everything that he saw within this world was exactly that, a dream, a most vivid and real memory.

"Where are you?" He continued to bellow repeatedly.

A key appeared out of thin air, to which, he reacted with deranged childish laughter. It was a small key, shaped in a way that the head of the key resembled an X. Atlas gripped the cold brass with relief and hurried, pressing it into the lock. The metal faded and blew away like dust as the chest opened with a click, making the pirate captain smile. Oh, how Atlas wished his little brother could be here to see this! In all the vast world he had ever sailed upon, the chest in front of him was probably the only thing that would make that overly talkative idiot shut up and stop his blasted singing!

Placing both his hands just below the latch, Atlas slowly opened the box; he was savouring the surprise of seeing all his ill-gotten childhood gains again, and he fondly remembered all the adventures he had stealing from others as he and his friends ran across the sand dunes of their home. With the lid fully opened, Atlas gazed in wonderment and pride; everything was as he left it! Even the last thing he placed in the bottom was still there, but at this he scowled. It was something that brought Atlas great pain and a heavy heart – a singular green bean. Atlas looked at the bean with sadness, picking it up between his fingers. This simple seed looked ordinary enough, but held a monstrously devastating power that wrought a giant weed-like monolith from the earth, destroying everything around it. That was one of the reasons why Atlas was always told to never ever wander the green spaces.

As the pirate captain recalled what had happened that day, the bean suddenly sprung from his hand and rolled its way to a pile of dirt that had arisen in the corner of the skeletal structure. Oddly, Atlas had not noticed this happening and the pile of dirt opened a hole in the ground for the bean to burrow its way into. The dirt welcomed the bean, embracing it in its warmth, like a warm blanket on a cold winter's day. Then, at the side of the dilapidated stonework, water started to trickle towards the dirt. The seed began to expand and grow. It grew larger and larger and began to eat away at the stonework. Within moments, the hole had expanded to encompass the whole of the stone hut - aside from the small corner in which Atlas and his treasured chest now stood. The hole began to eat away at the tip of his boots. Soon Atlas would have no choice but to jump. The bean wanted him to jump.

"Damn you." He muttered to himself.

He glanced up one more time at the wall behind him and at the two ravens sat above, blinking their beady eyes. One held a wilting lily between its beak. There was no possible way that Atlas could climb the wall. Any attempt would most likely end in him slipping and falling into the hole. Exhaling, the pirate captain looked down into the abyss below. Then, without warning, the ravens; giving a great cry, swooped down from their lofty perches and dug their talons deep into his back. Atlas was thrown from the wall, falling headfirst into the deep, dark, unending hole with nothing but a choked breath escaping his lips.

Act Two:
The Illusion of San-Journ Island

9

It seemed as if he leapt from the abyss; from deepest, darkest nightmares, and suddenly Atlas shuddered from sleep, dripping from head to toe in ice-cold sweat.

What a crazy dream, he thought.

He looked beyond the curtained window of his bedroom, finding the sun high above the smooth curved dunes. Today was a day for adventure. Throwing off his covers, he packed a bag from the long chest, putting his illusive dream to one side. Everything he would need was pulled from the bowls of that chest, ready for the big adventure he had planned. Nothing, not even a bad dream would put a stop to it. He then went to go see his brother. He would hate Orion to miss anything, and he stormed into his room without warning or invitation.

"Morning." He beamed, grinning from ear to ear. "What are we going to do today, I wonder?" He gave his brother a glimmer of foreboding curiosity in his voice, to add to the sense of mystery.

Of course, Atlas already knew what he was going to do today. It was just a question of whether his brother would join him.

"I don't care, Atlas. Go away, I'm sleeping!" Orion groaned, burrowing beneath the sheets.

A small gap appeared in which his sleepy gaze crept from a hidey-hole within the white linen material, and he stared at Atlas.

"Just let me sleep, father isn't even up yet, and mother is out at sea again."

The younger sibling then pulled the covers back around him, trying to resume his slumber. Atlas, however, was having none of it. He wouldn't miss adventuring.

"True, but mother will most likely be back today, or even any moment for that matter, so you might as well get up."

He grinned. Atlas was determined to convince his brother to join him. Orion rolled over in bed and looked tiredly at his grinning brother's face. What had he done to deserve a brother such as him? One who would wake him at any given moment? Orion hoped that if he managed to do that to Atlas, it would put him in a foul mood.

"Fine, fine, I'll get up." He croaked, rolling his eyes. "What are you thinking about doing today anyway?"

As Atlas had hoped, Orion asked with an ire of curiousness and his grin became even wilder as he walked further towards the bed.

"The beanstalk." He spoke. "I want to go up. You really think there are giants at the top?"

Orion looked at him in disbelief. Atlas couldn't be serious about climbing a beanstalk, could he? They were in a green space, and no one was ever allowed anywhere near those!

"Atlas, you know we're technically not kids any more, right? You're seventeen, I'm fifteen." Orion argued.

He hoped reminding his sibling of his actual age would dissuade him.

"Still, we're not adults." Responded Atlas, as he threw his brother's bedclothes away from his reaching grasp. "And I want to have one last great adventure with everyone, before I turn eighteen next month."

"Wait, everyone?" Orion gasped, trying to snatch his covers back - he was unsuccessful.

"Yeah, I asked Gillian and Silvers last night!"

Atlas was getting more excited by the second, walking away with the bedsheets and throwing them in the corner of the room. Finally, he would see what was at the top of that massive obelisk, and all his friends would be there with him to see it!

"But how are we going to get there?" Orion interjected, running after him and into the kitchen. "The nearest beanstalk is easily ten dunes away, that's a four hour walk at least! Father's going to be furious."

Atlas then gave his brother the most devious smile he possibly could. He had already thought of a way to get across the blistering sands and scorching heat.

"What?" Orion asked, crossing his arms.

From the sour look on his face, Atlas could tell his brother wasn't as excited about this as he was – there was a way to go to convincing him.

"I'm going to borrow some of father's Wraiths." He said eventually, watching as Orion's eyes widened, frantically shaking his head in opposition.

"No, no, no! Father would castrate you the moment he saw you riding one! Plus, they're incredibly difficult to control."

Atlas rolled his eyes.

"I have a plan, you know."

They continued to argue and bicker about how they were going to deceive their father over breakfast. They did not eat much. Food was hard to come by; the Navy was keeping it all to themselves.

On the table, their father had left them a note, saying he had gone to the market. Despite having the farm, they hungered for food and water. Wraith meat was not exactly edible, it had a hard rubbery texture when cooked, and when eaten raw, the juice excreted was poisonous if consumed.

A wicked idea came to Atlas, one that came from myth. It may have been real, it may not have been, however, he knew it could bring his brother on-board and it poised on the edge of his tongue, slithering to escape, like the low hiss of an awaiting snake.

"You know, they say giants can grow a vast amount of food on top of their beanstalk, it's because they catch all the rain." He whispered, eyes glowing as he sat across the table.

Orion raised an eyebrow at that.

"It's why the land we live on is so dry and barren. Besides, even if we don't get any food, I'm sure we could swipe some of the treasure and sell it for the Navy's share instead."

"Don't you mean *our* food?" Grumbled Orion.

Atlas smiled. He had him now.

His brother was right. It was their food. The Navy had taken it.

"Okay then, how would you do it?" Asked Orion, taking the bait.

Atlas knew he was thinking about the prospect of eating an unlimited amount of food.

"You'll see if you come along with Gillian, Silvers and me." He teased.

Orion rolled his eyes in response, finally giving in to his brother's incessant demands. After all, what was the harm in going adventuring?

"Fine, I'll come." He said, crossing his arms. "But father better not find out about the Wraiths… And I'll only do it for the food. We almost got locked up the last time you wanted to find some treasure."

Atlas smiled again, remembering the bandits they had encountered when the Navy had captured them. He and his brother were taken too, and their father had to threaten the garrison commander with his war-axe.

With a broad cat-like grin, Atlas pressed a hand to his chest and swiped a finger across the arch of his sand-encrusted knuckles.

"Cross my heart, little brother. I promise, we'll only go for the food."

"You don't have a heart, Atlas."

"I know." The older boy chuckled, and then all fell silent.

A loud bang sounded at the Vain's door, echoing against the desert wind.

"Shit! Is that father?" Cried Orion, springing from his chair, thinking they had been foiled.

Atlas gently patted his brother on the back, calming the boy's terror ever so slightly. Peaking around the flimsy piece of wood, Atlas found two boys about his age standing on the front porch, gazing at the dusky, newly risen sun. One had wavy pink hair, about medium length to his neck, the other had short hair, like his brother, but was coloured brown.

"It's okay, it's only Silvers and Gillian." The boy called back.

Orion breathed a prolonged sigh of relief.

Atlas turned back to his friends.

"You found everything okay then?" He asked. "Did you bring it?"

Both the boys nodded, and Silvers brought out a small pouch from his pocket, showing it sneakily beneath the shadow of his coat. Inside the bag was a white coloured powder with tiny specs of obsidian. It looked relatively normal, however, the boys knew the Navy wouldn't keep it under lock and key for just any reason. To this day, their desert homeland was at war with the neighbouring island at sea and it had stripped them of the little it already had. Atlas and his friends were just taking back what was already theirs. The Navy garrison commander demanded tariff upon tariff of their village, causing many to take to the life of piracy and bandit-hood to feed themselves. Atlas's father forbade his sons from taking to sea, and for the life of him, Atlas did not know the reason why. His father was older than his mother, and it seemed to the boy that the man had lived a life before choosing to sojourn in the land of blazing, burning sands.

Atlas looked at his friend in amazement.

"Silvers Kent, you're a dog!" He cried, and a smile emerged knowing that they had just broken the law to steal the small brown pouch from the Navy Lock-up.

The garrison commander would shit himself if he ever found out about this – not that they cared, mind you; they were going to have this adventure, nothing was going to stop them!

"What makes you think we can control those creatures with this?" Gillian asked, unsure why the powder made his friend so happy.

The truth was, many weeks ago, as Atlas explained it, he was travelling down to the market with his father and had seen the Navy shoot a dart with this powder at a Wraith. It caused the beast to stop dead in its tracks, which was something his father said at the time was impossible to do with just a simple dart. Their father had built trust with his Wraiths before he was able to ride them. They were big centipede-like winged creatures, that scurried across the sand and soared through the air. The males were coloured in a yellowy shade of brown, tentacle-like antennas sprouting from their face. They were extremely dangerous beasts to keep.

"What now?" Gill asked.

"Now, now we go." Said Atlas.

* * *

The walk to their father's farm took the boys just over ten minutes. Because the beasts they kept were so dangerous, it was safer for them to live in the village and then travel to the farmstead for work. The day was stifling, and more so than usual. The early morning sun was burning hotter with each passing moment and sweat began to drip down their faces as they ascended the hill. Eventually, the farm appeared in the distance, under a distorted mirage. Atlas took out the tattered brown map from his bag and checked the several points he had drawn earlier, making out a large, thick metal fence, that covered the perimeter of the farmstead. The paper felt coarse in his hand, as if all moisture was sucked dry from his skin. They needed to get away from the heat.

"So, what now?" Silvers asked, as they all made it inside.

He was gazing at the line of neat boxes drilled into the rock face at the back of the farm, and the massive, snarling creatures that were contained within. Atlas put his bag down and started rummaging through it. He brought out the small pouch of white powder and darts, along with the blowpipe.

"Pick the Wraith you want and go stand by it." He ordered. "One of the smaller ones should be big enough."

Silvers walked over to the nearest Wraith cage, stood by the lock, and waited for Atlas. The Wraith he picked was small and fat, like an overgrown bulbous spot, its tentacles slithered along its back.

"Ku-ku-ku-ku-ku." The beast snored.

"What's it doing?" The boy asked, nervously.

The Wraith shifted in the warm sand beneath and dug itself deeper into its burrow. This was the first time he'd seen one of these beasts up close. Atlas smirked at his friend's dismay. The eldest child of Ragnar Vain knew how the Wraiths behaved. This could go either very well or very, very wrong.

"Relax, he's just sleeping." Laughed Atlas, as he slid the dart into the blowpipe. "At least for now anyway. When he gets a load of this, he won't be for much longer."

Atlas loved to see things in agony. It was like a carnal desire exploding inside him when he saw something suffer. It was exceptionally pleasing if the creature had caused him, or someone he knew, any pain. For years and years without fail, a Wraith would escape the farm, making his father go after it. The old Ice-raider was ageing, thought Atlas. The once luscious black beard of the man he admired had begun to see flecks of grey, as it withered and grew pale. Orion had said once that the desert island heat was seeping into his head, and some in the village even whispered he had become foolish for not remaining on his home island in the barren North Sea. This would finally be Atlas's chance to get revenge.

Gently, Atlas pressed the blowpipe to his lips and nodded to Orion to open the pen. The doors creaked with a rusty scrape, brushing against the hot sand. The Wraith began to stir from its sleeping position, continually moving about the sand, shifting from side to side in the pen as if it were a snake. Silvers backed away toward Gill, a horrified look on his face.

"Um, Atlas? What is it doing?"

"It's waking up." Said Atlas, naturally.

The Wraith let out a screeching wail that caused the boys to cover their ears. It was like a torrent of cannon fire, and Atlas felt a warm fluid trickle slowly from his lobes. Suddenly, the beast coiled its tentacles and lashed out at the boys, striking with extreme accuracy. First, it went for Gill, who narrowly managed to avoid the beast's striking whips and a plume of sand erupted from the ground where the tentacles had struck. The sand hissed and sizzled, each individual grain beginning to decompose by the toxic acid.

"That was close!" The boy breathed.

The Wraith coiled yet again for another strike, and he hunched over the ground as he saw the creature's blood red eyes follow him.

"You might want to fire that dart now, Atlas!" Yelled Gill.

"I'm getting to it!" Responded the eldest Vain.

However, he couldn't get a good line and Orion cowered too close to the creature's behind. The Wraith continuously weaved and slithered, and Atlas needed to be as accurate as the beast for it to count. Suddenly, the Wraith struck out again, and to the group's horror, its blood eyes shifted from one boy to another. With great force, it made a beeline straight for Silvers. Gill and Orion raced towards him to help, but it was too late, the tentacles wrapped around his neck and viciously pulled him across the sand.

The boy was gasping for air. Atlas could see the look of annoyance in the creature's eyes as it tried to pull more than it could and it released a wash of venom, making Silvers scream.

Suddenly, there was a thick, sharp, thwack sound from where the Wraith sat in its cage, and the boys looked over to see a dart protruding from the beast's forehead. Gradually, its eyes began to turn the purest white. It was like a glaze of white fog seeping over a sea of red. Atlas had done it and the beast's tentacles began to loosen from around Silvers' neck.

The look on his face was a mixture of relief and pain. The boy was still very hurt, and a ghastly red scar encompassed where the tentacles had been. However, the whole situation seemed odd. Wraiths only attacked when they felt threatened or hungry. So, if that was the case, why hadn't the Wraiths been fed? Even more questions appeared when Orion found the last cage lay open, its occupant gone.

Suddenly, Silvers screamed out in agony. Orion had poured a bottle of water over his friend's wound to neutralise the acid. Slowly, the ring around his neck stopped sizzling and his brother explained that the smaller the Wraith was, the less acidic its tentacles were, and it reminded Atlas why the females were to be feared.

"Are you alright?" Gill asked, offering a hand.

Silvers grabbed on and was pulled to his feet.

"Yeah, I'm fine now, no thanks to you three." He coughed. "Why did that happen? I thought you said they were safe!" He glared at Atlas.

"They are, they are." Orion repeated, looking to his brother for answers.

Silvers then ran at Atlas and knocked him to the ground with a tackle. Orion tried to intervene, but Gill stopped him.

"What went wrong!" Silvers roared, slamming his fists across Atlas's jaw. "This was your bloody idea to begin with, and now look what happened! Look at me! Look at me!"

The seventeen-year-old took every blood-soaked punch from his friend. He knew his anger was warranted.

"All right, that's enough!" Gill yelled, but Silvers kept raining attacks down on Atlas. "I said that's enough!"

Gill then grabbed his friend by the wrist and the boy looked down at a battered Atlas, covered in blood-stained sand and dirt.

"Why?" He spat.

Atlas smiled. He never thought someone as crafty as Silvers Kent would have it in him to hit someone out of rage. In fact, Atlas probably liked him more because of the whole ordeal. However, he had to tell him why he thought the Wraith attacked.

"They hadn't been fed." Atlas said, as plainly as he could.

The boy in front of him boiled with rage.

"Well didn't you check first? Surely, if you knew we were doing this, you would check to see if they'd been fed or not?" He seethed.

Orion looked down into the metal container laying broken on the ground next to the pen and confirmed his brother's suspicions. It was just as he thought.

"They're empty, see." He gestured. "There's no point checking, they eat everything, and it would have eaten you, so, can we move past this, or do you want to argue more before this heat becomes unbearable?"

Silvers sighed, seeing that there was no point arguing with his friend anymore. He had seen Atlas fight seriously once before, he'd let him land those punches, and he was grateful that Atlas didn't throw one back.

"Fine, let's go." He muttered.

The Wraith sat as calmly as a sleeping kitten, watching the boys with glee as they worked to get everything ready for their trip.

"Which way now?" Gill asked.

Atlas pointed to the old brown map in his hand, making Gill swallow long and hard. He had picked a hell of a day to go on an adventure.

* * *

Luckily, the four friends were no longer suffering from the immense heat that came with the long desert days as they flew upon the back of the Wraith. Small birds and creatures passed by as they journeyed; fascinating animals that emitted bright colours, setting apart the dry desolate ground below. One of these birds - a small crested-sparrow; its bill sharp and pointy - chirped and sang alongside them, fluttering to keep up. Orion made a promise with himself that he would have to catch one and keep it as a pet.

Ahead of them, lay a sizeable rocky valley. It was filled with an overgrowth of green vegetation as far as the eye could see, amassing a vast array of different shades of flora, devouring any sign of the dusty red rock beneath. Vines climbed over everything in sight, and the boys could hardly believe such a place existed if they had not seen it with their own eyes. It was common knowledge that everyone in the village could see the giant stalks, but they would have had no idea that a green and luscious jungle existed below.

As the boys flew closer, a menacing, shadowy structure began to reveal itself from above the clouds, and they could hear the sound of rushing water as the monolith in front of them became more vine-like.

"This is it!" Atlas cried in delight. "This is the beanstalk!"

"Great, so we can land now?" Asked Gill, who couldn't wait to get off the smelly beast they had ridden.

Atlas nodded excitedly, pointing to his tattered map once more. He just couldn't believe they had actually made it, when all the adults had told them they should never even try to venture it.

The creature would soon run out of energy, and suddenly, it folded its wings behind its back and all the boys felt panic flood the pits of their stomachs. All the clouds rushed past them in a downward spiral. The Wraith howled a deep, menacing wail.

10

Atlas placed his hands on the table and lifted his phased and weary head. The amulet glowed beneath him; so bright was the light that emanated from the purest gem, that even the gods would've had difficulty in distinguishing day from night in the platonic dining hall from which he now arose from slumber at the head of the table. He had no idea how long he had been asleep, but he didn't think much time had passed. He still felt drained of energy, even more so than before, as the map below finally came into hazy focus.

"Orion! Gillian!" He groaned, in a deep, rough voice.

The harrowing silence of the boarded-up mansion dawned on him that he was utterly alone… or so he thought.

Orion appeared from behind one of the red curtains that covered up the many long glass windows. His face was dull, looking slightly glum, perhaps nervous? Atlas had been right about someone coming into the room, and he wasn't at all surprised that it was his brother trying to sneak up on him as if they were children again - just as they had been a decade ago. Orion tiptoed to where Atlas resided and seated himself next to his brother without a word.

"What is it?" The pirate captain asked bluntly, guessing something was amiss through sleepy and groggy eyes.

A moment of silence followed.

"What. Is. It!" Atlas roared, slamming his fist down.

The table rocked back and forth like a child's rocking horse. Atlas was fed up with the secrets that his crew kept from him out of fear. He was going to get what he wanted. Throughout his time as captain, he had given his crew everything – he had worked towards their goal with no end and refused to cease.

Now, when it was finally in their grasp, everyone treated him with impatience and impertinence. Did they not know they were being hunted? Did they not know what was coming for them!

"Out with it!" Atlas repeated, his temper beginning to rise once more.

His eyes were piercing, throwing daggers to anyone that dared look.

"Erm, well, you see, the patrols still haven't found the guardian or his accomplice. However, I did find two corpses in the tunnels, wearing Navy uniforms." Orion spoke quickly.

The pirate captain felt his rage subside, and his knuckles began to relax. At least some news he could control. How were two dead Navy crew going to affect his plans? Not having found the guardian was disappointing to hear, nevertheless, they had plenty of townspeople to pick from to do their work. By the timid look on Orion's face, Atlas knew there was more to come.

"Go on." He urged, as he started to feel a small portion of his energy crawl back to him.

Atlas watched as his brother's smile grew into something resembling a crocodile's.

"We found the antechamber, but the door is jammed shut, covered by earth, and littered in the runes that father once knew. We could give those we captured more Ash, but they could cause trouble. I could redirect our efforts from the diamond tracks -"

"No!" Atlas interjected. "We need those jewels for the Trolls and our crew! Need I remind you of the weasels that tried to mutiny? If they're not paid, more will spring against us! Have the townspeople stay put and work them to the bone -"

"But the money?" Orion gulped, rubbing the black spot on his hand as Atlas rubbed his own.

His brother had a knack for making him feel at his worst. Orion wasn't in this game for revenge like his older brother, yet the spot oozed and pulsated constantly. One day it appeared on the back of his hand with no knowledge of how it got there.

"Enough, little brother. Pass me the cable phone, I need to call Silvers." Atlas commanded.

Orion paused for a moment. His brother still hadn't fulfilled his promise, still, he nodded and walked over to the wall where the phone was located. He dialled in the number for the restaurant and waited as the line beeped.

"Yes?" The quartermaster answered.

"It's -" The vice-captain began but was interrupted by Atlas grabbing the phone from him. The captain brought it to the table and spoke instead.

"We've found it!" The captain cried. "But two Navy are dead; I trust you can find more to continue their work?"

Silvers chuckled in response.

"Really? Well, that's a shame, looks like I'll have to find a couple more 'volunteers' then." He mused sarcastically.

"Is that a problem?" Atlas asked, raising an eyebrow.

"No, no problems here. I can handle things."

With a pause, Atlas brought the phone away from his ear and handed it back to Orion, who then slammed it down on its pedestal.

"What now?" He quizzed, looking at his brother, continuing to rub the black spot on his hand.

"Now, we go claim what we have uncovered." Atlas stated simply, grabbing the map and gently rolling it up and attaching it to his belt before getting up from the table and walking towards the door in an exaggeratedly lethargic manner. His energy was still immensely drained from his illustrious venture.

"Atlas?" Orion asked suddenly, still looking at the spot on his hand. "How did this happen?"

He raised his hand up as if to study it, growing angrier at the prospect of how he had been treated.

"You did promise me, and I don't remember getting something like this. I don't even remember leaving Kaine - how did that happen again? We were on good terms with him. You've been maddening this last month. Our wealth has been squandered, not to mention your questionable dealings with Lazarus, the Hoarder-king!"

Atlas halted in the doorway, and stood deadly still, despite his condition. He decided to tell Orion the truth about why they were running – no more lies.

"I had your memories of what happened taken."

He turned away; he could not bear to see the betrayed look on his brother's face, not again. The last time Atlas had seen that look, they had been mere children.

"Silvers!" Orion swore.

He looked to his brother's own dark mark on the back of his neck and fell silent for a moment, wondering if other memories had been altered as well. It reflected Atlas's personality perfectly. He was cold, dark, and manipulative, however, that didn't explain how and why they'd all come to acquire Kaine's legendary black spot?

"Continue." He whispered, feeling his throat start to swell and his heart sink with the riches they had lost for not continuing their protection with one of the five pirate lords of the wine-dark seas.

"Kaine was so mad at us after he finally realised that we were the ones who started the war. It was only a matter of time. The troll-kings were always whispering in his ear, and when he found out, he wanted us dead. He still does want us dead. So… we stormed the beast's lair, and of course it didn't work. I even lost father's axe in the struggle. But to cut the story short, he caught you, giving every man present the death-mark. He could have killed you in an instant! With a snap of his fingers. It took everything to get you free, and in the end, he said he kept you alive because he wanted to make me suffer as I watched you die. It's because of me that his trolls are after us."

The look on his brother's face was that of rage, the likes of which mirrored Atlas's own, yet Orion did something that surprised himself and his brother even more so – something that he had not done since that day in the village - he wrapped his arms around Atlas and gave him a firm hug.

"Thank you." He mumbled into his shoulder, patting his brother on the back.

Atlas felt emotion well within him, and tears stung his eyes. He loved his brother, despite all the visions, the voices and the pain, he had never doubted his love for the man that now held him firm, and his forgiveness meant everything.

"Gill said you would need more sleep, so why don't we both go down to the antechamber, and you can get some rest while you're there?" Suggested Orion, releasing his brother.

Atlas nodded, and both of them left the room to find the antechamber. After a few moments, Orion spoke again.

"I suppose that makes sense now... why you made that deal with the Hoarder. Why we've always been hurried from one place to another. You know, he'll have sent the others, right? The ones with the tool to find the mark, just like I said they would when I first saw this on the back my hand and upon your neck and just like I said when you made that deal. It could be days! I told you not to fucking trust them, they have spies everywhere and more than most. I'm surprised it's taken them this long if they know where we are. So I ask you again brother, which of The Three Kings are coming for us?"

Atlas smiled.

"Have little fear, what is below will see them away, however, you are right. We probably have days before they get to us. Although it could be worse."

"How so?" Orion asked.

"Mother could know where we are..."

* * *

Fire flickered from Fryedai's hand as he gingerly hobbled through charcoal black tunnels. He had escaped the mass panic of the pirate rally when fire swept across the stage. Somehow, he had managed to break free of his bounds and used the disarray that followed to gain some distance from his captors. Others, however, were not so lucky, and Fryedai, remembering the path they had been forced upon, descended back into the tunnelled jungle undergrowth and towards the hellish mines that dwelt within. He'd not been able to do much when the pirates first captured them. The first thing he remembered was waking up in a long-boat that was bound for the shore and manacles of cold steel rubbing against his then pale skin. He'd looked to his left and to his right, finding that all his shipmates had been bound in a similar fashion, the crisp morning air blowing against them, along the island. The pirates then forced them to trek through the jungle-growth, reeds of bamboo extended level to the tall trees that dotted the area, and eventually they arrived at a mound with two tracks appearing from its dark pits as if it were a pair of skeletal sockets.

The pirates that had led them to their toil laughed to themselves as they went.

'Wait until the quartermaster gets a'hold of you lot!' One of the dirtier fellows had sniggered. 'He'll make you work, and the vice-capt'n will extract the wealth from the land, and we'll all be rich! No more running, not for I, that's what I say!'

The fire afforded him a dim light and he had to be careful not to draw any attention. He had to find his crew and save them. He listened to the hollow echoes of the tunnels as he bent to peer behind a cleft of rock. Fryedai regretted that he'd been unable to do anything when the pirates attacked, resulting in Captain Robbinson being taken. He felt as if he had let them down; that he had failed them. It had all happened so fast.

In the gloomed and murky distance, clanging pickaxes bashed against stone to reveal a glimmering prize. Fryedai now knew what that prize was; diamonds! Hidden treasure wasn't the only thing the pirates were after, they needed to somehow fund their crew. The diamonds underneath the town provided the perfect answer for the murderous and vile brothers to stay in control. Power was everything to them - the power to destroy and the power to control.

However, now the navigator of The Inspectre had to wander around in the darkness with only the flames in his hand to guide him. He had thankfully found a supply of Ash at the entrance to one of the narrow crevices that populated the underground mining system. Long abandoned by the townspeople of the island, the mine was eery, decrepit and whispered to the very soul of a man, through echoing passages and walls. Something dwelled in the deep shadows of its carrion depths, Fryedai felt, and it was something that the pirates had disturbed from a long and ancient slumber.

"Faster worm!" A brutish voice shouted from the dark, the echoes reverberating along the slender gaps in the ebony rock.

Fryedai gulped, crouching deeper behind where he hid and extinguished the flames in his palm.

"I want those diamonds!"

The pirate continued to bellow abuse as he rained the whip down like a constant hailstorm with relentless cracks.

"Hahahaha, there you go, Worm! Would you look at those precious jewels!"

The pirate reached down to pick up a handful of the shining rocks that glimmered in the gloomy light. The candlelight barely penetrated the encapsulating darkness. The pirate abruptly kicked the worker to the floor.

Fryedai heard the boot echo as it made contact and winced at the sound. He was unable to help the worker out of fear of exposure, and he shuffled to the right of him while keeping low to the ground. The pain in his feet was horrifying as he dragged a wounded leg against the ground. Sooty sediment made its way to the root, colouring his leg in its grimy dampness.

Damn these pirates! He thought as he made his way free in search of his shipmates. They had to be in the mines somewhere. He looked to his leg and grimaced. The quartermaster, Silvers Kent, had fired several shots during the rally that morning. One of them had found its way into Fryedai's leg, as the pirate made his escape from the explosive ensuing chaos.

Once more, Fryedai ignited the fire in his hand. It sparked in a brilliant mixture of orange and red that kindled and smouldered in his palm. Luckily, he had made his way through the cave and was standing in one of the earlier hallways the pirates had carved out. He hoped there wouldn't be any more traps left for him to uncover. Despite the pain in his leg, it was thanks to Captain Robbinson that he finally had a chance to get away, smashing the navigator's chains against the cobbles when the surge of people rushed through the market square. He had no idea where the captain was now, nor did he know where Commander Rockwell, Mister Rivers, Doctor Rudolf, Luke and his brother, Chris, or any of the other crewmen he had come to know over their voyage were. He was especially worried for the ailing crewman that had been confined to the Doctor's quarters, as the captain had mentioned that no one had seen them aside from the doctor for their entire voyage to the island. Nevertheless, he planned to save up as much Ash as he could, using it to try and aid in the escape of those enslaved beneath the earth.

At the end of the corridor of dark rock that he clung against, Fryedai began to see a blinding white light emerge as the figure of a ladder came into focus. He once again ceased his flames and mustered all his energy in preparation. If Fryedai were ever to meet up with the captain again in the outside world, he would have to try to reach the opening.

"Here." A voice said suddenly, holding out an arm.

Fryedai looked up and gripped it tightly, feeling the warmth of the familiar voice pull him forward.

"It's okay." The voice assured him, as Fryedai reached the top.

The navigator laid across the floor that covered the tunnels. His chest bounded up and down at a constant rate as he clambered for breath, the warm light of day seemed to release all the air from his lungs in unbounded happiness and he had never been so glad to be above ground again. The voice that spoke to him was warm and welcoming, Fryedai smiled as he opened his eyes, realising who it was in an instant.

"Sir, that's definitely you, isn't it? I'm not imagining things?" Fryedai rambled.

He felt his leg flare up and twist in pain again and moved his head to the side to get a better view of the captain, relieved at least that he had found the one person that could gather his splintered crew together.

"Yeah, Fryedai. It's me." Robbinson replied gleefully, he was overjoyed to see the young navigator and patted him on the back as he got his balance.

Robbinson was wearing the same slightly tattered leathers as Fryedai, and he grinned at the fact that they had the same idea to ditch their flamboyant and now greyed out uniforms, the leather being the only thing these particular pirates wore compared to the glorious colour of their previous attire.

"So, what are we going to do now?" A concerned Fryedai asked. "Because we need to figure out a way to get everyone out from there."

"I've already thought of that, however, we need to be careful. I'm going to try and place a call to Commodore Chesterfield. It should take him a couple hours to get here, but by that time we'll have freed everyone and be in control of the situation - leave him to handle the brothers."

Fryedai huffed optimistically.

"And how exactly are we going to do that, sir?"

Robbinson smiled.

"Well, that's easy, Fryedai. All we have to do is -"

Suddenly, there was a loud smashing noise coming from one of the other rooms, and the captain froze in place, falling deathly silent. The look on Robbinson's face said it all however; pure terror.

"What was that?" The captain whispered so quietly only mice could hear.

"I don't know, sir." Fryedai replied honestly.

Robbinson blinked and watched in horror as the grey curtained doorway swung in the gentle wind. Just then, voices arose from behind. They were getting closer and closer by the second.

"We can relax now, brother. May every man earn his fair and justly earned reward, remember?" One of the voices sang.

"We have the antechamber within our sights. The treasure, and its surrounding wealth are ours, and the Trolls and everybody else are none the wiser!"

Fryedai rushed to the gap in the curtain as fast as his lame leg would carry him, hoping the voices were far enough away that they could still find time to move without being noticed. Fryedai quickly turned around and grabbed the petrified Captain Robbinson from where he stood and dragged him stumbling into the next room.

"What are you doing?" The captain hissed with great urgency. "We are not in control of this situation, what are we going to do?"

The room they stepped into looked like a cloakroom with many wardrobes and cabinets in which they could hide. Fryedai gripped the captain's leather jacket tightly and pulled him towards the closet that was closest to the exit. At least this way they would be able to make a quick getaway.

Unfortunately, due to Robbinson's barrel-like size, the two men were unable to close the doors.

"I don't know how long we'll be able to last like this." He said quietly, unable to stop his face from pressing against the golden blonde hair of Fryedai.

The young navigator squirmed in response and quickly had to tell the captain to stop fidgeting and be quiet. He had just about managed to close their hiding place shut. Through the curtained doorway, two tall men emerged.

"Damn! You'd think the mayor would have put some doors in this place." The slightly smaller man laughed.

The other glared at him, his crystal blue eyes menacing as they slowly made their way through the room. Captain Robbinson let out a small gasp.

Something about them looked eerily familiar.

Fryedai recalled what the captain had told him about what happened on the ship, however, both of them remembered fragments. Fryedai barely remembered how the dagger-like waves rose out of the water and horrifyingly shook The Inspectre to near tipping point, battering the hull.

"That's Atlas and Orion Vain." The captain informed Fryedai against his ear, pausing with slight apprehension. "I told everyone to fire, but he was too quick. He looks different now though, more tired and worn..."

Fryedai looked up at the captain and away from the brothers.

"Sir, why do you do it?" Fryedai asked abruptly, though this was hardly the time to ask.

"Why do I do what?" Hissed the captain, his eyes remained fixed on Atlas Vain as he remembered the moment the colossal-tattooed man walked on to the deck of his ship and raised his vile and ugly head.

Was there no escaping the dire situations he was thrust into? He had weathered storms, monsters and pirates in his many years, and now as an old and tired man – not months away from retirement – he was trapped in a wardrobe with quite possibly the least capable and inexperienced member of his crew to date, a man he still considered to be a boy in many regards. It was then that Robbinson started to wish it was Rockwell standing next to him and not Fryedai. He could always depend on that man in a pinch; his skills in combat and unbreakable bravery were that of the best he had ever seen in the Navy, and it was only because of one particular incident that he hadn't already received a promotion from the Sea-Lord's Admiralty.

"This, the whole Navy-captain-thing." Fryedai asked quietly, as they watched the brothers shuffle around the room.

His heart was almost leaping from his chest and his legs started to quiver and ache from the long trek he'd endured through the mines, not to mention the wound he had sustained. Yet, Fryedai wanted to know. He wanted a long career in the Navy, he wanted to be captain someday. He hoped and this was the only time he had been close enough to the captain for long enough for him to gain some perspective on the man before he batted the question away and dispatched him to some other duty, and so Fryedai whispered as quietly as he could.

"You always want to remain in control of everything and yet you can't do anything, is that what it's like to be a captain? When something changes, you freeze. Isn't that the whole point of leading. You're meant to adapt, to change, to outwit the enemy?"

Robbinson sighed. The boy didn't understand a thing, and how could he? He was too young, too idealistic about the world around him and too green. This world was a dark and dangerous place. It was full of whispers and lies, murders and monsters, and things Robbinson himself didn't even believe in - and then there was the Seidr! The creatures! The guild of Alchemists, the government, and the Ash! So many secrets still lay uncovered, and no one could go through their world unchanged by what they bore witness to.

"Well, I may as well tell you." He muttered as the pirates neared the end of the room, being very careful to keep his voice low. "You see, long ago, I fell in love with a Nereridian princess called Adira and -"

"Like the Sea Goddess from the stories?" Interrupted Fryedai, raising an eyebrow.

"Very much so." The captain continued. "I met the mermaid by a waterfall, near the coast of my home on the eve of Izan's festival. It was a moonlit night, full of bitter chill and animals limped as you do now, trembling through frozen blades of grass. I had to wrap up warm as I made my way down Porphyro's hill and through the wood that was surrounded by mist. I was young then, I wanted to help people prepare for the festivities, and so I went to fetch the needed herbs that grew beside that fated place. I remember that numerous shadows haunted about me as I trekked the wooded-grove, and suddenly, as I reached the opening, a soothing song danced upon the air and yearned like a wandering wisp for me to follow it. I was taught to value every life above my own, Fryedai, and although the song was soothing upon the wind, it sounded as if its owner was in pain."

"It cried to me for help, it did – made my flesh tremble and caused my then nimble feet to run from beneath my standing. With a heart of fire, I rushed towards that cry, forgetting all about my need for herbs that grew along the rippling waters of the fall. And there, bathed in glorious silver moonlight, did I see her. O' by happy chance that night did celestial bodies burn brightly through the clouded apertures to grace their radiance upon that one blessed spot. She was trapped like a beast in a gilded cage of purest, shimmering argent. Her hair was of ebony; her drift, slender and lily-white; her face so fair and amorous that all would've gazed and worshipped for a chance – nay, a mere second to kneel, touch and kiss, and yet this beautiful creature, this goddess, was trapped betwixt two worlds of the waterfall and the sea, residing alone in that solitary pool. She sang to me, Fryedai, that she did. For when I approached her, languishing by the pool, she splashed her silken tail-fin high in the cold night's airy mist, revealing a latticework of vibrant shimmering sapphire, ruby, and ever-green-emerald."

He paused for a moment before continuing.

"Yet the sight of the goddess alone was not true love, by no means it wasn't, oh no. For when that luscious voice did sing, did it melt the hearts of men, and so Fryedai, beckoning me forward to where the water did swash and spin, I leapt with entire heart and soul into the freezing waters that lay within. Under her spell and with midnight charm, she pulled me toward her, and I looked upon her frail frame to find no disorder. With a single kiss she sealed my fate, to deathly and freezing darkness I was doomed to rest my weary pate. However, to my surprise I find a fisherman's spear-hook up-thrusted in scales and bleeding below. And so Fryedai, I ripped the spear-hook free, and then did Adira speak her name and swim free. But that was not the end, oh no, I followed her downwards to trenches deep, and found lying in my wake, a school of royal-guardian Mer-folk covering the princess's escape most haste."

"And then what happened, sir?" Pondered Fryedai, fully enthralled in the story, though the captain he admired so much conniving with mermaid royalty he found hard to believe.

Although they had been warned at the Naval Training Ground of people and monsters from the deep. Fryedai knew it could have been in the realms of possibility, as the first Nereridian kingdom had only been discovered a hundred years prior to his training as a navigator. Abruptly, their attention switched focus to the brothers at the other end of the room, as the pirates' conversation became more heated.

"You know, Atlas, I didn't want to tell you this until we found the treasure, but since we're being honest with each other, I think I should tell you." Orion offered.

"Tell me what?" Growled Atlas as he looked up.

Orion looked nervous and then explained the situation to his brother as best he could.

"One of our men came back from patrolling the streets, where they followed a woman. Apparently, it was the first time they had seen her in the town."

"Really? Gillian came straight to me after the rally, said he found nothing – ugh!"

The pirate captain closed his eyes as his brother held him.

"These cursed headaches, then we have a new arrival on the island we must deal with. Is it likely she might be one of the escaped Navy and found her way to shore?"

"Maybe." Orion replied. "I don't know, it's entirely possible. Gillian mentioned something about a girl being the guardian's accomplice, the one who's been giving us so much trouble with his traps in the tunnels. It could be Arabella, the mayor's daughter. She's being defiant with your plans concerning her, but she has blonde hair and the girl that was seen had red."

Robbinson and Fryedai's hearts leapt out of their chests upon hearing this, and Robbinson could barely maintain his excitement. Finally, they had some good news to think about. Perhaps they could make it off the island after all and save their crew. But a girl! That was most irregular, thought Fryedai, and through this his arm caught the side of the wardrobe's door frame and rattled the handle.

Atlas and Orion turned their attention towards the wardrobe. They peered at it with menacing curiosity, looking to it and then back and each other. Orion drew closer to look, at the command of his brother, leaving Atlas to slump against the wall, waving his brother on. With each step the pirate vice-captain took, Fryedai felt his heart beat louder and louder in his chest. Orion unsheathed his cutlass from his hip and stalked his way towards them with jagged steps as Blood-drip's tip scrapped along the tiled floor.

"Whoever's there, why don't you come out, little birds?" He cackled, his eyes wide with bloodlust.

He was dragging the sword across the floor in short, sharp bursts leaving horrible, ragged lines in the ceramic squares and his brother cackled with weak laughter as he did so. The pirate was taunting them to come out and face him, but Fryedai wasn't giving out to him.

The pirate reached the front of the wardrobe, and a wicked cat-like smile grew upon his face. Fryedai had to do something and tried to summon flames in his hand, focusing hard on feeling the embers and rising smoke spark from his fingertips. A second went by and nothing.

"Got you, little bird. You're trapped in a cage with nowhere to flee." Sang the pirate. "Well, let me help you."

Orion laughed as he raised his sword.

"Time to fly away, little bird." He said, voice dripping with venom.

He unlocked the wardrobe doors with the tip of his cutlass, revealing both Fryedai and Robbinson pressed against the hard wooden back.

Orion smirked.

"Why, Captain! How nice of you jailbirds to join us."

He then reached his full height, towering over both men, raising his sword to meet the Navy captain's stomach. Robbinson looked at the pirate; he was perfectly frozen in place, frightened beyond all belief as if he was trapped within Adira's pool again and unable to escape – Fryedai even wondered in that moment how the captain ever escaped the school of Mer-folk! It all made sense to him now though; why the captain was so afraid of sea creatures and monsters, why he was so unable to move in times of danger. He had been there before, and he returned to that pool every single time because of the mermaid's curse, because he had been tricked into falling in love with a mermaid princess on a frosty, fog-ridden night.

"What's the matter, captain?" Taunted Orion. "You and your man here aren't going to shoot my brother and me this time, are you?"

The dastardly pirate then thrust the hilt of his cutlass, pushing it deep into Robbinson's belly as slowly as he could.

"No!" Fryedai screamed as the man beside him keeled over.

The pain on the captain's face looked excruciating and unbearable. As blood fizzled out of the corner of his mouth, wetting the side of his shirt, the captain looked as if he had not expected to be stabbed, as if he was still lost within the tale of his story, cradled by his beloved mermaid. Blood trickled everywhere, and Fryedai had to back away from the gleaming scarlet sword, as crimson liquid splattered the floor.

Orion ripped his steel from the captain's stomach, causing the man to fall to the floor with a thud. Fryedai thought to himself of how twisted Atlas and Orion were in order to make light of someone else's misery in the way they did. What possible thing in the world had twisted them so perversely was beyond Fryedai's imagination. Because whatever made Atlas Vain that way, must have been twisted and wicked indeed.

Orion Vain turned his head and drew his attention towards Fryedai with the same cruel smile on his face. He again wondered what Orion had been through to make him like he was, or was that directly down to his brother's manipulations, which were so painfully obvious from the way they argued between themselves.

"You're next, little bird! May every man earn his fair and justly earned reward." He chirped.

Fryedai's eyes widened.

There was no way he could escape what was coming next, not without a weapon. He shut his eyes tightly, expecting pain to come. At least he had the satisfaction of knowing it would hurt less than his leg. He waited for everything to just stop as the darkness took him in and that would be the end of it, but before Orion's cutlass even drew near, the pirate heard captain Robbinson whisper something.

"What was that captain? I didn't quite hear you! You've got a little bit of blood just right there." Orian teased, kicking Robbinson hard in the gut.

Orion levelled his sword and bent down at the captain's side to antagonise him further. He then placed his hand to his ear and giggled to himself.

"Say that for me again, one more time."

"Ifrit..." Began Robbinson, as he struggled to say the words, trying to get his voice back.

Fryedai just wanted Robbinson to stay down and rest, it wasn't worth torturing himself for a few words when he could do nothing about what was going to happen. He then heard Atlas curse under his breath from across the room and watched a bemused Orion try to figure out what was going on. Suddenly, a ring of fiery pillars erupted around the wardrobe area, forming a perfect circle. Nothing burned aside from the fire, leaving everyone else trapped.

Orion looked astounded, and so was Fryedai.

"So, what if you can play with a bit of fire!" Roared Orion, swatting his sword in frantic arcs as he tried to bat away the flames. "We own the entire supply. This is nothing compared to what my brother can do! What are you compared to him? You can't do anything; we still have all the power!"

Robbinson shakily stood up until his back was straight and coughed up a small amount of blood. He then looked Fryedai dead in the eyes.

"I never did get to go to Izan's festival. You might want to try and run." He spoke.

Fryedai looked at him confused, he didn't understand, but the fat grey-haired man just smiled.

"Go, I'm finally doing something in my life that I can take control of, I'm saving people, and perhaps I might even end up saving myself if this works. People forget in the stories with all the blackness of the wine-dark seas that Izan gaze them light from the skies."

Fryedai felt himself grow hotter around the flames, he had always admired the captain, and now after all they had been through it felt like they were going to have to say goodbye.

"I don't understand, Captain? What are you doing?" He cried.

Fryedai hadn't even noticed that two lines of tears had begun to stream down his face. The captain then turned to Orion. The pirate's arms were still held at his side, like a soldier waiting for orders.

"I stole some of the more potent stuff from the guards after I got out of the tunnels." Robbinson coughed, holding up his hand.

A small pathway in the flames opened that curved just enough to make a hole big enough for a person to fit through.

"Fryedai, go! That's an order. Get away from here! I'll handle the rest! Find whoever it is who survived!"

Fryedai nodded, although he didn't want to leave, and he had no idea how long the captain would last against a person like Orion Vain. As soon as his foot touched the ground, the pirate leapt at the chance to attack, and Fryedai ran as hard as he could to the hole his captain had created. He could feel the pirate baring down on him, his sword waved high above his head as the flames twisted and crackled around them in towers of blistering fire. Fryedai looked behind him for one moment, and there Orion was, his sword poised and just footsteps away from him, his eyes glaring a hollow blue that echoed his urge.

Then suddenly, Captain Robbinson shouted one more time and Fryedai dove between the fiery gaps. A rush of flame erupted into the captain's hand, becoming a sharpened blade.

Fryedai looked at the pillars of twisting fire from the outside of the ring. He watched as the captain and Orion exchanged blows back and forth in a constant parry, neither one getting any closer to striking their foe. He realised he had more significant concerns than their fight, and slumped on the other side of the room against the wall and watching intently, was the dreaded Atlas Vain.

Although the pirate captain looked weak and drained, he still cracked a wicked, crooked smile and gently stroked his bushy black beard as an amulet of glowing indigo gemstone hung from his neck. Fryedai saw his look was one of amusement – after all, given their reputation, Atlas probably hadn't seen many people escape his brother and live. Fryedai guessed that a man of his cunning enjoyed a game, and he knew that Atlas did not want this to be easy. The pirate enjoyed playing with everything too much; the power, the town, the Navy. Fryedai had seen it all in the tunnel. He had to get away and fulfil his captain's order.

Taking one last look at the monster across the room, Fryedai watched him snarl like the creature he had become. The last thing the navigator heard was the clash of two blades against one another, and the terrorising shouts of Atlas Vain as he ran towards the open window and the perilous rocks below.

"Once we've done with this place, we're going to burn it all to the ground, every last piece of this pathetic island town will be gone. Remember this, I will see it all burn, along with the very last of Giant-kind! That prophecy… The Great Storm – it must be fulfilled!"

11

Back at the Trafalgar, the mayor shook with worry. He was sweating profusely, and his face was growing redder by the second. Silvers Kent didn't care about life, he only cared about ripping someone's spirit away. To him it was a form of entertainment.

"Now then, where were we? Ah yes, Jackson! You seem to have pissed off my men." The quartermaster chuckled, now steering his attention back round to the drunk as he put down the phone in the centre of the table.

"Just go." Jackson said rather drunkenly. "Just go and leave us all alone. Why are you even here anyway? We didn't do anything to you people."

"I'll tell you why we're here." Kent began, walking around the table towards the drunk.

He was as cool as the frost-coloured hair atop his head and showed it as he walked nonchalantly, as though he didn't have a care in the world. When he reached Jackson, Slivers placed a hand on his shoulder and bent down to his ear to whisper one straightforward line.

"Because we're pirates, that's why."

Jackson was too exhausted to move but he felt something boil up inside of him. He didn't care that he had taken a beating. Did they seriously think because they had the power to take over an island that they could do so, without any consequences at all? It was just benign! The pirates inflicted misery for no apparent reason. It was selfish and wrong. Jackson knew they were sick people, who wanted to do sick and horrible things to his home, whether it was for the sake of treasure or not, and for that, they had to be stopped. Jackson had to do it for the people he had left. Arie had given him reason to live again after Molly. Tom and Nelson had always been there for him, and Ann – what could he say about Ann? Somebody that he had hardly known for little under a day! That weird and hopefully optimistic girl had sped into his life and saved him from a storm of all things, so where could he even begin? There was the problem of her wanting to go to that cursed place, however, and the Ash she had found underneath his bed. He hadn't used the powder against the pirates because he didn't want to lower himself to their standards and there was no guarantee that he would win. But the way Ann had looked at the vial of Ash as she held it in her hand, it spoke of a shared pain they held between them. Perhaps she was trustworthy after all.

Silvers still hovered above him, and before Jackson could even utter a sentence or response, his stomach was hit with crippling pain; a white-hot ball of fire that twisted its way through his entire body. Jackson looked down in bewilderment as he saw Silvers' fist connect with his body. No hole had been torn and nor had his body burst, such as his stomach suggested. Instead, his vision became blurry and black, as if he were about to fade.

"You look confused, Jackson?" Silvers continued to whisper. "Let me explain to you how this is going to work, and how my friends and I deal with things around here."

Jackson groaned.

"You clearly haven't got it into your thick skull yet. None of you own this town anymore, we do! Atlas, he has it all figured out. He's very good with plans. We can save the world from that monster's tyranny. I truly believe we can do it. We've killed all of them so far – there's just one more to go. With my power of persuasion, it will be easy. We just need the treasure."

Everything was gradually fading away and the image of Slivers Kent's face began to grow distorted. Jackson knew he only had a moment or so left to stay conscious. He had to learn whatever he could before it was too late.

"It isn't real, it doesn't exist." He mumbled in a haze, struggling to stay awake.

He was unsure of what the pirate had meant; this treasure, the thing that the pirates had been looking for, he knew it wasn't real despite what Nelson and Tom had told him. The pirates had been here so long that they couldn't have possibly found anything. Could they? Again, it weighed in his mind along with the lingering image of Molly.

"Persuasion?" He asked groggily, as he just realised what the pirate had said.

His eyes widened. Ann had also mentioned that Silvers must have been a user too when he had mentioned the pirate putting Arie under some form of spell. He had been so stupid not to realise straight away that it had something to with Ash. It was the most sought after commodity in the world! That must have been why Arie had been acting so strange these past few weeks – she was being controlled by the power the pirates lorded over her, and yet for the life of him, Jackson couldn't figure out why this was only some of the time, as Arabella had rejected Silvers's invitation this morning to join him on Atlas's ship.

"It's my power." Stated Silvers triumphantly, placing another punch into Jackson's gut. "And you know what, Jackson? You're not going to remember this. I'm not gonna let you. Therefore, just because I feel like it, I'm going to tell you something that's just between you and me. Well, are you listening?"

Jackson hummed in response, he didn't care what the pirate's secret was, he just wanted Silvers to go away so he could get back to his normal life. The drunk now only saw the shaded silhouettes and outlines of dark shapes, even the pirate's voice was muffled as he slipped away. He guessed he had seconds before he blacked out completely.

"Your friends, the two you treasure most dearly..." Whispered Silvers. "I'm going to take them away. We have roles for them, insurances for if it all goes south."

Jackson trembled.

"They've hidden things from you, Jackson. Dark secrets indeed. Moreover, I discovered that they're far more valuable than they first let on. We have connections, vested interests concerning the mayor's only daughter – people would be very concerned if she were ever..." He paused then, as if to savour the sweetness of his words. "To go missing. Ha-ha. And the cook, his tale is even more delightful...I still haven't told Atlas, you know..."

Jackson did not hear the end as his eyes finally closed and flooded with a rushing and unrelenting field of black.

* * *

Ann leaned her forehead against the foggy windows, placing her hands on the thin panes. She was now at the back of the restaurant, the sea wind blowing in from the coast whistled through her scarlet hair. She hoped so much that Jackson was okay. There was no possible way she could reach Black Ridge without him. If Jackson died, then her friend died too, and she couldn't let that happen. Prisoner 220118 was due to be executed in three days! She had to convince Jackson to help her, and fast, otherwise she would never make it.

Suddenly, the door to the left of her burst open with a clatter and a host of pirates stampeded to towards her. She quickly clung to the sidewall and hid behind the door to avoid detection; her fingers locked in a death-grip. It looked like they were all rushing up to the manor house on the very top of the hill.

Nelson had told Ann about what the pirates had been doing on the island when they had met this morning before Jackson had given his monologue at the bar. Nelson had asked why she had helped save the drunk, even though they did not know each other. Ann explained her reasons to him as she had done to Arabella. The cook said that if she could show Jackson a reason to go with her, then he would probably help. That was just the sort of person he was, and that was why Ann had to keep him safe. She glanced towards the hill. The manor house itself looked like an offshoot of an old castle, like that of what a traveller might find while wandering through a forest. Its outside was littered with boarded-up windows covered with wooden planks, and the main doors were graced with two stone columns on either side. It had one blue-slated spire on the top of the middle roof, supported by a massive white windmill.

With the pirates now gone, Ann looked to see if the coast was clear. She peered through the doors at the back to find the kitchen staff clearing up the mess that the pirates left in their wake, it seemed like they were cursing their very existence with the amount of work they had to do. She spied Nelson hastily looking through the service hatch as Napoleon sat next to him, wagging his curly tail.

"What's going on?" She asked, sneaking up on him, causing him to jump as she crept through the kitchens.

"Gods, you're quiet." He exclaimed. "And well, Jackson flipped-off some pirate named Brent."

"Is that all?"

"That said pirate then transformed into a giant gorilla and tried to beat him senseless." Explained Nelson, pointing at the large, heaped body on the floor.

"Ah." She nodded. "I can see how that may be a problem."

"Yeah, and now he's just met Silvers, the brothers' quartermaster."

"We've met." The red head sneered.

Ann looked over to see a person clapping. He was tall and slender, and everything about him was white – aside from a thick purple scar spanning the width of his neck. White hair, white eyes and very, very pale skin, making him look sickly.

The moment was interrupted when the phone rang, and Silvers Kent picked it up. Ann was very interested in the conversation; it seemed that the pirates too were in a rush to get off the island, the only question was why?

All the while Ann whispered to Nelson and told him of the situation regarding Tom. The cook looked fearful as she described the guardian's predicament but stopped just short of telling him about the old man knowing he had Alchemic-blood flowing through his veins. As this went on, Silvers continued his monologue, it was all somewhat villainous, and Ann could not help thinking that he was a bit of a bore. She liked the people she fought to have some character or quirk, at least that way the fight would be fun and somewhat decent. All Ann was getting from Silvers was that he was cruel and efficient, and she was just about ready to get up and go knock the lights out of him, when Nelson pulled her back.

"What did you do that for?" She grunted, annoyed that she'd been stopped.

The look in Nelson's eyes said it all. The man was terrified. Ann was not so reluctant, however. Perhaps it was because she had not lived for weeks on end under pirate rule, or maybe that she was not scared of someone that had powers.

"Just look at what he's doing!" Urged Nelson, who kept peaking over the countertop.

Ann rolled her eyes, peering over the counter herself so she could get a better look.

"And?" She shrugged, noting that Silvers' fist was a ball of molten white energy.

It was not the first time she faced someone like him, nor would it be the last if she were to face Atlas.

Jackson collapsed to the floor in a slump, and the pirate turned around to face the kitchen, raising his arms to his sides triumphantly. A hot bright light surrounded both of his hands and the pirate sniggered. Mayor Johnson was by his side and begged him not to take his daughter. Clearly, he had heard what Kent had said, and Ann desperately wanted to know what was going on.

"Come out, Chef!" He shouted. "I know you're there!"

Nelson's eyes widened as he saw Silvers march towards the kitchen. Then, turning to Ann, the cook took her hand and politely told her to go. He somehow knew Jackson would be all right if Ann stuck by him. After all, they both needed each other to get what they wanted.

Nelson didn't know what he got out of the arrangement. What did he achieve by being friends with them and going against the pirates? Ann got to go where she wanted and save her friend, and Jackson, he got his payment for taking her. Nelson didn't really get anything. One question still plagued his mind - it was something that he had to know if he was going to die at the hands of these pirates. The question was his sister. Where had his sister gone and why had she never called or even written a single letter? He had to know why. She wouldn't just up and vanish. That wasn't like her at all, and it was something he'd been wondering about ever since her disappearance. He trusted Jackson completely, although he still wanted to know the truth about what happened to Molly.

Then an idea struck him. He could go with Ann when she left. At least that way he might have some say as to where they might go?

"Go hide." He ordered Ann, making up his mind.

He wasn't going to die here.

"You need to be there to tell Mark what happened when he wakes up."

He hurried Ann into one of the store cupboards.

"What, why?" She complained. "And weren't you afraid of Silvers just now?"

Nelson smiled at Ann's confusion.

"I was, but at least now I know that his ability doesn't kill you. Mark was still breathing when he fell."

"Let me help you, I know how to fight!" She argued.

"No!"

He was adamant that Silvers had to take him if any of them were to survive. For some reason the pirate wanted him, and Nelson had no idea why.

"I'll be fine." He assured her as he opened the doors to a large food pantry.

Ann continued to protest, but Nelson was having none of it. He needed to do this.

12

Great! This was just perfect, thought Ann. She was a sucker for trusting her friends – well, future friends, she hoped. She slouched against the locked door and held her head in her hands. How foolish she had been! She felt an odd layer of irony on her lips and grinned at the prospect. Confined again! This was only slightly less bad than all those other times she had been torn away from those she loved and cared for.

A thousand thoughts raced through her mind. What was going to happen now, now that she wasn't there to protect her friends? Ann shuddered. This cold, confined pantry reminded her too much of her childhood and the times her father spent in the dark. In retrospect, Silvers and his Ash powers weren't that bad, not compared to then. She looked around the pantry, willing herself to be sensible in order to find some form of resolution. She wasn't going to let those events repeat themselves a second time.

As Ann got up to her feet, she sighed, thinking about what everyone on the island had been going through at the hands of these pirates. Just how much devastation they had caused? It reaffirmed the choice she had made; the choice to save people without violence, not if she could help it at least. Ann remembered the broken mess the outskirts of the town had been in when she first arrived this morning. Thankfully, the information she obtained was right and she had found Jackson. The people weren't used to seeing strange kinds of power out here in the West-Sea; Nelson had made that plain. Perhaps that was why he'd hid the fact he had Alchemic blood? Ann knew from her father that Ash, and Ash-users, were more common on the Devil's Doorstep. That place was like a hornet's nest for those kinds of people, and it was far more dangerous than any of the Outer-Seas.

The Doorstep was the central ocean of the world, surrounded by the North, East, West, and South-Seas. It was when you reached the Doorstep, that the seas stopped converging, blocked off by doldrums and harrowing monsters. Although Ann has been born in the South-Sea, she had once heard a traveller to their home say that the Doorstep had double the amount of island chains than all the seas combined, but that was not true - The Doorstep had double the islands than all the seas combined. It was known as the chain of a thousand islands; the Devil's domain, a place that drives all men insane!

But that wasn't going to help her now. Ann put the thoughts of the Doorstep out of her mind, preferring to focus on the task at hand. She had to get out of this damned pantry! Unfortunately, she was locked in. Nelson had turned the blasted key!

"There you are chef." She could hear the slime in his voice.

His words were as cold as the snow-coloured hair covering his head. Silence soon followed.

Ann did her best to do as Nelson had said. However, she couldn't bear the waiting any more, not when her friend was in danger. She walked away from the door to the back of the pantry, getting out one of her guns from the inside of her jacket pocket. She gripped the pistol tightly in her hand and aimed it at the lock, pecking the ribbon on her wrist for luck. As she gently squeezed the trigger, a shot fired from the barrel, making a loud bang as it rattled through the air. The latch exploded into shards and Ann ran forward, kicking down the pantry door with a thud, sending up a plume of dust.

Nelson and Silvers were nowhere to be seen. It was almost like they had vanished.

"Shit!" Ann cursed, lowering her guns.

Somewhere in the kitchen she heard a swine-like cry, and Ann realised that Nelson must have hidden Napoleon away too. She followed the piglet's cries till she found her rosy companion in one of the back cupboards of the kitchen. She opened the cabinet door to find the pig squealing at her in terror.

"I know, I know." She soothed sweetly, lifting the pig from his hiding place and onto the surface nearby.

Napoleon squawked in response and rushed along the countertop to where the pantry door had fallen. Without a moment to waste, the piglet jumped down from the worktop, trotting along into the dusty space and snuffled about the many jars and boxes as he went about trying to climb the shelves. Ann was amazed, she had never seen a piglet try to climb shelving before, nor had she been one so concerned for its master as she realised the little pork-chop must have known something had gone terribly wrong. As Napoleon worked his way around the first two levels of shelving (which he had used a cardboard box to gain access to), he squealed at Ann, to what she could only assume were instructions to lift him higher to the third row of shelves, where Ann saw that Nelson kept strange bottles of luminous coloured liquids. They sat at the back of the shelves, glowing in the dimly lit gloom.

"What is it you want?" Asked Ann, as she lifted the piglet higher.

As much as she knew Nelson cared for the pig, she was much more concerned with the well-being of its master, as well as Jackson and Tom – the latter of which was bleeding to death in an alleyway. Now with Nelson gone, she had no way of saving the old man who she knew would probably die. Nevertheless, the piglet snorted back at her as he scurried to where the peculiar jars were. Moments later, the moody Napoleon called out for Ann with what seemed like a happy cry – not that she could tell mind you. The piglet nudged a jar of blue liquid with its snout. The jar rolled forward and was pushed to the floor by Napoleon. It smashed on impact and the viscous liquid oozed across the flag stone flooring of the restaurant's pantry.

Ann quickly backed away and looked at the piglet in amazement. For a beast so clever in the way he acted, why would he do a thing that was so silly?

"What did you do that for!" She cried. "We don't have time for this. I don't have time for this."

Ann spoke to Napoleon as if the pig were human. The animal replied by once again squealing at her and then quickly jumped down with his little hind legs to where the blue ooze spread across the floor. To further Ann's astonishment, the pig lapped at the puddle with his tongue happily till there was no more and belched as the flagstone was licked clean.

"Ah, that's better!" Belched the pig. "Never thought that master would let me speak again with those pirates around, fuck me!"

Ann jumped back from Napoleon, her eyes almost popping from her head. The pig spoke!

"You- you can speak! you're swearing! How can a piglet as cute as you have a mouth so foul?" Cried Ann in amazement.

Of all the things she believed in, of all the tales she had heard. How could pigs speak? It must have been something in the liquid. Something that Nelson had somehow concocted with Alchemy.

"Alright, calm down love." The piglet huffed, a mocking tone on the air of his newly discovered voice.

Ann continued to glare down at the pig in disbelief.

"First of all, I'm an Alchemist's familiar. Master is not a particularly good one, but that's beside the point. A familiar that just so happens to be in the form of a Teacup pig. It wasn't my choice believe me, but that idiot fucked up the contract ritual on his eighteenth birthday, and I got stuck as a pig. I wanted to be a Labrador. I told him, a nice big chocolate Labrador. We could've gone on walks! I could've had my belly rubbed, but was that what I got? No!"

"But you still get your belly rubbed, I saw Arabella tickle you this morning at the tavern." Said Ann, slowly coming around to the piglet.

Napoleon looked up at her in delight as soon as she mentioned belly rubs. His light blue eyes shone with excitement, his ears twitched and his cute little snout covered in dripping ooze shot upwards.

"Ah, Arie! She gives the best belly rubs I tell you, the best! But master commanded me to drink that concoction after I told him how to make it, so the pirates wouldn't discover he was an alchemist! Usually, I only have to keep quiet around his friends and during work hours, but they would have tortured him if they'd have known. That crew talks about what they did to the giants, how they used the slain creatures' blood to make their powers permanent. They whispered from the very beginning in the taverns and restaurant about what their captain would ever do to a man if he ever found out that he was alchemist. It would be a life of torture and imprisonment for Master."

"So, why are you telling me this? Plus, didn't Tom already know Nelson's secret? He's the one who told me to get your master; he's really hurt." Asked Ann, still concerned for the old man in the alleyway.

"Really? Fuck! He only knows about the secret because he caught me blabbing to Master. Jackson wanted to eat me. Bacon-butty my arse! Sorry to hear that he's hurt though."

"Yeah, that's why I need to hurry, and with Jackson out and Nelson gone, everything's become a mess thanks to the pirates!" Ann sighed in frustration as she turned to leave the pantry to see if Jackson was okay.

"I've got to go." She informed him. "Glad to see that you can talk again."

"Wait! I can help you!" Napoleon cried, trotting after Ann as she made her way through the kitchen.

"Why?" She asked the familiar.

"Because I want to save my Master, even though he may be a clueless idiot from time to time when it comes to magic. I can tell you the things you need to know to heal Old Tom too, everything is at my Master's house. A simple 'oink'-ment will do it. No Seidr needed for that one." Explained the pig as he waddled along.

Ann smiled brightly as she went to lift up the divider that separated the kitchen from the restaurant and allowed Napoleon to trot through. It wasn't the help she'd been expecting to get, but she was glad that it was help, nonetheless. She hoped she could get to Tom in time and do all the other things she had to do. Either way, she was going to bring these pirates down.

The divider was surprisingly heavy, and Ann just barely managed to make it through, landing squarely on the other side, amidst the broken furniture, where Napoleon sat waiting for her, wiggling his tail. Clearly, Silvers had managed to block the exit on his way out with Nelson. She manoeuvred over the broken furniture, near to where Jackson was still lying unconscious, surrounded by pieces of destroyed chairs and table restaurant decor. Napoleon followed closely behind.

"That's the best I've seen him in years." Commented the Teacup pig with a giggle, looking down on Jackson's face from above.

"Shhh!" Hushed Ann, as she went to see if the drunk was okay.

"What!" The familiar complained. "The guy likes red sauce, Master feeds me brown, can't a pig have preferences?"

"Napoleon, we're not alone." Whispered Ann, and motioning with her eyes Napoleon saw that she was right.

Sitting on the only surviving upturned-table across the room from them was Mayor Johnson, and he was staring right at Ann, apparently muttering to himself about what to do about Jackson. Because of the mess of scattered furniture situated about Jackson, Ann could use the majority of it to remain unseen by the mayor, his focus seemingly drawn towards the drunk's limp frame.

"Oh shit, yeah. Sorry about that." Napoleon whispered.

The small, rotund, blonde man was red in the face, and rife with worry. He continually whispered to himself about what he was going to do, and Ann wondered why he was doing that to begin with, seemingly in a state of shock as it appeared Silvers had left him in the room alone?

"No, no, no." He spoke under his breath, as Ann crept further forward.

She had to help Jackson and was stood just far enough away so that she could see and hear everything that was happening. Hopefully, the mayor would not notice her. Ann still wasn't quite sure if he was friendly or not. From what she had seen, the man that sat at the far end of the room had stayed silent all throughout Silvers's monologue, and Ann didn't want to take any chances, not with an unknown number of crazy pirates milling around outside.

"It wasn't meant to be like this, you stupid drunk!" The mayor cried, standing up from the table in a boiling rage. "I had an accord, that if I cooperated, my daughter would be spared from all this. It even included you and your friend too. Why did you think they left you be? So why? Why did you have to get drunk, and ruin everything?"

Ann was surprised to see the blistering anguish on his face. Clearly, she had gotten the wrong idea. Arabella had given the impression that all the townspeople were being forced to work for the pirates. It would have never occurred to the barmaid that someone would willingly work for the Vains after all the suffering they had caused. From the way Arabella acted, Ann figured that she was certainly not aware that the person betraying the town was in fact her own father. Ann thought back to the night Jackson had described when he first saw Silvers entering the mayor's mansion on the hill.

"They were meant to get what they wanted and leave! I was to be left with the diamonds!" The mayor continued, as he clenched his fists. "The Navy never helped us! We were all poor, so why should my town have to be destroyed when we can just work with them instead?"

Ann watched in bewilderment as she witnessed the mayor divulge everything. She hated how corrupt humanity could be, and how quickly the man in front of her had been able to sell out others. It was sickening to watch.

Suddenly, Ann heard the sound of a knife being drawn. The blade glinted in the midday light, and the mayor's nose ran with snot.

"It was all going so well!" He continued to whine, beginning to weep as he walked over to where Jackson lay.

Ann's heart almost skipped a beat as she saw the blade wobble. She couldn't let the mayor kill Jackson, there was too much on the line for her if he did, and her friend would never be saved.

"And now, thanks to you Jackson, I may have lost the diamonds I was promised! Atlas, he may turn back on our whole deal!"

Ann stepped closer.

"They're the whole damn reason I agreed to this situation in the first place. Do you know what I could have done with that much money? Or how many Threds those rocks would have got me on the underground market?"

Then, Mayor Johnson reached down, grasping the drunk up with all his might, dropping the knife, and shaking Jackson violently. For an older man, Rupert Johnson was surprisingly strong, and Jackson groaned slightly as the mayor kept a firm grip.

"This will teach you to mess with me and my daughter!" He sneered, and the drunk's face began to turn a dark shade of purple. "Don't think I've forgotten that you messed with her head too. To think you became like this all because your wife left you. How pathetic! You really did have it all, Jackson. Now look at you! You're nothing, with nowhere to belong, no place to be had, aside from that disaster of beach hut you call a home. You have no one. The pirates have taken your last friend from you."

Click.

"Well… I wouldn't say no one…" Ann began, with a smirk.

She was holding one of her guns against the blonde man's head. Mayor Johnson turned in surprise, all the while Jackson, still blissfully unaware that his life was in danger, hung by his quickly loosening grip and was promptly released to the floor.

"Who are you?" The mayor hissed as Napoleon came to sit by Ann's side.

"Drop him, and perhaps I might tell you. If you don't, don't think for a second that I won't be pulling the trigger. I won't let you hurt my friend."

The mayor laughed.

"Don't be silly, girl. Jackson has no friends left; how do I know that you'll…"

Bang!

Everything was silent for a moment, as Ann put her second gun back in her jacket with the barrel still smoking. Jackson was on the floor again and Napoleon quietly shook with swinish laughter.

"Let me make something clear. I don't like people like you, who manipulate the weak for their own personal gain. It's wrong, and I'll put a stop to anyone who uses people in this way. That includes this Atlas person everyone keeps talking about."

The mayor roared in pain, grasping at his perforated eardrum. Ann had fired that close to his head that the ear had actually burst, sending blood flying across the restaurant.

"Please, I have a daughter. You sound about her age. Please let me go. Let me go back to her, before those pirate thugs snatch her up!" He pleaded.

Wow, this person was really something, thought Ann. To go from threatening to quivering in an instant, it seemed that people were never really who they appeared to be. Ann then dropped her other gun from the back of the mayor's head but kept the armour-meant by her side. She still didn't trust the mayor, and he seemed like the type of person that would change at the flip of a coin. Still, she wasn't a murderer, she wasn't as cold as him or Atlas.

"Go." She ordered, flicking her pistol to the side.

The mayor turned and scurried towards the main entrance. To Ann's surprise, the door was not locked or even barricaded, the mayor simply burst straight through and continued down the hill towards town.

Finally, after peering out of the windows for several minutes, Ann was sure that the knife-wielding mayor wasn't coming back. She hopped off the ledge of the windowsill with a triumphant smile and tiptoed her way up to Jackson, who she had set next to an overturned table. Napoleon verbally berated him for all the times the drunk had threatened to eat him, which she guessed had happened a lot. She bent down in front of the navigator, looking at his sleepy little face. His shaggy black hair was messed up beyond all belief, and spread in every conceivable direction. It made the drunk look like he'd just spent a night with the pigs, only to then have water thrown over him when he was face-down in the mud – though Napoleon assured her that Nelson only gave the familiar the best bedding a pig such as him could possibly hope for.

"You know." She started, looking from Napoleon to the drunk. "Just because you don't believe in something Jackson, like this treasure, it doesn't necessarily mean it doesn't exist. It definitely does. These pirates wouldn't go this far if it didn't. To enslave an entire island is just mad, you know. I would never do it. Although, I suppose something is only legendary till someone proves it's real, right?"

Napoleon nodded in agreement.

"But who cares if it's real or not, right?"

"Erm, I care. I'm fucking real." The pig retorted as she continued to speak to Jackson.

"You wanted to be a Labrador!" Ann laughed.

"Point taken."

"Things like that, they should be about the adventure." Ann continued. "The discovery, and what you do with your friends while you're going to your destination, that's the whole fun in it."

Ann paused and thought carefully about what she was going to say to the unconscious Jackson. She hated feeling vulnerable, and the only reason she was saying what she thought at all was because it needed to be said. Jackson needed to know that someone was there for him. In truth, Ann liked the way in which the drunk didn't seem to care about other people's problems, when caring was all he ever did.

"So please, be my friend - because you and everyone else have suffered so much, just like me. I want to help you all. After all this is done, I want you to come with me, okay."

13

It took half an hour for Jackson to wake, and the first thing he saw was Ann. She was sat right in front of him, looking at his nose and up into his nostrils.

What was wrong with this woman? Had she never heard of personal space before? Ever since they had met this morning, she had continued to always be in his way in some form or another, and he was starting to become concerned. She was only ever serious when she needed to be. But that wasn't even the strangest thing.

"What's up, fuck-face? Hells, you're ugly."

Jackson looked to the right-hand side of him and sat there with a grin about his chops was what the drunk would have classified as his breakfast.

"What did you say, Ann? My head's still a mess." He mumbled groggily, as if his head had been shaken.

It seemed for a moment that Nelson's pet had talked! Jackson looked at where he was and found that he was somehow sat on the floor of a Trafalgar, but everything was unbelievably fuzzy, and his throat was scorching dry. He brushed his hand up and down his neck and found a small cut below his chin.

"Napoleon!" The red-headed girl complained.

How bizarre? Was this some way for Ann to get his attention? With the stuff he had seen her do so far, such as breaking into his home, there was no way he'd do what she wanted. The last thing he remembered was leaving the bar with the pork chop, Napoleon, in his arms. If this was Ann's doing, she was crazier than the pirates. Everything was just a blurry mess in his mind. He looked at Ann and tried to piece things together from the scene around him. His head hurt like crazy and pounded from side to side, as he tried to move. He looked down and found that both his rapier and flintlock had gone.

"Hey! Hey, Ann!" He shouted right in front of her face.

Ann just stared at him blankly with a broad and happy smile.

"What happened here?" He asked, turning his head more so he could see the wrecked restaurant. "And where is Nelson? He's meant to be here, where is he?"

Ann looked at him very gravely, not saying a thing. Suddenly, Napoleon jumped on his chest and his feet dug in. Jackson was now even more concerned for his predicament. Napoleon had never been happy to see him before, so something must have changed. He started to feel groggy, and his head ached continually, he tried again to remember what had happened, there was no way he could just appear halfway across town without knowing why. Besides, even if he were that drunk, he would still remember bits and pieces of what had happened.

"Watch this." Napoleon said to Ann. "Because Alchemists can create Ash, they're immune to its effects and their familiars can negate powers that have been inflicted on another - it's a bit of a comedown though."

The familiar pressed his legs into Jackson's chest, then it hit him, Jackson saw an image of light flash across his vision. Jackson was sure that only he could see it, though it was equally insane that he had just realised that Napoleon had been the one talking the entire time. The visions that the piglet imposed sounded eerily realistic, and around him, light shimmered as two people danced around in circles about the restaurant. One was a man, the other a woman.

The man looked like Nelson. Ghostly was his charming smile, however, Nelson was no longer wearing his worn bloodied butcher's apron and instead was dressed smartly in a purple shirt and waistcoat, with long black trousers. The woman, on the other hand, was a vision of beauty. The figure had the same glaring eyes as Arabella, but the flowing golden hair that looked an awful lot like Molly's.

Arabella, Nelson, Molly, he thought. They were so real, what happened to them? Where were they?

Jackson had to know, he had to find them! The images of light began to change, and both the figures were hunched over with picks in their hands. The light around them seemed dark and cold, like a pit had swallowed them whole. They were trying to get out, yet they appeared enclosed in a tight, unforgiving space. Without any emotion on their faces, they stopped what they were doing and turned to face Jackson.

"Free us. Free us, Jackson. We need you, please find us." They both groaned in frail voices.

It was as if the sound they made was echoing from a place that Jackson couldn't get to. They were trapped there in eternal torment and unable to get away. The drunk reached out to them as best he could.

"I will. I'll find you both, I promise." He cried out, his face flushed with frustration.

"Jackson, Jackson!" Ann said in front of him, but he was lost in blank eyes of dazzling white. "Jackson!" She cried again. "What is it? Who have you got to find? What's wrong?"

She shook Jackson's shoulders, and for a moment, there was not any reply, just deathly silence. Suddenly, Jackson gasped for air as his eyes cleared of white. He took big, gaping breaths, causing his chest tremble as it rose.

"Are you alright?" Ann asked concerned, placing a hand on his shoulder for support and looking to Napoleon, who had jumped off the drunk.

The navigator continued to labour for breath. He looked at Ann who had her emerald eyes fixed on him, and then around the room again and at the piglet next to her. The place was utterly wrecked, and he could not remember why. Finally, he caught his breath, and his chest returned to normal. Ann then passed Jackson a cup that sat next to her, and he snatched it up in an instant, guzzling it down. The next thing Jackson knew, he'd sprayed the contents back into Ann's face, giving her daggers with his eyes as he sat against the upturned table.

"What is this?" He questioned in a serious tone, shaking the cup at her.

Ann looked at the cup, then back to Jackson.

"Told you he wouldn't like it." Whispered Napoleon.

"Water?" She suggested, giving him a tiny smile.

Jackson shook his head.

"What are you giving me water for? Haven't you got any Snake? Moreover, you never answered my question, what happened here? You have some serious explaining to do."

Ann tried her best. It took a few minutes for her to explain to Jackson what had happened; and why, subsequently, everything he saw around him was such a mess. Jackson still looked like he was in a state of shock. He'd said he had forgiven Ann for giving him water and not booze, however, she had a long way to go before he could even begin to trust her. Ann said this was fair, but he knew she thought otherwise. She still didn't know him very well, and the same might be said if the tables were turned, although with Ann it was unlikely.

"So, I fought Silvers?" Asked Jackson, still surveying the damage around the room.

"Yeah, that's right, although I was locked in a storeroom. Not my fault, if you were wondering." Ann replied, frustrated.

"I wasn't." Muttered Jackson.

He had a stern look on his face, one that Ann had not seen him use while she had been on the island. Maybe Silvers' powers had cleared his head just a little bit so that he was sober?

"What about him?" The navigator asked, pointing to the smiling and irritating piglet.

"Oh, I'm magic!" Napoleon exclaimed sarcastically and rolled over for Ann to give him a belly rub.

Ann rolled her eyes and rubbed the familiar's stomach.

"Ash?" Jackson asked.

"Yeah, let's just go with that." She trailed off, turning her attention to other matters.

Jackson paused for a moment as he took in the situation.

"Well…at least you don't squeal anymore." He spoke, rubbing his head as the pig stared at him.

"Oh, I still squeal!" The pig berated and the two of them began to argue about how the drunk had always treated his best friend's pet.

Outside across the hill, Ann could see the boarded-up windows of the manor house and the creaking windmill as it slowly wound its way round next to the spire. It was bringing up mounds of dirt from the tunnels below, but more importantly for the pirates, it was bringing up diamonds. She looked at the windows again and saw a bright flicker pass by. Something was going on in there, and Ann definitely wanted to find out what it was. No matter if it was some mystical treasure or ill-gotten diamonds.

"Oi, you two, stop arguing for a second! I'll make you an accord!" She called, turning around to Jackson, flicking her hair to the side of her bandana.

"No." He spoke, flat-out.

"What! Why not?" The redhead sulked as Jackson fixed his coat and made sure that everything was secure.

"Because you broke into my house, want to take me to a place I never want to go again, and told me I almost died in a fight I don't even remember."

"Well – when you put it like that, it does sound a bit dodgy, doesn't it?" Napoleon interjected, and Ann turned to scowl at the familiar; the pig didn't seem to realise that the more people they had on their side, the higher the chances were of them saving everyone they cared about, including his beloved master.

"For once we agree on something! Goodbye Ann. It was nice not knowing you, I guess."

With that, Jackson turned around and went to the door.

"Oh, and thanks for the contract and pulling me out of that storm, but no thanks." He declined, waving his hand in the air.

He would do this on his own. He had to try to figure out some way of saving his friends.

"What a dick!" Napoleon swore.

"You're the one who made him walk away!" Ann screamed in frustration. "What are we going to do now? You just made it more complicated!"

"Hmm, that is true." Mused the pig.

"Wait!" Cried Ann, she couldn't let her only chance of success walk out the door. "I'll help you get into where the pirates are keeping everyone, you can't do it on your own, and you're not alone any longer!"

Jackson stopped, his hand was on the door of the restaurant, and he supposed that there was logic to her words.

"Go on?" He urged.

"I'll help take down this Atlas guy, and in return, you can take me where I want to go. You don't have to come into the place with me. Sound good?"

"And you'll triple my pay?"

Jackson thought that he may as well earn a fortune out of the untold misery and trauma he was about to face.

"As promised." Called Ann, and after she had just helped him escape the mayor, Jackson knew that he could take her at her word.

A lot better than those dastardly pirates, it now seemed. If what Ann was saying was to be believed, he couldn't go wrong with this accord, of course, there was the trust issue, but they were going to have to move past that if they were going to catch Atlas off-guard.

"Fine, you have an accord. I'll do it." He grunted.

Ann smiled and nodded happily, as he walked back over to her.

"That's great. All we have to do now is…"

Bang!

Suddenly, a man in black leathers stumbled in. The stranger collapsed on to the floor in a heap. He was soaked through and wet to the bone in seawater and smelt of molten rock.

Who was this person? Jackson thought. He hadn't seen anyone like this in the pirates' crew before, not so bloodied and torn. Then he realised that Ann had mentioned seeing lights at the manor house. Jackson realised the Vains had started to move...

14

Fryedai opened his eyes to a blurry vision of shifting silhouettes and the white light of what he assumed to be a chandelier swinging above him. As he lay on hard flooring, both his head and wounded leg hurt beyond belief and he put that down to the way he fell from the high clifftop and into the water below as he tried to escape the pirates. He had washed ashore and made his way to the only building he could see not connected to the main town, as it was likely too dangerous to return to where he had last seen Commander Rockwell - at least Fryedai thought it was him? He remembered the captain saying that he didn't know anyone stronger in a fight when they had sailed together during the voyage. The captain, he thought again. O' almighty gods, the captain! His mind fizzled into terror as the figures became clearer. He'd left Captain Robbinson to die in that room, only to run as a coward would and now there was pirates here too.

"Get back!" He shouted as a girl with crimson red hair smiled at him and a rough looking man scowled.

His vision now came into clear focus as he shuffled along a cold stone floor and his leg burst with pain.

"I'm... I'm warning you, I'm with the Navy!"

"See, Jackson? Not a pirate." Said the girl, happily.

The man called Jackson continued to scowl as Fryedai sat fully up, his back moving to rest against a broken, splintered table. What in the world had happened here? Fryedai, looked around him to see a weirdly grinning piglet by his side.

"Y- you thought I was a pirate?" He stuttered, still looking around at the devastation about the room.

Tables were turned upside down, chairs were broken and drinks and shattered glass were laid bare across most of the space.

"Well, you are dressed like one." Jackson retorted.

"And therefore, I must be?" Fryedai replied, still trying to figure out what was going on and why these two people, also dressed in a similar fashion to the pirates, were going to the trouble of asking him questions.

If they were the Vains' men, why didn't they just finish him already? After all, he had already gotten away twice. Then Fryedai realised, the girl before him had red hair! Just like the woman the pirates wanted to find, the one that they had said was from his own crew and had been causing havoc all across the island. But how was that possible? Everyone on his crew that he knew of had been male.

"What's your name?" The girl asked softly.

"Fryedai." He answered after a moment, rubbing his leg.

He thought back to the long voyage they had been on the past two weeks onboard The Inspectre and what the captain had told him about the attack. No one had seen Doctor Rudolf's mysterious patient since the crew member had boarded, and throughout his time as navigator, Fryedai had learnt that medicine-men could be notoriously fickle when it came to reporting the truth. Robbinson had ordered an update from the doctor and because of the pirates' attack, it was an update he never received. However, it all suddenly made sense now! As sailors, Fryedai being no exception, the entire Navy was superstitious when it came to the ways of the Sea; monsters, creatures and The Goddess, they all played a part in the way the waves shifted and turned along the tides, and it was well known that some women brought with them the death of the siren's song when they stepped onboard a vessel. If a crew were ever as unfortunate to stumble upon a mermaid during their voyage, and there was a woman among them that rivalled in beauty to that of the sea creature, then Merfolk would become envious, and doom the entire crew to the wine-dark depths by whispering a sweet lullaby. Fryedai was worn and tired and looked at the two people in front of him with absolute disbelief as he waited for them to decide what to do with him. He was about to ask the girl what her name was, but as soon as he opened his mouth to speak, he was quickly interrupted as he had been when he sailed on board *The Inspectre.*

"Well, what are you doing here then?" Asked Jackson abruptly, before Ann could say anything else, however, he was glad that at least the pig had chosen to keep quiet and not freak out the man even further than he already was.

"The Navy around the island is all but destroyed! Fat lot of good you did, too. But shouldn't they be after you?"

"That doesn't matter now." Ann muttered, as she continued to urge Fryedai to tell them more and to ignore Jackson's comment as best he could.

To Ann, the drunk seemed grumpy about the prospect of dealing with The Navy as well as the pirates, but they did have a deal, and he was being paid for it. Much like everyone else, Jackson was along for the ride.

"It does!" The drunk warned, he folded his arms as he glanced out the window, peering out over to the manor house. "These pirates leave no loose ends; remember how they trashed my house!"

"I assume he's a local?" Fryedai asked, to which Ann nodded.

"*I* wouldn't call it a house." Napoleon added, chuckling quietly beside the drunkard.

The pig was sat on the windowsill next to Jackson and the drunk glared at the Teacup pig as menacingly as he could before his oink-ish shrikes of laughter finally stopped. Ann paid them no attention. She wanted to know as much about what Fryedai knew as she possibly could.

"You can tell us what happened. We're not with the pirates, we can help you." She assured.

"I... I got free at the rally." Fryedai finally admitted, trying to come to terms with the prospect of his new reality.

Would he find anyone else? Was his crew lost? The captain was gone it seemed, and all that he had were the people in front of him. They were the only ones willing to face what the pirates' terror had wrought upon the island, and so, Fryedai told them all that he knew.

"With all the confusion, only one or two of us managed to escape." He began slowly. "But I don't know for sure. I came back to save everyone else, moving through the underground tunnels they brought us in by, but I saw no one. The pathways were numerous and my captain... he was lost to one of the brothers before we could find anyone else. Gods! We were only carrying food for the island as ordered, that's what our manifest said. I fell as the pirates chased me, fleeing to the cliffside with this wounded leg of mine, thankfully I found my way here after washing up on the shore."

"Wow!" Ann gasped in excitement.

She leaned forward in her seat and twisted her hair into a knot.

"How did you survive the fall? My friend in town said that the hill is the highest point on the island. You were lucky to make it out of that one, especially with your leg."

Fryedai was about to say something when Jackson interrupted yet again.

"Okay, first of all, Arie isn't your friend. Not everyone on this island is your friend! You only just met her – you only just met me this morning, along with Nelson. We are not your friends!"

"Yes, we are, you just don't know it yet." She smiled.

Jackson glared at her as if he didn't really know what to say, rolling his eyes. Ann just kept surprising him with her many views and personalities.

"Besides, I'm sure Arabella will warm to me. I grow on people. I'm like a barnacle. Just you wait! And yes, I know not everyone is my friend. It's just that when I meet people, I tend to trust them, and if I trust them, they're my friends."

Jackson clenched his teeth.

"Are you done?" He asked.

"Yeah, I'm done." Ann replied.

"As I was saying, the manor house also acts as the island's only mill, its offshoots reach out into the sea, that's why the pirates can move all that dirt as they fish for diamonds."

Fryedai's face lit up, in stark contrast to the doom and gloom he had shown so far.

"Yeah, that's right. How do you know about that?" He asked, still rubbing his wounded leg.

"I um, live here." Stated the drunk, giving Fryedai a look of disbelief. "I, erm, was also sleeping with the mayor's daughter." He added, with a hint of regret.

"So, you would know how to get in and out of that place undetected?" Asked Fryedai, smiling as an idea came to him.

"If I can do it drunk and in the dark, I can see no reason why I can't do it in the day surrounded by a bunch of murderous pirates that want to kill me."

"They want to kill us all." Noted Fryedai. "Atlas was raging about a prophecy being fulfilled, something called The Great Storm. It sounded as though the treasure they found could help them wipe out everything - change the world even."

"Yep, I think you'd be right there, Fryedai." Quipped Ann, moving to look out of the window.

"Why'd you say that?" Jackson asked, turning his head.

"Because they're heading right towards us."

Ann raised an eyebrow at the mention of the prophecy.

"Crap, we gotta go!" Exclaimed Fryedai, as he tried to scrabble to his feet, taking a hand from Jackson.

"Guess you're coming with us then. Hells, I hate these pirates!"

They all headed for the doors, only to see a wave-like horde of what must have been a hundred pirates, race down the hillside. The pirate captain had sent his cannon fodder to finish what his quartermaster had started, and Jackson quickly pulled the doors closed again, realising he wasn't as prepared as he ought to be.

"Okay, who pissed off the pirates?" Jackson asked, as he rushed to find his rapier and flintlock, Napoleon quickly following behind.

Ann checked her guns, and even Fryedai managed to pick up a large cutlass and used it as a support for his leg.

"I think we've all done that today!" Ann retorted.

"Say..." Jackson called, as he rammed his rapier into the scabbard and looked out the window again. "There are a lot of them, so how do you suppose we get out of here fast enough with that guy's leg?"

Ann had finished checking her guns one last time and glanced back to Fryedai.

Great! She thought. She hadn't considered their latest companion's injury.

"We could leave him behind?" Suggested Napoleon with a cruel smirk as he trotted up to Ann.

The girl looked down at the pink piglet and glared. Did all familiars run their mouths this way? She wondered to herself, as Fryedai hobbled along.

"Make a run for the carts." She ordered, seeing the horde growing ever closer.

"Why, what are we gonna do?" Jackson asked, noticing a few of the contraptions were a little further down the hill from where the checkpoint had once been earlier that morning.

Thankfully for them, it now seemed to be abandoned, as all the pirates had made their way back to the manor house when their lunch was over, only to receive new orders to continue once again down the hill.

Ann abruptly bolted from the doors before she could even give Jackson a reply. The pirates were barrelling their way down the winding path that led from their hideout, racing towards the palisaded checkpoint as their leader shouted for them to surround the restaurant on both sides. Yet, Ann ran and ran as fast as she could, trying to get there before the pirates did, their footsteps causing the ground to rumble. So powerful was their rampant disregard for the way they brandished their weapons, that when the pirates reached the carts before her, they caused the barrels that were loosely strapped down to the carts to snap free. As the barrels crashed to the floor, the pirates did not seem to care. Dirt spread everywhere on to the green, grassy ground, some of it glittering with a mixture of gemstones.

Ann was amazed. So that's how the Vains were getting the rocks and diamonds off the island! The brothers were carting them off to the docks to be loaded, hiding the diamonds in barrels as something they weren't. It was a clever plan, remarked Jackson as he saw the mounds from outside the restaurant as he rushed to catch up with Ann, but she continued to run further forward, headlong into the horde of pirates at an ever-quickening pace, and he couldn't leave Fryedai and Napoleon alone. The piglet would have the poor boy for dinner!

Nothing was as it seemed. If the pirates came across somebody they couldn't blow out of the water as they had done the Navy, the brothers would have a way to trick them in the search of their treasure and gold. Ash had gone up the hill, and dirt, diamonds and dust came back down. It wasn't enough that they had to take away their freedoms, their food and their booze; the brothers had to abduct and use Jackson's friends too. Atlas and Orion were stripping the island bare of everything that his home had to offer, and by what she had done so far in comparison, Ann had finally given him a reason to trust her.

A couple seconds more passed, and the pirates were ever closer. The leader of the horde was roaring at the top of his lungs, a cutlass held high above his head. He had blood-lustful eyes, a long shaggy beard, and yellow, crooked teeth. In all probability, he was one of the lower ranking members of the brothers' crew and wanted to make an impression with his captain. Suddenly, Ann heard a pistol shot roaring through the air. She turned and saw that Jackson had taken out his flintlock, aiming a shot into the first pirate at the head of the group.

Smoke sizzled from the gun as he squeezed the trigger and the catch flew back, igniting the powder and sending a tiny ball of hard iron hurtling towards its target. The shot sliced past Ann's bandana, narrowly missing the edge of the delicate silver material. The leader fell backwards, landing on his backside and howled in pain as he grasped near to his neck. Ann could see his teeth were now stained with scarlet red.

"Come on guys, let's go!" She shouted back to Fryedai and Jackson.

She climbed on the cart just ahead of her as the horde rushed to catch up. The two of them had barely covered half the distance she had and she looked at them with worry. Moreover, the other pirates were almost upon them, only mere moments away with sharpened blades. They had to hurry!

Ann had no choice. She leapt to the front cart in the column and released the break. She saw how Fryedai grimaced as he tried running harder towards her, but on that leg, they would soon catch him. Continual shots blared out from Jackson's flintlock as the drunkard cradled his friend's familiar in his arms. They were never going to make it! The cart Ann was driving began to roll forwards and she swerved the wheel around in an iron grip, her knuckles turning white. She was heading straight towards the head of the pirate group and her friends.

She had to hold on for as long as she could, she had to reach her friends in time! Like the first one that had gotten close, a small off-shoot of cocky pirates exploded from the main group and pounced upon the struggling Fryedai. However, they weren't the only ones to pick up speed, and upon the second they had reached him, Ann appeared by his side as her cart rambled on, slamming into the unsuspecting pirates.

Both her friends looked up at her in bewilderment as the pirates slowed their advances, Ann had only meant to swing by them and catch Fryedai as she drove past, bringing him safely and quickly aboard the cart. She hadn't intended to use the few runaway pirates as breaks.

"Jackson, you okay?" Shouted Ann to where the drunk now ran.

"No bullets left." Jackson informed her as he neared, starting to climb on board, placing his gun back in his coat.

Ann could have sworn by the sound of Jackson's voice that he was beginning to enjoy himself. Both of them rushed to help Fryedai into the back of the cart and Napoleon jumped from Jackson's arms and into the back. A smile arose on her face as she flicked the cart forward and down the hill. Dust kicked up from the ground and pirates next to them were beginning to get smaller and smaller as they sped closer to town.

"They won't be gone for long!" Shouted Fryedai, over the noise of the rumbling cart. "You did an excellent job hiding away and blending in with the pirates though!"

"I did?" Ann cocked her head in surprise.

How had Fryedai figured out she'd said she was from the Navy? Had Jackson told him as they were running across the hill?

"Yes, yes I did Sir, that's what I was going for." She said, putting emphasis on the sir part.

Ann held her breath.

She said she was from the Navy, wasn't that enough? She had paid the Doctor plenty of threds to keep her name quiet.

"I, erm, swam." She lied, trying to hide the cringe on her face by looking forward at the winding road.

She wasn't completely lying to him, she indeed had to swim to shore, but it had been via barrel – more floating than anything.

Suddenly, another cart burst out of the horizon and clattered to the ground like an exploding cannon. Jackson sat up instantly and drew his rapier from his belt and Napoleon squealed in fright before swearing. The pirates continued to follow in pursuit, barrelling their way down the hill, this time headed by a pirate Jackson seemed to know very well. It was Patchwork Jake.

As Jackson stood up, he counted how many there were - easily ten pirates per cart - and all were packed in tightly. The drunk gulped as he prepared and wished he had a bottle of ale with him for courage, as Fryedai asked if he had just heard Napoleon shout.

"Oi!" The drunk yelled to the front. "We got company!"

"Crap!" Fryedai cursed, pulling his cutlass out from his belt, somehow managing to fall to the floor of the cart behind the driver's bench.

The drunk pulled him up by the scruff of his neck as the pirates began to roll level, snarling at them with rotten teeth.

"Are you going to be okay?" He asked, as the cart still rumbled.

"Yeah, I'll be fine." Fryedai assured him, in a slightly sickly manner, his face turning somewhat green.

The pirates were right on top of them, barrelling their way down on either side of the hill. Suddenly, a few of them built up the courage and jumped across from the back of their fleeing cart. There were three of them all together, including their scarred leader. They dropped from either side of the pursuing carts, landing next to the diamond barrels with a thud. In an instant, the pirates brought out their knives, short, sharp stubs of grey metal that twirled through the air.

The pirates hissed at Jackson and Fryedai with teeth bared like hungry jackals.

"Ready for this, boys?" Patchwork Jake growled.

Both men either side of him grinned and sniggered in response.

"Good, I was getting bored of those townspeople and the Navy any-ways. The hunt is just so much better."

Then, as if on cue, they all stepped forward with massive strides. Both Fryedai and Jackson were pushed against Ann, forcing her to shuffle forward and perch on the very edge of her seat, her feet were mere inches from the ground.

"See, didn't I tell you this was going to be fun!" She called sarcastically from the front, trying to keep hold of the reins.

"You didn't!" They both shouted back, too engaged to offer a full response.

"Well, I should have done!" She cried.

Patchwork Jack laughed from behind as he kicked Fryedai backwards with the heel of his boot. Fryedai lifted his sword to try to stop the impact, but it was no use. He felt the boot connect to the back of the blade and a jolt of force pushed him in the opposite direction, narrowly avoiding Jackson. When he landed, Fryedai's head bashed against the division of the back of the cart and Ann, knocking him out cold.

"Ha-ha-ha!" Jake roared in triumph, his pig-like snout twitching in the air. "How do you like that, Navy dog?"

The other pirates laughed in response; their blades ready to lash out as their crewmates had. Jackson knew that wouldn't be happening. The drunk reached into his trench coat and brought out his flintlock once more, and the pirates took a small step back, teetering on the edge of the cart as their heels hung perilously close from diving to the road.

"Hey, wait a minute!" The pirate to the left shouted. "We have guns too!"

"Too bad." Jackson replied, as the pirates rushed for their side arms.

He gave them a cocky smile as he slowly squeezed the trigger. Their faces twisted in horror, and they raised their arms up for protection. It wouldn't do any good. Any moment now, Jackson would blast them in a smoky haze of gunfire.

With the mounting tension, two of the pirates jumped off the cart, leaving only Jake in the middle.

"Cowards." He muttered.

Jackson then pulled the trigger inwards to the butt of the gun.

Nothing happened…

"Shit!" He cursed as he looked down at his gun in confusion.

He could smell the last residue of sulphur trying to burn with the charcoal and saltpetre, but why wasn't anything happening?

That was when he remembered that he used all the bullets as he climbed on to the cart. The pirate laughed and drew his own pistol, pointing it directly at Jackson's temple.

"Run out of bullets, eh? Too bad for you, ha-ha!"

Jackson looked up at the pirate and his several missing teeth and mangled black hair.

"Yeah." He grinned, staring straight down the barrel. "Too bad for you."

Suddenly, the cart jerked to one side, throwing the pirate off balance, and the barrel of the gun pointed up into the air. Jackson quickly grabbed one of the diamond barrels from the corner of the cart. He laid the barrel on its side as the pirate regained his footing and was careful not to get in his line of fire. With one push, the barrel rolled forward and crushed Jake's feet, making him howl in pain. Jackson rushed forward, raising his rapier above his head, and slashed at the pirate as he fell back. For good measure, the drunk lifted his leg up high and kicked the pirate square in the chest, knocking him from the cart. The pirate tumbled to the ground, the diamonds quickly followed him in a spluttering, but their soft chiming could not be heard as the other carts continued to give chase. It was then that Napoleon came out from his hiding place and sat at Jackson's side as the other two carts followed.

"Are they about to..." The pig trailed off as he watched the pirates race after them.

"Yep, man!" Jackson called out in relief. "Atlas really does want us dead if you guys are willing to run each other over!" He taunted at the pirates that drew closer.

With a tremendous bang, the carts bashed against each other with a brutal force, and wood on both sides splintered away. A powerful screech sounded from the back of their own cart, and they immediately jolted to one side.

"Jackson!" Ann called, as she struggled to keep control. "What is going on? Don't tell me we lost a wheel or something!"

Jackson leapt over the divide between the driver's seat and the back of the cart, landing squarely next to Ann. Ann took her eyes off the road for one moment and looked at the drunk's concerned face.

"Is it bad?" She asked.

She could feel the mechanical pieces that propelled them were about to give way.

"Gods yes!" Napoleon cried.

"Well, I wouldn't say bad, more like our lives are in a spot of mild mortal peril." He said simply.

Another bang rang out. One of the pirate carts crashed into them and had caused their own to shake from side to side.

"I think we're down two wheels now!" She informed, as they veered into the central part of town.

Ann took hold of the controls with one hand and drew one of her guns from her jacket. With an outstretched arm, Ann shot a market stand as they passed by and a snowy ice-like projectile spewed from the barrel of her gun, freezing the post in place. Turning around to the back of the cart, the red-haired girl switched the settings on the dial of her gun, firing a second shot off as the pirates following them came level with the frozen post. Lightning shot from her gun in the blink of an eye, shooting its way to the exact same spot, cracking it instantly. Icy sparks erupted from the stand and both pirate carts crashed. Pieces of wood and metal machinery flew everywhere, along with the shouts and frantic cursing of the pirates.

"Is Fryedai okay?" Ann asked Jackson a couple of minutes later.

Finally free of their pursuers, they veered to a stop. The pirates were nowhere to be seen, but she was sure they would soon catch up. It seemed like a total after thought, but Ann was still concerned for Fryedai and they also had to recover Tom if he was still alive. She felt terrible about leaving him in that cold and damp alleyway, and as soon as she could, she would go find him.

"Yeah, the kid is knocked out in the back." Jackson mumbled.

"What do you mean kid? He's older than me!" She complained.

"Why, how old are you?"

"I'm nineteen!"

Ann jumped off from the driver's seat and began to look around. They desperately needed somewhere to lay low while they figured out what to do, and how to get into the manor house.

"Hey, doesn't Nelson live around here?" She asked. "I sort of remember this area, but it was a lot darker and stormier."

"Yeah, he does." Said Jackson.

He still wasn't feeling like himself. He thought the fight with the pirates had taken it out of him, but lights were flashing across his vision and whispers echoed in his head. Out of nowhere, a white spectre ran across the road, and once again it smiled and laughed just as Molly did those many times when they had sat on the tide together and watched the sun go down. The ghostly apparition even looked the same as her and the wind that followed wafted her scent through the air, ruffling his hair.

"Do you have a key?"

"Hey, drunkard!" Yelled Napoleon.

"Huh?"

Jackson rubbed his head.

"Fryedai needs to rest, and we need to put a plan together, preferably somewhere the pirates won't find us."

"Okay, okay." Jackson groaned, putting his hands up. "I'll go get the key."

Ann nodded and went to grab Fryedai from the back of the cart, as Jackson began walking down the street. This would be his chance, he thought. He could swing by *Looty and Booty* to make sure that Arabella was okay on the way back from his hut and everything would work out okay.

"Try not to get in any trouble." Napoleon called out jokingly.

"I make no promises, but I'll try."

Please let her be okay, he thought secretly. Please. Let Arabella be okay! The winds began to grow cold, and it made his stomach churn. He simply couldn't lose anybody else...

15

Atlas was feeling most pleased with himself as the amulet dangled from his neck. That stupid Navy navigator had fallen to his death, and he had sent the men that he could spare down to the docks, so that they could prepare for their departure from this wretched island. Everything was finally coming together.

He and his brother had worked their way down through the tunnels as soon as Captain Robbinson had been dealt with. A childlike giddiness washed over him; his own mutiny had been crushed and they had wealth from diamonds and jewels gathered from beneath the earth, and a workforce that would slave for him night and day. Just that girl who attacked them and the guardian remained, along with that other loose end - the last thing he required to appease the Hoarder-King. Atlas only had to open the antechamber and flee with the first treasure piece in hand, as tonight was the one night they could finally sail free.

He brushed his hand against the dark, coarse rock of the tunnel, as he and his brother walked by, feeling the ebb and flow of the power that carved it out, smelling the stale air as it coursed through his body. What a fantastic smell, he thought. To him, it was precisely like death, and Kaine was next...

At the end of the tunnel, stood waiting for him, were Gillian, Silvers, and Taylor the last surviving twin, who had managed to secure another *'willing'* volunteer.

"Is it open?" Atlas croaked, using his brother for support.

The amulet glowed more than it had ever done before.

"Not yet." Replied Gillian. "We came across many traps on our way here, but it will be, soon. What does it say? I can't read the runes."

The blinding indigo light from the captain's amulet spread across the hollowed-out cavern as he reached towards the circular stone door. Atlas snarled as he saw he was being watched by the volunteer. He glared at him with a mixture of interest and disgust, as the pirate captain glimpsed over the runes and read them quickly. The door was shaped as a tortoise's shell, with engravings reaching all around the edges. Atlas recognised the writing from the map and its many riddles, and he translated the Runic-Language aloud so that everyone could understand.

"For those who enter here, be warned." He began. "Death approaches swiftly for those who abuse this power! Blood will be tainted for those who speak these words."

"Mph!" Huffed Atlas afterwards. "We do not fear death, and she will not come for us, she is too afraid. After all, we've almost single handily sent her an entire race to watch over. Now, stand aside."

He took an orange leather bag of Ash from his belt and opened it by pulling on the strings that fell by the sides. Its black contents sparkled with flecks of white and a chilling, frosty blue. An elemental ice-type. Perfect, he thought.

Atlas brought the bag up to his nose and breathed in profoundly, allowing himself to become one with the power, for he was ice and winter itself. His eyes glowed. Atlas no longer needed Orion's help to stand, and his brother just merely let him go as he walked towards the door of the antechamber and placed a hand upon it. A spark of frost erupted from his hand and covered the entire stone doorway in a deadly winter freeze.

"Gillian, would you do the honours?" He spoke in an icy tone, looking to his first mate.

Atlas tore his hand away from the frost. The only sign he was ever there was the thin layer of snow that covered his hand. Gill drew his serrated blade from behind his back and looked at the ice-encased doorway.

"Piece of cake." He muttered, pressing the button on the end of the sword.

The small little motors in the palm of the blade began to rumble, each individual piece began to move. Then Gill pushed another button, and yellow electricity began to flicker and strike the air.

"You see, Orion. This is what I meant when I said you could add Ash to your weapons, you should try it sometime." He called.

"Just get on with it!" Roared Atlas, growing ever more impatient.

"Yes, sir."

Gill struck the middle of the doorway, cracking the frozen stone. Lightning spluttered everywhere, yet the door did not budge and remained firm, the indigo markings of the runes glowing even more with each stroke of the blade.

"Again!" Atlas demanded. "Again!"

Even after a few attempts, the stone was as immoveable as it was before. Nothing had changed, and the pirate captain brought down a barrage of ice upon the doorway in a fit of rage. To come all this way! He thought angrily, as the ice struck and chipped at the marbled, grey surface. To come so far across the world when they had been chased to its very oblivion, only to be denied by an ancient stone doorway! It caused Atlas's anguish and temper to flow beyond the edges of what any one man in that chamber could've thought was possible. The amulet told him it had to be so! The light continued to shine form the crystal, so hotly and brightly that the captain could feel it cling to his neck in slick sweat. Suddenly his head erupted in pain, and the low, dulling ache that he had once felt presided once again.

"Atlas, Atlas..." Something whispered to him, louder in his head than it had ever been before, causing his bloodshot eyes to burst open.

What was whispering to him inside his head? He didn't understand. The voice was different to that of his memories of Kaine hissing to him in his sleep; when he would watch the foul beast's yellow eyes follow and torment him from across the seas. This was very different, and unlike any he had ever heard before. It was filled with pestilence and malice, reeking of age and time as it spread across the caverns of his mind, older than the giants from a dark undergrowth he knew not where. Was it some form of madness or a curse? Nevertheless, the voice would have to wait until he reached his prize. Atlas had to see if the treasure he sought lay beyond that door as he was promised, or all else would have been for nought.

None of it mattered to him now; what the voice said or made him do. Atlas had to complete the prophecy so he could slay the Devourer, to save his brother and himself from the beast that would come for them. But why hadn't the Ash worked as it always had? It should have blown the stone door to dusty pieces, and yet it was still standing! The amulet, the map, the Runic-Verse, even the association with the Trolls and the Giants, it all told him that Seidr was involved, and when something was created by Seidr as the door was, Atlas knew that by Seidr it must be destroyed!

It was then that Orion spoke as he looked at the blonde volunteer that had been glaring at Atlas all this time, then to the door. The others simply scratched their heads.

"That's funny." He spoke, only remembering what his brother had told him about the powder in the past. "Ash powers don't seem to be working on this one either?"

Atlas turned around in a rage as his brother interrupted his thoughts. But when Atlas realised that Orion was right, the pirate captain began to grin and laugh. His brother had spoken true, the man's eyes behind him weren't glowing white as they should have been when exposed to Silvers' persuasion, and the pirate captain remembered the old tales about Ash and Alchemy that his father had taught him. Those with alchemic-blood were immune to the effects of the powder. Finally, Atlas had discovered a fabled Alchemist.

He looked to the door once again, running his eyes across the markings and grooves etched along the stone. In the very centre of the doorway, Atlas made out a small notch in the cold and grey surface as he wiped away the chilling frost, only to uncover a crescent-shaped mark, matching only that of his glowing amulet.

"I wonder..." He started, drawing his ruby-hilted cutlass from its sheath. "Taylor! Bring that man here!"

The brute of a man did as the captain bid and grabbed Nelson the chef; the blonde man kicking and screaming as he did. He threw him down before Atlas and the tip of his blade. The pirate captain sneered at him. Nelson, on his knees and in the light of the amulet, looked up at the terrifying and ailing captain.

"Please, don't do this." He croaked. "You can still leave, the Devil's Rush is still-"

"Silence!" Atlas bellowed, his patience for the Alchemist wearing thin. "All this time you have hidden from me in plain sight, and now I shall take what is rightfully mine!"

And with that, Atlas grabbed Nelson's hand and guided the cutlass's blade across the chef's palm before letting the crimson droplets fall onto the glowing disk of the amulet.

"And now the door shall open, and we shall see if destiny awaits us inside."

Atlas placed the bloodied amulet into the crescent sized hole, itching in anticipation as the tortoise shell stone began to twist and turn. Runes once again began to light up and form words in the dazzling indigo light. The pirate at once began to read them out. As Taylor dragged Nelson away, a name began to form. It read: 'Dive into the deep river; speak my name and enter'.

"Grimgorth." Atlas bellowed, and suddenly a crack reverberated around the cavern and the door began to crumble to mouldy, dusty pieces as the centre of the antechamber was unveiled.

Atlas and his crew stepped back as the last of the stones from the doorway fell, bathing them in a golden light. In the centre of the chamber stood a short pedestal about half the height of Atlas, on top of it rested the most beautiful sight the pirate captain had ever laid his eyes upon. It radiated a bristling heavenly light. The golden treasure of myth, the one the map and riddles had only whispered about. It was all true! It really did exist, and Atlas could not contain himself.

"We've done it!" He cried.

His goal could become a reality. He could finally get his revenge! He rushed over to the fingers, pondering with hardened eyes.

"Silvers." He barked, soothing over his prize as he had done the Ash.

Nothing would distract him.

"Rouse everyone, we're leaving tonight as soon as everything is underway. I want the Alchemist on board too, not just yet though. I want him to see what his blood has uncovered."

He reached for the treasure. Silvers left the chamber and delivered the news while everyone else stood in awe. The voice began to whisper in Atlas's head yet again, drawing him closer.

"Atlas, Atlas." It rang out, singing a sweet melody as smooth and alluring as a siren's song. *"Come, claim your conquest, wreak havoc on the world and the one you aim to topple. All will burn at your heel. Reunite my pieces and I will help you claim what you rightly deserve, freedom – and the power to rule an empire."*

"Brother, perhaps you should wait. Let us be away from here." Orion cautioned.

However, Atlas did not waste another second in listening to the voice that called to him, nor did he to his brother. He had already decided what he was going to do, and he put the fingers on to his right hand, quickly snapping them into place around his skin. The fingers glowed a dazzling red and sunny light.

"Atlas!" Orion cried as he reached out with his hand.

Gillian rushed towards him too, but he was too late. Atlas tried to speak but the pirate captain fell to the floor in a dream-like haze as whispers once again carried him away to the realm of sleep. Everything had turned to black.

Act 3:

What Lies Beyond the Shadows

16

Atlas awoke with a thrashing headache and the sound of a pleasant chirping in his ears. The singsong of a small, crested sparrow lulled harmoniously next to him and whistled with a soft light tune that caused him to look around where he lay. In bitter contrast, the second thing he heard brought a change to that pleasant song. It was a hard, shallow, thumping sound; holding a constant beat as it echoed across the rocky jungle valley.

Thump, thump, thump, thump. Thump, thump, thump, thump, it bellowed, like striking a stick across a drum. Atlas couldn't see or hear his friends anywhere!

"Damn it!" He cursed to himself.

He found that his hands were bound, and he was sat propped up on a straw cot. A tent draped over his head, and through the thin material, Atlas could still see the dark and imposing vines that made up the deadly jungle. Now, he realised why his father had told them never to go to the green zones - it was just their luck that someone had to be out here and that they winded up getting captured.

A light abruptly flashed in his eyes, and a small, frail weed-like man sat in front of him. From the corner of his eye, the boy peered over behind the man, and Atlas got his first glimpse of the outside world they had set upon. Beautiful arrays of luscious flora trailed along the jungle floor, entwined with the many insects that darted to and fro. Even though he and his friends were on the same island, this place felt like an entirely different world than the one they'd been used to. Suddenly, he was reminded of the man in front of him, thanks to the constant thumping coming from outside the tent. Atlas once again began to wonder about the state of his brother and their friends.

The man staggered towards him with a limp, his bony legs trembling. His skin was the colour of rich coffee, and his body boasted a small frame. From his neck, an ornate necklace made up of colourful feathers and finger-sized bones dangled freely. The coming truth was evident. Atlas was about to be invited to dinner.

"Where are my friends!" Atlas roared, twisting in his bonds. "Take me to them!"

"You boys will visit the sky god. The gods must be appeased for the sins of this island." He croaked out.

The man hastily placed a hand on his bloated, swollen stomach, and rubbed it greedily as he licked his lips. Atlas thought back to the stories his father had told him.

Izan! He and his friends were going to be sacrificed to the sky god, Izan! Not only were there tales of horrendous giants that lived in the sky, but also of green men that lived in the jungles below, who devoted their lives to the gods by forming murderous cults.

Outside, the drums continued their hollow banging sound as the sun beat down upon them and Atlas was quickly brought to the beanstalk to join his friends. Around him, Atlas could see several more green men; they were busy toiling at their many jobs and chopping wood for a fire. He kicked and struggled, demanding that they let him go, otherwise they would suffer the consequences, but the two men that held the young boy just laughed, knowing that they would soon be munching on his bones. He was then lifted on to a podium so he couldn't escape. His mouth had been gagged, his shouting becoming nothing more than a chorus of gurgles. Next to him, the boy saw that he'd been placed in a row with his friends who had been tied up and placed in the same way he had. Fortunately for them, they hadn't woken up yet.

The savages' whole village seemed to surround the thick green stems of the beanstalk as though it was a place of worship. To them, the stalk was everything. It was sacred. The old man walked out of the tent and staggered towards them. He was carrying a large, curved knife. As he waved his knife in the air, the savages once again cheered in unison. Moments later, a group of women appeared and began to lay bits of wood and vine at the boys' feet. The peculiar man was very obviously the chief.

The chief ushered a green man with a pierced nose to come forward.

"The sky god comes for you; we shall praise him." He rasped out.

In a split second, a blade was thrust against Atlas' neck.

"This one shall honour us and summon the sky god from his home." The chief announced.

As soon as he called out to his people, an uproar of cheering and merriment began, and the drums continued to increase in speed. The sky quickly grew darker, as a great shadow loomed overhead. The bright sunlight of the daytime turned into a cold biting frost, setting a grim, atmosphere over the luscious green valley.

"YA-YA-YA-YA-YA!" A commanding voice called from the heavens, and the green people below continued to celebrate as they had before.

"He's coming!" The chief called to his people. "The sky god will make them pure, and we shall consume that pureness when their bodies return from the heavens!"

The one with the nose piercing brought forward a lit torch and thrust it on to the kindling below. The timber and vines started to smoulder and wilt as flames began to emerge and rise higher and higher. Atlas could feel a mild itching pain start to spread across the bottom of his legs, even his friends next to him were starting to shift and wake because of the pain. He had wanted to find the giant and possibly steal some treasure so he could get some food from the navy, he didn't intend for his friends or himself to become food!

Smoke filled their lungs and Atlas could do nothing but cough and splutter, thanks to the gag across his mouth making him choke on the acidic fumes. This was it, he thought. This was how he was going to die.

He had survived living in a desert. He had survived Wraith farming, yet he could not escape one lousy fire? Pathetic! He didn't even get a chance to see one of the fabled giants up close. As the flames flickered and climbed their ankles, Atlas heard another call race across the sky.

"YA-YA-YA-YA-YA!" It bellowed, then suddenly the green men's drums fell deadly silent, and a massive shadow appeared over the top of the boys, blocking out the blistering sun.

Atlas looked up, wincing in pain, to see glowing orange eyes as black smoke began to cloud his vision. For the second time that day, he drifted into hazy unconsciousness, as a massive arm reached its way towards them.

A great, monstrous hand swooped the four boys up with relative ease as it descended from the sky, climbing the great stalk. With every gargantuan step, great green vines tore away, plummeting towards the earth. The hand that held them hurried, with a few more gigantic steps the creature that tore them away would reach its high hold. It gripped the cold foundation-stone that lay on top, as its belly grew ever hungrier. The creature was in fact what the four boys had been looking for all along, a terrifying, fabled giant. Its vast hold was surrounded by white, velvet-like clouds. A castle towered in front of them as they struggled against a vice-like grip. As they would later discover, it had four great towers at the corners, spiralling even higher into the heavens. The central section of the building was again a massive column, high walls and a large open gate leading to a drawbridge.

Once inside the doorway, the giant frantically looked around the stone corridors as he clutched the human children firmly. It was rare they had guests wander this high up into the sky, where no one ever reached them.

The halls of the castle were lined with torches, casting dim shadows over everything and making the ancient oil paintings ghoulishly creepy.

"Oni!" The giant wailed. "Oni, I need your help, some humans are hurt!"

He did not know if they were in pain or not, but indeed something must be wrong with them to travel this high into the sky. He opened his mammoth palm and the fattest one of the human children groaned in what the giant could only perceive as pain. The other boys were still out cold.

"Oni!" He cried again. "Oni!"

There was still no reply.

Oni always roamed or stalked about in the corridors somewhere, it wasn't like him to be preoccupied with something, unless he was tending to the plants.

"Oni!" The giant repeatedly shouted, racing up the spiralling stairway. "Humans, normal humans are hurt, we must help them!"

The giant reached the top of the stairs and burst through the double arched doors that led to the springs. Inside the room, a wall of thick, misty steam greeted the giant, as the vapours from the bath bubbled up in a menagerie of colour. The human child was continually groaning louder and louder, and the others were beginning to wake. The giant continued to race down the stone pathway and frantically looked at the bubbling springs and pools.

"Oni!" He called out again, in the hope that his friend would tell him which pool to use.

Suddenly, the giant heard a louder, deeper groan erupt from one of the springs, followed by the pattered slashing of water on the hot stones. The giant followed the noise, cradling the injured boys in his massive hand. The sound of splashing water could be heard again, and the giant was close enough to see that in the distance, two massively large and long red limbs stretched out of a pool of glowing, golden water and placed themselves at either side.

"Oni, there you are!" The giant exclaimed in relief as his friend climbed out of the spring.

Oni was not entirely trusting of humans. They both hated thieves that were foolish enough to climb up to their castle and steal from them, although, they made an exception for those in need. Slowly, the giant hoisted himself out of the water and revealed his long, slender face; as dark as the deepest shade of crimson. His eyes were sharp and bloodshot, and he brushed a clawed hand along his face, wiping the white and grey bushelled moustache that grew outwards, towards the bones of his cheeks.

"What do you want, Kabuki?" He asked, wicking the water from his face, flitting it to the edges of his fingernails.

"Humans." Kabuki began softly. "They need healing."

Oni looked them over as he peered out of the pool.

"Not that it will matter, though. These little ones will be dead soon enough."

"You don't know that!" Kabuki screeched.

Oni swiftly exited the entirety of the pool and stood before his friend, looking him straight in the eyes. He was beginning to grow tired of Kabuki's sentimentality towards the small creatures that lived below. All they ever did was steal and plunder, and no good would become of them.

"And just look how well your heroics have gone? We now have a human roaming the castle, doing who knows what, and you now want to save more of them? Praise the sun the last human never saw the trove!"

The giant dipped his head.

"I know, but I have to try. They are only young, and nobody deserves to die like this. What's the worst that could happen?"

Oni huffed, knowing it was useless to argue.

"Go on, heal them then. We are magical creatures as they would call us! I might as well go find our other guest. He's bound to know something about their anatomy. It's the air up here they can't take at first."

With that, Oni walked away, leaving the giant to decide how he was going to save the children. Kabuki gently scooped up the fatter human boy from the floor. It seemed his pain was far worse than any of the others. He had to be treated first.

A huge smile began to grow on Kabuki's face as he started to use his Seidr, grabbing some ground herbs that he carried in a small pouch attached to his belt. The boy started to groan and twist more fiercely than he had done before.

"By the maker's hammer!" He yelled, biting his tongue before quickly moving to pick up the boy by his ragged clothes.

He didn't think that the herbs would have worked as quickly as they did, providing additional air for the boy to breathe at the castle's altitude.

"Ahg, ahg!" The boy groaned, his eyes beginning to open and close, fluttering in and out of consciousness as he swung beneath the giant's fingertips.

The swinging must have been very disorientating for him, thought Kabuki.

"G g-giant!" He shouted. "Giant!"

* * *

"You! You did this, didn't you? You're trying to eat us. I'll kill you. I told him this was a bad idea." Orion exclaimed, moments after seeing the giant.

He could see the bright glint of orange in his eyes and the smooth, round curvature of his big nose. The part that scared Orion the most however, was the sharp, yellow, crooked teeth, that were arranged like scattered fence posts.

"Woah, little one. I am not that kind of giant anymore. I'm trying to help you, so stay still." Insisted the beast.

Orion glared at the orange-eyed giant with malice, but then quickly realised from the look on the giant's face that his captor wasn't joking.

"I'm Kabuki." He said kindly, helping Orion to his feet.

The boy smiled cautiously, gave his name in reply, and raised his eyebrow as his hunger began to subside.

"You sure you're not going to eat us?" Asked the boy.

Orange eyes laughed at this.

Orion gulped as he looked at his unconscious brother laying by his side. The knot tying back his hair had come undone, and his wavy black locks spread across the stone. He knew his brother had so much pain and anger built up in him at how people treated their family. What father had suffered through when farming the Wraiths was atrocious, and he knew that Atlas wanted it all to burn. After all the pain he endured, Orion knew that Atlas wanted things to change for them.

"What's the matter little human? You seem lost." The giant asked.

"It's nothing." Orion spoke, as he tried to ignore Kabuki's concern.

He could not let on as to what his brother planned to do.

Atlas had promised him food. It was why he had agreed to follow them in the first place. Everyone, including himself, was getting hungrier and hungrier by the day thanks to rationing. The war on the seas with the neighbouring island was putting a strain on them all, and the Navy hogged whatever they took from village stores.

Soon enough, the giant had healed his brother and his friends. Sadly, none of the others had awakened to the shock that all their childhood tales were real. They paused at a tall brown oak door, before being carried to a room. The door opened with a long creak. Orion followed the giant inside.

"This is where you will stay until dinner tonight, little one. Be sure not to touch anything, we giants are very protective of the things we own." He warned.

Orion nodded as if he understood and jumped off the giant's hand and onto the large bed he was presented with. Then, with a quick grunt, Kabuki left the room, leaving Orion alone in silence.

At the end of the bed, next to one of the four posters, a man sat gazing out of the far-away window. Orion remembered that the giant had said that there was another human in the castle.

"Are you alright, boy?" The man asked in a grizzled voice, as his legs dangled helplessly off the edge.

"Father!" Orion gasped in surprise, recognising his voice. "What are you doing here? We saw a letter. It said you were going to the market. Is this about the Wraiths?"

"What was that about *my* Wraiths?" His father questioned sternly, looking him straight in the eyes.

His great beard hung down from his chin in braided knots, and hung on his back was his beloved war-axe. The head glinted in the light as the man descended to meet his son.

"Nothing, nothing." The boy said nervously, trying to avoid the question. "Nothing happened to the Wraiths. They're all safe and sound."

"Then why are you here, Orion? I doubt that you could climb one of the stalks by yourself. Atlas could maybe, but not you." His father peered at him.

"Wait, you're not mad we're here?" Orion asked curiously, raising an eyebrow.

His father laughed at the idea.

"Let's just say, I've yet to make up my mind." He pondered.

"Why, what are you up to? You're hiding something aren't you? What's going on, why are you here?" Orion continued to ask.

His father turned around to him, tired of his questions. His face had grown red, and there was a look of rage and madness in his eyes.

"Stop with your questions, Orion. I don't know. Why are you here, hmm?"

Orion stood in front of his father in silence, looking down to the floor. He hated it when father was like this. Atlas could always handle it better than him, but then again, Atlas had learned from watching his mistakes, and that was why father preferred him.

"I, I, I-" Orion stuttered.

"Enough!" Roared his father, and suddenly there was a groan from on top of the bed.

"I've had enough with you babbling about. You were probably following Atlas on another one of his adventures. Don't you both realise that I'm trying to keep you safe! Your mother-" He was cut off by more groaning from the far side of the bed.

"My mother what!" Shouted Orion, but his father didn't answer. "Father!" He called again. "Father!"

What was more was that he had rushed to Atlas' side. Orion had no clue as to what he was truly up to, or what he wanted. He knew that his father wasn't one for adventures like him and his brother were. He was just meant to be a simple Wraith farmer, so why was he here, on a beanstalk in the clouds?

* * *

Atlas sat at the windowsill to their bedroom, looking out at a darkening orange sky. He was filled with amazement as he watched the clear glistening stars above the cloud line. He still couldn't believe they actually made it. They were here, the stories were true.

But a darker feeling passed over him. It had been an hour since they had woken in the castle in the sky. War and famine raged below. He spied the giant that his brother, Orian, had called Oni, harvesting massive crops of pumpkin and watermelon, clutching a great scythe.

"I wonder where they got the seeds from." Gill asked, as he joined Atlas; his wavy pink hair fell just short above his eye, and he sat beside his friend, crossing his legs.

"I have no idea." Atlas began. "It's just difficult to believe that they have so much food, more than the two of them can eat and we have so little. It's not fair!"

"I know it's not, but what can we do?" Gill shrugged, patting Atlas' back.

"I want to make them suffer!" Atlas exclaimed, a morbid glint in his eyes. "They helped us for sure, but they're now holding us as prisoners in this room while we wait! I'm fed up with waiting!"

Gill smiled.

"It would be nice if the food we stole went to us for a change. I'm tired of scraps. There is one problem, however -"

Atlas raised an eyebrow. He always loved and despised how his friend found the flaws in his plans. He just loved to pick things apart and pull at that one thread until there was nothing left.

"And what would that be?"

"How do we go about stealing the food in the first place? Let alone how we're going to get out of here." Said his friend.

Gill understood why Atlas wanted to get back at the giants for keeping the food to themselves. After all, this was their country too, and everyone was starving across the island. Why should they get to keep the food?

"Do you hate them?" He asked curiously, looking up at the stars, full of wonderment.

"No." Atlas stated calmly. "I just want them to learn that they can't keep everything to themselves. The way I see it, they're keeping us here. They've kept father here all day, locked away in this room, and haven't let him leave. The whole village depends on him, on the Wraith farm for their power. Without him, everyone there would die. I want revenge."

"Revenge – is that all you care about?"

"That and the food. I'm just tired of not doing anything anymore. Something needs to be done. If it can't be good, because the Navy won't let us join the war, then it'll have to be something bad."

Atlas paused. According to Orion, the giants would come and fetch them when it was time for dinner, so getting to them would not be a problem. They just needed to come up with something before then, otherwise, every single one of them would become dinner, and not the dinner guests.

"I might have an idea." A voice said from behind.

Both boys quickly sat up on the windowsill in surprise. A second later, Atlas' father walked out from behind a gigantic waterfall-like curtain and looked at the boys.

"How long have you been standing there?" Gill asked, his eyes glaring at the ghostly farmer.

"Long enough. So, since I've been here longer than you four and have not been knocked out, I might add, I might know more than you, don't you think?"

Both the boys sighed and allowed the farmer to continue, although to Atlas this was strange, as his father had never offered him help with anything before.

Sometime later, after the sun had set, did the giants finally come to collect them. A hollow knock banged on the bedroom door, and seconds later Kabuki emerged. The giant was dressed in dashing gold and emerald robes that flowed down to his ankles. He looked drastically different to how he looked when he was farming, and Atlas still could not believe the vast size of the creature that stood before him. He must have been easily twenty-four feet high and looked a lot scarier up close.

"I see you are ready. You must be hungry, little ones, after your long journey. I am sorry for the wait." The giant reached down with his hand towards Atlas, and the long black-haired boy backed away slowly.

"I am not going to hurt you, little one." The giant whispered softly, then grappled Atlas' bags from him and tossed them aside.

They fell with a thud in the back corner of the room. Everyone's faces looked worryingly shocked.

Terrible thoughts rushed through Atlas' head. Was their plan going to work? Were the giants going to eat them there and then? Orion had said that the Giants didn't want to eat humans anymore, but Atlas could not help but wonder and capitalise on the word '*anymore*'.

The giant bent over and got as close to Atlas as he could, so close that his jagged teeth sat mere inches from the boy's own. Atlas' heart was starting to pound. Was the giant going to figure things out - that they were planning to take their food? As the giant glared at him, his orange eyes reflected off the gold in the room, and his beard swept across the carpet. It gave a long, hard stare, before it finally turned it's gaze away, looking at the others and then to the bags.

"Hmm, that's good, little one. I see you aren't a thief. We hate them most of all, along with killers." He whispered ominously.

The beast's breath swelled with the scent of sweet honey and strawberries. It was uncomfortably warm, like a raging inferno. Kabuki stood up and glanced over the room once more, checking that nothing was out of place.

"I trust there is nothing else in the bags the rest of you are carrying?" He asked.

Everyone else shook their heads.

"Follow me, little ones. Leave your bags here, you won't be needing them." The giant instructed, thus, they left their bags behind and ventured onwards into the hall.

"Did they touch anything?" Oni snapped.

The thinner giant stood by the doorway, eagerly watching as they exited the room.

"Doesn't look like it, but I knew they wouldn't. I told you when I saved them, they were good people. I could tell as I brought them up the beanstalk."

"You've been wrong before." Oni quipped, crossing his arms.

Atlas noticed that he too was wearing the same gold and emerald robes that the other giant was. The giants seemingly adored gold, considering how much of it was spread across their room and the design of the hallway. No doubt the rest of the castle would be similar.

"They didn't take anything. I checked their bags, we can trust them."

Oni threw back his head against the wall, and the whole hallway rumbled with an earthquake-like shake as he groaned.

"Ugh, fine. Let's eat, I'm starving anyway."

With that, Kabuki shut the bedroom door with a slam and walked with Oni to where they would be eating. Atlas and the others trailed behind them, taking note of everything they passed on the way.

"We shouldn't be doing this, Atlas. They helped us remember." Orion suddenly and quietly urged as he walked next to his brother, not wanting to draw the giant's attention as they thundered along in front of them.

Atlas looked at his little brother. He had been doing a lot of singing over the past couple of hours and he wrapped an arm around his back, whispering in his ear. It was a low soft whisper; the kind father would use when he was angry and wanted to underline his authority.

"You're the one who wanted to come because of the food, remember? Because all we had this morning was a measly crust of bread." Atlas could almost hear his brother gulp as he tightened his grip on his shoulder. "We came because of you, little brother. Even Silvers and Gill agreed; we are simply getting more food for the village while we are here. We are saving people's lives, are we not?"

"But you're not here just for that, are you?" Questioned Orion.

Atlas fell silent, maintaining his iron grip. He glared daggers with his eyes at his brother. If he did not keep quiet now, he was going to ruin the whole thing. He might even get them killed!

"You're here for the adventure, for the glory. You're totally and utterly selfish, yet again." Orion continued. "You even said so this morning, and then promised me you would only go for the food. You lied, yet again."

Stop! Just stop talking, Atlas thought. The giants were now glancing behind them as they turned the corner towards a large spiral stairway. If Orion did not stop now, this would all be for nothing.

"Hey, Kabu-" Orion began to shout, but his mouth was quickly covered by a hand and dagger held to his back.

Atlas turned his head, standing firmly behind his brother was Gill.

"Shut it!" The pink-haired boy spat, as silently as he could. "That's enough from you, we can't afford to muck this up."

Atlas was glad that both of his friends were on his side for this, despite all that had happened on their journey here, he could always count on Gill and Silvers.

As they descended the last couple of steps, the waft of food became ever-present and seemed to pull everyone in. The smell of assorted meats filled the air and rushed into their lungs, filling every fibre of their bodies with warm delight.

"Here we are, little ones." Orange eyes bellowed at the front, as they approached a massive set of oak doors. "Dinner is served." He finished, taking a curt bow.

Thankfully, Orion was no longer under the threat of a knife due to the wafting aromas and had decided to keep quiet. The doors creaked open, and a line of slithering firelight seeped from the room, revealing a beautiful, dark purplish table, the colour of obsidian, encrusted with gold leaf and pillared as high as the eye could see with mountains upon mountains of toppling food.

"Excuse me!" Orion shouted from below the table, his voice struggled to be heard as it fought against the sounds of the crackling fire.

Crap! Atlas thought. He was going to run his mouth!

Oni reacted immediately and bent down, leering at Orion, narrowing his eyes, as if to study him.

"What is it, human?" He spat.

Clearly, he had more disdain for their race than the other giant.

Orion gave the giant a sheepish smile.

This was it, the moment of truth, Atlas thought. He gritted his teeth. Either his brother would give in to his hunger, or he'd become the food himself.

"What is it, human?" The red giant asked again.

Orion reared his head up slightly and chirped in a sweet, timid tune.

"How do we get up there?"

The giant turned to his partner who nodded, sitting down in his own chair across the table.

Oni groaned reluctantly and closed his eyes in frustration, extending his long bony fingers from the palm of his hand, telling everyone to jump on. The giant hoisted them up in the air and deposited them on the table where they were greeted with the most glorious sight ever to behold. Wondrous meats, sizzling pink, intact rainforests of unending fruit, and sugary valleys of frosted caramel delights. To Atlas and the others, it was an unlimited cornucopia, and nothing was going to stop them from taking it all. They were going to strip the giants of everything they had.

17

The giants ate greedily, stuffing their faces with anything they could find, causing food to tumble from their assorted piles. Even when food rained, Atlas felt nothing but malice towards the giants. How dare they scoff their food in front of those who had almost nothing!

"To your health, partner." One of them roared, raising a cup the size of a small lake high in the air.

Deep lush liquid rushed down hairy vines like a gushing waterfall, making droplets seem like glowing gems, sparkling under the firelight.

"We should toast to the little ones?" Kabuki suggested.

Oni, who was sat at the other end of the table, groaned woefully.

"Do we have to? Whenever we save people, they always wind up being a nuisance. They try to leave. They take the waterfall and end up dying anyway. What makes you believe that these ones will be any different? None of them are paying attention to what we are talking about, they're too busy munching on our hard grown labours."

Kabuki nodded slowly, agreeing with his partner. He then raised his cup, encouraging his fellow giant to do the same.

Atlas laughed quietly to himself, so he was not overheard. The waterfall! So, there was a way out, he thought. His friends may have been fixated on the food, but by no means did that mean he was too; he could stave off the hunger a little bit longer if it meant he could find what treasures the giants were keeping. But was there a way out of the castle that avoided them dying altogether? Atlas hoped so.

"Little ones." Kabuki began. "Although you've not been with us more than a single day, I feel an immense bond and attraction to you, like our fates are intertwined…"

"Father, father?" Atlas whispered over the giant, as his mind began to work.

He was crouching down under a field of broccoli and found his father sitting on a block of Emmental cheese, eating a small piece of bread.

"There you are, let's go." He ordered, taking him by the hand and dragging him off the cheese stack.

"Can't you let me finish eating first?" He complained, taking one last bite of the bread.

"No, I can't. We need as much time as we can get. Have you seen the size of them! They're a few over two stories high."

His father warily rose from the floor and brushed himself down, annoyed he was not able to finish.

"What did you expect, Atlas? The stories are true, Giants exist in this world, and they live at the top of towering Seidr-like beanstalks. Size is irrelevant, we can't do anything about it."

Atlas was about to say something, however, he heard Kabuki finishing his toast and knew he had to hurry with father to the table's edge so they could get away unseen.

His father glared at him with a menacing scowl, then suddenly, thwack! His hand shot up to the side of Atlas' head and a raw pain erupted.

"Ow, what was that for!" He exclaimed, as an aching pain banded back and forth at the side of his temple.

His father pointed a long finger at him. He could see the vicious blue fury in his eyes.

"That." He paused ever so slightly for emphasis. "Was for being an idiot - you don't listen."

Atlas rubbed the side of his sore head as they walked through the forest of overgrown vegetables.

"Yes, I do." He stated after a while.

A carrot was blocking their path, and his father walked over to clear it.

"What?" He grunted, feeling the undersides of the vegetable.

"I do listen to you; you just never look to see. I do it in my own way. The result is still the same." Muttered Atlas.

As his father lifted the carrot, seemingly not listening to a word being said, a bag fell from his pocket and Atlas walked over to pick it up. Upon closer inspection, the long-haired boy realised it was the Ash that Silvers had stolen from the Navy. His father had brought it with them and eluded the giant's search, however, Atlas distinctly remembered Silvers only had time to steal a very small amount and he had used that when subduing the Wraith, which begged the question: how did his father come across another bag of Ash?

"Hey, dad? How come you have this anyway?"

His father grumbled in response, as if it was a bad memory. He continued to clear the fallen carrot from their path.

"Your mother." He began, lifting the carrot up over his head with great effort.

Once he had set the blockage down, he turned to Atlas.

"She deals in the trading operation between the Navy and the N.S.T.C."

Atlas looked up from the bag.

"So, she's a merchant then. Funny, I never knew what she did. She leaves for nine years at a time, so I guess that explains it."

His father grunting, not really giving a tangible response, continued working his way to the edge of the table. He never liked talking about their mother and Atlas was beginning to wonder why.

"You don't remember her, do you?" He pondered, using his mighty axe to hack at a row of vegetables that blocked their path.

"You know Orion said she'd be back soon." Atlas went on as he shook his head. "I was thinking about sneaking out of the village to see her at the cove-"

"No!" His father snapped, turning back around.

Atlas could see rage fill his eyes.

"Stay away from your mother. She's dangerous!"

"Why? She's only a merchant, like you said."

"I never said that!" His father bickered, frantically pointing his finger at Atlas' chest.

"Ah!" He screamed, pulling away. "Why do you think we cower on the doorstep of where nothing grows! She's just a very dangerous person, Atlas! One that I should have never gotten myself involved with –"

Then he paused for the briefest of moments, as if re-living a painful memory.

"The woods decayed... The woods were decayed when I found her, and I fell victim to the weeping vapours of her tears because she seemed so helpless at first and I thought it was love as it grew. When I refused at first to give her what horrible thing she had asked for, she turned upon the ground beneath us and she formed the sands of this place, leaving all untouched, aside from these beautiful monoliths. It amazed me that she lured even more people to settle here, only to feed herself and her desires for when she returns home at the rise of the moon. She wanted sons! So lulled everything to sleep to make me suffer and wore me down as time marched on! That is why few birds sing in this place – her island of paradise where we all sojourn. The lakes have withered, and I see a lily on my sons' brows for her to kiss, filling her lips a bright red. She's an utter monster. A demon is what she is. So you promise me, son, that you and Orion will stay away from Lilith Saturn!"

"So, that's her name. After all this time, you finally tell me my own mother's name!" Atlas began to shout.

He was getting madder at his father; he had kept so many things from him, that all of the feelings he had been holding in were beginning to well and spill over the surface. Again, there was little reaction, and they continued to walk towards the edge of the obsidian table without a word passing between their lips.

"I did it for your own good, to protect you, you must see that. To the Devil, I will not send my sons! I came here to gather wealth and enough food for a new life with you both before Lilith returned. She would not leave the island when you both were so young, but now-" He started, after a while.

"I don't care. I just want to get out of here." Atlas said quietly as they approached the part of the table where Oni the giant sat.

They hid behind a stack of meat, just in front of the giant's plate. Quickly, Atlas' father brought out the bag of powder. The white specks were glistening like colourful gemstones that had fallen from the night's sky, yet he was hesitant to go any further. After all, the secrets his father kept were hurtful and damaging.

"If you want to get out of here, then do it and be done with it." Said his father, scooping up a handful of the powder, ramming it up his nose.

After a second, the farmer's eyes began to glow a radiating white.

It did work! Marvelled Atlas. With the Ash they could finally steal what the Giants had. This is why the Navy huddled it away as they did in the village. They knew that any type and amount of this extraordinary substance was paramount for victory, and only the powerful could command the supply. Atlas' mind filled with rage. If that was true, the Navy were deliberately dragging out the war and making people go hungry.

Atlas drove his hands into the powder. He had always found power to be an attractive quality, and he felt something dark surge within him, something that hadn't been there before.

"That's good." Ragnar soothed. "Now... Just breathe, let the power free you."

Atlas did as he said, breathing in slow, deep breaths as the beads of charred powder flowed through him. The effects were instant.

Suddenly, the dark shadow of a crimson red limb hovered above, plucking both father and son up from their improvised hiding place. Two red fingers held them up as they dangled helplessly in the air, unable to do anything.

What power? Thought Atlas.

"Mhhh, what was that, human? You like my cooking. Amazing, is it? Well?" The giant mused, as he narrowed his eyes, studying them intently.

He had heard everything.

"How do you like this?"

In an instant, Oni dropped Atlas and his father, letting them fall a little before scooping them up with his other hand. They were corralled in a cast-iron grip; the only place for them to go was down should the giant choose it, thus they faced back-to-back against his palm.

"Partner?" Kabuki asked suddenly.

Both father and son heard the panic in the red giant's reply and quickly felt shaded from view.

"Yes?" The giant replied, quickly moving the humans under the table as far as he could.

Oni didn't want Kabuki to see that he was about to eat his precious humans.

"Something the matter?"

"No, no, no, nothing the matter at all." The red giant lied.

Under the table, Atlas' father asked him a simple question.

"Can you move your hands?"

"A little bit, but not much." He said, gritting his teeth.

They were being pressed into a pulp and everything was getting tighter.

"Try to focus on what you want the giant to do."

"What!"

"Just do it!" His father demanded.

Still, the orange-eyed giant had not caught on to what the other was doing, but Atlas and his father both knew they could use that to their advantage.

Atlas breathed in and tried to press his hand to the palm of the giant's – he wanted the creature to let them go, to tell them where they kept their most valuable item. Suddenly, the giant's fingers loosened their grip and he set them back down on the table as white light flowed from Atlas' hand. Thankfully, the other giant had become too interested in his meal to take any further notice of what the other was doing, and Atlas hoped that his friends would stay clear.

Oni looked down to them, and Atlas and his father backed away. Deep crimson eyes peered into their flesh and sharpened teeth hissed at them.

"The treasure vault is down the hall." The giant stammered, his face a wide, painful grimace.

Red facial muscles were aching, trying to force their horrendous foe from divulging his secrets.

"Follow the hallway down to the end." He continued. "The vault is the last door you will see. It is not locked; we haven't needed to do that since the sands came."

It was then that Atlas' father ran at Oni's chair and used it to make his way down to the floor.

"Father, what are you doing?" He called.

"We need to get to the vault! There's no time. The Ash won't affect him for long, he'll come looking for us, they both will, and when that time comes, we all need to be out of here."

Atlas nodded and followed his father down the table, when they got to the bottom, he placed his hand on the giant's leg.

"What are you doing?" His father hurried. "Come on, we've got to go!"

"Hang on."

His eyes glowed white.

"Oni, I am ordering you. You will not tell anyone where we have gone, or why. Do you understand?"

The giant nodded and Atlas let go of his leg, following his father out of the room. They ran down the hallway as quickly as they could and soon found a large wooden octangular door.

"This has got to be it." Announced Atlas, as he stared into the ornately carved wood.

The design showed just how much the giants cared about their culture, displaying images of vast heaps of jewels and gold. The door was supremely heavy, and the two of them only just managed to slide through a wafer-thin gap before their strength gave way, sealing them inside. Atlas was breathing heavily. His muscles burned and ached, hunching over with his hands on his knees. Aside from the vault door, the entirety of the room was walled off with the thick stone blocks. There were no windows, no torches to set the slightest glimmer.

"This is amazing." Ragnar uttered, astonished as he surveyed the vault.

The utter darkness was drawing them in further, calling to them to venture closer.

"What do you mean?" Breathed Atlas, still looking down at what he believed to be the floor.

His breathing was starting to return to normal and he could taste the stale air that hovered around the room. The dull pain in his arms gradually began to fade, and Atlas lifted his head to see an impossible shimmering shade of yellow light reach across the room.

The light was coming from piles upon piles of vastly heaped golden coins and treasures. They were everywhere, strung across the cold stone flooring and rising above their heads like the menacing beanstalk. Blown away by the vast enormity that faced him, Atlas had no words that could explain this strange occurrence of dazzling and bewitching light. What kind of crazed treasure had they stumbled upon?

There was all manner of jewels set into the gold. Blazing blue sapphires, as deep and rich as the ocean depths, blood-red rubies, stained crimson, and shining emeralds that looked sharp to the touch. It was all here. The riches of an entire world! Moreover, it was his!

Rushing over to the nearest heap, Atlas scooped up as much as he could in one go. Just a single tankard of this treasure could set them up for life, and he was going to try to take it all! Greed had overcome him. He looked at the richness, letting out a deep cackling laugh as it slid between his fingers. This trove was truly out of this world, and he understood why the giants had gone to the lengths they did to protect it. This is what they had come for, not the food. The hunger didn't matter at all, not when they had all the power and wealth in the world.

"Atlas, come look at this!" His father almost squealed from atop another pile of vastly hoarded treasure.

Atlas shook his head, breaking his gold lucid trance and slid a handful of coins and gemstones into his pocket. He couldn't let anyone else take this treasure from him, not a single piece would leave his sight.

"What is it?" He asked, ascending the slippery mound.

"Take a look at this, son." His father marvelled.

A massive black and brown leather book was placed in his arms, easily the size of the Northman's chest, but to the giants, this enormous hunk of text would easily have been just a normal book. The tome was worn and tattered, its pages the colour of dirty mud-stained water.

"What's so great about an old, tattered book? We're here for the treasure, aren't we?" He asked, raising an eyebrow at the blotted script.

"Not all treasure is gold and gemstones, Atlas." His father pointed out, turning a fragile, wafer-thin page. "You said to your friend you wanted revenge, didn't you?"

Atlas gritted his teeth in frustration and nodded.

"His name is Gill! You've never been good with their names! You couldn't even tell me my own mother's up until a moment ago!" His voice echoed.

The look on his father's face was stern.

"I had my reasons!" He bellowed.

Atlas cringed in fear. He had never once seen his father this angry with him and he had to snatch the book away from his enraged and vicious grasp.

"Now, that will be the end of it! Give the blasted book here, and I'll tell you what it says."

"No!" Atlas cried, clutching the ancient tome to his body.

Suddenly, he began to feel the coin on which he stood shift, and, like a changing sand dune, it flew, sending Atlas hurtling towards the stone. His father reached out in a mad dash, barely grabbing onto his arm in time.

"Hand me the book." He commanded.

"Or what?" Seethed Atlas, struggling to latch his arm around the text. "You'll drop your eldest child?"

"I would be doing you a favour, boy. Never forget that." His father replied.

There was nothing but cold contempt in those eyes, so Atlas threw the frail pages back, not wanting to be impaled on an encrusted gemstone and was finally pulled to safety.

"See, not all treasures are expensive jewels, some are worth little to one person, and yet, have great meaning to others."

"Yes, I get that, but what does it say? Moreover, why can you read ancient languages? You're just a farmer." Atlas asked impatiently, now situated on better footing, and wanting to know what his father found between the pages.

"It's Runic-Verse. I taught both you and Orion how to read it when you were younger, you just never bothered to practice enough." He said and then he continued to read from the frail pages.

"If you aim to kill the thundering beasts, that tower above land and sky.

You simply strike them where sight does not reach. Thus, they will fall and die.

Where others may be hard to reach some will simply fall. However, some are harder still, and you must take their limbs or more."

"So, we have to kill them where they can't see us…and maybe sever some limbs at the same time?"

His father smirked.

"I doubt my axe can cut that deep - it would take hours, if not days to cleave a head from such a host, and as we've already found out, they're not exactly what you'd call passive." He explained, closing the book and rubbing his head, trying to figure out if they could find any form of weapon powerful enough from among the treasure heap.

"From the looks of things, this book has all sorts of notes on giants. I caught a glimpse at the other pages, and there are many types of them, aside from the two we know of."

"Plus, there is something else you should be aware of." Noted Ragnar.

"What is it?" Asked Atlas.

"It's a prophecy, almost invisible at the bottom of the page I just read to you. It's almost as if it was added after the tome was completed."

"And, what of it?"

"It's about a Great Storm: a mammoth reckoning that will change the world, bringing civilisations to their knees."

"Like the giants?"

"Yes, boy. Like the giants. It says that a child born of devil's blood will bring decay to all that is near. Giants will fall; men will crawl; and monsters will roam the sky. A man, black of heart, mind and will, will control it all. A son of death, a mother in red, and two ravens flying across the sea – for they will pay the ultimate price and all monsters shall roam free."

Atlas gulped. It all sounded very serious, and he began to wonder; with what his father had told him about his mother, could he possibly be the child born of Devil's blood? After all, his goals did seem to align with that of the prophecy and his father was black of heart, for he too wanted to steal from the giants.

Suddenly, the room began to rumble, treasure rattled down from its heaped slopes, spreading even further across the cold stone floor and the sound of thundering footsteps grew ever present.

"Little ones!" An enraged voice yelled in the distance.

It was Kabuki.

"Little ones, I know you're there. The fat one told me so!"

"Quick, grab what you can. I'll take the book." His father urged.

Atlas nodded, and they both jumped off the mound of coins, goblets, and gemstones, landing unevenly on the hard floor.

"Little ones!" The giant bellowed again, this time he was a lot closer and pounded against the octangular door to the treasure vault.

At first, the door splintered, showing giant fist marks against the frame, then moments later, two bellowing mammoth hits came, sending the door flying, and smashing it to hundreds of tiny pieces against mounds of treasure. It barely missed Atlas and his father, yet all the boy could think about was how his own brother had ratted them out.

Before them in the doorway stood the giant. Tears were rolling down his angular face as if it were a twisted waterfall and debris continued to fall.

"We saved you! We fed you! And this is the thanks we get!" The giant roared, showing his misshapen teeth.

Oni then appeared behind his partner, waving his closed fist. Atlas caught his eye and could make out the faces of his brother, Gill and Silvers locked within the giant's palm.

"Let them go!" Shouted Atlas.

"No!" Snapped the giant. "Why would we let this little songbird go?"

Atlas could see the giant's long, thin, pointed teeth. Clearly, Oni was the type of giant made for eating people. Perhaps now, Orion could see what true monsters their hosts really were.

"Come on, partner. Let's just eat them already. We can make some lovely bread with their bones."

Kabuki nodded, and the giant made his way towards Atlas and his father at a frightening speed.

"Atlas, do you remember when I first trained you and Orion to handle the Wraiths?"

"Yeah, but I don't see how that works here-" He cried, as the giants were all but on top of them.

"Roll!" His father shouted.

Atlas lurched forward and dived between the monster's gaping legs. At that moment, his father swooped to the side, picking up a golden spear that lay newly uncovered by the escaping treasure. The elder steadied it in his hand and launched it at the giant with a tremendous thrust. The spear flung through the air, and the giant quickly moved his hand to protect his face. Oni dropped the boys in an instant as it struck, letting them fall on to a heap of mounted treasure below as he screamed.

"Run, Run!" Atlas shouted as the giants bounded after them.

Kabuki hurtled past and slammed into the back of the vault. They had to hurry.

Atlas and Orion's father guided everyone outside the castle, through the winding labyrinth of twisting staircases and corridors as the giants chased them every step of the way, but thanks to their size they were able to hide in the cracks and shadows for what seemed like hours. It was pitch-black when they reached the outside world. Still, rampaging stomps chased them, and the humans were pressed to the precipice of the waterfall that flung from the keep.

Orion, out of breath, wondered if it was the only way down.

"YA-YA-YA-YA-YA!" Their foes cried in pursuit, a horrid scream rippling across the stone-clad citadel.

"Down the beanstalk. Now!" Suggested Gill, who ran to the side, grabbing onto a dark leafy vine as he slid down, colliding across the different off-shoots.

The rest followed his idea. Better that than falling through a watery veil to a hard grave below, where vicious mouths waited. They scurried down the beanstalk as fast as they could with the giants giving chase. Their massive limbs were no match for the speed and swiftness of smaller human ones. Despite their size and strength, the giants tore off vast chunks of emerald green as they followed, not having the time nor delicacy as they had when Kabuki had saved the boys from the hungry mouths of the creatures below. They were enraged now, raining down on Atlas and his friends a storm of thick and twisted flora. Suddenly, the stalk began to bow and sway in the darkness of night. The boys quickly realised that the beanstalk could not hold out for much longer, as it began to creak with an almighty groan. Without a second thought, Ragnar gripped the giant's tome tightly in one arm. In between his teeth, he had been gripping his axe as he climbed and he shouted a muffled cry to Atlas as he began to wrap vines around his leg with the heel of his foot. Atlas looked up, seeing the giants and his father above him as the Wraith farmer called. In the glint of silver starlight, the head of the blade gleamed, and when his father opened his mouth, the axe fell from his grasp through the dark air until the boy reached out as far as he could and caught it in his grasp. Without warning, the beanstalk cracked and creaked, making the giants wobble and press their weight in even further.

"Use it!" Ragnar bellowed, and so Atlas set to, and with several vicious strikes, he hurriedly began to hack away at the emerald monolith.

Above him, Atlas could hear the giants swear in anger and rage. Then suddenly, Snap! The beanstalk plummeted to the ground, and thunder reigned...

18

A blood tinted moon rose over a blackened night's sky, and blinding dust blew in every direction. The fallen beanstalk lay across a dry, windswept land; its corpse battered and broken, started to shrivel in the sand. When it had fallen, desert dunes flew into the air. The night's cold, howling winds had gathered them, sweeping all into a blanketing cloud of dust, faded with the visceral red of the moon. Atlas coughed as it filled his lungs. He could hardly breathe in the gathering sand-squall, and with his vision hazed, he lowered his head to find his feet, covering his eyes from the bombardment. He stood upon a part of the fallen corpse of the giant's monolith; he remembered that when he had struck with his father's axe, it had been felled with the weight of everyone and everything that clung to it. It had exaggerated the cracks and tears already present, causing the tower to spin and splinter. Even the waters from the fall had quenched the desert land as it fell, and now the sands moved to drink the pools and droplets up.

As he finally found his feet upon the broken thing, Atlas squinted to see the outline of giant footsteps through the haze of the squall, snaking their way across the land, the size of a horse or a cow. Barely visible even to one such as him; who had spent a lifetime on this isle of burning sand, but they were there nonetheless! They had survived!

"Is everyone okay?" Called Atlas.

He rushed in undoing the green holds that had saved his life, peeling and hacking them off with his father's axe, as sand attacked his dried, parched throat. It was a miracle they had survived, he thought, as he peered into the distant dunes, jumping down onto cooling ground.

No one replied. Had they truly made it? Had they been crushed? Had he been lucky? The giants certainly had - they too, clung to the vines as he and his friends did, as the once high emerald tower had twisted and turned. Atlas knew at once he had to hurry as he looked at the footsteps, wandering off into the distance. Everyone else must have landed further away, he thought reassuringly, as his piece of the stalk lay segregated from the rest when it had broken apart in the fall.

And so, Atlas began to make his way across the sands of his home, running to follow his prey amidst a sandstorm, their deadly trail the only hope he had of finding the others. After what seemed like hours of running, the sand-squall cleared, revealing the silvering light of the red blood-moon that was hoisted high above him. His eyes widened in terror, and his heart began to beat at a quickened pace. Ahead of him was the ruins of the giants' crumbled fortress, stuck between the intermittent trunks of jungle beanstalk. He stood there for a moment in shock and awe as he caught his breath. The treasure of the giants' horde had survived too, it glittered against the sands in scattered clumps and shimmered in the moonlight. It looked so innocent and was ripe for the taking! Presently however, a massive shadowy hand appeared above him, its fingertips long and bony.

"Look out!" A loud bellowing voice shouted, one Atlas recognised as his father's, but it was too late.

Before he could look above him, the hand reached down, grasping him once again in one fell swoop. As Atlas squirmed in the giant's grasp, he saw far off into the distance under blurred vision, a plethora of dimly flickering orange lights, hovering over twisting sand dunes. His home, his village! The giants were so close, and the boy thought that they would surely seek recompense for what had happened, as he was lifted to see a sneering red face with a sharp, tapered grin. His father's axe fell from his grasp as the giant squeezed, falling to the sand. Atlas felt as if his bones would shatter under the strain.

"I'm going to make you suffer, human!" Oni spat.

Black blood was seeping from the red creature's forehead and there was a crazed look in his hatred filled eyes as he smothered his lips with a long-forked tongue. Below them, Atlas' father was too far away to do anything, pushing himself harder to run faster across the dunes, watching the shadowy figures struggle, his voice barely raised above the growing wind. He had tied the giant's tome behind him on his back with broken vines and now he ran towards his son and the red-limbed foe.

"Atlas!" Ragnar exclaimed over and over, trying to gain the giant's attention. "Atlas! Hold on boy! I have what you want creature. I have your tome of riddles, so come take them if you dare!"

"Father!" Atlas cried, as the giant opened its gaping mouth.

The boy stared at the darkness within, looking to his father for one last time. He didn't want to die like this, not in this way.

"I'm sorry." He screamed. "Did you hear him, monster? We have your book!"

The giant paused for a moment as he considered what Atlas said, giving Ragnar time to catch up to where Oni stood. Suddenly the red giant screamed in blood curdling pain as the old warrior found his axe among the shifting ground, and drove it deeply within the thing's flesh, dropping Atlas several feet upon the sands in the process.

"You lie!" Oni seethed.

"Father!" Atlas cried once more, heaving, and running haphazardly over to Ragnar against the desert sand.

As his father cleaved the axe from the giant's ankle, and black blood whetted the sand around them, the red- limbed foe reached down as he did once before and beheld Ragnar, plucking him from the ground. Atlas' heart thumped yet again as he looked in rage to the shadow that carried his father. The giant squeezed the Northman, harder than he had done Atlas. Oni had the pleasure of knowing this time nothing could be done, and before Atlas had even reached his father, the giant had dangled the man above its spiked teeth. With a spare hand and Ragnar shouting, Oni ripped the tome from the Wraith farmer's back and flicked the axe away. Atlas was forced to watch them, helpless and alone, as he pounded at the wound seeping from the giant's ankle and tears streamed down the boy's face. The giant hissed as Atlas threw punch after punch, none of it helping his cause, his father still dangling.

"Atlas!" His father called to him. "Find your brother now, boy! I will not send the Devil two sons this day. Save him, do not let your-"

"Enough of this!" The red giant wailed, loosening his fingers, before chomping down his teeth in several vicious bites.

When it was over, the giant threw what remained aside, letting blood saturate the dry earth. Atlas felt as if he had aged years in one horrifying instant, as the giant now looked down to sneer at him. A hollow, unending rage blanketed over Atlas' guilt, as he now ran from a clawed reaching hand, his eyes empty like a bottomless void. The land reeked of death as he ran to find his brother; a horrid acid smell filling his lungs, burning them with pain, making his eyes swell with water. He was now a child of death, born anew in a wash of blood.

Atlas swore to himself, every single giant in the world would suffer a payment for what had happened this night. He would become a monster for the monsters to fear and stand atop of their bones, victorious.

He now had no idea where Orion was. Atlas had to find him before it was too late. He had to make sure that his little brother was safe, just like his father had asked.

"You're going to pay!" He cursed, pushed on by rage.

Its red eyes gleamed in the distance, flickering in the cold moonlight with a menacing glare. It taunted him, growing closer and closer, stalking its way towards him in a slow, antagonising pace as black blood trickled behind. Atlas' heartbeat grew faster with every shuddering step. Sat in the cold, pale moonlight and the twinkling stars was the village - his village. If only Atlas could make it that much further, he could try to convince the garrison to help him, though with the sight of two giants, he didn't think it would take much convincing on his part.

"Every single one of you will pay tenfold for what has happened here!" He roared, taunting the giant further on.

Now the terrifying cries of people began to rest upon Atlas' ears as he neared the settlement. He realised that the rest of the beanstalk had fallen just short of its walls, with a number of scattered pieces littering the desert. He was sure that to the people of his village, the giants were a sign of pure horror, as no one apart from him and his friends had ever believed the tales of the creatures that lived in the sky.

"Run!" He ordered, wanting to be their hero.

"Run for your lives!" He screamed, knowing he would bring ruin to the giants.

Nothing seemed to work as he continued alongside the fallen green corpse. Where were the Navy? He wondered as he climbed through the hole that had been made in the defensive wall. Had they abandoned them? Were they dead? His wantings, his whispers, fled into the night, they all fell silent next to the screams echoing from the village. Kabuki was already inside.

Atlas ran towards the marketplace, the ground rumbled amidst frantic shouts. The hustle and bustle from this morning was gone, and vendors' products were spread across the ground, still not a scrap of food in sight. Atlas balled his fists as he searched. A thought quickly crossed his mind: where was the one place his brother would go if he was frightened? Orion would go home. Atlas would bet that Silvers and Gill would be with him too, if they had all survived that is.

The ground shook once more.

"We will find you!" Roared Kabuki, viciously stomping with no remorse.

The giant was only one or two stories higher than the small homes at best, and yet, when Atlas looked up, the giant seemed to tower above everything, as if there were no end. He quickly thought back to the book, and the pages father had shown him. How was he meant to deal with these creatures when he had been so helpless a mere ten minutes before! Atlas remembered there had been other giants hidden in that book. What had been listed on those tattered pages seemed far more substantial, far more fearsome. He was beginning to think the world would be a far safer place if they didn't exist.

Ahead of him, his tiny home was untouched. Atlas ran to the door and knocked, hoping the giant hadn't caught sight of him.

The door flew open, and Atlas was dragged inside. He fell onto the floor, landing on top of his friends. He had never been so relieved to see all their dirty faces.

"You made it!" He cried as he lifted himself off the floor.

"Of course we did." Mused Silvers, who looked back at the others. "Who do you take us for? We can outrun giants any day."

Atlas then turned to his brother, wrapped his arms around him, and held him tighter than he ever had before.

"I'm sorry." He wept, tears streaming down his face.

He was no longer able to hold back his emotions.

"I'm sorry for everything that has happened, but you can see how they're nothing but monsters."

"I know." Sniffed Orion, as he returned the hug. "After just one little thing, they just turned on us in an instant. Although you are still to blame for some of the things that have happened to us, and there is no way you can fix what you've done now. Have you seen father?"

Atlas fell silent for a while.

"Orion... I..." He began.

His brother turned white. He pushed Atlas away from their brotherly embrace and the elder could the familial rage brewing in his bright blue eyes.

"Then his death is on you." He said at last. "And I will never forgive that. He was cruel, yes, and nobody shall sing the Haven Song for him, but in his own harsh way, he loved and protected us both. Your ambition, your adventures, Atlas, what have they wrought? Nothing but death and danger, and because of that we are poor as always, and now berthed. You have doomed us all!"

"Then you leave me no choice." Wept Atlas, placing a hand on his brother's back as he turned from him.

"Huh?"

Suddenly, Atlas' eyes glowed a bright white light, and he whispered something into Orion's ear. The world would go blank. He would completely forget what Atlas had done to him. He would only know that the giants were to blame. His brother flopped to the floor in a heap, and Atlas carried him to his bedroom. All around them, the giants still called for the boys. The house shook, the ground shifted and rumbled, and the village burned. Had this all really come about because of his actions? It was his father that had climbed the beanstalk first, and he, by his own admissions, would have stolen from the giants to escape their mother. What had Ragnar meant when he said would not send the Devil two sons? Did he mean the giants? He wondered. Or was it destiny, a prophecy or someone twisting the threads of fate on a loom? If the book was right, it seemed he would have a greater part to play.

Suddenly, there was a tremendous shaking, and the roof of the house was torn from over their heads.

"They're over here, partner." The giant said to Oni, beckoning him.

The red-eyed giant was a few houses away but peered from afar. Atlas bawled his fists. He tried to cry out, to shout at the giant and take them on as his father had, thus he swore he would not be as helpless as he had been. Kabuki the giant loomed over Atlas, his fingers crumbling the thinly built walls to dust as his deep orange eyes glared at the boy. Atlas stared back. So vicious and so fearsome was his gaze that Atlas thought it caused the giant to tremble. But why should it? He thought to himself as he stepped forward to affront his attacker. He was a child, helpless! And, as he had seen before, he could do nothing. All Atlas could do was watch as the giant bellowed, laughing as he crumbled the walls to his childhood home. He thought of his friends now, of their fates as Kabuki waited for Oni to arrive, the giant licking his lips in anticipation of gnawing flesh from bone. Silvers and Gill had dived underneath the kitchen table when the roof had begun to crack, but still the giant looked to Atlas.

"What are you waiting for!" He yelled, bringing his arms out wide in challenge, only on this occasion he realised he did not have his father, or his axe for protection.

The giant laughed yet again at his challenge, and his eyes flicked across the house. He smiled. Kabuki reached down to coldly clutch his brother from his bed, surely dragging him to a known, yet unknown fate. As he did, a strange metal wiring sound could be heard from nearby, and the boys peeked out from under the table. Above them, a small shadowy figure spun in the moonlight, propelled by what looked like two thin wires.

"Get away from them, they belong to me!" The figure shouted, landing on the shoulder of the giant.

The voice was distinctly female, and Atlas could see two small boxes attached to the figure's waist. Unfortunately, he was unable to see who the woman was, but continued to hear the wiring ticks of gears as they spun. Whatever it was, the woman had used it to sneak up on the giants with surprising accuracy, after shooting the thin wires into the buildings next to her.

With one swift motion, the woman reached behind her back, pulling out a long-curved blade. It bore a striking resemblance to a scimitar, with several nocked chips, and was as black as a raven's wing. The woman quickly jumped off the giant's shoulder, plunging the blade deep into its neck, making the giant howl with rage, dropping Orion from his grasp. Oni rushed over to help his partner, swatting at the figure with his sharp fang-like fingernails. She narrowly avoided the attack from the red-limbed giant and dove to catch the tumbling boy.

Atlas could see his brother fall, horrified that he could do nothing to stop it. But swooping down, the woman caught

Orion in mid-air before he hit the ground and Atlas breathed out a sigh of relief.

Just then, Oni caught the wires attached to the building and pulled. The thin cables snapped, making the woman and Orion veer off, and slam into the ground, where Atlas could not see. The red-limbed monster reached into the house and flicked the table away with his long fingers. The giant smiled and the boys could see his sharp pointed teeth, as thin as needles.

"I'm going to enjoy eating you, little ones. You've caused us much pain, and now it's time to say goodbye."

Atlas knew the giant was taking his time by how he licked his lips with his long snake-forked tongue in anticipation.

Then as Oni reached down, and to Atlas' surprise, a small thin wire shot through the giant's neck from below and attached itself to one of the taller piles of rubble. A second later, there was a final tick and a flash of roaring steam. The wire broke free of the pile of rubble, and the hook slammed into the back of the giant's neck.

As this was happening, the woman drew from her back another raven-coloured scimitar and held it to her side. In one clean blow, she struck at the giant. Blood erupted from the wound, covering the woman in a scarlet shower.

"Oni!" Kabuki screamed, pinned to the ground. "Help me, I can't get this free."

His hand scrambled at the blade, but there was no reply.

Atlas rushed out from where he and his friends were, and over to the woman.

"Who are you, and what happened to my brother?" He demanded.

The woman was now wiping her blade against the sand. She looked at him carefully, in her scarlet jacket, drenched in the giant's crimson coloured blood and wiped a slithering droplet from her cheek, licking the tiny orb clean from her gloved finger.

She smiled at him sweetly, before tossing him his father's axe from behind her back. Atlas saw she had deep brown eyes, and that they were almost loving.

"Don't worry, my dear. I put him down just over there." She said, pointing to a pile at the other end of the destroyed village street. "As for who *I* am, don't you recognise me?"

Atlas winced slightly, looking at her more closely, and saw that she did indeed look familiar.

"Mother?" He gaped in amazement.

The woman smiled at him again, nodding her head.

"Yes, my love. It's me." She spoke softly, and dove her arms around him for a hug.

Atlas was very confused as he tried to search his memories for answers.

A mother in red, he thought. He may not have known her name up until recently, but he had a vague image as to what she had looked like when last he saw her. The problem he was having was that she looked the same, and not a day older.

"How is this possible?" He stammered, and his mother placed a blood-soaked finger to his lips.

"Shush." She said quietly, turning her head to look at the squirming Kabuki. "I'll tell you when you're older, but for now, what do you want most?"

Atlas turned to stare at the giant, gazing at the damage all around and the chaos they had caused.

"I want them dead." He said plainly.

His mother smiled brilliantly and stroked his face. It was something that he had missed for a long time and had not known why, perhaps it was the feeling of being loved?

"You are most certainly *my* child, Atlas." His mother beamed, and she placed a hand on his back and led him towards the giant. "Come, let's start to make your dream a reality. This giant is almost dead, take your revenge. I will help you get started so you and your friends can take care of the rest. I know they share your dream, how can they not when they've been with you the entire time. All you need to do is push."

Her fingers curled around his shoulders as they approached. Every footstep felt hollow, heavy, like it was full of importance, every step he took led him further down his destined path. Atlas climbed up the giant's back by his mother's side. They trudged over the tattered and torn emerald and gold robes, as if they had not a care in the world. Finally, they reached the back of the giant's neck, and Atlas felt the heavy breathing of the creature as it exhaled. In front of them, his mother's raven-coloured, blood-soaked sword lay notched in place. Atlas gripped the hilt.

19

Atlas found himself on the hard, cold floor of the gauntlet antechamber and his black mark ached as the violet amulet shone. Above him, he saw the now thinned and bone-like face of his younger brother.

"Atlas, are you okay? What happened?" Orion asked, offering a hand.

Atlas gripped him tightly and let Orion pull him to his feet. On his right hand, he wore the treasure; golden metal twisted and seeped around his long and massive hand. Atlas was slightly amused that although the treasure looked solid while on the pedestal, they actually slithered continuously around his arm.

"Fascinating." The pirate said aloud.

He twisted and moved in all sorts of directions and the wet fingers quickly followed. No longer did he feel tired or drained. The gauntlet glowed a golden-red as it shimmered with light, and he backed away from Orion slightly, unsure of what it might do.

"Did it show you something?" His brother asked. "You were out for quite a while?"

"I had a continuation of my dream." He said, gazing up at the shifting fingers.

One moment they were normal, then they were a pointed blade or a slithering snake.

"It was as if the gauntlet somehow tapped into my Ash-ridden dreams, showing me our past in the exact detail it happened!"

"Oh?" Orion quipped, raising an eyebrow and cracking a smile. "You had hair then, right?"

"Yes, I had hair then, you stupid fool!" Atlas bellowed in rage.

He had not realised that the fingers had transformed his hand into a gun, and that he was pointing said gun towards his brother. He didn't have time for mockery. They had to leave quickly, before Kaine's hunters finally found them.

Orion's smile dropped from his face, and his brother backed away slowly.

"Sorry." He huffed, putting up his hands. "I meant no harm by it, Atlas. You know, I think that thing is messing with you a bit, but at least it gave you your energy back, eh?"

Atlas smiled, lowering his hand.

"Is the Mayor still here?" He asked with a devious smile, stroking his goatee.

"Yeah, he's just around the corner. Shall I send him in?"

Atlas nodded.

"Please do and get Gillian while you're at it. I may need him to do something for me." He replied.

Orion then stepped out of the chamber and passed the snow-melted ruins of the once frozen doorway. After a few moments alone, his brother returned, followed closely by Gillian and the Mayor.

"Ah, there you are!" Atlas exclaimed, greeting them both with excitement.

To Atlas, his first mate looked the same as he did when they entered the chamber, but the small blonde Mayor looked far more shaken.

"Why Mayor, is something the matter?"

Mayor Johnson was silent, only looking at Atlas with worry. Suddenly, the pirate captain bent down to meet the little man's eyes and breathed in sharply.

"What. Is. It?" Atlas spat, his face turning bright red, veins popping out of his forehead.

Even the sound of the shout itself reverberated across the tunnel walls and echoed with a loud snarl. A flash of red and gold light erupted from the fingers, turning the liquid-form of the fingers to a large blade, one that balanced on the end of the gauntlet. Atlas moved the knife over in front of him, pointing the edge at the soft part of the Mayor's neck.

"Tell me now." He whispered. "Or I will gut you where you stand."

The Mayor gulped, stepping out from beside the first mate and trembling with terrible shakes.

This is not what he wanted, the Mayor thought to himself. This is not what he was promised! Diamonds and jewels beyond his greatest belief, and now he had a golden metallic sword thrust against his neck.

"We've had a report." The Mayor trembled. "The Navy woman you wanted to be captured has escaped, along with the drunk, Jackson, and another Navy officer. We thought he threw himself off of the cliff, but he survived, and I believe she knows everything. We can't find them, and a few of the men we sent are dead."

"What!" Atlas roared. "You mean to tell me that the only person to escape the mines is now with someone who could quite possibly bring this whole thing down on us, and you let them get away?"

The Mayor dipped his head.

"Yes." He shivered, and the pirate captain erupted in a bellowing rage.

"Gillian, go bring me this whelp's daughter. We will bring them to us. I believe Mister Johnson was talking about this Jackson before. He will come for her, as well as that cook outside. I am sure of it."

The pirate captain could not afford any loose ends. Not now. Not when they were so close to getting away with what they quarried. Atlas was going to make sure the Mayor did not get a gram for what he had done.

"Now then." He tutted, twisting the golden blade slightly into the Mayor's neck; blood trickled slowly down the side. "This is what you get when you fail me, Rupert. Any last requests? No? Good."

Then, with one effortless thrust of his fingers, the golden blade shone dimly with a red light and the edge extended slowly towards the Mayor's neck.

"You can't escape Kaine." He uttered, trembling as the sharp finger-blades travelled towards him. "He'll find you. So long as you bare that pestilent mark. I've heard stories about him, and he'll eat you alive."

"No!" Shouted Atlas. "*I*, am the child of destiny! *I* am the hero of this tale! And I will cleanse this world. I will watch it burn for what it has done to me. Goodbye Rupert. The prophecy will be completed."

In a second, Atlas flicked his fingers at the Mayor, killing him. The old man choked on his blood until the very last, holding the open gash with his hand. Atlas saw the light fade from his eyes, and at that point, tore the blade from his throat. The pirate captain then held the golden weapon close to his face and watched in fascination as the blade changed and transformed.

"Fascinating." He said again, circling the pedestal.

He then laughed maniacally as he watched it shift and change.

"Just think of all the fun you and I are going to have together."

20

"So, who has been snooping where they don't belong?" Jackson said to himself quietly.

It was the first time he had gotten to look at his hut since Ann had arrived, and he kicked the glass from the broken Ash vial around with his foot. From what he had seen of Ann, she had so far been all encompassing, forever the constant centre of attention despite saying otherwise. Jackson shook his head. Because of her, Tom had been hurt, Nelson had been kidnapped, they had been chased by a pirate horde and dragged headlong into the centre of the island's problems – just where he didn't want to be, and now Arabella was in danger too. Yes, he wanted the pirates gone, he had said it often enough, but not at the cost of losing yet another person. Simply put, Jackson just didn't know if he could ever bring himself to trust Ann completely. The outside world was made up of a kingdom of thieves. People often spoke in half-truths, if only to get what they wanted. The pirates, The Company, The Lords who sat in government, they were all the same in his eyes, yet his sense of honour told him that making a deal with Ann had been the right thing to do.

That damn girl, he thought. Even if he was repaying a debt by going to that place again, he had to admit, the Navy really did know how to search a place.

Above the bed, dangling from a hook and a piece of small thread, was the key to Nelson's house. The slightly green, bronze-coloured key, swung with a slight motion as it scraped against the grainy wood of the back wall. The hollowing silence floating in the air made Jackson shiver, as if a cold spectre were hovering behind. As his fingers wrapped around the cold metal, a mysterious force grabbed him, forcing his arm down sharply. Jackson looked at the sleeve of his trench coat, seeing the unmistakable marks of a man's hand pressed against the leather.

"Show yourself!" He demanded, swinging his arms around and drawing his sword.

Suddenly a voice sprung up in the air and chuckled deeply.

"Why? What would be the fun in that, Jackson?" The voice cooed.

Jackson gritted his teeth, spinning around once more.

"How do you know my name, Pirate?"

"That's not important." The invisible foe taunted. "I just wanted you to know this: that everyone in the tunnels are talking about you. They say your wife abandoned you, that you were forgotten about, that it all meant nothing to her and that she simply left you to rot. Is that true?"

Jackson gritted his teeth once more.

"You know nothing of me!" He roared, as tears began to roll down his face.

He hated it when people judged him for matters that were not their own.

"What happened was not my fault, who are you to judge!"

"No reason at all." The voice said calmly from behind him.

Jackson could feel his warm breath push the hairs up on the back of his neck.

"There is absolutely no reason for me to judge you. You see, Atlas wanted me to do something for him. I came here first to see if it would work, and I am pleased to say it did. So, take that key, and run along to your little friends."

"What? Why?" He spat, feeling a sense of familiarity to his words, but he did not know why? "Why are you doing this to us?"

The voice laughed.

"Because, we all have something we want, Jackson. And there is always something that everyone runs from, no matter who they are. Sometimes we are drawn to these things and people, and there are those that will always keep our hearts, no matter how many times things go awry. Atlas, and our pirate group are no different; we just wanted to make the world a safer and better place. I do this for him. Now we have the first piece of that puzzle we can do that. An accord must be fulfilled with the Hoarder-King. I just wanted to see for myself what she means to you. You're quite the popular man on this island. Always someone to care for and yet nowhere to belong."

Jackson glared at the empty space before him.

"That's not a reason at all. It's madness in fact, to cause such heartbreak! What have I ever done to Atlas? Just because you are something does not mean you have to act like it! You can be better than that. You can be a good person and not cause suffering to so many just because you want something. That is how obsessions start!"

The voice snorted at this, and Jackson could feel him getting closer as he saw a man's footprints press across the wet sands before him.

"It's not you! You're no one, Jackson. Someone simply in our way, connected to the people who matter to us. Arabella for example, we've marked her for the Troll King, Lazarus. A payment-in-kind for information we received. However, she was still connected to you. Anyone would have done, but that girl has fire in her to make her a queen, and it suited our plans with her father once we sent word to the Troll of her beauty. It was Silvers' job to take care of that, but your friend the Alchemist got in the way with that silly bracelet charm of his and it messed with his powers. Now Atlas has charged me to do it the way real pirates do best."

"Wait, you mean Nelson? He told me to give Arie that ribbon?"

The pirate laughed.

"Hehe. I wonder, how many secrets are they keeping from you? And how many are you keeping from them?"

"Shut up!" Jackson yelled.

Suddenly, a shimmer flashed in front of him, and his invisible foe appeared as if out of thin air. The man in front of him had spiked pink hair, blue eyes, and a plump button nose. He wore a black leather jacket, the jolly roger of the Vain Pirates attached to the shoulder. Another User. This time Jackson wouldn't let his guard down as he had with Silvers, and so he placed the key securely around his neck.

The pirate beckoned him forward to the beach-shore, placing his hand behind his back, gripping the serrated blade. Jackson rushed outside to greet him, planting his feet firmly in the soft sand as he went. He was not going to give up an inch of ground, not this time, not if he could help it.

"Brave?" The pirate taunted, raising an eyebrow, as well as his sword.

"I see you're not running away yet. Silvers said you would. That at least has to count for something." The pirate chuckled to himself. "It's a shame I have my orders, I really would like to fight you and succeed where Silvers failed, but I will say this; you should probably go check on your barmaid friend."

And with that, the pirate leapt backwards into the air, vanishing as quickly as he had arrived.

Arabella! Jackson panicked. Was all that just to mess with his head? Still, she was all alone and had no idea what was going on, or what had happened. Once again, the drunk found himself running to Arabella's tavern as fast as he could, only this time it wasn't for a drink. Sweat cascaded down his face. He was dramatically out of breath by the time he arrived, taking alleys and off-beaten paths to avoid the three of four pirate patrols circulating around the town and the docks as he climbed up the hill at a heaving pace. Breathing in profoundly when he reached the double doors, the drunk pressed his hands against the wood and nervously wondered about what he would find inside. Was Arabella going to be there behind the bar? Jackson only hoped he would see her smiling face unharmed.

He pushed the door open and there, stood behind the bar with a scowl plastered across her face, was Arie. Shit! Thought the drunk. Not what he had hoped for when he had just imagined her 'smiling face', but at this point after the interaction he had with the pink-haired pirate, a scowl was more than welcome; though he feared more for whoever had caused such a visage. Jackson smirked. He supposed that that pirate had been right about one thing, Arabella had fire enough to become a queen. Troll or not, whoever the pirates planned to steal her away to did not deserve her in the least.

"Yo." Jackson greeted, catching his breath and resting his arms on the side.

His eyes were frantically searching around the room.

"What are you doing here?" Asked Arabella, wiping the bar. "Aren't you busy taking care of business with my dad? And what about Ann? If the brothers find out someone got onto the island there will be heads to roll."

Jackson smirked slightly at this, but still gave her a very concerned glare.

"What?" She asked again, throwing down the tablecloth in annoyance.

"Has anyone been in here?" Jackson asked, breathlessly panting.

Arabella scowled at him once more.

"Of course, people have been in here. It's the only place open on the island. Pirates have been in and out like crazy, and now I'm closing. Is everything okay, you seem... off?"

"I just needed to see if you were okay, that's all -" Jackson began, but was cut off by the barmaid. He wondered if Arabella knew that the reason the pirates had allowed the tavern to remain open was because of the interest they had in its owner.

"What have you done?" She asked, causing Jackson to screw up his face.

"Nothing." He muttered defensively.

Arie crossed her arms, and eventually Jackson gave in.

"They said they'd come after you!" He exclaimed frantically, and once again searched the room for invisible foes with his eyes.

Arabella's face grew darker as she stared at him, and she reached over the bar, raising her hand high in the air and slapping him as hard as she could, making him recoil.

"I told you not to mess with them, didn't I? We're already in enough trouble as it is."

Jackson grimaced and he knew he had to tell her about her father.

"What?" Asked Arie.

"I think your dad was more involved with them than you know. He tried to kill me at Nelson's, but Ann stepped in."

"Then you should just get out of here. This place is bad enough as it is. Get away while you can. Just take your contract from Ann, go see the world. You've spent enough time wasting away on this small, little island, so just go, get out there. Do it for me and do it for Molly."

Jackson smiled.

"I'll see if I live through this first."

He grinned, glad that everything was as it should be. He clutched the key around his neck. If he really did decide to leave the island after this, he knew the Navy would follow him. Black Ridge Prison was no joke. Was this his final chance to say goodbye, he wondered. With Molly, he had never gotten that chance.

"One more drink for old times' sake then?"

* * *

Fryedai and Ann stood crouched in an alleyway, corralled by dark bricked walls and hot brass tubes. It was the same alleyway she had hidden Tom in, but on arriving there with Fryedai in search of her wounded friend, they found that the old man had disappeared without a trace, leaving Ann sick with worry and concern. As they waited for Jackson, her head peaked around the side of the brickwork. Her red hair dangled in front of her eyes as she watched swarms upon swarms of shadowy-figured apertures run by, frantically scouring the streets. The island had grown gloomy with fog as they waited, and it was now mid-afternoon.

"There are dozens of them." Fryedai whispered in her ear from behind, as he too moved to get a better view, picking up Napoleon in his arms.

"And we need to find a way past." Added Ann, looking at the Alchemist's familiar.

The piglet had fallen asleep some time ago after all the excitement of the morning. The endless ranting about how Jackson had talked to him when Nelson had forbidden him to speak, had tired the poor little familiar out. Fryedai then commented on the weather and how much it had changed on the island from what he had seen during his time above ground during the day. Perhaps they could use that to escape the unwanted gaze of those that searched for them? It surely was a strange, bordering on bewildering, place for the young Navy navigator as he wondered about the strange weather and what had caused his arrival on the island.

"Is this caused by Ash, or something else?" He questioned aloud.

Ann wasn't quite sure herself. Ash-made weather usually portrayed the characteristics and intent of its user, and the fog she had encountered this morning had been different to that of the one that surrounded them now. That one had had a malice to it, a foul and evil intent that was the same as its master's, cold and cruel. The present fog seemed natural and calm yet filled with gloom all the same, as if it had travelled from a dark and foreboding place. Ann assured Fryedai that this was the case, as she knew it was because of where Ale Town sat on the Leon Archipelago.

The chain of islands was frightfully close to Central Sea. It seemed to Ann that the Navy navigator only had knowledge of the weather in his home region, so she continued to explain to Fryedai that all the wisps of the wild elements that managed to escape over the top of the doldrums' walls would eventually wound their way to the shores of the settlements that dwelled the closest; the last island in the chain being the island town in which they were now situated. Several hundred nautical miles was all that separated them from the invisible wall surrounding The Doorstep. Brushing her scarlet hair aside, so it rested just past her ear, she sighed. Ann was now beginning to get frustrated, and this Atlas was really getting on her nerves. She wondered where Tom had got to. Was the old guardian okay? Was he still alive even? It all played out in her mind for the people she had only met that very morning, yet she still called them friends. They had helped her, and she had helped them. Only one question remained: what in all the world was taking Jackson so long with that key?

Suddenly, there was a noise of frantic panting from afar, groaning as if a ghoul had arisen from a long-filled grave. It caused the restless, searching shadows to flee, and both of them peered out the alley with weapons to hand. In front of them, was a dark, shifting platonic figure, swaying from side to side. Ann could hear the scrapes of its misplaced steps as they dragged against the cobblestone. As she raised her weapon, and placed her finger on the trigger, she could hear a familiar hiccupping sound, and she squinted more violently into the distant fog to see what it was.

"Jackson? Jackson, is that you?" She called, peering down the barrel of her gun. "Have you got the key?"

"Don't shoot, don't shoot! It's me, it's me!" The shadow cried, and Jackson stepped forward from one of the steam vents that littered the pavements and roadways of the town.

"Is anyone there?" Called Ann, wanting to know if all the pirates had gone.

"Yeah." Jackson hiccupped and then proceeded to wipe his mouth.

"They're all gone, scared em off. I even managed to swipe this ale along the way, strong stuff. Did you want a bit?" He asked, offering the jug of dark liquid to the red-headed girl.

"Okay."

She supposed one small drop couldn't hurt her after all they had been through, so she swiped the bottle from Jackson's outstretched hand as he toddled off to open Nelson's door at the far end of the street. Ann took a deep swig.

"What are we going to do now then?" Asked Fryedai as they all gathered inside, and Napoleon was laid down in his bed. "It's not like we can just storm the place, can we now?"

Jackson chuckled to himself as he led the group forward, rummaging through the kitchen.

"There's not many ways to get into that place." He explained and then muttered something that nobody heard underneath his breath.

Ann looked at him strangely. She hadn't expected him to be so blunt about his response and she wondered what he had said afterwards.

"And what about everyone else? All those people trapped in the tunnels, working for the brothers, what about them?" She questioned.

"What about them?" Shrugged Jackson.

Clearly something had changed. He then opened the cupboard above him and found another bottle of ale, which he quickly downed.

"They've done nothing for me." He hiccupped. "Everyone apart from Arabella, Nelson, and Tom, left me to rot like a piece of waste, floating in the gutter. I've given my life to this town, and what has it got me in return? Nothing but misery and bloodshed, that's what!"

Ann suddenly felt a pit of rage boil up within her as she watched Jackson drink from the neck of the bottle. After everything she had been through today, she could no longer hold it back and she was about to unload.

"Hey!" She barked at Jackson. "What gives you the right to say that? You said you'd help!"

Her eyes were now flaring, and her hair seemed like it was burning awash with a torrent of flames.

"What did they ever do to you that was so bad in the first place that you would completely abandon them in their hour of need?"

Jackson glared at her.

"Don't pretend to know what it's like being me. You don't know the half of it!"

Ann glared at Jackson as he raided the cupboards for another drink.

"Perhaps I don't know what it's like being you, but at least I know when someone is in pain and know when to help. This entire island needs help, and so do you. Let me help you, I can give you a place to belong." She whispered, growing louder with every word.

"What do you know, Ann?" Jackson boomed suddenly.

He pushed her away with one forceful shove, and her feet crunched against the specs of broken glass. Ann's eyes widened in shock at what he just did, she even noticed Fryedai raise an eyebrow in curiosity as he watched from the hallway. However, she had no choice but to let Jackson continue.

"You know nothing of me, or what I have been through, so just back off, alright!" He said in an almost drunken scream.

Ann seized this opportunity, quickly moving forward to snatch the bottle from him and holding it firmly in her hand. Jackson lurched desperately but Ann was too quick for him and kept the brown, glassy, bottle well out of reach.

"Then tell me." She urged smiling, reminding herself of the way they had met that very morning.

"Fine, just give me my drink back, and I'll tell you all there is." He pleaded, looking up.

His black hair had swung over his red, bloodshot eyes and Ann could tell that all he wanted was another swig of the drink. However, if that continued, they would have no chance to get the upper hand on the brothers and Jackson would continue to be a withering wreck. Huffing, the drunk stormed over to a chair at the other end of the room, collapsing in its embrace and glaring at Ann in a degree of detest. The girl raised an eyebrow as she twirled her hair around her finger.

"Ugh, fine!" He sighed. "You're worse than Arie, but you leave me little choice. You want to know why I'm like this? You wanna know why I prefer to be alone, drinking all the time, despite how much I sorely miss my Molly?"

Ann nodded and placed the bottle on the side of the kitchen counter and walked over to where Jackson was sitting.

"It's because of that place you want to go to so much; Black Ridge Prison." He muttered with a look of dread and fear on his face.

Ann could almost see that the last of his colour had drained entirely.

"I spent two years in that monstrous pit of darkness they call a prison, for something I didn't even do. I don't ever want to relive those memories, those horrible black walls, that evil, unending labyrinth. You want to go diving into that place, for one person? It's impossible!"

"What was it that they said you did?" Ann asked softly, resting her arm on the fireplace.

Jackson clenched his teeth then looked over to the hallway to see if Fryedai was still paying attention.

"Molly and I, we... we took a contract for the N.S.T.C, a simple consignment of goods that we were meant to deliver to some fishing town at the top end of the archipelago. The whole delivery was meant to take about a month, two at the most."

"So, what happened?" Asked Ann. "The Navy doesn't arrest people for trading simple goods on a contract, especially one from the company, no matter how vicious they may be."

Jackson nodded and looked out to the hallway again.

"That was the problem, it wasn't a simple goods run we were doing. The food was packed with illegal and stolen Ash. Molly and I had no idea. We tried to show them the contract, which they checked, but they said the company had never made such a deal and we were arrested and taken to Black Ridge." He explained.

"I'm sorry." Said Ann.

"Don't be. It wasn't your fault, it was those People at the company, who hide behind their government puppet masters, The Lords. They are the ones responsible for what you see before you, this entire world even."

"But that's why I want you to help, to stop the same thing happening to someone else, only this time its way worse. She's going to be put to death, besides you've already said you'd help me get there, did you not?"

Jackson nodded, damning his sense of honour.

"Thank you." Ann said, smiling. "Now, what to do about the pirates?"

Suddenly Fryedai walked back into the room holding the module for the broken cable-phone he had found in the hallway, he too was grinning from ear to ear. Jackson saw what the blonde man was holding and said it wouldn't work; the pirates had gone from door to door when they had arrived and broken all forms of communication.

Fryedai smiled.

"I've modified and fixed it, so we should be able to get a signal out to the nearest transmitting ship."

He seemed hopeful.

"That great!" Grinned Ann, who walked over to have a look at the Navy officer's work.

Fryedai tried to explain to her that anyone listening on particular frequencies would be able to hear them so they would have to be short with their message.

"So how are we going to work this thing out?" She asked after a while, looking at the modified phone with interest. "I can't imagine the brothers are just going to welcome us with open arms as we come barging at their front door."

"And what about the treasure in the tunnels?" Interrupted Fryedai with a concerned look on his face. "They'll surely have that by now and want to leave as soon as possible. Atlas is afraid of someone; he won't risk staying a moment longer. I heard them talking before Orion tried to kill me, they're both running from someone who really wants them dead, badly too."

"Wait, what? Atlas is afraid of someone?"

Both Ann and Jackson were caught in surprise. They looked shocked and wide-eyed, and could not believe such a tyrannical person would have someone to fear. However, the buck stopped at hurting people the way Atlas did, and she would never endanger people like that, not even once.

"Do you know who he's running from?" Ann asked.

"Haven't a clue, but it must be someone awful to go after the man who single-handedly started the war that almost wiped out the giants. There is only one left now, but the Navy files I read say he's reclusive; though I don't believe that for a second."

"Why, who is it?" Ann asked, flicking back her hair.

"One of the Demon Five. His name is Kaine, but he doesn't have much to do with the world. Captain Robbinson heard that all he does is sit in his castle atop a volcano, he's still pretty powerful by all accounts, just he's asleep most of the time."

"Oh, so he'll want revenge if he's the last one, right?"

Fryedai waved his hand in the air and dismissed the idea.

"I doubt it, once giants go to sleep, they're out for almost a year at a time. That's why they grow so much food, so they can feed themselves when they wake up. It's likely that Kaine doesn't know a thing about the wars as he's so far within the Doorstep and just agreed to take the brothers under his wing anyway. Most of the giants lived here in the Outer-Seas, so there was no reason for the brothers to travel that far in on their crusade. But if he does know..."

"Still, that doesn't mean he's the one behind this mess. For all we know he could be sound asleep on a volcanic rock pile somewhere. That's why I don't think the brothers are running from him, it could be someone else."

"Then who?" Asked Ann.

"Haven't a clue, to be honest with you." Shrugged Fryedai, who then turned to ask Jackson a question.

"Still, how do you know they won't leave right away?"

Jackson chuckled.

"You've never sailed around these waters have you, Navy?" Laughed Jackson standing up from his chair and walking back over to the kitchen area, where Ann stood protecting the bottle of booze.

"No." Said Fryedai cautiously, as the drunk stalked around him and into the kitchen.

Ann backed away slightly, and Jackson planted his hands on a smoky brown bottle.

"No, of course you haven't." He huffed, lifting the bottle up to take a big swig.

He gulped as the liquid poured down his throat.

"The Navy outpost you're from doesn't usually come this close to the Archipelago. You're from the South-Sea, am I right?"

He pointed a long swaying finger at the blonde navigator, who stood frozen in place. Then suddenly, Ann snatched the bottle out of Jackson's hand, and sweet ale dripped down his mouth.

"What was that for?" He exclaimed.

Ann crossed her arms with a triumphant look on her face.

"You've had enough. Just get to the point already, would you?"

"Ugh, fine. Are you from the South-Sea or not?" He groaned in a fed-up manor.

Fryedai nodded.

"I knew it, I can tell by the tan colour of your skin. We don't see a lot of Southern-Seas people on the edges of this chain, so I'd say you're inexperienced."

"And what about me?" Ann asked.

"West?" The drunk guessed, looking at her with intrigue and at the complexion of her skin, her red scarlet hair. "The neighbouring archipelago to this one, Taurus?"

"Not even close. Northern-South."

"You're from the Rapids!" The drunk gawked.

Fryedai huffed.

"So, what if I am from the South-Sea? Outpost Forty-two is still the closest command point to here and far nearer than the one in the Taurus chain. That doesn't mean I'm a bad navigator, I just see no reason as to why Atlas would wait. How do you know he'll be around when nightfall comes?"

"Simple, it's because of the Devil's Rush." Said Jackson boastfully, and Fryedai looked even more puzzled than he had done moments before. Even Ann had no idea what the drunk was on about.

"Explain." Ann insisted.

Jackson moved to pat her on the back, but Ann pushed him away.

"Alright."

He looked disappointed.

"It's a local event only found on islands that are closet to the gateways leading into the doldrums zone. The tides of all these islands rush out into the open ocean all at once, and once a month, when it's a full moon, people can get into the Doorstep without getting caught in the doldrums. It also means that no one can leave the islands at night because there is no tide to catch, that's why this sea is one of the hardest to navigate, because things constantly move."

"Okay, when does this Devil's Rush start?"

"It usually starts around eight and goes on to the early hours of the morning, the tide appears back somewhere in the region of five or six o'clock the morning after."

"And tonight is the night a Devil's Rush is going to happen?" Fryedai asked.

Jackson rolled his eyes.

"Yes, Fryedai. That's why I mentioned it, they won't be able to go anywhere."

"Well, that's good news at least. Now we just have to stop them." He mumbled sarcastically.

"Hey, what about that message?" Asked Ann, pointing at the phone still sat on the kitchen counter. "Didn't you say we could reach the next island with that?"

"Yeah, but we'll only be able to send a short message, anything longer than a few seconds could blow the system and we'll only have enough power to do it once."

"Guess we better make this quick. Put something like this: Pirates come quick...help needed... Atlas Vain. I think that should be short enough, what do you think?"

"Yeah, that should work!" Nodded Fryedai with a smile, and he quickly set to work tuning in to the Navy's signal and reattaching the keypad.

A breeze passed by from an open window and the room filled with a frightfully cold chill for a midday afternoon. Ann clutched and rubbed her arms to keep warm as she wandered next to the bed that lay in the corner, her eyes full of sleep. She'd had a long and tiring day so far and she looked back to the Familiar sleeping in a bed of his own. Napoleon had the right idea.

"I'm going to sing a song to send myself off to sleep. I have a feeling we'll need the rest."

Jackson's eyes widened.

"Wait, you didn't say anything about singing..." He protested but it was too late, Ann had already started to sing, tossing logs onto the fireplace as she went.

They crackled to a spark.

"O, the year was unknown, and I do not know,

O, how I wish I were a braver man!

When a letter of chance slid from the deep,

To the scummiest ship that was sinking beneath,

I damn you all!

I was told we'd ride the waves for Company gold, We'd fire no guns -shed no tears.

Now I'm a broken man on a sinking ship, with a bottle in hand and nothing to sip,

I damn you all!

Have some fear!

For it's the last of Barrett's Privateers.

Now, Captain Barrett, he was said and done,

O, how he wished he were a braver man!

His crew all dead and he the only one,

He damned them all!

For he sat and drank his life away, until one day a mate did say,

What ills you friend,

I was told you were sailing the waves for blood n' gold,

Did you fail?

No, my man – I just lost the crew, to Jones' locker by the Kraken's hand slew,

I damned them all!

Now I'm sailing the waves for Company gold,

Firing no guns-shedding no tears,

And the Kraken will be had by the end of the year,

For I'm,

The last,

Of Barrett's,

Privateers!"

Finally, Ann had finished loading the fire and now the roaring, crackling flames danced across the logs in the space underneath the hearth, warming the room.

"Wow, that was amazing, shame it was a pirate song. Other than that it was absolutely perfect."

Fryedai was almost lost for words.

Ann blushed.

"Why thank you, Fryedai. Now, if you don't mind, I'm going to get some rest."

And with that, Ann left the room, shutting the door behind her, leaving a slightly tipsy Jackson alone with Fryedai.

21

As he lay awake, Jackson kept thinking about that moment repeatedly in his head.

'You should just get out of here. This place is bad enough as it is. Get away while you can. Just take your contract from Ann, go see the world. You've spent enough time wasting away on this small, little island, so just go, get out there. Do it for me and do it for Molly.' She had said.

He listened to the harrowing wind and the pouring rain as it sprayed the outside world. Then he wondered: Was he really going to Black Ridge again? Maybe he wanted to. As Arie said, then he would at least be away from here after this pirate blockade was all said and done. That would at least give him some freedom to get away from town and everyone he knew. They had always been judgemental of him, and when Molly had gone, they blamed him for her leaving. They lost their best brewer that day they said, and Ale Town would never be the same again.

Nelson – he hoped they got to him soon, that nothing terrible had happened to him. Unfortunately, the streets were flooded with Vain's men and the only time they could get away was when night fell.

Perhaps he should go away? He thought again. Ann had saved him countless times today and by that alone it made her worthy of his trust. Besides, going away would give everyone a chance to forget about him, especially Nelson. Nevertheless, he still did not know for sure, and with that, Jackson closed his eyes, his mind finally cleared as the fresh ocean wind drifted over him and he sang himself a lullaby as he rested by the fire.

It was the first thing Nelson had taught him when they were kids, and it always brought him comfort in hard situations as it reminded him of carefree days.

"Tie and hold that rigging down lad,

Turn to port and set that sail lad,

Set your course and venture on lad, You will now be

sailing.

Cannons blast all around us,

Captain's dead, so it's just us,

Navy's still gaining on us, We must fire back, sir.

Catch the wind and hold them back now,

Do be brave they might still catch ya,

If they do they'll probably kill ya,

Cos you are a Pirate!"

"Ann, I trust you now." He spoke. "Try not to mess it up."

Act 4:
A Monster's Rage

22

It was now approaching seven o'clock, and it had been many hours since Jackson – or anyone for that matter – had come to visit the bar.

"Damn that Jackson!" Arabella cursed, as she thought about what the drunk had said a few hours earlier; an invisible pirate, he had told her.

She surmised at the time he was probably off his rocker, but then again perhaps not, with all the weird and strange powers these pirates had. Still, she could not keep herself from feeling sorry for Jackson as she looked at the ribboned bracelet charm that he had given her. It gave way to the fact that she did believe him a little, in some small form or another, because what reason did a stupid drunk like him have to lie? He did care about her after all, despite all she had said to him during the past few weeks since the pirates had arrived. It had broken his heart and hers when she had described the small, lingering feelings that had grown for the silver-haired quartermaster. Something gnawed at her when she thought about him, pulled her away into the background of her thoughts until a white light glowed, but then the light would stop, and a warm feeling would wash over her until she felt like herself again.

Suddenly there was an enormous crash from behind the bar, and kegs of ale erupted, sending splinters and gallons of ale across the room.

"Aw." A voice doted, sounding amused, as if out of thin air. "I've been sat here quietly watching you for the last couple of hours now, it's a shame that we have to go so soon, but oh well, I guess it's time to close up shop."

Arabella's eyes widened in horror, as a man appeared in front of her, almost from thin air.

"Nice place you have. You won't be needing it anymore, not where we're going anyhow. Atlas says that you're to come with me."

Arabella crossed her arms in defiance and flicked her hair to the side. She could see the determination in the pirate's eyes, but she was not going to let him win, as she once again felt that warm feeling washing over her, giving her strength.

"And why would I do what a pirate says, anyway? I'm not going anywhere, that's final! So, get out of my bar right now!" She exclaimed, pointing her arm to the door in anger.

She wasn't going to run, not if she could help it. She wasn't a coward like her father was, who keeled over at the first chance he got in the way Jackson had told her he had.

The pirate laughed again.

"Certainly, my dear." He quipped in a contrastingly relaxed manner.

A twinge of fear raced down Arabella's spine. Jackson had warned her this might happen, and she ignored it entirely as a part of his drunken ramblings.

"But I'm bringing you with me, whether you like it or not."

Arabella turned to the door to run, but it was too late. Suddenly the pirate reached to grab her. She ducked down as fast as she could and bolted towards the double doors, however, the floor had become wet and slick awash with a golden stream of alcohol that had spread across the tavern floor when the kegs had exploded, and she immediately found herself skidding. She screamed and squirmed in protest as the pirate grabbed her, but Gillian just ignored her calls all the same.

"Let me go, let me go!" She cried repeatedly, flailing her arms thunderously across his back.

The pink-haired pirate sighed.

"Oh, do shut up!" He groaned, holding her tightly. "These are my captain's orders. Otherwise, I'm going to have to put you out, and well, that would just ruin the fun for me. One more word out of you, and its nighty-night, do you understand?"

Arabella turned on her side as much as she could, blowing her frizzy blonde hair out of the way so she could see what the pirate was doing, and where he was taking her.

"Bite me." She growled, and surprisingly, the pirate set her down and glared at her, a furious look on his face.

His pink tangled hair matched his flustered appearance. His button nose scrunched up tightly.

"Run!" He scowled as he turned around, going back to the bar to fetch his blade.

Arabella heard him heft the sword on to the top of his shoulder. The next thing she saw was the pirate running at her, blade entirely drawn and sparks flying.

"I need you to run!" He screamed as he ran down the road towards her.

This time Arabella did what he said, she ran. Her footsteps struck the hard cobblestone brickwork, and she bolted down the street, the palest silver moonlight illuminating her way. All she had to do was keep on running as fast as her legs would carry her. She had to try to keep away from the raging monster, hot on her tail. But where could she go? To Jackson's? To Nelson's? They were too far away for her to run and survive. How would she ever get away from the pirate that now followed? Most of this side of town was relatively broad and open, and there was no way she would ever make it to the train station in time. In addition to this, Gillian could turn invisible, so there was no way of knowing if she had truly gotten away for sure.

"Got you!" The pirate growled.

Arabella felt a hand grab her and everything turned to black as the hilt of a blade knocked her clean out.

23

When Arabella came to, the first thing she heard and smelled, was the unrelenting dripping of what sounded like running water and the stale smell of fermented alcohol. She felt the rough texture of cloth on her skin, and rope around her wrists.

"Hello, is anyone there?" She called. "I need help!"

She was desperate for anyone to reply. She couldn't bear not being able to see what was going on.

"I'm here." The pirate cooed, making Arie's heart sink. "But I'm not going to help you. Why would I do that when you tried to run away from me so vigorously."

"But you told me to run. You wanted me to run, didn't you?" Arabella replied.

She could tell she had touched a nerve because the pirate stayed quiet for a moment, so much so that she heard the individual drops as the water fell.

"I did, I did, but that's because I enjoy the chase so much." He growled. "Unfortunately for you, you weren't any good at it, but still, that is not the reason you're here."

"Then why?" Arabella cried, just wanting the whole experience to end.

"You are here." He continued. "Because Atlas needs you to be here. We made a deal with one of the three Troll kings, and you were the price agreed upon."

Arabella gritted her teeth in horror.

"So, they were real." She whispered to herself, remembering the tales Jackson used to tell the others in the tavern about how he would keep close to the rock of a bay or island at night when in certain parts of the seas.

"You think you can get away with this? Does he think the Navy will just let him get away with the violent murders he has committed? And now you add abduction to the list! Atlas won't get away with this. They'll catch you when you get out to sea."

"Why don't you ask him yourself? He's on the line right now."

Abruptly, the pirate ripped away the blindfold and Arabella could see that they were sat in what looked like the cabin of a ship. The walls were wooden, sodden with seawater, and thick with an algae crust. The pirate then shoved a microphone in her face, and Arabella's neck shot backwards. The black mesh of the receiver crackled and spat as the signal came through, and each static pop held a moment of dread as the voice of Atlas vain echoed across the room.

"Gillian, is she there? Have you got her?" Snapped the pirate captain.

Gillian turned the microphone towards himself and held it at his mouth.

"Yeah, I have her alright. Can't wait to get out of this place and blow it sky high!"

Wait, what? Arabella thought.

"You'll have to wait a little bit longer, the tide has just started receding, and we can't get off. We're collecting the rest of the diamonds from the tunnel. Put the girl on." The captain commanded.

Gillian then smiled and turned the cable-phone back towards Arie.

"Hello, girl. I'm sure you're wondering why you are here, so I'll put this simply for you. Your father traded you for wealth and fortune. Out of all the women on this island, he chose you. His own daughter, to be discarded to a hideous Troll, and now he is dead! That drunken boyfriend of yours is the one to blame. You see, he let someone essential get away from us and I just could not allow that to slide. Now all the diamonds will belong to us, and your town, by the morning, will be no more. You can have faith that his face will be the last friendly one you will ever see."

24

The skies turned from a bright orangey-blue to an encapsulating obsidian-like black. Letting the stars shine through its darkening blanket like pure diamonds. Ann looked up in wonder as she thought of what it would be like to fly through those stars. The moment would have almost carried her away if Fryedai had not tugged on her arm as the three of them sneaked up the dark green hill that had grown pale in the eclipsing moon. Jackson was leading them to the manor house, and soon they would find a way inside.

As they stalked up the hill, the windmill at the top of the house creaked and churned. As it spun, an orange torchlight shone out from the top window as the sails passed. Ann had a feeling that Jackson would want to sneak in there, as who would be crazy enough to climb a spinning windmill?

They kept low to the ground, trying to stay free of any unwanted attention, and Ann whistled in a low pitch for Jackson to make the first move. The drunk ran forward as the mill blocked out the window of light, grabbing on to a rudder as tight as he could, allowing the sail to carry him. When he reached the top, he dived into the open window, scuffling around as he did.

Ann now did the same, the sail's thin blue material fluttered in the slight wind against the constraints of its wooden frame.

"Just grab on and let it take you." She heard Jackson whisper from above as she was about to grip the sail.

Ann scowled at him.

"Well sorry if I haven't done this before. I don't sneak into my ex-girlfriend's house every night!"

"Watch out!" Jackson pointed from below, as the sail got nearer.

Then suddenly, thwack! The sail hit Ann in the face, and she staggered back.

"You could have warned me!" She hissed, looking up as the bandanna she wore fell to the ground.

Ann turned to see Fryedai, chuckling in the grass next to her, and she glared at him.

"I did." Replied Jackson.

He kept looking around the room, just in case any pirates appeared.

"Now get the next one quickly. We haven't got the time, remember?"

Ann rolled her eyes and flicked back her hair to its usual place. She stood to the side and grabbed the next sail as it passed her by and was gradually lifted off her feet. The windmill sails creaked and groaned as they worked their way around, and Ann could feel herself losing her grip as she struggled to stay on. Eventually, she reached the top and Jackson pulled her in.

"Let's get Fryedai up quickly so we can get moving. The sooner we can stop them, the better." Stated Jackson, looking down at Fryedai through the window.

"Wasn't there an easier way to get into the house?" Groaned Ann, getting up from the wooden panelled floor.

"Not if you didn't want to get caught there wasn't." He muttered, signalling to Fryedai to get moving.

"You two catch me up." Ann said. "I'm going to see if I can find these tunnels."

"But what about Fryedai? He knows where they are." Argued Jackson, slightly shocked at how eager she was to take on the brothers.

"I'm in a hurry." Pleaded Ann. "I'm sure you can understand that."

"Ugh, fine." Jackson sighed. "Go down the hatch, then through the kitchen and follow the rooms till you get to the hall. According to the 'Navy' down there, the tunnels are in the back rooms, down another hatch."

Ann nodded and headed down the stairway and into the kitchen. Strangely, as she reared her head around the end of the stairs, she saw that no one was there. Kitchen equipment had been left abandoned on the side of work counters, as well as empty sacks of grain; their previous contents scattered across the stone floor. It looked like the pirates had finally started to ship out, and Ann knew her eagerness had been justified. She rushed through the many combined rooms, flailing back the curtained doorways and soon reached the main hall, where a long table sat in the middle of the room. At the back was a tall wicker chair with a smaller table and a bowl.

"Pathetic." Ann mumbled to herself as she stepped up to the chair to investigate.

So, Atlas Vain fancies himself a King? She thought.

Next to his so-called throne, Ann saw an empty bowl with specks of Ash surrounding it. This did not surprise her at all, but what did was what sat just behind it, covered by a grey cloth. She ripped the scrawny rag away to reveal more stacks of empty brown bowls, all surrounded by the remainders of many powders.

No wonder he was so feared. Ann now realised the true magnitude of it all and wondered how much power one mortal could accumulate. The pirate captain was an addict!

Behind the wicker chair, Ann found an open doorway, just as Fryedai and Jackson had said, covered by a draped, tattered curtain. The curtain waivered almost in anticipation, and Ann crept forward, slowly reaching to pull the ragged sheet back. She passed through the curtain, seeing that the doorway led into yet another room. But where were the pirates? Where was Atlas? Was she alone?

At the end of the room was the hatchway Jackson spoke of. However, unlike what Fryedai had mentioned, the wooden and cast-iron door was sealed shut, a lock bolted across it. Ann hurried over to the lock and pointed the barrel of her pistol down the keyhole. Out of seemingly nowhere, she heard someone creeping along the old wooden floor and her heart thumped as she thought about where the pirates had got to. If they weren't ahead of her, then they could sneak up behind her, so she turned her gun to the doorway, as she didn't have the time to blow the lock.

The curtain peeled back. The manor house had been silent as she had wandered through it. Not a soul she had seen, not a pirate in sight, and now her heart and head leapt for joy as she saw Jackson and Fryedai patter cautiously in.

"Geez." The drunk sighed, bursting into the room once it was clear that only she was there. "Did your parents ever tell you to look before you shoot. I know mine did, you could have killed us!"

Ann laughed in relief.

"My mother home-schooled me." She explained, taking her finger off the gun. "Wen was the one who taught me to shoot. She always said to trust my instincts."

"Well, your instincts need work. Who's this Wen, anyway?" Asked Fryedai.

"My best friend." Responded Ann sadly, once again looking down at the closed hatch.

"She's the one in that place, isn't she? The one you want to rescue?" Said Jackson.

Ann flicked back her hair once again.

"Yeah, she is. She means a lot."

Jackson grunted.

"Well, let's get a move on and kick Atlas' arse. I'm tired of paying too many Threds for my drinks! Hopefully we can find Tom and Nelson down there. That old fool thought he was the guardian of this place – fine job he did."

Ann gave him a small smile. It was nice to see some humour and light-heartedness, given their situation. She then pointed her gun towards the floor and the barricaded door and squeezed the trigger, causing the lock to fly free with an almighty bang. If the pirates didn't know they were here before, then they would definitely know the three of them were coming for them now.

"Well, here we go." Said Ann and they started to make their way down the hatch, down into the confined spaces that Ann knew would torment her.

When they reached the bottom, she could feel stale air pass them, it made the hairs on the back of her neck stand to attention and both the boys shuddered. From what she could see in the darkness, the walls of the tunnel were covered in hard, ebony rock.

"It's a little down this way." Fryedai stated, walking forward into the darkness and gloom.

It left Ann and Jackson no choice but to follow him, and neither of them knew where it led. They could feel the temperature around them skyrocket; the damp sprinkling of dripping water in the distance, along with a relentless groan, from what sounded like tormented ghouls, made the caverns feel haunted, yet alive. How anyone survived under here for any amount of time was a mystery to Ann. Feeling the dark rocks enclose around her made her feel a sense of claustrophobic dread and it cemented the anger she felt towards the brothers. She hated feeling enclosed and trapped. She was always a free spirit, she needed room to breathe and run free as she pleased. At the very least she wasn't alone this time, and she wasn't confined to a cabin for weeks on end nor was she trapped inside a cellar, unable to escape. Ann had friends with her, friends that she could trust and rely on.

Jackson let out a clear sigh. These caverns and tunnels were as dark and twisting as the Hells of the Underworld, and it was Fryedai's job to lead them through the tunnels as he limped his way through the dark crags. They had to rescue everyone they possibly could if they were going to stand a chance. Not making any noise was key, so that the pirates - wherever they were - couldn't catch them. Ann smiled slightly given the circumstances. She guessed that Fryedai was excited to finally have a chance to save everyone on his crew, and she found it admirable that he had remained as upbeat as she had. A strong heart and a strong mind will do a lot for a person in this world. She had told Jackson those very words this morning, and now she had to console herself with them, as the three of them wandered further into the awaiting shadows. The right side of the tunnel was scorching hot and vented with steam. No wonder the entire town had chosen to capitalise on it when it generated so much heat. Ann was beginning to see why the pirates were getting so many diamonds from the temperature and the pressure.

The group abruptly came to a halt, although there were still none of the brothers' men in sight. A small orange torch flickered between them. It stood on a metal stand in the middle of a divide. There was a choice to make now; two tunnels, two openings.

"Which way?" Jackson whispered.

Fryedai hesitated for a moment, confused by what was before him.

"Oh, come on kid. Even the talking sandwich would have an opinion on this!" The drunk complained, his eyes bulging out of his sockets in frustration.

His wavy hair twitched in front of him, giving him an unnerving edge.

"I... I don't know." Stuttered Fryedai as he looked at Jackson and then to the openings. "This wasn't here the last time. I don't know."

Jackson glared at him, and Fryedai winced, causing Ann to step in.

"It doesn't matter now. Let's just pick a way and choose that one. I can hear the groaning coming from both of them, so no matter which one we choose, our friends might be down either."

"I have to save my friend, you understand?" Jackson said pleadingly, looking to Ann. "I can't lose him, that pig will give me hells! And I can't lose another person because of something I did!"

"I understand that, trust me, I do. But shouting at him won't change the fact that we have a choice to make, and I for one think we'll cover more ground if we split up and investigate both."

Jackson frowned, looking to Fryedai and then to Ann as the orange light flickered.

"I can't believe we left the pig back at the house." He uttered. "Looks like you're following me then."

Thus, Jackson pushed passed them both, picking a crag to venture down. The slim openings left little room for them both to fit and Ann breathed in as she brushed passed the dagger-like teeth that grew from the rock, leaving Fryedai to follow the other path.

"Do you think the kid will be alright?" Jackson asked her after a minute.

Ann paused.

"Yeah, I think so. He's dealt with this place once already today, so what can be the harm of going back? I mean he's armed, so he can handle himself. Why, did he say anything to you before coming here?"

"No, not at all. He just wants to get your crew back. He just does it in a different way than you or me, that's all."

"Aw, look at you caring."

Jackson blushed.

"You saw how I care for Nelson just now, how I care for Arabella. I'm just saying that's a dangerous place to be when the people you love are in danger."

"Yeah, I get that." Ann replied, thinking about Wen and what her closest friend in the world must have been experiencing at that very moment.

"Hells! That's the whole reason you are here, right?" Continued Jackson. "So, you can pay me to give you passage to save your friend? But I've been thinking about it all day. That's not the kind of thing the Navy is known for."

Shit, Ann thought as she quickly realised where the conversation was leading.

"In my experience, once you're guilty, you're guilty. They don't let their members go off to rescue the people they've incarcerated. So why are you so different, that you would risk their wrath to go to such a place as Black Ridge Prison?"

Ann was silent for a second, wondering how much he had figured out. The two of them continued to walk forward as they went along the side of the tunnel wall. They listened to their feet crunch against the ground and to the tiny droplets of water splashing in the echoing distance.

"Well?" Jackson asked, but for once Ann didn't know what to say.

What could she say to him that would make sense; that he would believe? She couldn't lie to the man that had finally accepted her offer of friendship. Over the last couple of hours, they had opened up to each other so much and she didn't want to throw that friendship away over a technicality.

"Did they give you a secret mission or something? Because I can't think of another reason, or have you just gone rouge?"

Ann's heart swelled in her chest, and she felt her palms begin to grow cold and clammy as they had done during her game of Scourge with Arabella. What in all the world could she even say to him? The drunk was so untrusting of strangers, of The Company, of pirates! Ann struggled to think of something to say that would appeal to Jackson's hubris; his sense of honour, which would make him believe she was a truly good person. There were so many things that Ann feared. Secrets, along with whispers that remained hidden behind dusty shadows, and grim, Stygian countenances. Many things to do with Ash, The Company, and The Lords. So many things that she had had to overcome in her life and even more awaited her. How could she possibly begin to convey all of that to a man that judged all too quickly? Still, there was a similarity to them both that had drawn them together. Jackson had lost Molly, and Ann would be damned to the Hells if she or him lost anyone else.

"Jackson -" She began.

Her red hair clung to the rocks slightly behind her as they passed by, and her palms began to grow firmer as she decided on what she was going to tell him, but suddenly, the navigator's eyes widened, and he quickly shouted something back that Ann did not understand through the echo of the cave. All of a sudden, Jackson reached back and tackled her down to the floor. Ann had the briefest glimpse of what was happening, and ahead of them something shimmered and flashed in their faces like a silver shooting star. Jackson rolled Ann over on the ground, but all she could hear was the very slight but constant buzzing around her ears. She looked at the drunk in a daze as she held her hands up to her ears. Despite his mouth moving, there were no words escaping in his usual drunken slur. Her vision faded in and out, between coloured blurs and black blotches, even Jackson's face seemed twisted and distorted, and it turned into something horrible from her past.

"Get away from me!" She yelled as she saw scales, teeth, and fire!

Her arm erupted in a flare of stinging pain, and a speeding silver star scraped across her leather jacket as she continued to move. Ann gritted her teeth to stop a scream from escaping her lips and suddenly the vision faded. The fire was gone, the hissing was no more, and the dragon-like scales that crawled across Jackson's skin had disappeared. After a few moments of rolling around and scraping against the rock, her vision returned, and it was then that all the words Jackson mouthed to her came blaring out in an audible rush.

"It's okay, it's okay, I've got you, I've got you." He assured her softly.

Ann looked to her side and saw that her jacket and arm were completely undamaged.

She wondered what had happened, as she patted herself down just to be sure. She could have sworn that a spinning blade had crossed against her side and a monster had come to feed on her, so why wasn't she dead?

"What was that?" She gasped, glaring at Jackson and then to the floor.

Jackson looked at her softly, though with hints of anger and annoyance.

"One of the pirates' traps, I imagine."

The look on his face told the teenager all she needed to know; Jackson knew this pirate well.

"Silvers?" Ann questioned.

Jackson nodded and shrugged as he let Ann go, though he barely remembered what it felt like the first time the silver-haired, purple-necked pirate had messed with him and Ann continued to question what had happened as it played tricks on her mind.

"I wouldn't put it past him. When you fell to the floor and started groaning, I saw Nelson and Arabella in front of me running further into the tunnel. You looked a bit worse for wear though. It's probably because of what you allowed Napoleon to do to me at the Trafalgar that I wasn't seriously affected."

Ann shook her head, a deadly seriousness about her.

"They're trying to separate us. Have you still got the Ash I tried to steal from you this morning?"

"So, you did try to steal it?"

Jackson quirked an eyebrow, as he looked down to his money pouch, still filled with the electric blue and red powder.

"Yeah, but there's not much left."

"Take it now." She urged. "We're going to take them out. No one messes with my head and gets away with it."

Ann then staggered away from the wall and picked up her pistol that was laying on the floor. Her head was heaving, a dull ache pervaded and now she could hear whispers hissing to her mind of memories far off into the past. She had to think of happy thoughts to push all the pain away; the memories of family dinners and breakfasts she no longer had, her mother Alice, brushing her hair. She thought about the times when she sat in her father's workshop on the side-bench (after he had caught her sneaking in), as he went about his work in the moonlight, or of the Traveller coming to their house every year since Ann could remember and getting a gift and a story. But most importantly, Ann thought of Wen, and the time they had spent together, along with that of a little boy, smiling brilliantly and as radiant as the sun.

"Okay? But isn't that kind of dark for a Navy officer?" Jackson asked, raising an eyebrow yet again.

Ann shook her head clear.

"You have to think like these people to beat them."

25

Fryedai was pleased that he finally found something to make a torch out of as he wandered down the dark tunnel path. What he was less pleased about however, was the fact that he was left to wander it alone. It was hot and even worse, it was cramped.

He approached the next crack in front of him, which whistled and groaned as a breeze passed through, making the water on the walls glisten with a black gloss.

"I hate these things." He whispered, shimmying along the crack.

After a few moments of struggle, he finally pushed his body through and leapt out of the other side, where his leg once again exploded in a dull pain. It was pitch black, and he felt helpless without the safety of the warm torchlight. There was no turning back, however.

He trudged further into the tunnel, his forehead dripping with sweat. Suddenly laughter erupted and echoed around the rough walls, and Fryedai froze in fear. It bounced off the rocks like a ricocheting bullet. As he drew nearer, he recognised whom it was that the sound came from; Orion Vain!

"Work, you dogs, work!" Orion barked as he cracked a whip.

He was standing over a group of enslaved townspeople as they toiled against the dark rock. Sparks of ice erupted from the picks with every hit. Fryedai recognised someone in the group from his crew, and realised it was Commander Rockwell along with one of the twins that he had befriended on their voyage. The Commander was alive, to his surprise. He was covered in bloody cuts and gashes, his once great brown beard tangled in a messy and muddied knot. Fryedai rubbed his leg as he peered over a rock. He saw that the Commander still had that cold, hard, steel look in his eyes that he was known for on the ship, and he gave the pirate a look of solid defiance. Sadly, his hair had been torn at, his skin broken and blistered in places, and Fryedai had to blink twice before he recognised his friend, chained to Rockwell in harsh iron.

Luke, the Bosun, dropped to his knees in exhaustion, collapsing on the floor in a sweat. The navigator remembered Captain Robbinson telling him about the Ash sickness that people developed from the overuse of the mineral. It started first with hallucinations and dreams that gradually became worse over time. A fever would then develop, shrouded with cold sweats, and the person would lose consciousness from time to time, slowly turning them crazed before they died from exhaustion.

"Work, you good for nothing sea-brat!" Orion roared.

He brought his whip down on the Bosun repeatedly, like an axe felling a tree, and the crack echoed throughout Fryedai's side of the tunnel.

"Stop!" Fryedai interrupted, appearing from the darkness into the bright torchlight.

He couldn't bear to watch people suffer any longer, and he took out the dagger from his side-pocket.

Orion turned around and smiled at him with a broad, cat-like grin.

"Well, well, well, what do we have here?" He snarled, cracking the strap down, causing Luke to wail in pain. "Look who crawled back into the gutter from whence he came. Looking for another beating? Or do you want me to kill another one of your crewmates right in front of you?"

Fryedai gripped his dagger tightly as he watched the psychotic pirate laugh and kick his friend.

"That's enough!" Fryedai demanded.

Orion turned his head to one side, glaring at him with a dilated bloodshot eyeball.

"What was that you just said, little bird?"

Fryedai began to tremble, but he somehow managed to maintain his composure. He had to remember that he was here to save everyone and get justice for what happened to the captain. Only then could he forgive himself for running away.

"I said enough!" He yelled.

Orion smirked once more, slightly surprised.

"Great!" He mused, turning to look at Luke's strained face as he unbuckled his sword from his belt, dropping his whip to one side. "She has found her voice, your friend, hasn't she? Well, I hope you can fight as well as you scream, because I'm itching to kill something, and I really want to make you scream!" He roared, pointing his cutlass directly at Fryedai's chest.

Fryedai raised his dagger in response.

"You're the only one who's going to be screaming, pirate!"

Orion lowered his sword slightly and began cackling like a starving desert dog.

"Well, that's funny, because I remember your captain saying the same thing right before I gutted him and hung him up to die!"

Fryedai froze in terror, his bravado suddenly gone; he still made sure to grip the dagger. He watched as Orion's cutlass dropped down next to his leg. The pirate continued to play with it as his monologue continued.

"O', the look on his face when he realised that he was going to bite the dust, it was priceless!" He grinned, now within a metre of Fryedai. "I don't ever think I'll forget it for as long as I live. The way he sobbed and pleaded was music, like a dream. You Navy really are something, aren't you? You're all so weak and helpless. Not like Atlas. Not like my father. It's like you're asking me to kill you, and what do you know? When I'm just about done with killing you all, you just turn up on my doorstep out of the blue, offering yourself up on a silver platter!"

Orion was now stood towering over Fryedai, gazing down at him. What was he going to do? What was he going to do against such a terrifying foe like this sniggering jackal? Fryedai had to do something about his snarling, grinning face and he had to put things right. The captain would have wanted him to stay strong.

* * *

It had been a while since they split from Fryedai. Jackson already felt like he needed another drink. He stumbled along the path, dragging one foot in front of the other as they scraped across rocky black dirt. Ann was a little ahead of him. She offered no support or encouragement as they continued to venture on into the depths of the tunnel. For her, he guessed this was becoming personal, and again he continued to question why. Who was she? He wondered; this red-headed girl with alloyed heart of iron and gold.

Jackson saw how she hated the slavery that the pirates had placed the people under with a passion at the restaurant. He guessed it must have had something to do with her own past, which she wasn't entirely sharing with everybody else.

Why? He thought again.

Jackson had noticed how Ann had particularly avoided telling the young Navy officer her name, even though they were supposedly apart of the same crew. Had he been right then? They had a deal, of course. She was going to help take care of the pirates, and in return, he was going to take her where she wanted to go, but that didn't mean he couldn't find every little detail about her first. Who was this person he had placed his trust in? Ann who? Ann...

"Hey, Jackson?" She called back to him from up ahead.

"Yeah." He replied, snapping back from his thoughts and focusing on her in the poor light. "What is it?"

"Have you taken that Ash yet?"

Jackson shook his head, looking down to the filled money-bag on his belt and the small little ball he had made.

"Well, you better do it soon. We're coming up to an opening, and I see a bunch of lights. We might be near Silvers and that antechamber that Fryedai mentioned?"

Jackson groaned slightly, picked up the pea-sized ball from his money pouch and holding it between his fingers. He was going to do it. He was actually going to take Ash for the first time despite all the trouble it had caused him. He let himself have one more small memory seep back into his head before taking it. It was the day The Company approached him, and despite his misgivings, Molly had urged him with a smile, telling him that everything would be all right and work out in the end, that it would be an adventure. Just the two of them.

It didn't work out in the end though. Would this?

As he took the Ash, Jackson felt a jolt of energy burst into him. All his senses felt heightened, and he could move faster than he ever could before. His hands were a blur as he pushed them back and forth in distorted, faded lines. The Ash he had just taken gave him the power to run at almost impossible speeds and control the kinetic energy around him. It was like getting over a hangover in an instant. Like having a boundless, constant rush of energy flow through him for the rest of a conceivable lifetime. Finally, he was ready to face the pirates.

"Ready." He stated to Ann, and they both squeezed out of their narrow walkway into a large cavern space.

It was dark and black, dimly lit by orange and blood red touches prostrated down either side of a worn track. Bamboo scaffolds, taken from the jungle forest, propped up the sides of the cavern and narrowed to a point where the torches converged with green-yellow limbs and twinkling diamonds. Ahead of them, Jackson and Ann could hear far off voices from somewhere inside the cavern, and they ran into the domed antechamber ahead. Could that have been Nelson or Tom?

As they rushed to save their friends, they noticed rubble littered the ground in frozen clumps around a circular opening of what looked like cracked tortoise shell. The shell was scarred along the edges, and the middle had strange writing that Ann had never seen before carved within. It was scrawled with harsh, primitive, jagged lines. The girl could make no sense of what it said, she only knew it was old. As old and as ancient as Tom had told her. Perhaps as old, as ancient, and as dark as the island and caverns themselves.

"Where is everyone?" Asked Ann when she eventually caught up to Jackson, as he was far ahead, peering around the room.

The walls of the dome were engraved with golden drawings, beyond the like that Ann had ever seen. Some were straight and symmetrical, others had flowing, wavy lines. It began on one end of the room and continued all around. Firstly, Ann was drawn to the six majestic golden figures that stood below a behemoth Ash tree. From the looks of things, the drawings illustrated a story. From what she could assume, there was one of three men and three women, as half of the figures had long and flowing hair in the central image that held vigil over the empty podium that sat in the centre of the chamber. Half of the figures held weapons. A man with sky-blue eyes emblazoned by sparkling sapphires carried a spear. Then a woman positioned next to him, in golden leaf, with equally coloured eyes of topaz, held a trident. Her hair was coloured in a dark-liquor plaque, encrusted with flecks of gold. It flowed through the drawing as if it was a body of water, until it reached the final man brandishing a weapon, who stood apart from the other five. He was wielding a bident, a two-pronged fork with ends as sharp as any spear. This man only had one of his eyes coloured, the socket filled with a deep amethyst and in the other hole, nothing, as if he or the chamber had been robbed. Ann's eyes quickly scanned the chamber as she and Jackson raced further in, and she was surprised to find the treasure room baron and bare, with the exception of the golden-leaf engravings and the empty podium. Had the pirates taken everything already? Around them, there was nothing but flickering shadows, dancing next to dimly lit touches. The entire place had been stripped bare.

Out of nowhere, from the very edge of the room, came a sniggering laughter, followed by a terrible howl, and two men stepped out from within the shadows. One of them was Silvers, snow-white hair, and bulging purple-red scar, slithering around his neck. The other was bald, with a black goatee beard and standing an immeasurable foot above the pirate quartermaster. Jackson knew in an instant this was the elusive pirate captain he had heard so much about. Tattoos sprawled across his arms like vines of black ink, and held in his right hand, the glistening golden fingertips of what looked like a piece of an unfinished glove.

The treasure! Jackson thought - if that's what it really was? It was awe inspiring to him, and more than he dared ever imagine. It seemed to be alive. The whispers, the rumours, everything had been real!

The pirate then spoke.

"I can assure you, girl, Mister Nelson and your other friend are quite safe for now. Rather, at least we think they are. We have the cook safely stored away under protection, along with the rest of the rats."

Jackson gave Ann a worried glance, as he watched the golden metal of the fingers twist and change between various weapons and appendages. The other friend - did they have Arabella like that pink-haired pirate suggested? No, that could not be. Jackson had made sure he had left her safe back at the bar. He turned to look at Ann as she fished out her guns from her jacket. She just shrugged, as if it was nothing, as if there was no immediate danger at all.

"Who are you?" She asked the pirate captain, merely leaving the rest of them shocked.

Jackson could see the pirate's eye twitch in a crazed flutter, not knowing what to say. After all the stories he had told Ann about Atlas, not one had gone in!

"What?" Atlas barked, "Doesn't the Navy keep a poster of me? Do you not know who we are?" He hissed, pointing between himself and Silvers Kent with a finger.

"I know who he is." Ann said, pointing at the white-haired pirate. "That's Silvers, the man who took my friend away and we're going to kick his arse for it, but I have no clue who you are."

"Erm, Ann?" Jackson muttered, leaning over to her across the podium and whispering in her ear. "That's Atlas the pirate captain, the one everyone was telling you about."

Ann looked at them both and turned her head while holding up a finger to both pirates to wait.

"Oh, so that's Atlas? But Fryedai said he looked pretty weak, so that can't be him, can it?" She questioned aloud, so that everyone could hear.

Jackson nodded, only to see Atlas continually glaring at them both with a growing madness.

"Shit! Well, I've stepped in it there, haven't I?" She uttered, this time keeping her voice lower.

"*Weak!*"

"Weak!" Atlas shouted, curling his fist and making his fingers glow red with rage.

"You think me weak? *I*, who have a bounty totalling fifty thousand Threds! *I*, who hath begun the Great Purge of Giant-kin, tearing islands aflame! *I*, who hath hunted every last of that demon race across the seas. I am not weak!"

"Ann, I would shut up now if I were you." Jackson said nervously.

Even with the incredible speed of his Ash power, he did not think he would be able to avoid the deadly looking weapon that was ensnared along Atlas' arm.

"Well, from what I hear." Ann continued. "You just sit there and do nothing while your goons do your work for you."

Atlas began to look even more furious at what Ann was saying and flicked his hand to Silvers. The snow-haired pirate launched himself down the centre of the antechamber, and Jackson quickly had to jump in the way to stop him from getting at Ann, who at this point, was still verbally belittling the captain.

"I thought you were meant to be a big, bad pirate captain, but from what I've seen, you're only a quaking coward who likes to hide behind a bit of Seidr and a shadowy curtain. You've even proved my point. Your goons do all the hard work for you." She rambled.

Meanwhile, Silvers continued to attack Jackson, first striking left, then right, then right again in a continuous motion.

"Hello, Jackson. We meet again, do you remember me?" He grinned from ear to ear. "Of course, you don't. I bet your friend there had to tell you. I wiped part of your memory and gave you those crazy dreams. How is Arie by the way? I hear she's swamped playing with Gillian at the moment."

Jackson clenched his fist as he held his rapier steady under the rattling blows, and he balled his spare hand to strike at the quartermaster. Jackson did his best to block the attacks and the glowing fists that perused him as they shone a white-hot light that countered the edge of the drunk's steel blade.

"Shut up, you crazy pirate. Arie is safe. I saw her with my own two eyes!" He insisted, moving around to the side to follow Kent's every move.

Out of the corner of his eyes, he could see and hear Ann firing her guns multiple times at Atlas, as he stalked his way menacingly towards her. She ran in circles around the room, continually shooting at his golden-like red fingers.

"But can you really trust what you see and hear, Drunk?" The pirate snarled, the purple scar around his neck bulging as he did and the grey bandage around his hand falling clear to the floor, revealing a deathly-looking and oozing black mark.

Images of Nelson, Arabella and Molly danced in Jackson's vision as both men ducked and weaved. Jackson sped up his attacks and yelled at the pirate that what he said wasn't true! He was trying desperate uppercuts and kinetic blasts using his Ash power, but he had no idea how long it would last. Silvers gritted his teeth and swatted the first volley away as if it was nothing.

"Do you think you're the first person to try a trick on me?" Kent jested, seeing the powers Jackson was using. "Atlas has made me fight him constantly over the years, and thanks to his habit, I've fought against pretty much every Ash power there is. You can't beat me!"

Silvers' white hair and scarred face then changed, transforming into one Jackson was much more familiar with, and causing him to back away.

"Nelson, is that you?" He asked, seeing the wavy blonde hair of his friend.

"Yeah, Jackson, it's me." Nelson assured, holding his arms out to hug his friend.

Was this real? He thought. It certainly looked it.

"Ha-ha!" Silvers laughed triumphantly, still using Nelson's voice to mess with the drunk's memory and then striking him across the face.

Jackson flew across the chamber from the impact and slammed into the rocky walls of the engraved golden dome, causing a crater to form.

The pirate followed him up.

"You are so easy to trick, Jackson. Have you come for more of the same yet again? Because, I have lots more to show you. Nelson has told me lots about you that I could torture you with, not that he said all this of his own free mind, of course. I took every single word out from under his lips, and all his secrets came tumbling out."

How dare he. How dare he! Thought Jackson, enraged.

How could he use his own friend's words against him?

"You lie!" The drunk yelled as he tried to raise his rapier to strike.

With his arms outstretched, Jackson held his sword in a vice-like grip, even after he was sent hurtling into the wall. Was it the Ash? He didn't know for sure, but he knew it was giving him some form of protection that he wouldn't otherwise have if Ann hadn't played to his sense of honour and 'fair play' to face the pirates, and he realised the girl had been right! Sometimes he did have to think like these people to beat them! The answer was quite simple. It was because Silvers was a pirate, and pirates didn't have any regard for others, like he or his friends did.

"Never mock anybody else's dreams!"

Suddenly, Jackson managed to raise his rapier and he blocked Silvers' next punch and threw it to the side, causing a wave of worry to crawl across the pirate's face as Jackson curled his fingers. Then, with his other hand and all his collective might, he struck out against the snowy-haired foe, hitting him square in the chest, and sending him flying back across the room. Silvers was catapulted with the scalding heat of a kinetic blast to the opposite wall of the curved domed chamber. The pirate screamed with pain, stuck in the shattered golden crater he had made, unable to break free of the burning heat and ruined, delicate drawings that had once been. He strained his neck forward and eventually his back began to peel from the wall with his skin turning the same red as the scar around his neck. But if that happened to the pirate, then why didn't that happen to him? Then the drunk realised again, and in the heat of the moment he had forgotten. It was the Ash! His body's energy had moved so quickly that the heat hardly had an effect!

Silvers fell to the floor, collapsing in a heap as Jackson began to peel himself away from his own crater, and watched to see if his foe was finally down. His back ached with the impact from dark rocks and fist-sized diamonds that had been hidden within the caverned wall. He ran over to the pirate in an instant with power and looked down upon him as the quartermaster had done many times over the last month with how he had played with both his and Arabella's feelings. It was kind of ironic that the diamonds that they were so desperately searching for were now seared into the pirate's skin as he laid unconscious upon the cold and broken floor; a constant reminder of his greed, obsessions, and the price everyone has to pay.

26

Orion Vain was relentless as he continued to bash his cutlass against the small dagger Fryedai held. Hefting the blade to above his head and holding it in the air for all around him to see, Orion brought it down in a vicious flash. In a few hours, Atlas was going to destroy the island – a precaution against Kaine and his dogs if they dared to follow the pirates.

"Your Captain is dead, Little bird." The pirate taunted, snarling, and grinning down at his foe, placing his cutlass on the side of Fryedai's shoulder. "He's dead, and there is nothing you can do about it that can change his fate, you've failed him. You've failed everyone you hold dear on that precious crew of yours."

Fryedai looked up and saw the light reflecting from the glint of the blade.

This was it? He thought again, for what must have been the fifth time today. Was he really going to die?

"Everyone." He began. "I'm sorry, I messed everything up."

"No!" A voice suddenly screamed out, and Fryedai opened his eyes just in time to see the confused look on Orion Vain's face.

Running at him from the side of the tunnel was Commander Rockwell, dragging alongside him a screaming, ashen-faced Luke, who abruptly tackled the vice-captain to the ground. Everybody else in the tunnel watched in amazement.

"What is going on here?" Demanded Orion, who was being forced to roll around on the floor by the two men who held him down.

Suddenly, the whole tunnel system shook. Rocks fell from the ceiling as the dark earth below them shifted. Luke and Rockwell were thrown from Orion as the pirate swatted them away with the back of his blade, and the pirate got up to run down the length of the tunnel.

"We have to get out of here and find the others quickly, before this whole place collapses!" The commander urged above the noise of the crumbling rock.

Luke nodded in agreement, and they both chased after Orion as he scurried down the tunnel, freeing everyone as they went. Whatever had happened must have been significant. Fryedai just hoped Ann and Jackson were all right.

* * *

As Jackson was fighting Silvers, Ann knew that Atlas Vain would come straight for her, and unfortunately, that is precisely what he did. The pure embodiment of what Ann liked to call pissed off. His hulking form stalked his way over to her in heaving, monstrous steps as a glowing amulet swung from his neck. His peculiar looking golden-red fingers began to glow, and Ann wasted no time in bringing her guns out and firing to take him down.

However, it didn't all go according to plan. It was never, ever, that simple. Upon firing the first shot and squeezing the trigger, Ann went all out, firing a volley of cold, icicle projectiles from the barrels of her gun as she switched the cylinders. Ice flew at the pirate captain, causing cold ripples of water to run through air and freeze almost everything they touched. As they got closer, Atlas leaned to the side and dodged each of the three, one by one. He thrusted his shoulders in and out and from side to side, as if he hadn't a care in the world. He then looked at her from across the treasure room with a withering stare.

"You still think me weak, girl? This is all according to my plan!" He yelled. "And soon you shall be dead, and I will be away with the prize in hand. One step closer to my goal without you Navy-brats interfering. I will, we will have our vengeance on the giant race and kill The Devourer where he sleeps!"

"So that is what all this is about?" Ann quizzed as she clicked the cylinder back.

She was now firing off normal rounds that she hoped Atlas couldn't see. However, the brutish pirate captain had transformed the golden liquid metal into a shield and was effortlessly swatting the bullets to one side with ease as they pinged off the surface.

"Yes, vengeance! The prophecy must be fulfilled." Atlas cried, morphing the shield into his own personal canon. "The giants destroyed my home; took my father's axe, so I've made it my mission to destroy everything else that was theirs, including this town. Now that I have its treasure, it no longer has a use. We're going to burn it to the ground, and you along with it. Everything will decay."

Ann's eyes widened as she saw the long golden width of the cannon pointed at her head, and dropped to the floor, rolling beneath the podium. A massive blast sounded around the treasure room. It was as if an earthquake had just erupted out of nowhere. Small amounts of dust and rocks were thrown up from the floor and the delicate artwork that was inscribed around the inner surface of the domed room began to peel and crack away. Ann looked around, desperately out of breath. Next to her, she found a medium-sized crater had appeared that would easily have fit a person. She heard Atlas snarl.

"Jackson! Jackson!" She shouted as the dust cleared, coughing slightly, as some reached the back of her throat.

She did not get a reply, and two bodies hurtled themselves across the room.

"Great!" She muttered to herself and ducked down again.

She had to do something about that strange, mysterious weapon before it killed her and everybody else on the island. Suddenly, she heard the fizzle of a fuse and an almighty bang. Ann quickly had to dive out of the way. One after the other, pieces of the cavern roof came crashing down in boulder-sized rocks and she ran to and fro to avoid them.

"Is this what you really want, Atlas?" She yelled as she continued to run from boulders.

Atlas' face sat twisted, contorted in frustration. Breathing in deeply, he summoned the Ash power he had consumed earlier and channelled it into the gauntlet, squeezing the trigger of his makeshift gun.

"I want you to stop moving and die!" Atlas boomed, his crystal blue eyes becoming ever brighter as he used the power of the gauntlet.

"Yeah, that's not going to happen." Smiled Ann in return. "I would never hurt anyone that didn't have a true and deserved reason for making me do such a thing! So, I am going to stop you right now, and save all these people."

"I think not." Growled Atlas as he channelled yet another power from the gauntlet, as the amulet around his next still glowed brightly.

Suddenly, a bolt of purple lightning emerged. Ann swerved to avoid it as it curved around the treasure room in a terrifying arc of power, causing her to keep firing yet more iron balls in Atlas' direction. She couldn't keep avoiding everything forever, and another bolt of energy was blasted towards her, giving Ann barely enough time to move as it sliced through the air. The lightning struck her within an instant, and Ann felt as if every molecule of her being was on fire. The blast stung and seared parts of her arms black with small scathing marks.

"How do you like that now, girl?" He spat as he walked up to her and stared her in the face, eyes blazing.

He had changed his weapon yet again, now presenting a gleaming golden spike as long as a spear. Atlas began to speak, taunting her about what she had done to him for her to deserve a fate such as this, and he slowly rotated the spike little by little into Ann's side, causing her to emit a bloodcurdling scream in pain. She had to make it through this if she could, and not focus on the searing pain. Out of the corner of her eye, as the pain became unbearable, she saw Jackson punch Silvers Kent into the side of the treasure room wall, revealing a trove of glittering raw diamonds. She tried to get the words out to call for help, but sound only escaped her lips as a stutter.

"What is it, girl?" Atlas laughed. "Something on your tongue? My crew should have made their preparations by now and we will soon be underway. It's a shame, I'm sure Lazarus would have liked you."

He was completely unaware of what had just happened to his fellow crewmate, and he tore the spike from her. Droplets of blood fell from the tip, and Ann gasped.

"Look over there." She spluttered, forcing a pained smile.

Atlas turned around in horror and confusion to find Jackson standing over a fallen, diamond-studded, Silvers.

The look of horror on Atlas' face was absolute as he gazed at his fallen friend. He screamed as Jackson ran over to them both at incredible speed. However, he wasn't fast enough, and the golden gauntlet began to burn red as it became hotter and hotter. Within a moment, Atlas let out a terrifying cry that shook the entire room and even the dark and twisting tunnels around them. Bolts of electricity shot out from the fingers, sending both Ann and Jackson flying as the drunken navigator reached out.

"Now this island will burn!" He howled. "May every man earn his fair and justly earned reward!"

It was all a blur to Ann, who collapsed to the hard floor as Jackson ran over to her, watching as Atlas ran away, bolting for the nearest exit and the island's doom. They still had their friends to find, and now they had to hurry all the more before Ale town became ash and smoke!

"Are you going to be alright?" Shouted Jackson to Ann, as rocks continued to rumble and fall around them.

"Now you know why I called him a psychopath back at the tavern. What was that thing on his arm anyway? It looked like it was eating him alive, was that the treasure that they were looking for?" Jackson asked, still bewildered that it was actually real, as he helped Ann to her feet.

More rocks fell, and they raced out from the domed, treasured antechamber as the dark earth filled it from above, covering the golden artwork and the empty vault for time everlasting, never to be uncovered by anybody ever again. Now looking along the tunnel whence they came, Jackson and Ann could hear the frightened screams of those left remaining within the diamond mines as they too raced for the exit. From what they had found out in the antechamber, only Atlas and a couple of figures from his group had remained within the mines to set up the disaster they were now experiencing; the rest were townspeople, captured slaves left by the pirates before they made their way to the dock, where their galleon lay in wait. Ann trembled at the thought that they could do this to the entire island. Her sides stung from where Atlas had wounded her, and Jackson had to carry her so they could avoid the crumbling rocks.

"Can you see Nelson at all?" He cried as they came up on a group of townspeople.

They too were running towards the shaft of light that had opened in a crack between the rocks and they all scrambled up a deep incline as a boulder crashed and slammed. Many people didn't make it, but thanks to the Ash Ann had made Jackson consume, the two of them helped to usher as many people as they could to safety and towards the light. Finally, they reached the crack of light. Ann, Jackson, and five others. They pushed and squeezed through the gap as quick as they could, and above them when they reached the other side, was a shaft of twinkling moonlight shining above them as the last of the mine collapsed. They had made it, and yet so many others had not. Now they had to chase the pirate that did this and stop him before he could do anything else.

Jackson quickly helped Ann jump to the worn rope ladder that dangled in front of them, and the girl wondered if Nelson or Fryedai had made it out. The ladder looked frail and tussled, but sure enough, it was able to take her weight and she slowly scrambled up with the rest soon following. When they got to the top, they were sure they were the last ones out of those deadly tunnels alive. No one else seemed to be down there. Ann desperately hoped that her friends were safe. She would hate it if it had caused the loss of a new-found friend.

She looked up at the night's sky and rested her hands on her legs. She truly would have been dead if it weren't for Jackson, and she could hear the drunk breathe a hefty sigh of relief.

"Is it always this crazy with you?" He gasped, wiping his black hair back from over his face. "Because I really need a drink."

Ann laughed despite the circumstances, and the rest of the group they had gathered thanked them and began to walk into the jungle as they explained to them that the pirates had fled to the docks.

"Yeah, it is." She grinned, breathing heavily. "And that thing you mentioned crawling up Atlas' arm was definitely the treasure they were after. Everything in that room was gone and bare. Did you see those crazy carvings scrawled across the walls?"

"No?" The navigator quirked a brow. "What of them?"

It was at that point that Ann held up the unrolled circular map she had swiped from Atlas' belt. The pirate captain may have been smart and all-powerful, but he wasn't smart enough to notice that when she had pointed out Jackson to him, she had swiped the map that had hung from his belt.

"I haven't a clue, but I'm sure this scroll can tell us. Atlas also mentioned something about a prophecy." Ann informed him, a wave of excitement growing inside of her.

"That's not very Navy-like of you." Jackson said, raising an eyebrow again.

It was moments like this when he wondered how Ann made it into the Navy, despite many of its members that were rumoured to be corrupt.

"Hey, I go where my moods take me. Can you blame me after who we've just had to fight? If I'm going to die, I'm at least going to make it worth my while." Ann explained.

"Well, never mind that now. We've got to find Fryedai and Nelson before we do anything else, plus on top of that, Tom was nowhere to be seen and we've got to find and rescue Arie, otherwise you and I have no deal, remember?" Jackson reminded her, and he began to walk into the distance.

"He seems to want to take both of my friends from me!"

"Where are we anyway?" Ann asked, looking up at the glimmering, starry night's sky, and the dark green forestry around them.

Jackson grumbled.

"Jungle, we're in the jungle. It's no wonder you need a navigator so badly, you can't bloody get anywhere by yourself! Come on, the train station is this way."

Together they ventured down the path that others had left, with Jackson leading the way in search of Fryedai, Nelson, Tom, and Arabella, and hopefully the rest of Fryedai's crew, not knowing truly if any of them were alive. All Ann was thinking about as she walked behind him was the strange markings that had been etched across the tunnel's treasure room walls. Hopefully, she could also think of a way to deal with Atlas, and she gripped the map, hoping it would reveal a clue to her much-needed answer. Perhaps it was the prophecy? Unfortunately, the map was scrawled with harsh letters and lines, the same she had seen on the golden engravings of the antechamber and its door, and she could not read what it said as she matched up the many different pictures and islands drawn across its surface. It came to resemble the shape of Ale Town Island; of which she had seen in Doctor Rudolf's quarters.

* * *

Arabella still couldn't believe what that monstrous beast had told her over the Cable-phone was true. She continued to weep uncontrollably as she sat confined to a chair by the iron chains Gill had wrapped around her.

"You monsters!" She spat as she watched Gillian step from shadow to shadow in the darkness of the cabin. "You absolute monsters. How are you able to do this, how are you able just to stand by and watch as you, and other madmen, tear people's lives apart with the misery and torment you cause. Do you not know right from wrong? How many fathers have you killed? How many families have you broken with a single sweep of your blade? Do you not think about what the responses will be to your actions? Why are you doing this?"

The pink-haired pirate stepped out of the shadows, out of all the members of the brothers' pirate crew Arie had met, the 'Hacksaw' - Gilligan Mayers - was the most methodical and the most callous. He bent down in front of her, as a predator would to its pray, keeping low to the ground with his shoulders hunched and head bent low.

"No." He said simply, raising his head up to look at her weeping tears. "Too much has been taken from our group, and I would rather chase the whole world to get it all back, than let it all go. Atlas' plan is the only way to do that, and no matter what I care for, or what I do to stop his habit, nothing is going to stop him getting back what we lost, and I will be with him to the end. Does that answer your question? No one, and I repeat, no one, is coming for you."

Arabella felt her tears well up again.

"Not even Jackson?" She whimpered.

Gillian smiled and shook his head with the sound of metallic jangling behind him.

"Especially Jackson." He responded, watching the horror unfold on Arabella's face. "Silvers should be able to take care of him, but I have my doubts. I'll do it myself should it come to it. I suspect he's already been taken care of by now though."

"You liar!" Gasped Arie.

Gillian continued to laugh and shake his head.

"Just you watch, pretty girl." He mused and went to stroke her cheek with the pad of his finger. Arabella bit down on his skin, making the pirate scream.

"Arr, you little so and so! My orders are to take care of you until the captain arrives, but don't think I won't make you suffer in the meantime! When Atlas gets here it will be his decision on what to do with you, and I can't wait for what he decides. Lazarus wants you, but that Troll didn't say in what condition."

Arabella then watched helplessly as Gillian produced some chains out from behind his back with a smile and attached them to each leg of the chair, making sure they were secured. The metallic chains rattled and shook as he tied them, and he pulled down hard so that they wouldn't come off. When the pirate had finished, he took out a piece of fabric from his jacket pocket and moved closer to the girl. The barmaid shouted in protest, threatening again to bite the pirate. However, he just sniggered at her with a vengeful smile. No one was going to come for her it seemed, and she felt a tear stream down the side of her cheek. Gillian used the fabric as a makeshift blindfold. Whatever it was he was going to do filled her mind with horror. She heard the chains rattle from side to side and water drip. The chair lurched forward, and Arabella felt it tip back, as she was gradually hoisted up into the middle of the small cabin, hearing the pirate laugh as she swung there.

"I can't wait for this." Gillian giggled. "We are going to have so much fun when Atlas arrives!"

Arie continued to sob, and the tears leaked through her blindfold and down on to the floor.

"You didn't answer me before." She spoke. "Why? Why are you doing this?"

"Because I can." He stated and glared up to her. "I have had enough of the world taking advantage of me, so I'm taking advantage of it, and helping Atlas is the best way to do that."

"But doesn't that mean Atlas is taking advantage of you? From what I heard from my dad, all he really cares about is his brother and his stupid quest to get rid of Kaine, which is impossible. You've been running from him, haven't you? That's why you want all the diamonds so you can pay people off."

Gillian frowned.

"So?" He growled. "What of it? We've been friends since childhood, all four of us have. There is no way Atlas would use us like that, we made a promise!"

"So where is your other friend? Because I guarantee Atlas will be with Orion, so where does that leave you? Friends don't betray friends."

"Shut up!" The pink-haired pirate roared. "What do you know?"

"I'm a barmaid, I know people, and you're going to be abandoned for a brother's love."

"I am his brother! I'm his friend, his council. I am more than that for my captain! I've dived down a giant's beanstalk for him. I've had to watch our entire village burn for him, just so we could steal some food to eat because of a damned war!"

"All the same." Arabella sobbed. "You will be abandoned by him in the end, even if no one comes for me, like you say."

27

The jungle was hot and bothersome, even at the dead of night as they tracked through the long sways of bamboo that populated the south of the island, and the sound of humming crickets buzzed through the air like a melody. After speaking to most of the group, Fryedai knew that the majority of the people who had escaped from the tunnels were out for payback after what happened. They seemed to have rescued the entire town as they raced through the tunnels, desperately freeing people as they went. The rest of *The Inspectre*'s crew had to urge the townspeople to let them handle it. Moreover, Fryedai soon realised that most of the crew, including Mister Rockwell, had no idea what was going on, and it was Fryedai who would have to explain to them what had happened. In the tracks below their feet, massive footprints littered the ground amidst the odd broken growth of tall bamboo, snapped like a twig from the head-height of most men. It made the navigator worry that not all the pirates were at the docks like Orion had proclaimed. Pirates often lied. Fryedai knew he would have to keep his guard up as he walked back further down the line of throngs, and to the first officer, who was technically now in charge.

They were heading to the town through the darkness of the night. Rockwell had ordered that they safely return everyone to their homes, hold off the pirates until more reinforcements arrived, or wait until the cures had finally grown bored and left. The Commander had a grief-stricken look on his face as he clung tightly to his blue and white Navy coat, and before the words even came out of the officer's mouth, Fryedai knew he was about to get hammered for dressing out of uniform while on active duty.

"Where in all the seas is your uniform, Fryedai?" He growled.

"At the bottom of a mine, sir. Un-salvageable, sir." Fryedai said, standing to attention and almost forgetting to salute his superior officer out of the habit and friendship that had formed between him and Ann these past hours.

"Very well, Fryedai." Rockwell sighed. "Report. I want to know everything."

Thus, Fryedai explained all he could as they wandered on. He put some things delicately and others he did not, remembering that the majority of them had been toiling away as thralls and had little clue about what had been transpiring in the world above. Ann for example, how she was a woman hidden away on their ship and not a man as they suspected all along. That specifically went against their rules and what the captain had preached while at the Outpost – yet over the last day, Fryedai had learned that those rules were neither right nor fair in some cases. His captain had been wrong, no matter his experience with the Siren-women of the sea. Ann was a good and trustful person. She was his friend. Were those prejudices the reason why she had chosen to keep herself hidden on the ship perhaps the Doctor would know?

The jittery man walked beside them as they talked, a deathly sheet of paleness spread over his skin like a rash and his eyebrow raised when Fryedai mentioned the red-headed girl by name, a small glimmer of sweat running down the side of his face. Was the ship's Doctor always like this? The navigator did begin to wonder why hadn't they seen Ann along the jungle path? Had she and the drunk made it out of the mine before the caverns and tunnelways collapsed? Then there was the help he'd received from Jackson and that talking pig. How could he explain to Rockwell that he had to rely on people he hardly knew after the death of the captain, people that had saved his life so many times now.

"I see." Rockwell said glumly.

Fryedai could feel his ire burn through the front of him, as he looked the first officer in the eye.

"Is there anything else that I need to know?"

"No Sir, I've told you all I know."

"But what about this Ann?" Rockwell asked, he too raising an eyebrow, which also drew the further attention of Doctor Rudolf, who stepped forward to further listen in on the conversation.

Fryedai was about to say something but was interrupted when they heard a roar from further within the bamboo jungle which they now trekked.

"What was that?" The Doctor cried, his cracked, dusty broken glasses jumping to his head.

"It - it sounded like an animal." Fryedai guessed. "A large and overgrown animal."

"That would explain the marks on the ground and the tears in the jungle growth." Stated Rockwell.

The pale bamboo around them began to rumble, and the roar of a distant monster's rage grew closer...

* * *

As Jackson led Ann on through the jungle, all he thought about was how he was going to find his friends. He swiped his rapier against the overbearing brush as he walked through the glistening rays of silver moonlight and below him, he saw the freshly imprinted tracks of a creature, barely an hour old. He peered down and grasped at the dirt with his spare hand as the other gripped his sword tightly.

"What is it?" Asked Ann from behind. "Did you find anything?"

"Maybe." Jackson replied, thinking he had seen the very feet that had made these marks before. "Have you figured out those scribbles yet?"

Ann squinted her eyes against the worn map paper and held it against the argent moonlight, the blood-red lettering twinkling.

"There's some drawings and islands that I don't know the look of, but I still can't understand this strange writing."

"Let me have a look." The drunken navigator grumbled, striking his sword at another green vine that crossed his path and peering over to the map as Ann held it out.

"That can't be right?" Said Jackson, stopping in his tracks as he stared at the drawings and traced them with his finger against the brown paper.

The light of the crescent moon amidst the clouds made the map shine, and Jackson could feel it almost hum, as if it were alive. Just as it had been with Ann, Jackson found that he couldn't read the writing either, making head nor tail of the harsh lines and marks that littered the scroll. He wondered how ancient the map and its treasure truly were. It was then that Ann remarked that the drawings had changed since she had held it in her hands, saying that it was a strange and twisted form of Seidr. However, one or two of the drawings that flickered across the surface of the map he recognised, though the islands looked unfamiliar to his eye. Painted across the scroll in glittering crimson ink, where once had been a podium and a broken bottle, now lay a twisting serpent with wings. Fire spewed from its gaping mouth as it clashed against a tortoise shell. It bore a striking similarity to the door of the domed antechamber that had rested deep below them. Next to this was an image of what Jackson saw as a shinning castle or city. It was broken down in parts and vines and smoke was scribed across the image in equal measure.

"Why?" Ann asked. "What's wrong?"

"Because the kind of creature depicted here is like the giants, they're all but dead, well aside from The Devourer." Jackson added. "No one has seen any for the last one hundred and fifteen years!"

Ann looked up from the map in amazement.

"Wait don't tell me that's a -"

"A Dragon." Jackson finished her sentence.

"Nelson's dad had this book on them when I was a kid. The Ifirt some people call them, or Draigs. *Izan's Kin* it was called. In the myths of our ancient times, the war-leader of the gods created the serpents through his haggard brow, when racing the sea goddess Adira, across the world. Adira, riding a great beast of her own, challenged Izan for his war-seat after she caught the god with her high-priestess. She was so infuriated that she caused wild squalls to brew, towers of water to rise and fall from the oceans into the clouds; and all the while Izan ran and jumped from cloud to cloud with a quiet rage growing for being interrupted with the priestess. There was fire in his belly, coldness in his blue and jovial eyes, and thunder in his step. From pole to pole they raced and east to west, covering every land and element, and Izan ran so fast that slivers of Seidr ran from his brow and crawled across the lands till they seeped into the sea and Adira came. Izan won the race of the gods, as he had reign over all the sky and was untethered by that lands that blocked Adira's Sea. And when the race was done did his serpents come crawling from out the waves that had nurtured them and they were of many types, as both Adira and Izan had given them life, if somewhat intentionally. Adira, furious that Izan had used her precious seas as a birthing ground, spurned the god, but as a prize for having won the race, she allowed the creatures to live, taking as a consolation those without wings as her own as they felt most at home in the sea; and that is how the serpents of sky and sea were born."

"And the Dragons who dwelt with the goddess then created fish to feed from and other sea-life, whereas Izan would lavish his spawn and bring them anything that roamed the mountain peaks that touched upon his realm, hunting with his great spear." Said Ann. "I know the stories too, and so the god couldn't interfere with her worshippers again, Adira turned them into Mermaids, Sirens – their voices still alluring and as beautiful to praise their goddess with, yet the sweet songs to any mortal would drag them far beneath the waves."

Jackson sighed.

"It seemed like the whole family was in a cult over that book, but Molly and James never gave it any mind as their parents did. Both are gone now, missing..." Replied the drunk. "Trust me, the keeps atop those mountains that the god made for the Dragons – they all burned."

Ann smiled.

"So, you do believe in something?" She laughed, flicking back her hair as she followed him through the bamboo groves.

As she did, Ann clenched her teeth as her side ached in a sharp pain and she looked down. The wound Atlas had inflicted; it still had bite and stung viciously. However, Ann resided herself to the fact that at least the bleeding had stopped. The burns from the blast of lightning had seen to that and had healed some small amount as they walked. She was lucky for Jackson jumping in when he did as surely the pirate would have killed her. Still the gash ached, and Ann had to tie it off with what remained of her silver bandanna before she could attend to it properly.

"The book and now this map tell me they are real, and that thing proves it." Jackson stated as a matter of fact. "How they came to be, well that's just a bedtime story. If I'd seen this map a month ago, before that twisted treasure today, I would have told you what Atlas sought was a joke and laughed it off. I always questioned it though, but there was just no evidence to support what everyone was saying, until now."

"You know, you really are great when you're sober, just like Nelson said you were!" She smiled in surprise, wrapping her arms around him from behind and wincing as she did.

"Woah, wow. When did Nelly say this?" Jackson questioned, wanting to know exactly what his Mohawked friend was telling her.

"This morning." She smiled again, brushing back her red hair over her ear and twisting it into a curl. "You were knocked out cold. I was tempted to draw a moustache and glasses on your face when I first saw you, but Nelson said calling you a good navigator would embarrass you enough – said you just need some positive reinforcement."

"Well, that's just great, isn't it? I suppose that's why you're hugging me?"

Ann nodded with a girlish giggle and let the drunk go, but again she winced as she did, and this time Jackson noticed.

"I'll thank him for being such a mate when I next see him." He groaned. "Are you going to be alright?"

"I've had worse." Replied Ann. "But what are we going to do about these footprints?" She said, motioning down to the floor where Jackson had scrapped the dirt from the track.

The jungle then seemed to draw silent, and the sound of the island's crickets stopped. Just then it dawned on Ann that something about the overly large footprints didn't feel right, and in the distance, they suddenly heard the roar of a great beast yell into the night.

"Doesn't that sound like..."

"A gorilla?" Stated Jackson, once again finishing the sentence before Ann could even suggest what the sound, or thing, even was.

The open jungle quickly began to feel like it was too open. With the night once again drawing deadly silent, they both continued walking in the direction they had before and towards the footsteps. Whatever the creature was, they both knew the pirates had something to do with it.

Could pirates have been nearby? She thought, frozen in place as she realised that Atlas' crew had been so vast from what she had seen. They could have been surrounding her this very instant! She then tapped on Jackson's shoulder repeatedly with worry as he hacked through the jungle vine.

Were they about to be outnumbered?

"Jackson?" She whispered into the jungle night.

"What is it?" He asked louder with annoyance, not even taking the slightest caution to whisper.

Jackson simply rolled his eyes and lowered his sword. All the pirates would be at the docks if they wanted to escape the Devil's Rush, but still the noise ahead worried him.

"How much time do we have?"

The drunk already knew what Ann was talking about, his mind had been on nothing else since they escaped the tunnels. They would need to find and stop Atlas and his pirates to save their friends. Jackson was certain they still had Nelson. Neither he nor Ann had seen him in the mines, nor had they come across him on the jungle path since they had departed from the townspeople that had escaped with them as they had quickly run ahead to chase down Atlas. This bamboo jungle close to his home had deep memories for Jackson. When he and Nelson were young boys, they would play here. This was before he was the town drunk, and he still had fun and mischief in his heart. They would try to leap from treetop to treetop, swinging on vine after vine and brushing leaf after leaf as they ran. Their goal was as always to beat Molly, in a race down to the waterside, where Jackson's hut now sat. She was always the fastest runner, and neither of them could ever beat her in a race. Despite this, Jackson would always play tricks on her in the hope of winning, and the optimistic ideas he came up with were always overflowing. Ann reminded him of this. Once the poor fool had actually travelled their usual route ahead of time and built a series of traps and mud pits to try to slow them, however none of that worked in Jackson's favour, and he had forgotten where he laid the traps. He remembered the roaring laughter he saw from his friend as he wiped the fresh, brown drooping mud from his face, and it filled him with joy.

It was this naive optimism, which he saw in both Ann and now Fryedai. Because despite everything that they had been through in the last day, he was still willing to see the hope in everything, which was something Jackson had long since forgotten. If anything came out of this horrendous ordeal, it was that he might finally see some optimism again and Ann was just the person to make him see it.

"Hard to say." He spoke softly, looking up at the moon, and its position in the night's dark sky. "I would say in the region of an hour to an hour and a half; the tide will be back. It usually happens around dawn. If you listen closely, you can hear the waves crashing against the shore."

"Can't you run ahead, like you did in the mine?" Asked Ann as they trekked nearer to the island's South-station and the sound of the animalistic, gorilla-like roar.

"No, I can't. The Ash has worn off, so it's the hard way from here on out."

"And when's dawn?" Asked Ann nervously.

"Around five, six o'clock. It can vary from day to day."

* * *

"So, who is she, Fryedai?" Pondered Rockwell with a look of confusion about him, wanting to know how a girl had managed to get onto his ship.

"Ann." Said Fryedai, reaffirming what the commander had just said, and still Mister Rockwell looked at him blankly.

Doctor Rudolf shuffled uneasily as they walked. They heard the monstrous roars from far ahead, and a few of the local townspeople that led them said it sounded as if it came from within the South-station. Fryedai made a note that that was where the footprints were leading, where Orion had run to before they had lost sight of him from within the mines.

"Doctor?" He asked, remembering that Ann had stayed within his cabin.

In turn, Commander Rockwell gave the Doctor a hard, menacing stare and turned to the officer, placing a firm hand on his shoulder.

Doctor Rudolf continued to sweat nervously and even tried to pull away from the man that held him. Both men found that odd.

"I took a bribe." The man cried, caving to the pressure of the looks his crewmates were giving him.

He couldn't stand to keep the girl's secrets any longer than he already had. What had he got for it? A pouch full of measly bronze Threds when she had promised silver! Captured and tortured by pirates in return for nothing!

"I don't know who the girl really is, but I do know that she has a goal in mind and that she thinks she is doing the right thing. She said she had joined the Navy but paid me a pretty penny to keep her name away from you all, with that I could continue my research!"

"Or your other habit!" Rockwell growled, disgusted by what the Doctor had done to go against the Navy like he had, against people that the captain had called his family and wanted to help.

Fryedai even had to step in front of them to stop him from striking the man.

"I only know what you all know." The Doctor flinched. "That her name is Ann, aside from that, it is a mystery as to who she really is."

Fryedai was shocked, although something to him had seemed off about Ann from the very beginning, despite her friendliness. When she said she was in the Navy, Fryedai had believed her.

As they all continued to walk through the jungle path, Fryedai stayed at the back of the line with Doctor Rudolf as Rockwell went up and led the group in the moonlight. The sounds of that monstrous roaring continued grow and it made Fryedai feel uneasy when the commander ordered him to watch over the snake of a physician.

"So, do you really think we can trust her?" He asked him, not knowing if lies or the truth would come out.

Captain Robbinson had hidden things from him too. Fryedai didn't know who or what to believe any more after the day he had had.

The Doctor looked at the blonde navigator with a mixture of pity and remembrance. In front of them, a clearing finally opened within the jungle, and it led from their curvy dirt path, plagued with insects, to one of red brick and greyed out cobblestone; the place where the roaring was coming from. Suddenly the group came to a stop and Rockwell raised his fist up high in the air. Both Fryedai, the Doctor, the Bosun twins and the helmsman, Mister Rivers then hurried up the line to meet the first officer at the head of the group as the townspeople whispered amongst themselves.

"What is this place?" Rockwell asked as he spied the brothers going inside a building from afar.

"Erm, it's the train station, mate. Can't you tell?" Luke's twin Chris pointed out and Rivers laughed to himself, pointing out the sign next to them that said South-Station.

It was covered in bird droppings and jungle moss. It looked as if Atlas was now helping his brother get inside quickly. Rockwell asked Fryedai if there was another way into the station aside from the glass door ahead of them in the distance. Fryedai didn't know, he hadn't been to this area of the island when he had stumbled through his escape earlier in the day. He needed to be confident now that the captain was gone, so he nodded and said that he did, thus a plan was hatched.

* * *

After twenty minutes of scouting the area, Fryedai and the Bosun twins made their way towards the train station as quickly and as quietly as they could. They kept in a single file line, staying low to the jungle shrubs so that nobody could see them in the dead of night. Fryedai was at the front of the group, hurrying the others over to the glass doors and ushering them inside as it gleamed with the artificial light of the station. They couldn't let the pirates escape. They were behind the brothers by about forty yards and saw that they were hobbling across the foyer with Atlas' arm thrown over his brother's shoulder as they walked arm in arm, the benches and upturned seats of the lobby lay in their wake, surrounded by decadent brickwork and brass-copper tubing that bent and weaved like tendrils throughout the building.

"Is that them?" Whispered Chris as he hid, crouching behind a splintered bench. "Are they the bastards who murdered the captain?"

His dark eyes were staring directly at Orion Vain. The others peered around the lobby. Most things in the station lay in ruin, aside from the cleared tracks that were free of rubble and discourse with two trains held securely on their rails next to one another.

"Shush!" Said Fryedai as he thought about the plan Rockwell laid out.

They were only meant to scout the area and then report back. This was so they could all approach the building from one side and take the pirates unawares. However, now that they were here, Fryedai had other ideas as he watched the thing on Atlas' hand move up and down his arm.

"That's them." The navigator spat.

With only the brothers in view, Fryedai was sure that with the help of his friends they could jump them, and as he turned to look at his two shipmates, he saw a grin curl to his friends faces as they looked to one another and nodded in agreement. He was about to say something when suddenly a huge and monstrous beast came crawling out of the shadows beneath an open train car. The car was designed with a massive iron-cast door and opening, attached from the back of the train's engine and before the winding trail of seemingly never-ending passenger cars. It was big enough to hide the beast completely from view as it came out to greet the two pirates. It was a massive creature - grey and silver-haired and angry, moreover, held in its grasp was the man Jackson had described as Nelson.

"Taylor!" Atlas announced, overjoyed to see the beast, as his amulet glowed, the smatterings of blood around the crystal visible to see. "I see you've kept my Alchemist in safe hands!"

Both the brothers sniggered as the beast nodded and huffed, and Atlas took his arm away from Orion so he could look closer at the prize the ape-like monster guarded. Fryedai had had enough as Nelson was brought forward for them to inspect, his semi-conscious state drifting through mumbles and murmurs. He had had enough of the countless times that the brothers had gotten away, escaped justice, and always seemed to be one step ahead. They had thought they had killed everyone with the destruction of the mines, and now the pirates sauntered at their leisure to the next destination. Fryedai would have none of it! If they worked their way back to Rockwell now, the pirates would be gone and there would be no chance of catching them again. They would be free to the wind, and no one would be able to put a stop to them.

And so, the Navy navigator stood from his hiding place and breathed in deeply, letting his voice carry over the station lobby. For once again he would have to try and be brave and face his fears. For the captain. For his friends. For himself.

"Stop!" Shouted Fryedai, his voice echoing across the lobby.

He surprised himself that he had been able to speak so clearly and so loudly, and both his friends raced after him as he began to run towards the pirates. He was no longer the shy and timid sailor that he had been this morning; that had carried maps and charts along the decks of the Inspectre, dropping them at every possible step. He had changed and grown with his experiences and the people he had met. Both the brothers turned their heads over their shoulders. All three of them now raced after the pirates as they headed towards the tracks and Fryedai's leg once again began to ache with pain.

"You can't win." He huffed, still undeterred by his desire to make things right.

They would be arresting the pirates here and now. As they neared the car in front of them, Fryedai saw that the steam train was ready to depart, with a few members of the brothers' pirates rammed into the cars.

"Don't think it will be that easy, Navy." Sang Orion as he hauled himself onto the iron car where the gorilla sat.

A smile grew on his face. Was the pirate pleased that some of them had made it after all? But then Atlas turned to face them as the train whistle rang out, and the strange metallic object that flowed up and down his arm began to glow a deep blood red. With a flick of his wrist, Atlas sent out a volley of sharp projectiles, golden tipped and shining, that cascaded towards Fryedai and his friends. The spikes struck and covered the ground with a thick layer of ice, spreading like wildfire across the lobby's floor. The twins who had run in front of Fryedai rolled out the way as more of the golden death-traps flew over their heads before the ice had reached them. Chris crashed into the ticket booth that sat at the side of the rails. The last projectile had sent a sharp cut across his forearm, and he yelled in pain.

Fryedai barely managed to avoid them as the wave of ice struck. Quickly, he rolled over only to find that everybody else had been glued to the floor by the frozen sheet and his leg was jammed. He could not believe the pirate captain had gotten the better of him again, and he stared at Atlas as he struggled to get up. The pirate, glaring at him with intense malice, once again raised his fist.

"Be gone." He spoke.

Suddenly, another volley of golden spiked projectiles barrelled their way towards Fryedai and his friends. There was no way they would be able to avoid this next attack while they were trapped on the slippery sheet of ice beneath their feet. Everything was frozen in place. A bang erupted out of nowhere in the station, and a wave of fire washed over the rapidly approaching spikes, throwing them to one side in a clatter.

Fryedai looked to the side of him and saw Ann and Jackson further down the platform and running towards them. Smoke was billowing from the cylinder one of Ann's pistols and Fryedai had never been so glad to see them in his life. Atlas on the other hand, was more enraged than anything else the navigator had seen thus far. The pirate captain hung on to the rail at the side of the passenger car and fired multiple projectiles at the approaching duo.

Again and again, constant explosions rang out as Ann fired shot after shot at the golden spikes. Thunder, ice, and fire all met their targets, and Atlas screamed in frustration. The train whistle sounded with a sharp scream, and the train gradually rolled along the tracks and towards the end of the station.

"He's getting away." Stressed Ann as she got to the platform and freed everyone from the ice, along with help from Jackson.

"And they've got Nelson!" The drunk hissed.

"Taylor!" Atlas shouted. "Finish them off!"

And with that, the great ape jumped from the iron passenger car as the train moved onwards down the tracks and on to the lobby, making the layers of ice that had grown across it crack and crumble. Another shout came from the pirate captain as he and his brother fled.

"No, you fool! The Alchemist! You still have him!"

However, there was nothing Atlas could do as the train rolled away, and both Ann and Jackson smiled as the ape holding Nelson snarled and roared at them, their friend laying within its grasp.

"We're going to have to be careful." Said Ann as she once again changed the setting on her pistols so that her shots wouldn't spurt fire, roasting their friend.

"And since when have you ever done that?" Jackson asked, pulling his rapier from his trench coat, and standing ready so he could win Nelson back.

Ann pondered for a second as she looked at the animal that reared up before them.

"Fair point." She said and shot the ape in head.

The ape bellowed in rage as it leaned back on stout grey legs, with Nelson held in one arm, the monster slammed its other into the sheet of ice and threw their friend towards them like a rag doll. Jackson dropped his sword and ran towards Nelson as he flew through the air to catch him. All the while, Ann continued the fire at the beast. Raising its massive arms in front of its face to protect itself, the animal roared at the red-headed girl before turning to flee and race after the train as it fled along the tracks. She had enraged it now as it returned to its masters, its pride bruised. Yet if they were to put an end to what Atlas had in store for the island, then Ann knew that they would have to face the beast again.

"Now what do we do?" She questioned, looking to both Fryedai and Jackson for advice.

She was relieved to see that everyone was okay. Jackson had managed to slow Nelson when the ape had thrown him and the two had slid across the lobby before coming to a stop. It was still troubling that Atlas had managed to get away on the back of a train. Who knew how long it would take him to get to his ship. Jackson pointed to another train as he helped Nelson to his feet. The cook shook his head from the shock of being thrown and crashing into his friend.

"Will that do?" He asked.

Ann was so happy they were both unhurt by the event that she jumped up and hugged them both.

As they got over to the train, the six of them found it was strangely quiet as they climbed up the iron steps. Ann had to pinch one of Fryedai's Navy friends, Chris, for likening it to a ghost train and told him that he should know better, to which he scowled.

"Hello, is anybody here?" She called as she walked down the middle of the row of seats.

Atlas was getting further away by the second, so they had no time to waste in getting after him. If anyone was on board that could not help, then they would have to be thrown off. Further down the row, as everybody else scanned the seating, Ann could hear a slight whimpering, but she didn't know who, or what it was. She turned to look at the seat next to her and found that an old man was crouched down, hiding in between the gap.

The man looked up, and Ann smiled.

It was Tom. And not only that, he was joined by Napoleon too, who was rubbing in a strange concoction to the guardian's poorly bandage wounds, something that looked as if he'd done it himself.

"What are you doing here?" She asked them both.

The pig answered that he had prepared the ointment for the guardian's wounds when they had left Nelson's house and that he had gone to look for Tom and his master when it was ready. Being that the familiar knew that Tom was also the island's conductor and that he was hiding from the pirates, he also explained that he knew that it was a possibility that he was hiding here to recover, in order not to get further dragged in by all the chaos that Ann had been causing across the island.

"Hey!" She complained, looking down at the piglet and pointing to Tom. "I'm not the one causing all the trouble. He was the one who disappeared on me!"

The rest of the Navy was searching the train and its cars with Jackson, and Napoleon was overjoyed to hear that his master was somewhat safe and sound.

"Only because you were taking so long." Tom said and sat up from where he was crouching.

Below him, Ann found that he was sat on a pile of weapons that he apparently intended to use against the pirates. Ann looked at him in astonishment. Did he think that he was actually going to fight against Atlas with all this?

"I swore to protect the chamber, I told that drunk he would have to, too."

"Wait, did you just say that drunk?" She uttered with a weak smile, and looked back over her shoulder to Jackson who was further up the aisle. "Hang on for just one second." Explained Ann and she held up a finger. "Yo, Jackson, get over here; I found someone you know."

"Crap." Cursed Jackson as he walked towards her. "It better not be Clive. I hate that guy, he rides the train at night, he's got one eye, and he always looks at me funny in the bar."

"Erm, it's not Clive." Said Ann, and Jackson felt relieved. "Although, I do think I met him earlier? Was he the creepy old guy with the leather braces on his face and the missing socket?"

"Yup."

Jackson then saw who was getting up from the floor and smiled.

"Tom!" He said in happy surprise.

"Screw you, Jackson. I asked you to help me this morning, and you just brushed me off. Now Atlas has the treasure!" Tom barked.

"So, I'm going to take that as a yes."

"What do you think? I warned you this morning, didn't I. He's going to destroy everything." He said, and he bent down, picked up a sword and held it to Jackson's throat.

All the while, Ann just stood and watched as she was happy for some brief entertain after walking through the jungle and the beating she took. She was not going to let Atlas get the better of her again and she held her side as she winced. Napoleon noticed this and trotted over to her and offered the ointment he had used on Tom, to which she accepted as the two men argued.

"Erm, I'm gonna go with no, however -" Jackson began, raising up a finger and looking down at the sword at his neck. "All we've got to do is yank it off of him to get it back, right?"

Tom huffed and put the sword down, throwing it on the pile with the guns and all the rest of the weapons he had been sat on.

"You fool, it does more than that. I should know, I've been its warden for over fifty years."

"Why? What does the treasure do?" Asked Ann, being unable to read the writing scrawled across the map.

Tom sighed.

"Well, I do not know exactly. It could destroy everything. It whispers to you, twists a man's mind, and as far as past guardians have been able to tell, it houses a soul."

"A soul!" Napoleon piped up. "That's Troll Seidr!"

"So, it's bad then." Jackson said.

"Very." Tom assured, as he pushed past them and walked down the aisle, his eyes full of determination.

Ann had only seen that look on his face once before, when the pirates had cornered them at the rally. This time she hoped that the old guardian wouldn't be so willing to race to his death. He then turned around and opened his arms, bowing low to the floor.

"We can't let Atlas get away. I'll start the train, the pirates took the slower one anyway, so we'll catch them up in no time. Welcome to the Ale Town Run."

28

The train hurtled along at a startling pace, rattling violently against the tracks. Ann and her friends shot down the line towards the pirates, and ahead of them was the outline of a small box, with steam billowing from the roof as it ran. To Ann, the island's surroundings seemed to pass by them in a rickety blur, and she started to feel a little uneasy. Her stomach curled, washing around the stew she had eaten at Nelson's.

"What's the matter?" The cook asked her gently, as they all huddled together in the only car that was attached to the engine.

Fryedai along with the twins began to laugh at her as they cleaned out the weapons Tom had given them.

"This is your first time on one of these things, isn't it?" He quipped, pointing to the way Ann held her hands around her belly whilst Napoleon ran along the floor.

Ann nodded grimly, continuing to look outside the window.

"Don't worry about it." Nelson said, drawing her attention away. "You'll get used to it soon." And he patted her on the shoulder and whispered softly in her ear so that the others could not hear. "Thanks for saving me back there. I should have had more faith in you, even for someone such as yourself."

Ann turned her head and looked at him dead in the eyes with slight confusion. She hadn't had the chance to speak with Nelson since Silvers had abducted him in the kitchens, and even then, Nelson had locked her away in the pantry with nobody but Napoleon for company. She hated to feel confined, but she knew in the back of her mind that the chef thought he was protecting her, and for that reason alone she had forgiven him. She couldn't have imagined what he had been through in the last few hours they had been apart. Ann could tell by his face that he was tired and drained by it all, but just as with his drunken friend, Ann knew that he still held some glimmer of hope that they could all come through this. They had so much to talk about after all. She had originally wanted to hire Jackson in order to rescue Wen. Not very 'Navy-like' she knew, but she had gained so much from her time on the island. Truth be told it was the pirates' fault. She even began to wonder if all her posturing had given her away. First Jackson and now Nelson. Had they figured her out? Even Fryedai and the rest of the Navy looked at her with some suspicion.

So, in response and with slight worry, she flicked back her scarlet red hair with a twirl and answered Nelson's question.

"What do you mean by someone such as myself?" She whispered.

This time she was more fixated on the question. Her green eyes were alarmed with worry, no matter how much she tried to hide it and her heart beat faster with every moment she waited. Ann could feel herself starting to develop a cold sweat, and it gradually began to ripple down the edge of her pale skin.

Nelson looked around the car. Jackson was upfront, near the engine with Tom as they rattled down the tracks and the Navy were busy cleaning out the weapons they were given. They talked amongst each other; laughing and joking for the first time in hours and were only a row or two away from where Nelson and Ann sat towards the centre of the aisle in the middle of the car.

"Do you know?" She asked even more quietly.

This time she looked around to see if the others were paying any attention.

"Follow me." He ushered, and they both got up and walked further down the car, where they could not be heard.

Ann was now severely worried about what was going to happen. Just how much did Nelson know about her, and what exactly was he going to do about it?

At the end of the car, Nelson opened a small door that led to a closed off terrace at the end of the train car, and held it open for Ann to walk through. The train continued to rattle. Once through, Nelson closed the door behind him as softly as he could. Was it because she knew about his Alchemic blood? He had probably concluded that Napoleon had told her at some point during the day because now he muttered under his breath, cursing his small and pink familiar - that and the fact that Atlas had shouted it for all the world to hear.

"I know." Nelson said, turning around to her.

Ann's eyes widened, but she could still turn it around. Nelson was not specifically saying what he knew and therefore it could have been anything.

"You know what? I thought you brought me out here to thank me?"

She was jostling her hair with her spare hand as she held on to the railing of the car.

"I know that you're not who you say you are. Jackson and I talked it over once I came round."

Ann gulped.

"It's clear you're trying to do the right thing by saving this island though. You're not like any 'Navy' we've ever come across. Though you hold up their best ideals."

"So, who are you?" Nelson asked.

For a second, Ann thought about giving the cook the same answer she had given Jackson when he had asked. '*I'm me.*' Then again, she looked at Nelson's face and knew that this time wouldn't slide and there was no way she could lie to him after what they had just been through.

"Jackson thinks you're on a secret mission or something. You're an open person Ann, so it's the only reason we can think of as to why you're such a mystery." He said suddenly. "Is that why you want Jackson to take you to Black Ridge? Your friend, they have something to do with it, don't they?"

Ann breathed a sigh of relief. Nelson was the one who had just weaved her a tale and not her. It was not lying if she just went along with it, was it? She didn't entirely know, and she didn't want to lie any more to her friends than she already had when it came to her *secret mission*. Nevertheless, if Jackson ever found out who she was before they got to the prison, she could kiss everything goodbye, and she could not allow that to happen. She knew how much he distrusted the Navy as it was. Too much was on the line for her to not say something to Nelson, even though deep down inside she desperately wanted to. He had been so kind to her, and she wanted to repay that kindness by bringing him along for the ride when this was all over, just as he had wanted. But she also knew that Jackson wouldn't help her if anything went wrong. Everything she had done so far had led up to this journey of getting Jackson to help her, and she was so close now that she was hanging by a thread.

Damn it! She thought. Why was her head so conflicted? Just tell him a little bit, Ann. She thought to herself. The teenager sighed. She had to tell him the whole truth now. Otherwise, Nelson wouldn't trust her, and Jackson certainly wouldn't. He may as well just have stabbed her right there and then and thrown her off the side of the train while it was still moving.

"The truth is the Navy wants to uncover the corruption in their own organisation and the North Sea Trading Company, and my friend Wen has the information I need."

"So how did you know about Jackson and him getting to the prison? Surely other people could have got you there, why come here?"

"Can't exactly let the rest of the Navy know about what I'm doing, can I? They'll say I've gone rogue! But when I started to look for my friend, I found out she was being taken to Black Ridge and I overheard some N.S.T.C officials talking about Jackson." She explained.

"What were they saying?" Asked Nelson and Ann threw her arms up in the air.

"Have no clue. I didn't catch all of their conversation, but they said that he'd been inside the prison before and that he owed them contract money, so thought he'd be perfect. I don't like those trading company guys anyway."

"Why not?" He asked, now even more curious as to who Ann really was and why Jackson had been inside the prison; why had he lied?

"The trade minister for the World Republic Government, the guy who runs the Company, Lord Roscoe Davidson-Duval, he burnt down my family home with my parents still inside and took my nine year old brother captive. He's a black-hearted man if ever there was one."

"Damn." He said, now understanding why Ann needed his friend.

As far as everybody on the island knew, Jackson had been away for a few years travelling with Molly, before Nelson's sister had mysteriously vanished whilst at sea, or so Jackson had told them. His friend had spent time working for one of the higher up company officials. But when Molly disappeared that had all stopped, and Jackson had become what he was like today. Nelson began to wonder whether the Lord was the cause of it all.

"And do you know where Davidson is now?" He asked.

Ann shook her head. She then brought out the small little book she kept in her pocket on all that she had found and opened it up, showing Nelson one of its pages. Nelson took the book from her and looked at it intently, reading each sentence in extraordinary detail and soaking up all the information.

"Along with Davidson, there's a Jonathan Draig and an Admiral Tenka, plus two other names which you've blacked out and I can barely read." He looked at her with a cold, silent judgement that then turned into a look of warmth. "These people have put you through a lot, haven't they? Just like how Atlas and his pirates have done with us this last month."

Ann felt as if she was about to sob her eyes out. Finally, after all this time, another person understood what she had been through.

"Don't tell anyone, Nelson!" She yelped. "I want to keep it a secret, at least until we get off the island. The Navy would want to kill me if they found out I had a book with the crimes of an Admiral and a Minister in it. I have enough trouble with breaking into a prison, I don't want to stay in one forever. I have more people to find afterwards."

Nelson smiled.

"Wait, you said *we,* so Jackson is definitely coming with you?" He asked hopefully.

His friend needed some time off the island, out at sea.

"Yeah, we had an accord." She explained. "I was kind of hoping you'd come along as well. I could use the help."

Nelson was silent for a second. This was finally the chance he needed to go out and look for his sister, and even though he decided to go anyway, it filled his heart with joy just to be asked.

"Yeah, I'll come." He chuckled. "Can't let that drunken fool have all the fun, and don't worry, I'm good with keeping secrets, but you've probably figured mine out already."

Ann smiled, saying that he was right, and Napoleon talked too much. As they made their way back inside, they saw that the entire group was sat together in the rounded leather booth that was closest to the doors.

"Right." Fryedai muttered as he loaded the gun in his hand and strapped it to his back along with all the other weapons – swords, daggers, pistols, they had it all.

The twins also had the guns they had been cleaning strapped to them, they were locked and ready to go with fire in their eyes, and for once Ann thought the Navy looked like a formidable fighting force. Fryedai then informed her and Nelson that Jackson had taken it upon himself to sit in the cab of the locomotive with Tom, and that they were now in jumping distance of the pirates' train.

And so, they went up to the cab of the engine as they continued to rattle along the rails.

At the front, the dials of the cab danced up and down measuring speed and pressure, and Tom the conductor sang merrily to himself as he shovelled coal into the engine's fire, making it fizzle and roar with heat. They were so close to the pirates' car now and Ann could make out the silhouettes of the people in the back, as their own almost touched the railing of the exterior terrace. In the corner of the cab, Ann saw that Jackson was slumped to one side trying to balance on his eerily wobbly elbow. The drunk was taking swig after swig of liquid from a metal container and was gradually falling further to one side. That was until Ann, Nelson, and Fryedai grabbed him, and stopped him falling onto the tracks.

Nelson turned to Tom and grabbed him by the shoulders, tearing him away from the controls of the mechanical train.

"Tom!" The cook shouted. "What in all the five seas did you give Jackson? He's completely knocked out!"

The conductor huffed and waved his hand in the air tipping his hat off. Nelson looked shocked, and Ann could see that despite the cloud of steam blocking the vision that both men were drunk.

"What did you give him?" Nelson asked again, but Tom started to sputter and laugh.

"Snake – he said he wanted a drink, so I gave him one. No harm, he-he!" The conductor laughed aloud and giggled the way a child would.

Nelson dropped him on the floor to crawl back to the controls.

"Crazy old man, trying to get us all killed." He muttered underneath his breath, and he turned to look at Ann and the others, who had no clue what was going on.

Ann especially had no idea what this 'Snake' was, and she was about to ask, when all of a sudden, Chris the Navy Bosun, took the words out of her mouth. She decided to see what it was and picked up the flask Jackson had dropped.

The container was much more substantial than she initially thought, and it seemed as if not even a quarter of it had been drunk. Ann then decided to try some for herself and dipped her finger into the metal flask to gather the tiniest droplet. Once she felt the touch of cold liquid on her finger, she pulled it back out and looked at the glistening shine that now ran down it. The alcoholic liquid smelled of barley and sweet, sweet summer fruits, such as apple, raspberry, and pomegranate, although from Tom and Jackson's reactions she didn't dare to lick the shine away from her finger and decided to wipe it on her side. Perhaps she would try it later and placed the flask in her jacket pocket for safekeeping.

"Snake." Nelson said, answering Chris's question. "Is one of the strongest alcoholic drinks on the planet and it's almost as dangerous as Ash. It's mostly used in construction work, due to it being extremely flammable. It comes from the East-Sea, and it just so happens to be Jackson's favourite drink that isn't ale."

Suddenly, there was a massive bang as the train crashed into the back of the pirates. Everyone was thrown forward, and an almighty squeal was let loose. No one had been driving the train. At that very moment, the weight of the two trains was forced down upon the tracks, and they had no choice but to run forward and try to get on to the roof. The back jerked from side to side, and everyone held on to railings in the cab for dear life. Ann opened the roof compartment and ordered everyone through.

In the process, both Jackson and Tom, in their drunkenness, fell to the bottom of the cab, slamming into the black iron door with a thud.

"I'll be alright." Tom groaned.

There was a small grunt in reply from Jackson.

"You see!" Shouted Luke, as he held on to a railing and watched the two men being flung about like ragdolls. "This is what happens when you let a drunk drive the train!"

"Shut it! I have an idea! Somebody grab Jackson and Tom!" Ordered Ann above the noise of the screeching and groaning metal.

Fryedai looked to the twins, and they both sighed.

"Come on, Tristan." Chris ushered, as he hung from the opposite railing to his brother.

"Why do we have to do it?"

"Yeah, why do we have to do it?" The other brother complained.

"Because Rockwell put me in charge, that's why. Now get going, otherwise we're never going to catch the brothers!" Commanded Fryedai, and again both of the twins sighed.

"Fine." They muttered in unison and went down to collect Tom and Jackson.

"Hey, cook, how long does it take for them to get sober off this stuff?" Asked Chris as he threw Jackson's arm over his shoulder and hauled him up.

Nelson had no time to answer his question as the cab of the train started to twist and break apart, only having the slightest of moments to grab Napoleon as the familiar jumped into his outstretched arm.

When they had made it into the open air at the top of the cab, the group ran forward. Napoleon was safely nestled underneath Nelson's arm and the pig's eyes widened as he saw the front of the train buckling from where they had struck the car belonging to the pirates.

"Don't worry, this is all going according to plan!" Ann assured as they ran towards the enemy train.

She jumped over to the pirates' side, landing with a clatter. Ann looked around her to see if everyone was okay. Surprisingly, it seemed that everyone had gotten there in one piece, though they were haggard and out of breath from the abruptness of the event.

"What's the next step in your master plan?" Fryedai called from the back, as he gradually got to his feet.

The wind and steam from the train were blowing back his hair with the force of a gale and Ann could hardly see as her own was swept in front of her eyeline. The train continued to move, rattle, and clank from side to side, as it rocked down the tracks. Ann saw a hatch in front of her that they could probably open to get inside.

"Follow me!" She shouted, lifting the hatch with a strained effort.

The hatch clanked down on top of the carriage roof, and the pirates in the car looked up with confusion.

"Hello there." She chimed and dived in.

The pirates drew their swords. Ann blasted a few with her guns, allowing room for the rest of her friends to follow. There was another bang as they passed underneath a bridge, causing the hatch they had just come through to be torn clean off.

"Approaching West-Station, little birds. Toot, toot!" Orion Vain announced over the speaker, his voice singing throughout the car.

However, at this moment in time, they had other problems to deal with as a group of no name pirates surrounded them. Napoleon squealed and wriggled from the arms of Nelson and ran down the aisle with a cry.

"Great, well this is just perfect." Chris complained, and dropped Jackson in a heap on the floor as he got the long rifle out from behind his back, glaring at the approaching pirates as the pig weaved through their legs.

The pirates were all snarling viciously at Ann, as they had always done. There must have been at least fifteen of them pressed into the car, and she watched as the ones who had guns tap on their triggers. Suddenly, the few members who had swords charged forward at them and both she and Chris moved forward and fired their guns.

Bang!

A row of pirates fell in front of them, in almost a domino effect, and their shouts and screams could be heard throughout the car, as the furniture started to smoulder and fizzle. The pirates with guns stepped back and away from their burning comrades and cocked their weapons as they stood in a line.

"Get down!" Both Chris and Ann yelled to the others, and they all hit the deck while trying to cover their heads with their arms.

The first few shots flew over their heads, then slowly the bullets started to creep towards them as the no named pirates adjusted their terrible aim.

Ping, ping, ping! The bullets sounded as they sliced into the floor.

"Somebody, do something!" Chris yelped, and that was when his brother rolled to the side and used one of the brown leather seats as cover.

He appeared over the top of the seat with knives in his hands and threw them one by one at the neatly lined up pirates. Just then, the train jerked to a hasty halt, and Ann looked out the window to see that they had arrived at the station. As if out of nowhere, a rush of about twenty pirates, along with the brothers, erupted from the other train car and ran to exit. Ann swore to herself that they were going to catch them, and if she had to chase them all the way to their ship, that is precisely what she was going to do.

Out in the distance, past all the rows of houses, shops and vents of steam, Ann saw the sea around the shore of the island had disappeared; only a sandy, moist seabed remained. However, looming vastly over the town, was the giant pirate galleon of Atlas and Orion Vain. The pirates moved toward the west of the island. Fryedai, along with the twins, winced at the memory of facing it in the morning's storm.

How were they going to face such odds? Ann had seven people, herself included. How could they have the advantage against a crew as seasoned as the brothers, with only seven people?

"You know." Began Nelson, breathing heavily as they raced towards the port. "The pirates won't expect the Devil's Rush, and I'm sure with Jackson's help, as crazy as it might be, we'll be able to get them as the waves swell."

"And how are we going to do that?" Asked the rest of them in muddled words, looks of confusion plastered across their faces.

Nelson smiled.

"First, I need a kitchen. Thanks to the Rush, we might just have time."

"There's one on *The Inspectre* you can use." Fryedai spoke up.

"Great, thanks." Replied the cook, the whole group continuing to run down the street in hot pursuit of the fleeing pirates.

As they moved nearer into the port area of the west side of town, Ann began to see the small outline that made up The Inspectre. It looked smaller than it had done initially; the side railings of the ship dipped below the decking of the docks as it sat on the dried-out seabed, and the sails looked slightly worn and tattered.

"Why do you think they kept it?" She asked, looking over the hill as Fryedai caught up to them.

He replied in steady, sharp breaths.

"Who knows? Perhaps they may have wanted a smaller ship to haul extra cargo? There were a lot of carts coming this way when we were chased into town; the brothers could use it as a dummy."

Ann smiled as they reached the entrance to the port. She knew this was true, the pirates had been continually chasing them from the moment she stepped on the island, and now the tables had turned. The port took up the entirety of the western side of the island and could easily house at least fifteen galleons at the docks. At the side closest to the open stretch of water, sat the brother's galleon. The pirates didn't seem to care that they were being chased, their only concern was getting the sails and rigging ready for their escape when the tide came crashing back in. They had their treasure, and now they wanted to leave.

Finally, they all reached the dock that *The Inspectre* was tied to. Luke and Chris were severely out of breath and panting from carrying Tom and Jackson all that way.

"I am not doing that again." Whined Chris, as large beads of sweat cascaded down his face and he went to wipe his brow as he still clung to Jackson.

"Don't worry, bro." Assured Luke, doing the same as he hung to Tom. "Just a few more steps to go and then we can dump both these two on deck."

Chris laughed at that and decided to race his brother to the ship. However, there was something that none of them in the

group had noticed until they came within inches of the ship...
A group of pirates had beaten them to it.

29

Arabella sat alone in the dripping wet cabin as she waited for her insane pirate captor to return.

How could her father have been this stupid to have gotten mixed up in all this? If he were alive, she would have slapped him and told him that he was wrong, and now because of the decision he made, she was paying the price, along with her friends, and the entire island. The door to the cabin creaked open, ripping her from her thoughts. In walked Atlas Vain, closely followed by Orion, a brimming snarl on his lips as blood trickled from a cut near his eye, and Gillian, who was holding something she couldn't quite see by a long-chained leash.

"Arabella Johnson." Atlas snarled. "I am so glad you could finally join us aboard our humble ship. I hope my first mate hasn't made you too comfortable. We wouldn't want you too relaxed before we make way."

"For all the effort it took us." Snorted Orion.

Arie looked past Atlas, and his brother glared at Hacksaw Gill, who was grinning from ear to ear. The pirate captain had come back for him after all, to her dismay, and she couldn't help but think of what had happened to Jackson. Still, where was the other one? Where was Silvers, the man who had both courted and tormented her for the past month! Then Atlas continued...

"Unfortunately, your drunk friend got the better of us an hour ago. However, it's of no consequence. When the tide comes back in, I can blow him and the entire island to smithereens!"

Arie shuffled and moved about in the chair. The chains rattled in response. She was happy that Jackson was okay, but as soon as the tide carried the ship away it would all be over, and she felt tears begin to well.

"So, what now, you're going to sell me to a Troll?" She cried.

"Why, yes!" He quipped as the amulet about his neck gleamed in her eyes. "You're going to be a queen, Arie! According to the map I have in my possession, the next piece of the treasure should be located in Lazarus's domain. He's been hiding it from me all along, but to get it I need what was agreed. The Hoarder-king does very much like to keep people like you as pets. Just a simple trade will be all that's needed."

"We better get paid as that Troll promised, Brother. I still don't trust him, and the crew is -"

"Never mind the crew, Orion!" Atlas snapped, the gleam from his arm glowing golden-red, his brother growing silent as the form twisted and changed. "They will soon learn."

"You're a monster, Atlas. Do you hear me? A monster. I hope you burn!" Arabella spat at him, and the pirate captain wiped the glob of liquid away from his mouth with a smile.

"No, girl. I am a hero. I'm doing the world a favour by saving it, and if you want to see a monster, I will show you a monster. Gillian?" He ordered, and a twisted grin arose on the pink-haired pirate's face. "Introduce Miss Johnson here, to Polly..."

With that, the pirate captain and his brother left the room, leaving the large door wide open. Orion began to whisper to Atlas about the losses they had sustained as his raspy voice carried down the hallway, but beyond that, Arabella could make no more of it over what was said. The barmaid now had more concerning things to focus her attention on, and her eyes followed the long leash Gillian was holding. Amber eyes came into view from pits of darkness, a snarling black beast with teeth of dulled gold and ivory stared back at her, and all the while Gillian laughed. The barmaid felt fear swell inside her.

The creature was enormous! Just barely managing to fit inside the cabin as the pirate dragged it through, yanking on the chain.

"This is Polly." Gillian grinned.

The beast's antenna reached forward, and Arie tried to back away as far as she could. It touched her leg with the gentlest swipe, and she cried out in pain as it secreted its poisonous acid, making Gillian howl with laughter.

"She's a Wraith." He spoke simply. "And she can be a very fussy girl on who she plays with, but I'm sure you'll be the best of friends. She's going to be your roommate for the remainder of the voyage."

Gillian then laughed again and wandered down the corridor. He threw the leash into the cabin along with a barrel of fish that he was keeping at the side of the door. As he disappeared into the shadows, Arabella called after him.

"I was right, wasn't I?" Her voice echoed and Gillian Mayers stood silently in the darkness. "Where's your friend now? Where's Silvers? Because he would be here to share in this just as Orion was. Was the wealth you all plundered from my home not enough? Was killing my father not enough? He does not care for you, Gillian! Think about it! Atlas doesn't care about anyone past his own deluded goals! Surely you realise that by now through your devotion to him. Everything around him is beginning to crumble as he rushes to escape a fate that he himself has sown."

Gillian gritted his teeth. He had given everything to his captain and had gained much from doing so, but still Arabella's question made him ponder as the thought burrowed its way into his head and the Black mark he bore, itched. There had been mutinies against Atlas before, he told himself as he walked away, knowing only shadows could hear him. None of them had worked before, but then again, he and Silvers had always been there for the sons of Ragnar, and as Arabella said, everything around them was beginning to crumble. Could they really build a new future for themselves around the rumble caused by the treasure as his captain had always told him? Or was Atlas up to his old tricks again as he was with their childhood-ending adventure to the giant's beanstalk. Power begotten is power taken for powers sake and he was not a child any longer. He could make his own decisions, and so he chose to leave Arabella and her words alone, with only the terrifyingly large-winged Polly to keep her company. As he ascended the stairs to the upper decks of the galleon, he could hear her cry out yet again, and Gillian knew it would do her no good. Arabella's fate had been sealed and it now lay in the hands of a sweaty, grubby, fat, old Troll.

"Jackson... Nelson... Ann... Anybody?" She cried as she tried to avoid the stinging antenna of Polly, and squirmed once again as they got closer. "Please. Help me!"

30

Ann now had a lot of problems at once to deal with, and the pirates on-board The Inspectre were at the top of her list. As soon as Chris had thrown Jackson on board, the plagued scallywags had jumped on them in an instant, outnumbering them two to one.

"You're dead now, Navy!" Said one of the pirates as they stabbed at the second Bosun with their small switchblade.

"Not yet." He muttered, and he squeezed the trigger of his rifle, hitting the pirate in the chest.

The pirate, wide eyed, collapsed to the ground with a thud as blood swelled in the wound. One of the pirates called out in anguish.

"That was my best mate!"

He led the others in an infuriated charge. Nevertheless, Chris soon began to pull the reload catch of the old rifle he carried and heard the metallic scrape as the next round lodged itself in the chamber.

Once again, he steadied his aim, but as he squeezed the trigger, nothing happened. It was jammed and five pirates were almost on top of him with their swords. With their blades inches away, Chris threw his rifle up and jabbed at the pirates with the bayonet. It was no use though, and the pirates were too close. The Navy-man backed away to the mast of the ship, the pirates continuing to press him, their yellow mouths beaming. Then, an idea came to him, one that he had seen Mister Rockwell use before when they were practising at base.

Could that work? He thought. He supposed he could try, and it might keep the pirates at bay until the others got up to the deck. He lurched forward with a spinning step into the blades, twirling the rifle around his neck. Chris attacked as fast as he could, making sure that he pressed them into a defence that their long blades couldn't possibly hope to keep up. He stabbed them as many times as he could with his bayonet, and three pirates fell in his wake.

"This is for Captain Robbinson!" He exclaimed proudly and moved on to attack the other two.

As he did, he made sure that none of them would even get close to the knocked out, grumbling Jackson, that was now snoozing on top of the deck in an inebriated heap.

Meanwhile, on the docks next to the ship, the others had their hands full as the rest of the pirates came charging out from underneath the dry seabed. The no-names barrelled towards them, yelling, holding their blades high in the air above their heads. One of the pirates even fell over on his way and ended up scrapping the bow of the ship with his blade against the lettering; instead of *The Inspectre*, the letters now read: *The spectre*.

Ann got out her guns, but as she squeezed the trigger, she found that she had run out of bullets and the special Ash canisters that had been given to her were almost dry! The teenager had no choice now but to find another weapon and she ran forward to meet the charging pirates head on. She had no idea what she was going to do. She had to find some way to protect herself, and as she leapt and punched the first pirate in the face, she found the rest of her friends had come to join her. Many bangs and shouts echoed through the air for those few minutes, and gradually after finding a cutlass on the ground, Ann was able to help push the pirates back and they fell away swearing and cursing to the last.

"See, that's what they get!" Fryedai called as happily as ever.

They almost had the ship back, seeing the last two figures fade into the distance. All of them were out of breath. It had been a hard-won fight; sweat ran down their brows and cuts and bruises stung against their skin.

"You okay up there, bro?" Luke asked, looking over at the deck and to where he had last seen his brother standing.

"Chris?" Called Fryedai.

Only shouts came from above and the rest of them climbed aboard the ship to see what happened to the Bosun. Fallen bodies were cast about the deck from where the fight had taken place and Fryedai and Luke quickly looked over them in search of their friend and brother.

Then a shout came! The fight had been carried inside the ship!

A few moments later, Chris appeared from the steps of the hold, struggling with the last of the no-named pirates on deck. The pirate with a huff and bleeding forehead had managed to hook Chris from behind with his own rifle, and the Navy-man tussled, trying to throw the foe over his back. The pirate reached for his pocket, using all the remaining strength he had in his occupied arm to hold the Bosun in place as they wrangled to and fro. Suddenly a pistol was revealed, and Fryedai and Luke shouted out in warning, but Chris didn't seem to hear them as the sound of the creeping ocean had started to roar and he bashed the man into the interior panels of the hold's doorway. It was The Devil's Rush, Ann realised! It was almost at their door! The pirate moved his arm around, pressing his gun against the apple of the sailor's neck with his own head directly behind. With a blood-spattered, wolfish grin, the pirate squeezed the trigger.

Bang went the pistol, and both men dropped to the floor. Fryedai and Luke roared with rage as they ran towards the hold, unable to get there in time.

"What are you going to do?" Cried Ann as she looked around the deck.

Tears streamed down the faces of the men. The sea had started to flow in tiny drabs towards the docks as the tide rolled in on a gigantic wave, heralded by the sound of thunder. Ann knew they had to get the ship ready and that they didn't have time to grieve, otherwise they would be done for! Nelson and Napoleon scurried into the kitchen as he nodded to her and told her to lay both Jackson and Tom against the mast. Luke could barely move, and Ann couldn't blame him, but they had to do something as Fryedai started to run about the ship. She tried to help him and started to move the bodies of the fallen pirates off the ship until she came to that of his friend.

"We have to hurry!" Ann told him, looking over to the wave of water working its way towards the dry docks. "The sea is coming. We have to move him!"

Fryedai grimaced.

"This is none of your concern!" He snapped, as he rushed to untie the moors.

"But—" Ann Argued, her face in pain for him as she wanted to help.

"You just get to making sure Jackson is awake so that we can get underway. We need everybody, now!" And he wiped his eyes, motioning for Luke to help. "Get to it, help Nelson. Go!" He cried.

Ann knew it was helpless to argue with him further, but before she made her way to the galley, Ann hugged him for the briefest of moments. She felt his heavy chest heave in her arms, his salty tears brush against her check. She knew what that pain was like when fire and chaos burned all around. It could destroy a person if they weren't too careful, and Ann knew that people needed to be there for one another in times of hardship. She had to let Fryedai know that she was there for him, as she was for Jackson and Nelson and Arie. It was all she could do before she sped to the galley.

"We need to do this quick." Nelson explained as Ann raced into the kitchen. "The galleon will definitely survive because it's so large, but the only other person I've ever seen sail out of this port when it's like tonight, is Jackson."

"Is it that big?"

"Yes, colossal – it's a miracle that the island survives each time."

"What do I need?" Asked Ann as she frantically searched through the cupboards and moved Napoleon out of the way.

The Familiar had remarkably survived the train crash by clinging to his master's arm the whole while and had followed them all the way onto the ship, even helping in attacking the pirates on the dock, jamming his little trotters against the pirates' faces that she had punched to the ground.

"Everything you can find, especially chilli powder." Said Nelson.

"That sounds horrible." Complained Ann as she gathered everything she could.

Now she saw why Napoleon had said he was terrible at Alchemy and why Jackson had said what he said about the cook's food. Nelson was as only as good as he was when following a recipe.

"It does the trick. It doesn't have to be nice, and spice will wake anyone up, the tomatoes are just for texture."

"I see." Ann trailed off and she went out to go get Jackson and Tom.

Outside on the deck, Fryedai and Luke had unfurled all the sails so that they could fly free against the wind and had raised the anchor so they could get underway. However, this now meant that the ship was dangerously leaning to one side without the support of the sea, and Ann feared that they would soon topple over, as the rope that held them to the dock was starting to fray since Fryedai had released the moors. She proceeded to drag both Tom and Jackson inside, where Nelson poured the strange red concoction that he had come up with down their throats. They both awoke up with a start.

"Welcome back you two, we've got work to be doing. We have an island to save." Chuckled Nelson as Jackson looked at him with hazy eyes.

"Ugh, what happened. Where am I?" He questioned, rubbing his head. "Weren't we on a train a before?"

"Yes." Nelson sighed. "But then it blew up, and now we're on a Navy ship about to chase the pirates, before they have a chance to blow the entire island to bits and kill everyone we know and love."

"Well, isn't that cheery." Grumbled Jackson, getting up from the floor and helping Tom to his feet. "Is there anything else I missed while I was out? And ugh, why did you use that dreaded wake-up juice of yours on me, you know I hate it."

"Well, that's the point. The Devil's Rush is literally about to happen, and we need you to steer the ship."

Jackson then shook his head, shaking himself awake.

"Fine, I'll do it." He groaned, walking out of the cabin and up on to the deck.

Suddenly, there was a sound like crackling thunder and a monstrous downpour of rain.

"Look there, it's starting again. Hang on to anything you got!" Pointed the drunk as they climbed the steps to the wheelhouse.

All heads turned towards the left and the ragging tower of blue sea, barrelling towards them at an unstoppable pace. The waves were taller than any Ann had seen today, and even the power created by Ash could not hold a candle to the raw ferocity of nature that was contained in their monstrous world. The waves were high above them, like jagged mountain peaks, it came with the same winter's chill and roaring, frosted avalanches. In one swift movement, the entirety of the docks became flooded with crashing water, causing *The Spectre* and the pirates' galleon to be swept out to open sea.

They lurched forward, riding on the crest of a wave as they followed their hulking foe. Water bombarded all sides as they surged upwards into the sky. The entirety of Ann's crew held on for dear life. The base of the hull creaked and groaned, the sails and ropes screamed and shuddered as they began to slowly tear apart, piece by piece, but still for the moment they held. It reminded Ann of the Spider's glass that morning, and how the water, like an icy hand of death, was almost upon them. Death was carrying them now, and they had no choice but to hold on for the ride as it delivered them through the night's sky in pursuit of the pirates. An anxious surge pitted in their stomachs, and they fell through the wave, the bow of the ship crashing against the crest, causing them to descend further into the sea. The pirates fared no better, they had been cast a little further ahead, and only once the wave and sea had settled, did they follow at a straight course.

"What're we making?" Ann asked from next to Jackson at the wheelhouse as she looked towards the enemy ship.

"No better than nine knots with the incoming rush of seawater. We should be doing at least fifteen!"

"Not easy when you're trying to catch up to another ship." Luke added sorrowfully as he hung from the rigging.

"Well, we could always lighten the ship?" Suggested Ann, looking around.

"I know." Fryedai began. "But I hate to see us defenceless like the last time we faced them, least we should do is prime the cannons."

Ann shrugged.

"I'll wing it."

"Are you mad!" Screamed Fryedai.

Ann planned to try and close up to Atlas' ship then tear away at the last moment so she could jump on-board. That way at least she may have a chance of taking out the insane pirate captain before he used the gauntlet's power.

"Jackson, please say something to her."

"I'm not one for winging it usually." The drunk stated gloomily. "But I'll go along with Ann, if she thinks it's the right idea."

Surprisingly, he laughed to himself, making Ann frown.

"What is it?" She asked. "What's wrong?"

Jackson smiled.

"You are paying for this after all."

Fryedai huffed and stormed to the other end of the ship. He scanned the water that spun off the side as they cleanly skimmed and bounced over the waves. He knew that Ann and Jackson were making a mistake, it was his ship after all, and he knew it best. They needed the cannons, but they needed speed as well. The gap between them and the pirates might not be as close enough as they wanted it to be, and in the distance, he could only see their massive sails and boxed outline. The size of *The Extinction* itself had given the pirates an enormous advantage of getting away from them when the rush hit, as the weight of the ship had moved it further forward across the sea. Fryedai knew that depending on the angle of their curved sails, the strong headwind, and the movement of the currents, they could probably make up another five knots and be able to become level with the pirates – but still that would take time, time they did not have.

"Hey, Luke." He called up to the rigging. "Turn the sails south by south-east and angle the main mast to the port-hand side."

Jackson hollered in agreement; he saw Ann also climb the rigging to help.

Fryedai smiled to himself. At least now he knew he was not useless after all. He had been sailing on this ship long enough to know its speed to a fraction of a knot. He felt how much water pressed against the hull, and he knew when the ship was sailing easy and when it was sailing hard. Still, it would not be the same without his friend. They had so little time to prepare the ship that Chris's body still lay against the deck, covered by the rain and the wind and he knew somehow, they would have to let him go before the fight began.

"Hey, Ann!" He yelled up to her. "Do you know the Coxon's Call? I want you to sing it for Chris, we need to send him off."

Ann nodded and said that she did, and the Navy navigator nodded to Chris, now the only surviving Bosun of the crew, and he lifted his brother up in his arms and towards the railings of *The Spectre* as Ann started to sing, her voice carrying across the wind and the waves – he would be given a burial at sea, as a true sailor deserved.

"The Skies were red and the shores were gold,

Travel from these lands, onto damp olde unbeknown,

Let me carry you away till I wash against a prow, and look towards The Fields, which I know you have found,

So, row, my son.

Row deep and true,

May the Coxon's Call see you through.

Though, though we part on this long day, row across that river for me, and one day I will stay."

31

Arabella screamed.

The Wraith continued to wriggle its way closer to her no matter how hard she pushed away. Its acid-filled antennae slivered around her feet as the ship crashed against the waves, and she squirmed wishing that they would pass over the ropes that held her in place.

"Why won't you leave me be!" She cried once more.

She didn't want to be sold to a Troll.

The Wraith turned its head to the side and gargled at her sympathetically. Its fanged teeth spun in a circle around its jaw. Arie almost felt sorry for the beast, forced to be like this by the brothers.

"You're just like me, aren't you?" She asked woefully, and Polly the Wraith continued to turn her head, almost as if she were rolling over. "You've been made a pet by them as well. Say, could you help me get out of here, Polly?"

The Wraith shook her head from side to side, in a way she was like a dog, wagging its tail and antenna to tell Arabella that she wanted to play.

"Ugh!" Arie cried in annoyance and then suddenly, an idea sprung to her. "I tell you what, girl, shall we play a game?" She asked, and the Wraith nodded her head excitedly.

"Alright then, what game do you want to play?"

Polly abruptly left the cabin and bounded down the hallway with the leash trailing and rattling behind her. In the distance, there were shouts from angry pirates and Polly came back with a bright big red ball held in her mouth.

"You want to play fetch?"

Polly nodded excitedly and dropped the ball in front of the chair with her antennas closing around it.

"I'd love to." Said Arabella, looking down at herself. "But I'm tied up."

Polly growled, and out of nowhere, her antennas shot behind the barmaid's back and slashed the ropes open that held her in place. The ropes fell to the floor and sizzled away in the acid. She was free.

"Good girl." She whispered, trying not to alert any of the other pirates and patted Polly on the head, to which she groaned at happily.

Arabella then attempted to sneak out of the cabin, but Polly quickly turned around and barred the doorway, giving off a slight hiss.

"Okay, okay." Arie said, raising her hands. "I'll play with you."

The Wraith once again groaned with a happy chatter. If Arabella was ever to get off the ship, she would have to get past Polly...

32

They were closing on the pirates with each passing minute. Ann adjusted the upper edge of the mainsail as she had been told to do and the sea breeze blustered. She now had a clearer view of *The Ymir's Extinction* as it tried to escape over the horizon.

Atlas... She thought, shaking her head. Finally, someone is going to put a stop to your madness.

"How long now, Jackson?" She called from her lookout spot, clinging to the rigging.

The wind blew softly against her crimson-coloured hair as they sailed further into an up-draft. She was anxious to finally finish this chase. She didn't have time to play about any more, her friend was depending on her. She looked over the horizon and noticed a dim-orange and red glow slowly appear as it gradually started to lighten the sky. Dawn was coming.

"Won't be long now." Jackson responded from the wheel.

They still carried full sail, while The Extinction, with its massive weight and load, had dropped much of her canvas. Was Atlas trying to bait them to come closer? She thought.

Ann scuttled down the rigging and stopped just where it met the cannons. She stared through the shimmering glare of the growing sunlight as it shined against the glassy water. A vibration ran down the length of the ship. At the last moment, Jackson released the wheel, and it spun wildly out of control.

"Reef!" He barked, turning hard to starboard to stop the rudder from breaking.

There was another shudder, and Jackson knew what had happened as he wrestled back the wheel.

"The Rush brought it further along the seabed!"

The Spectre then twisted and turned, snaking towards *The Extinction*. Ann gazed out ahead of her as she raced towards Jackson. It seemed Atlas' ship was having the same problem, which was why they had dropped canvas, they were trying to navigate the reef but due to its gargantuan size, *The Extinction* had mowed across it, but Ann's ship was likely to be stuck.

"Shit!" Yelled Jackson, peering forward and he started to tell Luke and Tom to get ready on the cannons.

They came within inches of *The Extinction*.

"Make fast, we're coming around!"

Ann braced herself as Luke ran over and let the capstone fly. She poised her hand above her head to give the signal to Tom to let loose the cannon. Then, *The Extinction* turned, and echoing from across the gap of the two ships, Ann heard the one cry that everyone on the seas feared more than any other as hatches opened: "Fire!"

33

The sound of blaring cannons blasted across the sea like a thousand crackling thunderbolts. On board *The Spectre*, smoke began to rise as volleys passed close to the sails, burning away any catch on the wind.

"Dirty, good-for-nothing, pirates!" Jackson seethed, turning the wheel towards the east. "Hey, Ann! What do you suppose we do now? That bald freak has taken away our advantage!"

"Jackson, this ship is an experimental Navy vessel!" Shouted Fryedai up to the wheelhouse. "If you look in the centre of the wheel, you'll find that the middle centrepiece is made up of different slots and notches."

Jackson gazed down, feeling his hand over the slits and grooves. In the middle, there was what he could only describe as a traditional looking centrepiece, made from plain wood with decorative indents and a golden overlay. However, on closer inspection, he saw that Fryedai was right; the slots were actually numbered buttons connected to the housing, like miss-matched pieces of a jigsaw puzzle.

"What of it?"

Suddenly, cannon-fire roared again, and everyone on board ducked.

"Press one!" Fryedai urged.

With a push of his finger, Jackson released one of the outer pieces; the tiny groove labelled number nineteen. In a split second, the wooden panels that lined the hull began to shift and move, and Jackson could hear a mechanical wiring coming from the main box of the wheelhouse. In all Jackson's days of sailing, he had never seen a ship quite like this. Once the wiring finally came to a stop, three long, sharp hook-blades protruded from both sides of the ship. Barbed like the arm of a crab, the hooks to the port hand side buried themselves into *The Extinction*, cracking parts of the wooden hull into splinters.

"Woah, now that's cool!" He gasped, as they tore away from the pirate ship and sailed forward.

"Prepare to broadside!" Shouted Fryedai, and Tom and Nelson ran along the side of the deck with a torch, lighting all the cannons.

The ship turned to the side wildly, and Ann shouted out the word she had always wanted to say.

"Fire!" She yelled, and iron balls were set loose, flying towards the bow of Atlas' ship.

* * *

Polly the Wraith was groaning happily. At this moment in time, the massive creature was laying on her back, taking up most of the confined cabin with her slimy antennas sprawled out in front of Arabella. The ship shuddered and rocked violently from side to side, throwing Polly and the barmaid against the wall as an almighty explosion rang, breaking the chain that acted as the animal's leash.

Polly raised her wing to protect Arabella, whining slightly as the two of them got up from the now water filled floor. Water seeped in from holes dotted about one side of the room. Everything was soaking wet, and the sound of flowing water could be heard rushing into the cabin.

"We need to get off this ship." She said, and Polly tilted her head back, letting out a wail in agreement.

The two of them ran to the open door. At the end of the corridor was a set of stairs that led further up into the ship, followed by scores of diamond-heaped barrels. Plunder for plunders sake thought the barmaid as she remembered all the misery Atlas and his ilk had caused over the last month. It was all for deals, treasure, and alliances. Arie went up the stairwell first, and Polly soon followed. The Wraith bounded after her, the creature's red ball fixed firmly in between her spiralled teeth as her antenna dangled up and down.

"Alright, Polly." The barmaid began as water dripped down from her hair. "You go first, girl, otherwise those nasty pirates will lock us up again, and we'll drown."

Polly nodded her head and leapt up the stairwell in excitement.

Steadily, Arabella and Polly crept through the ship and stopped just shy of the top. The barmaid could see pirates rushing about all over the place as they worked tirelessly to scale rigging and reload cannon charges. Next to them, to starboard side, Arie noticed that Jackson, Nelson, Ann, and Tom, as well as two others were sailing next to them. She was so happy someone had come to save her from this nightmare, and she struggled for the words to escape her mouth. However, just as she was feeling an overwhelming sense of happiness, she heard Atlas bellow in rage from the top of his wheelhouse, and both their heads turned to look as cannon fire crashed into the bow of the ship.

"Argh, I've had enough of these games!" Atlas cried.

He was slamming his fist down against one of the arms of a massive throne. He really did see himself as king of the entire world, or at least the king of his entire crew.

"Orion, let's ram them head on, break them in twain!" He ordered.

Arabella ducked below the stairwell as shreds of wood covered her head like a sprinkling of snow. Above the roaring and wailing of cannon fire did she let out a scream when she heard the blasts; how foolish she had been to try and escape in the middle of a battle! Her scream carried itself across the ship, and she looked up in horror to find that the terrifying pirate captain was towering above her with an unnerving and menacing stare.

"And where in the Ten Hells do you think you two are going?" He growled.

Arie smiled nervously.

"Out for a leisurely walk to catch a glimpse of that morning sea view." She jested.

Behind her, Polly reared her head, nodding up and down excitedly as she held her red ball in her mouth and spat it out for Atlas to play with.

Atlas smiled, cold and wicked. It was a smile Arabella didn't like the look of, and the pirate captain bent down to pick up the slathering wet ball. He looked at it for a moment, holding it in his massive hand.

"Well, if you wanted a view, all you had to do was ask." He grinned and Arabella's face twisted in confusion. "Polly, do the thing."

"The thing?" Gawped the barmaid.

The Wraith suddenly leapt up on deck, spread her large black wings and groaned happily as she took into the air, she then circled around the canvases in a swerving arc before making her way back to Arabella. With sharp talons the Wraith proceeded to grab the blonde by the shoulders as she swooped by and lifted her up into the air. The creature flapped her wings wildly, carrying the barmaid off to the top of the crow's nest where she hovered in place.

Atlas stood in the centre of the ship then, his arms raised to his sides and his voice booming across the waves.

"Did you know that female Wraiths are bigger than the males?" He began.

Arabella didn't care what Atlas said, she just feared that Polly would let go.

"We found Polly as a hatchling just after our village was destroyed, and took her in. She's still a baby now, of course. My father once told me female Wraiths take fifty years to grow into their full size, compared to that of the male who take just two. Fascinating, is it not?"

"What's your point?" Arabella screeched, beginning to feel the majority of her blood rush toward her head as The Wraith had turned her round to dangle by her feet – the creature probably thought this was a form of play!

"The point is." Atlas bellowed. "Polly thinks of me as her parent and will do anything I command! Now watch as we finally destroy your friends!"

34

Ann hung to the side of the ship for dear life as *The Extinction* approached, she got the feeling that this was very much like the Scourge game she had played with Arabella; the only difference was that their roles were reversed, and this was on a much grander scale. The pirates were going to ram straight into their broadside, and because the anchor had been dropped, there was nowhere they could go to escape it!

"Hold on!" Shouted Jackson, as he desperately jammed his fingers into the buttons and grooves on the wheel.

Just as the ship was about to hit them, the blades that had appeared at the side of *The Spectre* retracted. Now the side panels of the ship opened, and two cannons appeared on either side.

"I love this ship." He muttered, and suddenly the cannons fired, blasting them a little further forward and out of the way of the pirates' ship.

The Extinction was now behind them, and the waves swelled, lifting *The Spectre* higher in the water for the last of the Devil's Rush. Ann now saw an opportunity to get on-board the pirate's ship, as they could easily swing on a rope and onto the stern. Quickly, she called Nelson and Fryedai over and together they tied up enough of the safety lines to throw them over the rigging and swing across.

"You're seriously not going to do what I think you're about to?" Questioned Fryedai as the winds raged.
Ann gave him a devilish smile.

"For Hells sake!" Cried Nelson. "At least let us go with you!"

"Alright." She shrugged, as she walked back across the deck for a run-up. "Here we go!"

Fryedai and Nelson looked at one another and rolled their eyes, together all three of them ran off the deck and jumped. The wind blew their hair, the salty seawater spat against them, but still nothing seemed to slow them down as they clung to the rope they had laid.

Just as they were in reach of the pirates' ship, Fryedai slipped down the rope that all three of them held, his grip loosening from the salty spray, and he slammed into Ann, resting on her shoulders. She had to hold on ever so tightly to keep herself from falling to a savage watery death, and every muscle in her arms and upper body burned with pain like it had just been set on fire.

"Fryedai!" She screamed as the three of them swung closer, the wind brushing through her hair. "You're quite literally going to kill me in a minute if you don't hold on!"

"Oh shi-" Swore Nelson from higher up as he saw where they were going.

Before he could finish his sentence, they crashed into the stained glass that made up the back of the pirate ship – an ornately designed skull – and fell through the window, breaking it into hundreds of pieces before landing in a large cabin.

"Well, that worked out better than I expected." Chimed the cook, as the three of them got up and brushed themselves free of glass.

In the room they were in now, the three of them saw that it was covered in old knickknacks and a cannon stood proudly in the corner. Above the cannon, there was a sign that read: 'Kabuki'. Ann recoiled in horror as she saw the fragmented remains of what appeared to be a giant's eye socket, rearranged into a bookcase. The shelves were lined with old leather-bound books and tattered sea charts.

"Some of these are Jackson's!" Nelson spoke in surprise as he too looked at the bookshelf. "Atlas must have stolen them."

Ann now looked closer at the stolen scrolls, some of which even shared the same ancient rune writing that was scrawled across the walls of the treasure room underneath the town, and on her own stolen map which she had taken from the mad captain himself. It seemed that the brothers had been searching for a very long time. Ann got closer to the bookshelf as her interest grew and Nelson and Fryedai looked very worryingly at the door, as shouts became louder. In a moment, the door to the room was forced open and pirates came swarming in, surrounding Ann and her friends in a matter of seconds.

"We've been expecting you." A pink-haired man said with venom in his voice.

It was the same man that had tormented her and Tom at the rally.

"Atlas will see you now."

Gillian Mayers ordered for them to be bound, and they were escorted up the couple of steps that lead to the main deck by gunpoint. They walked past the capstan and the rows of endless rigging that folded tenfold around the ship, and through the ragged and haggard scores of pirates that had remained and survived the island. They stared at Ann with hatred. If it weren't for Ann and her friends, they would have gotten exactly what they wanted and much more – only Ann was here to put an end to it!

Eventually, they reached the man who everyone had been talking about, and Gillian Mayers pushed them in front of Atlas, sat on yet another throne.

In the middle of the ship, Ann saw that Arabella was being dangled above them by a foul-some creature and the young girl was quickly forced against her knees as another gun was pressed to her back.

"Thank you, Gillian." Atlas spoke calmly before glaring at Ann.

The pirate smirked and continued his work as he headed towards the mast. However, before he did so, he stopped at the stand next to Atlas, filled up a pouch of Ash and went on his way, where a large gorilla-like man holding an axe waited for him. The man had a scar on his forehead the size of a bullet hole and was covered in bruises, what was more was that he and Gillian seemed to talk to one another in hushed tones for some time as Atlas decided what to do with Ann and her friends. Then she realised that this man was what had once been the giant ape that had attacked them in the train station: Taylor. She concluded that the Ash he'd been using had healed his wounds before his form had come to its inevitable end.

"Well, girl. I'm almost pleased you survived our last encounter." The pirate captain began, drawing Ann's attention back to the real monster on the ship – his indigo amulet glowing as the treasure slivered up and down his arm. "I have you here at last, welcome aboard *The Ymir's Extinction!*" He announced, looking at the red and gold shine that came from his hand and how his beard fell against the shining light. "May every man receive his fair and justly earned reward!" And to that the pirates around them roared in revelry.

"I see you've brought me back my Alchemist!" He went on as he lowered his hand for silence. "With this power, nothing will stop me from achieving my goal, I even have the map." The pirate boasted, looking from her to Nelson and down to his belt, but Atlas' smile soon faded, and his eyes widened in shock and surprise.

"What!" He roared. "Where is it!"

Atlas desperately searched around his throne and to his person to find it, knocking over the stand next to him that held the bowl of dark, emerald-coloured powder.

"Where is it!" He bellowed at his crew that now froze, some of them turning lily-white.

Ann smiled.

"What do you know?" Atlas screeched.

Ann said nothing, she didn't want to tell him that she was the one who had the map on her this very second and he slapped her with the back of his hand.

"Perhaps I will have two people to take to that hideous Troll-King, Lazarus! That map's Siedr was special!"

"You're crazy, Atlas!" Exclaimed Ann, as the pirates around her continued to grow uneasy and she looked to the remainder of the crazed pirate's crew that were not already dead by his hand, whether it was direct or otherwise. "Even your crew knows it."

Atlas looked around at the group that had gathered, and he saw they began to whisper and knave between themselves. He felt another headache brewing and his black mark itched at the back of his neck. Even Gillian, his greatest friend and love besides his brother, chattered and conversed in whispers. Had he not given them everything? Power, fame, and wealth now beyond imagining! Hoards of diamonds sat within the hold and hallways of his ship – he would not let the Hoarder-King have it, nor anybody else. With all the wealth he had amassed, he could find the remaining pieces to the treasure unopposed with an army, bought and paid for, at his back. He knew Orion would approve. His eyes had always glinted at the sight of jewels and golden Threds. Money held power as much as Ash, and with it he would uncover the secrets of the world.

"Am I now?" He jested, looking to Ann, and raising his arms with the glow and the hum of the red and golden treasure piece. "I gave them everything." He spat.

Atlas shouted to the rest of the crew of thieves and brigands.

"I gave you everything! All I see before me are four captured, no good, do-gooders, who couldn't stay out of my business. You almost ruined it all!" And he pointed to each of them with a long, accusing finger.

"A worthless coward who ran away, leaving his captain to die. A stranger, who appeared out of nowhere, disrupting everything. A girl whose daddy told her too much. And a cook... who just wouldn't keep quiet and went to get help from a stranger and a drunk." Taunted Atlas. "I should kill you all right now, for all that you've done! Alas, I need the Alchemist alive."

A murmur spread about the crew.

He had to make an example of them now. Tensions were once again beginning to rise as his crew stared at him. The pale crescent moon was low on the horizon as it straddled an emblazoning ocean. He knew that a dawn would come, that dawn was coming. Still, his crew whispered about him as his headache grew fiercer, and it was more agonising than he had ever felt before. The indigo amulet glowed, its white crystal shining as Atlas heard the voice in his head, the one that had spoken to him in the chamber.

"They lie to you, Atlas... They conspire and they plot. They want to take from you all that you have made, these people you now hold prisoner. Do not let your power waver. Kill them. I have never lied to you. Mutiny! You cannot allow it."

"I'll never serve you!" Nelson growled looking up at the captain.

Atlas was about to say something when his brother arrived before him, pushing through the group of whispering pirates as they uttered words such as 'Kaine', 'Devourer' and 'Trolls'.

"Oh, oh, Atlas! Atlas!" Orion cried.

The pirate captain rolled his eyes and gritted his teeth at the interruption as he decided what to do, shaking the headache off.

"Can I have the Navy to myself? I want to make him pay."

Orion pointing to the bloody cut that Fryedai had given him next to his eye, Atlas beamed as an idea came to him, a wicked smile curling upon his lips.

"*Yes...*" The voice whispered to him. "*You must make it a spectacle, for all to see. Are you not the hero of this tale?*"

"Sure, Orion." Atlas agreed. "You can have that one, but the rest are mine."

"Fight me." Ann said suddenly, as she realised the situation was running away from her. "Be a man and fight me, and not with your toy either. Show me what Atlas Vain, scourge of the five wine-dark seas can really do."

Atlas bent down and growled.

"So be it, girl. Let's have a little fun for a change, that way your friends can see you die before they witness everything they know and love burn to ashes. Lazarus can have the other one as was agreed."

Atlas' crew began to chant and thump on the sides of their ship.

"The captain's going to fight." They shouted, and the chanting started once again.

"Hum, hum, hum hum hum hum." They sang and steadily the members of the crew created a ring of people around the main deck.

"Hey, Atlas!" Orion shouted over the chanting, standing next to his brother as they all walked out into the middle of the deck, surrounded by the pirate crew.

"Can I go first? I'll make this quick, I don't think the little bird will be much."

"Fine." He grunted. "It'll be a warm-up match."

Atlas turned his head and looked over to his other side and glared at Ann. He quietened his pirate crew and held his brother's hand high in the air, and Ann noticed something was not quite right with Orion. A bandage on his hand covered up something gruesome and dark.

"My brother!" Atlas roared. "Has elected to go first and he will face…"

"You." Decreed the pirate captain and pointed at Fryedai.

Fryedai gulped.

"Wait!" A pirate shouted from the encircled group as Ann and Nelson were picked up by their bounds and tossed to the side.

Fryedai's own were cut by Orion Vain, and he was given a dagger to defend himself with as the pirate swaggered over to other side of the human-ring. They all paused as Taylor the brute bounded into the centre holding his hefty axe.

"What do we get out of this?" The brute questioned, holding his axe and arms in the air to encompass all around. "Should not every man receive his fair and justly earned reward, just as it was written in the articles that we signed when joining this blasted crew? Atlas has taken everything for himself that we have earned with sweat and toil, and now he wants more power, an unlimited supply of Ash from the Alchemist, that Silvers Kent himself captured! Where is Silvers I ask the captain; where is our reward?"

Atlas' fist tightened on his throne as the majority of the crew nodded in agreement. He stared at Gillian Mayers with hatred and bile in that moment as his crewman continued and the pink-haired pirate stared back. He shook his head and a single tear streamed down the corner of one eye. Where once had been love and friendship, brotherhood and trust, there was now only betrayal.

"Where is Silvers?" Gillian mouthed.

Atlas was about to give a reply when Taylor started again. All the fibres in his body wanted to strike the brute down. Atlas knew he was being backed into a corner, and he still needed the crew to man the ship. He had not left his blood-brother back in the caverns lightly. Silvers may have still even been alive if he had had the real concern to check, but he had made the tunnels collapse of pure rage for thinking him dead and it was true that still the whole island would burn once they had cleared the miles of bay. Was that not enough for them?

"Because it's not the diamond treasure trove we took, that's not our reward, that hoard is bound for the Trolls, so Gillian says. So, what do we get for our loses and hard work? Nothing! Atlas Vain will not keep his word to us – he is afraid of Ravens and creatures that hide in the night! All to protect his true brother, Orion. It is we who helped him wage war on the Giants, and for some fifteen years we have suffered because of the Sons of Ragnar. We all have the marks. Do we not deserve his love and protection too, for my brother is dead?"

"Enough!" Atlas demanded, rising to his feet.

Ann watched as the golden treasure, roaring red, turned into a sword, and Atlas grabbed for his own ruby-hilted blade and pulled it from his scabbard as he went to face Taylor. Thus, the bald and blue-eyed man held both blades to the brute's neck.

"We shall finish this after we deal with the prisoners!" He spat.

Taylor huffed, snarling at the blades that clung to his neck. He lowered his arms and pushed the blades away with the back of his axe before he walked away.

"What's wrong with a little fun first?" He quizzed, and the rest of the crew roared in excitement.

Ann knew they were getting exactly what they wanted, as she slowly worked her fingers to try and undo the tight bonds that kept her in place. She could use this to her advantage, and she gave a knowing nod to Nelson beside her.

"Can we begin now?" Orion complained to his brother as the pirate captain sat back down once again on his throne.

Atlas snarled, thinking over the situation that had come about as he passed his fingers through his long black beard. He was looking nervous.

"Let the execution begin!" He called and the pirate crew yet again jeered in excitement.

"Finally! I'm looking forward to this, little bird. I'm going to make you squirm!" Laughed Orion as he drew his cutlass, *Blood-drip*.

Fryedai was pushed into the circle and suddenly the menacing pirate charged at the blonde officer with an inhuman howl. Fryedai dived to the side wildly as he tried to avoid Orion's blade, falling hard against the deck.

"Fuck!" Orion shouted.

The pirate clearly wanted to give his crew a show to remember, and even his brother snarled at the effort.

"Why do you always have to be so slippery! That pig-captain of yours wasn't nearly as difficult to gut."

Fryedai breathed heavily, lifting himself from the floor. All the while Ann continued to work at her bonds, rubbing her hands together from behind her back, working to pull the twisting, fraying the knots so that she could get free. She had to help her friend. Orion would kill him!

"I'm not the captain." He said, reaffirming his grip on the dagger.

Orion smiled and brought his arms out to the side of him.

"Oh? Then who are you, little bird?"

"I'm Tristan Fryedai."

The pain he felt in his leg flared up again, and with all his might, Fryedai charged and ran forward at Orion. The look on the pirate's face changed from that of bravado to confusion. As Fryedai neared the pirate, the Navy navigator jumped up, wound up a shot with his fist, and curled his fingers around the grip of the dagger. In one swift motion, Fryedai let loose his punch, and the hilt of the dagger slammed into Orion's face, decking the pirate to the floor, and knocking him out cold.

"Orion!" Atlas screamed, as he rushed to his feet.

It all happened in a flash as Ann's bonds finally snapped free. Everything on the deck of The Extinction descended into chaos.

"We move now!" Yelled Taylor, stepping out from the crowd and raising his axe high in the air.

The pirate crew had now split into two factions: those too loyal or afraid of the maddened captain, and those that were tired of his unfair treatment and tyrannicidal rule – each were just as egger to kill the other in a fight for total dominance over the galleon, and now blood rained across the ship. It seemed Orion had been the only one holding the crew back from mutiny against Atlas, with his quartermaster gone. They had feared the snow-haired man too, as much as they once did their captain from what Ann had seen during their catastrophic rally to uncover the truth of the island and its antechamber. Perhaps that had been a result of his powers too, and why Atlas had kept him close for that very reason. However, Atlas had abandoned him once he had claimed his treasure, believing himself too powerful, and now Silvers, buried within a grave of collapsed earth far below the island, was dead and gone, and Ann's chance had finally come...

35

Arabella's head was a blur. High above on the crow's nest, Polly still dangled her by her legs. She begged repeatedly to let her up the other way as the wind whistled against the mast.

"Polly." She whined. "You have to help me, turn me the other way and I can play with you loads, we never have to stop."

Polly looked down and grinned with her spiralled teeth, a look of wonder in her sharp, amber, reptilian eyes at the word 'play'.

"Will you do that for me, girl?" Arie asked.

The Wraith nodded even more excitedly, grabbing the barmaid around the waist with her tail and flipping her around the other way, bringing her up to sit on her back.

"Good girl." She replied softly, and stroked the Wraith's long black tail as gently as she could, making the beast purr in a weird sort of low stuttered growl.

Her head was still a blur, but the blood that had rushed to her head slowly returned to where it should have been. Down below, chaos had erupted, many pirates shouting and roaring as if their lives depended on it. It seemed they were fighting against each other. What worried her the most however, was that Gillian had begun to climb up the rigging towards her.

"Polly, let's go." She urged, nudging the Wraith forwards.

"Polly!" Gillian roared as they tried to escape.

Polly looked back towards the rigging and turned her head once again with anticipation, arcing and diving towards the rigging. Atlas had been right, he and his fellow pirates were parents to Polly, and she could not resist doing as she was told.

Polly was a child and the Wraith needed to be told what to do, and what the difference between right and wrong was.

"Bring the girl here, Polly!" Gill shouted as he reached for his blade.

He had almost made it up to the crow's nest as cannon fire sounded. The sudden noise made the beast startle and jump into the air. What had once been a muffled sound for the creature being held down below in the depths of the galleon's hold and adjoining rooms, now came to life in blazing contrast and she let loose a wild shriek.

"Bad, Polly. Bad!" Arie shouted in what seemed to be the beast's ear as they fell, and Polly suddenly reared her wings, hovering in the middle of the air aft of the mast.

Arabella looked to her right in the direction of the cannon fire that had caused the beast so much fright. She saw Jackson circle around the pirate galleon in his own ship, blasting the pirates with a volley of cannon fire; his little figures working with him to move and hoist the ship's sails in the different directions. She knew it was Jackson by the way his long trench coat fluttered in the wind behind him, the figure which she peered at stood aside the wheelhouse, being slightly bent over in his posture from excessive amounts of drink as his long dark hair flitted over his eyes. Suddenly, her attention was brought back to Gillian as he revved his blade, the crackle of electricity coming from it sparking her ears.

"If I take you, then perhaps Atlas will finally listen to me again like he used to." He sang as the chains of his blades spun. "I no longer care if we're taking you to a Troll-king or not!"

"You're all talk, Gillian." Arie said. "Didn't you want me to run? I thought you enjoyed the chase or was that just talk as well?"

The pirate snarled.

"Chase this!" He shouted, swiping his blade across the sky in a wild swat as he clung to the mast, sending a blast of lightning racing towards them.

The barmaid was too late.

"Head up, Polly. Head up." Arabella cried as the white bolts scraped against Polly's belly, burning her skin, causing the poor creature to shriek in agony as they began to dive towards the deck.

Gillian now began looking even more unhinged.

"Try and run now, fools. See what happens when I tell you to run!"

He hadn't looked beyond what immediately lay in front of him, and his eyes widened in surprise as his prey rolled back towards him. Polly and Arabella were now colliding towards the first mate from above, leaving the pirate with no time to move out of the way before they smashed into the mast and him. They caught the mast-sail first, causing Polly to thrash around in the canvas of the black sail, wailing as they hurtled towards the deck. It seemed they had missed the pirate by a mere metre as she fell. Then it all seemed to happen in a blur for the pink-haired swordsman, and the beast's tail flicked from side to side, catching him in the chest as he clung to the breaking mast. Gillian Mayers was catapulted towards the sea like a spinning rock, flung from a trebuchet, where he landed with a massive splash, and did not emerge...

* * *

Taylor raged across the deck and towards Atlas, a steely determination in his eyes. He slammed his hefty axe down from high overhead in a heavy blow, which forced the captain to kneel as pirates raced around the foredeck of the throne; hacking and slashing at one another in an effort to slay their foe. These pirates, thought Ann and she shook her head. When

Fryedai had taken out Orion – a clean blow swiftly served – she knew that the entire ship would break out into chaos. She felt a smirk come to her face as she hurried to help Nelson, as she realised Jackson had been right! These pirates with their alliances, bonds of apparent brotherhood, they never had any intention of keeping any of it. Atlas was too narcissistic to care for anyone else but his own schemes and desires. This chaos was his own making, and that is precisely what Ann had been banking on. She grabbed a fallen knife from the deck and hacked away at Nelson's bonds. The pirates that had been guarding them during the fight had continually nodded and grunted with agreement during Taylor's speech, and now they went to slew their fellow crewmen with a gleam of bloodlust and vengeance in their eyes, freeing both Ann and Nelson of the guns that were pressed against their backs. Above her, lightning flashed across the sky, and the creature she had seen on the crow's nest narrowly caught the main sail as it fell, tearing it away as its tail smashed into a portion of the mast. To the side of them, Jackson rained cannon fire down on the pirates and the galleon began to slow.

"Are you alright, Fryedai?" She called, throwing the dagger away and picking up a much more substantial fallen sword, using it to deflect an incoming blow as a pirate bore down on Nelson.

Ann thrust the attacking blade away and ran the pirate through. Blood spurted from the foe's mouth and his eyes drew cold. It was now life and death, and she didn't have time to think. Fryedai looked at her, pure amazement spread across his face. He felt the feeling of euphoria tingle through him – he was still alive and breathing, he had actually won the duel!

"I'm going to rip you limb from limb for touching my brother, boy!" Atlas roared as he fought with Taylor.

The pirate captain's blue crystal-like eyes shone with rage and burning fury as the treasure twisted and morphed into something new, gleaming with its signature golden-red aura. Atlas now duel-wielded the sword from his scabbard combined with a set of sharp golden claws on his treasure-hand. Similar to what Ann had seen at the train station. They extended from the pirate's hand into a row of vicious projectiles. As Atlas blocked Taylor's latest heavy strike with his steel blade, he made a twisting and turning motion with his body, performing a single spin on the spot while keeping the head of his attacker's axe-head in the centre of his steel. From this position, Atlas blocked his attacker from behind whilst simultaneously pointing the golden claws in the direction of the Navy navigator.

"Fryedai, move, get out the way!" Ann screamed, waving her hand in the air as both she and Nelson ran towards him.

Fryedai dived out of the way just as the claws extended and shot forward. They flew through the air in three sharp points, the small blade in the centre of the trio reaching further forward than the other two. As Fryedai looked behind him, in a glance towards the pirate captain, he dove to the wooden deck as his legs came out from under him and the most exterior blade scraped by his cheek as. The other two passed by harmlessly as the pirate captain yelled in anger, and he quickly spun back around as Taylor hefted his axe yet again to strike. However, the maddened captain got there first, and struck out at his former subordinate. Atlas' treasure had morphed yet again as he turned, and he impaled the mutineer with the sharp tip of a spearhead.

Taylor fell to his knees as Ann and Nelson neared Fryedai, his axe falling to the deck as Atlas squarely kicked him in the chest to the ground. Ann helped the blonde navigator to his feet, but she quickly found that they were being surrounded by Atlas' remaining men. The pirates' mutiny against their captain was quickly coming to its end with its inciter felled, and Ann raised her blade to protect herself and her friends as the rest of the pirates laughed around her. She saw the fire and lust in their eyes, she could see both the pure fear and the joy of what Atlas inspired in their countenances, but all were broken in some twisted way.

A little further down the ship, and across the massive deck, the remainder of the main mast-sail of *The Ymir's Extinction* fluttered amidst the chaos, torn, and broken; Ann could have sworn she saw the black creature that had fallen from the sky move from within – she just hoped Arabella had survived as her own heart began to thump.

"Forget it, girl. You couldn't beat me last time with those guns of yours, what makes you think you can best me with a sword?" Atlas snarled, making his way leisurely over to the group that remained, and giving them orders to prime the cannons as still the galleon shook from the bombardment that Jackson, Luke, and Tom were firing upon them.

Small beads of sweat ran down the pirate captain's black beard and a shine seemed to emanate from the graphic tattoos drawn upon his skin. It was just the three of them now, and Ann took a breath before she called out to him. She wasn't afraid of Atlas, far from it, but she wanted him to know that she was different from him. From all that she had learnt on this adventure so far, Ann knew that it was of no use to be afraid. She'd been confined at first, but the friends she had gathered about her had been through so much more than she had, and they had stuck by her all the same as she had them. That was the difference between her and Atlas: Ann would never change who she was, using and betraying her so-called 'brothers' as Atlas did, nor would she abandon those she held dear.

"Because this time." Ann started. "This time I have all of my new friends with me, and I know with their help I can do anything, we'll stop you from hurting all those innocent people!" She cried.

Nelson and Fryedai gathered around her as she held the blade in her hand firm and Fryedai raised his own as Nelson muttered hurried words underneath his breath.

"Hah!" Atlas laughed, as he now faced the trio, telling the handful of men remaining that he himself would deal with them.

He began by swatting Fryedai to the ground with his treasure-hand, knocking him out; the steel blade the navigator held being the only thing that saved his life as it came into contact with strange golden-liquid metal. With a thrust of his free arm, Atlas threw his own ruby-hilted sword to the floor and used his menacing grip to lift Ann into the air before she could land a strike.

"Weakest first." He sniggered, throwing her towards the steps leading up to the wheelhouse.

Ann barely noticed that Atlas still hadn't laid a finger on Nelson. She landed with a crash against the ornately carved wooden features and her head was a blur as the tattooed pirate stalked towards her. Ann found her blade next to her where it had fallen, and she gripped it steely tight. She shook her crimson hair as it fell in front of her emerald eyes, and she narrowed in on Atlas. Cannons blared then as if from all around and Ann felt the ship begin to rumble.

"You see!" Atlas yelled in triumph as fire erupted from black iron. "You are not strong enough to defeat me! You are not strong enough to stop what is coming!" And he turned his head to see that Nelson was still uttering his incantation.

"No!" Ann uttered, her voice barely reaching her own ears under the blur and the noise as she tried to run back towards them.

"Oh, Seidr?" Quipped Atlas, amused.

The golden metal of the treasure began to shine and grow red once more.

"Give me your best, Alchemist! It appears you aren't even trained."

Nelson looked over to him and up thrust his palm towards Atlas as he finished his muttering of words. Nothing happened and his eyes grew in horror. Had he said a wrong word in his casting? Nelson thought, as he remembered the tomes that lined the bookcases of his home. The pirate should have been sent flying in a gust of wind and yet he stood not more than six metres away!

"A pity." The pirate sighed, almost sounding heartfelt. "It looks like I'll be killing you after all."

But before Atlas could be upon the cook, Ann found her voice again, her head now clear from the daze the pirate had inflicted.

"Hey, Atlas!" She shouted, holding up a frail roll of parchment in her hand, stopping in the mid-point of the deck and quickly pulling it from her jacket. "I'm the one who took your map! Don't you want to get it back?"

The pirate's eyes widened as he turned to see what Ann was holding. The brown paper she held above her head was awash with blood-red lettering and lines, constantly shifting in the pale light. It was filled to the brim with Runic-verses and writings that only he could understand, thus Atlas yelled at her at once more to restore it to his possession and he bounded towards her, and Ann returned the map to her jacket.

"I was like you once!" He yelled above the noise of cannon fire.

The treasure now morphed into a long reaching cutlass as Atlas stood before her, and the girl quickly swatted the attack away as the pirate slashed and chopped.

"I loved the fun of adventure, the smell of the sea, the thrill of finding the unknown. I can see it in your eyes, girl. I can hear it in your voice. Your pitiful friends over there, they mean something to you, and that tells me you've folly in your heart – I see that now. I gave everything for my friends and my dreams! Those creatures, the giants, they took everything away! But this treasure here, it tells me things. This treasure here, is my vengeance, and with it, comes a new age for my brother and I! Give me the map!"

Ann continued to swat and block the attack.

"Yes, but I know the difference between right and wrong and not to hurt all these innocent people!" Ann countered, and once again she had to roll away from the pirate's attacks before getting up. "Even if you see a justifiable reason, what you've done, what you're about to do, is just sheer insanity! Nothing can justify this, destroying an island so no one can find you!"

Atlas snarled again, and Ann thrust her attack from behind him trying to stab at the captain. This time Atlas parried, raising the treasure high above his head, blocking at his back as it morphed to protect him. Once he quickly spun on his feet, he slammed the treasure down in front of Ann, creating an axe that splintered the wood of the deck below him. Ann dodged the strike and moved to the side.

"Not even a brother's love? That is why I am doing this, girl. For him." Atlas cried, realising that his treasure hand had become stuck in the floor. "Would you not do anything in this world for your family?"

His face was strained, and he huffed in frustration at not being able to get at her.

"Yes, I would, but everything has limits." Ann responded, looking to see what he would do next. "There is only so much you can do. You clearly need help, your addiction for power has driven you too far!"

Atlas' face twisted in rage at her words, so much so that he pulled his arm free and struck at Ann's side, making a slit in her jacket as she backed off. She'd let her guard down again, attempting to humanise a monster. A stinging pain filled her, and she hissed trying not to swear as she staggered back.

"What makes you so right in these matters; has nobody ever hurt you?" He boomed. "All that I had was ripped away from me. I wanted to make those who had made me suffer hurt as well. If this island needs to burn to cover my tracks, so be it. I am the hero, and I will cleanse this world; it has already been written."

Somebody that had hurt her. She began to think as Atlas staggered towards her. He was looking drained now, but still Ann found herself backing up against the railings of the ship. She remembered what the Traveller had told her when she was little, then as if the memory had resurfaced from so long ago:

'Ann.' The kind man had said. 'If somebody hurts you. If ever they have the gall to do so – don't fight back. You wait for them to make that mistake, no matter how much they hurt you, and in the end, they will not win.'

Quickly, before Atlas could strike again as he raised his arm up, Ann ducked down and dived in between the pirate captain's legs, crawling through the gap. In a rage, the villain hit the railing, almost halving the entire thing in two as Ann got back up and ran towards Nelson, who had started his incantation again. He was stood in front of the wheelhouse above them, and she dived towards the stairs to reach him. Atlas quickly followed and morphed his arm into a massive blunderbuss.

"What's the matter, girl? Are you trying to run away? Well, I have news for you, don't think that his Seidr will save you; you're not going to get away from this." Snarled Atlas.

"That's right, kill her!" Something whispered.

He squeezed the trigger to the gun, sending a torrent of golden spikes flying towards her. Ann avoided as much as she could as she rolled across the splinted deck, trying to reach the stairs. She yelped in pain, dropping her sword on the sea-soaked floor next to her. Having taken the hit, she could hear Atlas starting his cackled laugh as he once again got closer, the last of his pirates still trying to fight off Jackson as he sailed *The Spectre*.

"Well, what do you say, girl? Are you a coward? Do you want to run away, like all your friends? Because I can tell you, none of my friends have. All my brothers stood their ground no matter how useless or treasonous they turned out to be. I love my brother Orion to the ends of this world, but he still disappoints me. Today is like that whole thing at the beanstalk all over again. I presume you saw what's left of Kabuki in my cabin?"

"Do it now!" It whispered again.

"Shut up!" Atlas yelled.

"You're a monster." Ann muttered as she pulled the spike out of her side, having no idea to whom the pirate shouted.

"Oh, and by the way, the name's not girl, it's Ann." She said, but Atlas didn't care.

He snarled at her as he took a few more steps and crouched down so she could see his face, his crystal blue eyes, his trimmed black beard. He was mocking her, and she knew it.

"Well, Ann." He cooed, having the modesty to call her by her name. "I'm going to put you right here, you're the first person in a long while that has ever managed to last this long."

Atlas then took one of his large fingers and pointed to the inside of his right arm, to a space not covered by a tattoo.

"Now give me the map."

"What happened to that one?" Asked Ann, stalling for as much time as she possibly could, noticing a tall and slim, black inked giant with red eyes.

Atlas smiled.

"He started this whole thing, killed my black-hearted father. We climbed to the top of a beanstalk and when we came down two giants followed, we had taken some food, and a treasure, more valuable to me than I could have ever known. The giants killed him for what we took, and now here we are, with only one more true monster to go."

Ann coughed and winced with pain as she laid against the foot of the stairs. The bang of cannons erupted with a fiery explosion from both sides. It was a miracle they had survived this long. Then, one iron ball was sent hurling across the sea towards the back of Atlas.

"The map!" He demanded.

The pirate captain sensed the projectile coming as something whispered yet again, and this time, Ann could have sworn she heard it too as Atlas turned around to block the iron ball, making an umbrella-like shield as the black orb smashed into him.

Everything in a small radius that wasn't covered by the umbrella burst into flames, and Ann saw this as an opportunity to try and make her way towards the wheelhouse and Nelson.

"You really believe you are the hero in all this, don't you Atlas?" She spoke when Atlas turned back around.

Again, the pirate captain morphed his weapon into something different, this time a pistol and clicked back the catch.

"Any last requests before I blow your brains out and take back what is mine?" He asked, pointing the gun at her as she crawled halfway up. "Being the honourable pirate that I am."

"*Yes! Yes!*" The whispers began.

Ann smirked as she steadied herself, her hand reaching into her jacket, and that is where Atlas made his mistake. Two black ravens had landed next to them and perched on the railing of the galleon, making the pirate jump. Ann could have sworn she saw a twinge of fear in his eyes. The ravens crowed and stared at the captain with ruby and emerald eyes.

"You're not an honourable pirate, Atlas." Stated Ann. "But sure, can I have a drink?"

Then she reached into her pocket and took out the metal container she had taken from Tom, holding it up. It seemed the pirate was still distracted by the enormous black birds plaguing his ship not to notice that she hadn't taken the map from her side.

"What are you doing here?" Atlas said to the ravens, still completely ignoring Ann, looking horrified beyond his wits.

Then, just as she had seen Jackson do so many times before, she screwed off the lid of the bottle and took one big swig. The Snake inside tasted of warm summer fruits and strong spices, but it was not her intention to drink, or swallow the liquid, instead she aimed her mouth at the flickering flame, sat against Atlas' treasure, still alight from the cannon ball. Suddenly, she spat the liquid out in an arc just as Nelson had completed his second incantation from above. From his hand, the cook let loose a light breeze, helping push the liquid forward. Nelson was amazed that he was even able to pull it off being so untrained and unpractised – having only ever been good at charms or potions. He and Ann had now doused the pirate from head to toe in Snake, spraying him all over, and ripping him away from the glaring eyes of the ravens, who flew away with a cackle.

Atlas wailed in pain as the flame immediately set him alight and engulfed his body.

"*No!*" Ann could hear something screech, though it was almost indistinguishable from the pirate's cries.

Ann watched as the flames crawled around Atlas' body, peeling away his crisp, dry skin. There was still a look of hatred in the pirate's eyes, and he looked to the shadow of the bird in the distance. With his arm outstretched, he cursed her as his body started to crumble.

"They'll come for you." He spat, and piece by piece he disintegrated into a hot pile of ash, drifting away in the wind's soft breeze.

In the end, Atlas got a monster's death.

"Maybe they will, Atlas." Ann said as she stood up and held her waist tightly. "But you won't see that. You won't be able to hurt people anymore."

And thus, all that remained of Atlas Vain was a pile of grey embers, smouldering on the deck of his pirate ship. On top of the cinders lay the treasure and the pirate's indigo amulet; its form undamaged, and the jewellery survived.

"*Ann, Ann.*" It whispered inside her head, an abyss calling out her name.

This must have been what Tom was talking about – how the soul that was said to be inside the treasure whispered to a person, giving them dark thoughts, she realised.

"Come, reunite my pieces, my treasures; you can bring them all back, everyone you lost can be returned and made whole once again... Ann..."

"No!" She screamed, holding her ears to keep the strange voice at bay. "They can't come back! I can't change the past. I'm not like him. I'm not like Atlas; I can move on!"

Ann now knew no one could have this treasure, Tom was right. Tearing herself away from the voice, she picked up the treasure and carried it to the side of the ship as quickly as she could. She told Nelson she had to get rid of it, nobody could ever find this again and he nodded in agreement as he made is way down the stairs and approached the side with Ann. The last of Atlas' pirates didn't bother them, they were too in shock at the loss of their terrifying captain.

"Ann... Ann." The treasure whispered to her. *"I can help you save your friend, but what would you sacrifice in return? An eye? An arm? A life!"*

Ann had had enough. She raised the treasure piece to the tip of her high-heeled boots and kicked it as hard as she could into the sea, wincing from the pain at her side. It now rested in a place where the whispers of the soul inside could never be seen or heard from again, and as it landed in the seemingly bottomless ocean, a small whirlpool appeared and swallowed the treasure whole, pulling it deeper into the murky depths. She did, however, decide to keep the amulet, putting it inside her jacket where she kept all her most important things.

Finally, the sun started to loom over the horizon, spreading oranges, reds, and blues across the sky. The cannon fire that came from the galleon had died out with the cries of Atlas.

They had run out of ammo or something else happened with the crew surrendering to shock, but the result was the same and the exchange had stopped. She had told Jackson not to skin the ship if they were still on board and it seemed as if their troubles were finally over. The tyrannical pirate captain was ashes to the wind.

36

Ann had a brief moment to relax as she walked down to the bow of the ship. Nelson had kicked away at the capstan, and it had let loose the anchor to halt the galleon in place, and Fryedai, now awake from his brush with Atlas was busily trying to help Arie from underneath the fallen mainsail. He jumped back in surprise when the barmaid emerged on the back of a black beast. Ann figured it was thanks to the creature that the blonde survived the fall, and she got off its back to talk with Fryedai. Presently, as Ann was halfway down the pirate galleon, she noticed the seas below *The Extinction* bubbled, awaking with a start as if they were alive and small outlines slivered below the water's surface. Was this the reason why the cannons had ceased?

The pirates that filled the lower decks dove into the water - these were the men that had surrounded her and her friends when Taylor's mutiny had failed. They began to scream. One by one, their heads disappeared in lapping, frothy waves, and Ann and her friends followed the bubbles as they continued to rise.

"Look there." She cried pointing as the rest stuck their heads over to look.

* * *

Jackson saw it from where he sat at the helm of *The Spectre*. To port, there was a churning beneath the surface and a bright, growling creature, came streaking toward them amidst the rising bubbles. He watched more intently, scanning below the darkening surface of the sea. It was enormous, he realised. A gigantic bag of flesh and scales, with long, suckling tentacles! One of its slimy, elongated arms, emerged out the water next to the pirate galleon in geyser-like eruption, reaching towards the craft as it parted wave and froth alike. In the water, the screams of *The Ymir's* once notorious crew were quashed beneath a pink sucker and a watery grave. Then as quickly as it appeared, it vanished! As if it was not even there to begin with.

Jackson's eyes widened in amazement. Luke, who watched from aside a cannon looked at him for an explanation, but Jackson could give none. That kind of creature he had never seen in these waters before, let alone such a monster that could appear and disappear at will! And just as the most reasonable conclusion had come to his head, did Tom speak for him and utter something that they were all thinking, yet the two sailors dare not say as they looked towards the galleon, where the waves continued to bubble and shake. The brothers' once steadfast vessel was now being rocked from side to side. Within a moment or two, the creature reappeared, its tentacles wrapping it's pink and green coils around the thick of the main mast post of *The Extinction*. It squeezed the life out of the appendage in a crippling grasp, its sail already torn and fallen, breaking it into splinters and chunks of driftwood as the creature took its hold.

Jackson grabbed at the wheel of *The Spectre*, shifting it to the side in one spin and making the ship turn. His friends and livelihood were still aboard *The Extinction*, and he wouldn't allow them to become the creature's all you could eat breakfast buffet. However, as he turned, something gripped them from underneath their keel and lifted them up from the sea as the wheel spun and spun! The creature, it seemed, was far larger than they had anticipated, and Jackson swore underneath his breath. Seizing control, the monster moved *The Spectre* from under the waves and further away from the pirate galleon. Jackson was knocked back against the upper deck, the breath in his lungs thrown out of him, gasping as Luke and Tom ran to him. Then came the wail – the terrified cries of a sea beast Jackson never hoped to face as a tentacle hovered above him.

"Kraken!" Tom howled, but the sound was distorted and blurred to Jackson, who rubbed the back of his head.

Whatever the beast was after, it wanted them to stay far away from *The Ymir's Extinction*!

* * *

On the pirates' ship, the sea-beast's tentacle rose from the deck and slammed back down in a tremendous crash that worked to tear the gargantuan in two. Arabella screamed as this happened, only managing to avoid the monstrous trunk with the help of Polly, who followed her. Her black tail grabbed at the barmaid's waist as it flailed to the side, with a push from its wing, trying to avoid the on-coming crash of the Kraken's limb.

"Good girl, Polly." She said, as the animal lifted her on to its back.

Arie patted the Wraith on the head to which it groaned happily. Fryedai hadn't been so lucky, however. The blonde Navy-navigator had been lifted up by a tentacle and carried across to another part of the ship when the sea monster had first struck, and Arabella had not seen him since as she and Polly raced towards Ann and Nelson. The sea monster seemed to have a will of its own. It picked up pirates and mutineers alike using its smaller appendages to separate or drown individuals in the crashing waves below. It wanted everybody alone so it could play and mingle and taunt, and it seemed to be personal for the beast.

"Looks like somebody made a new friend, though we've got a bit of a problem on our hands." Muttered Ann, and she swiped at a smaller tentacle that snaked towards them with the edge of her blade.

Ann was still bleeding from her waist as she swung the sword, and she flinched as she did, a hot pain running up her side from where Atlas' blunderbuss attack had caught her. She wished that now of all moments she had brought some of Napoleon's healing ointment with her, but yet again, she had been overconfident in her assessment on how to deal with the pirates. Nelson's eyes quickly widened in horror as another slimy tentacle-arm curled over the railing and twisted around her waist. Sharp, thorned suckers tore at her clothing, dragging her toward the rail, and it caused Arabella's beast to fly off frightened into the sky without its new master. Ann felt the coldness of the creature's flesh continue to coil around her.

Eventually, Ann overcame her revulsion, bringing out both guns from her jacket pocket. If there were ever a time to use the last of her remaining gift, it was now! As she was hoisted into the air, the teenager quickly set the canisters and pulled the triggers without a second thought. Fire spat from both barrels, hacking, burning and peeling away at the tentacled flesh encircling her, but still, the creature would not let go!

"Where did this thing come from?" She groaned.

It had incredible strength as it hovered her above the choppy and dangerous waters it had created. She fired her guns once again as her friends shouted after her and the monster wailed with a horrifying shriek. Greenish blood flowed down her legs, covering Ann in slimy goop. Then, abruptly, the tentacle released its grip, and she fell towards the chilling sea below.

As Ann fell, she held her breath whilst cold, icy water surrounded and entombed her. Tentacles were everywhere, snaking over the stern, encircling the bow, wrapping the keel, and coming up high over the deck. They were crawling and surrounding everything in sight as it started to bring the ship down and crush it below the depths. Bodies of no-named pirates dotted the water; they were food for rows upon rows of sharp spiked teeth.

She tried her hardest to swim away against the force of the sea, but the beast kept pulling her in. It could smell her blood. Soon, Ann was metres away from its gaping mouth, feeling the spiked tips pull against her feet. Quickly, she pointed her barrels at the dark, monstrous, gaping hole trying to consume her as the air escaped from her lungs and she switched the settings. Her vision was solely focused on where she needed to hit before the last of the air escaped. Gently squeezing the triggers, she allowed the caged lightning to be freed from its cannister, striking her foe from each of her pistol's barrels.

Zap!

That was the last of it, she thought as her vision started to wane – all her gift was gone. Writhing in agony, the Kraken stopped, grabbing Ann with one of its many arms and pushing her away. The creature flung her disdainfully, into the air, where she crash-landed back on the deck of the ruined pirate ship, which had almost been torn to pieces. As she struggled to get to her feet, she heard Jackson shout from across the water:

"Get back to the ship! Get below decks, hurry!"

They were being held by the raging monster too, as Tom and Luke tried desperately to reload the cannons in time to get off another shot at the beast. The bulbous body of the Kraken had started to move in the water and was now directly behind them, having been shocked by Ann. The girl was sopping wet and drained of energy and she looked up to the Wraith that circled high above their heads. If they couldn't make their way across to *The Spectre*, that black beast would be their only way out...

* * *

Fryedai found Taylor's axe laying on the splintered deck and hacked at the waving tentacle towering above him, Arabella Johnson, and Nelson. The very air glowed with the greenish light which the thing gave off, and the Navy-man gripped the large shaft with two hands as sickening green blood gushed at his face. The cook and the barmaid had rushed to find him when Ann had been taken and had jumped over the cracking deck before the monster had separated the galleon into indistinct pieces. The suckers lashed out, brushing against his bad leg, tearing at Fryedai's skin as the appendage backed off. But the monster was tricky, it snaked forward again, and wrapped around his leg in a vice-like hold. All of a sudden, he was dragged along the floor toward the edge of the ship's splintered segment, and Arabella screamed as she tried to chase after him with the cook quickly following behind. For a moment, he rode in the air, swung back and forth like a doll in the hands of a child.

With great struggle, Fryedai gritted his teeth, and with both hands as he slid across the sea-soaked deck did he grasp the axe fully and role his weight to one side, driving the axe into the undercarriage of the monster's tentacle. Astounded by its size, Fryedai realised it seemed to be trying to eat the ship, holding fast to the pieces it had craved with its many appendages and pulling them towards its gaping mouth. In addition to this, it had also gained a slimy grasp upon *The Spectre*, which had been brought above the churning waters of another end of one of the beast's many mouths. Directly beneath him, Fryedai saw one colossal eye situated above a pit of teeth – its mouth measuring seven feet wide and six feet tall, larger and wider than two average people put together. It seemed to rest in the very centre of the sea, positioned directly between the two ships. The eye did not blink. It had no expression other than pure rage. The pink pupil, surrounded by glowing, scaly, green flesh, seemed to survey Fryedai dispassionately to all the others as he had been the one protecting Arabella.

Had the creature in fact been trying to reach for the mayor's daughter and the black beast that flew above them? He thought.

"We have to get everyone out of here!" Ann shouted to him as Fryedai spied her on another segment of the ship.

Arabella agreed although she did not know how many people Polly could take.

"What about him?" Nelson asked, pointing to the knocked-out body of Orion Vain, as smaller tentacles started to squirm around the late pirate's vice-captain.

"Bring him with us, the Navy will want him!" Ann shouted from across the divide before Fryedai could form a reply.

Arie agreed with a sigh, shouting up to Polly to pick the pirate up gently. The beast cackled with a 'Ku-ku-ku-ku-ku' in response, as she began to weave around the suckers and tentacles that jabbed around her. Finally, she made it to the part of the ship that was the slowest to sink as water began to rise at their feet. Polly seized Orion in her jaw as she would a helpless toy, and Arabella and Nelson hopped on her back with Ann arriving just shortly after looking very frail and fatigued.

The Wraith emitted a chirping sound from its throat as the teenager looked at her friends.

"She can't take us all." Arie informed them. "We'll be too heavy! Though if we can make it to Jackson, she might take one more."

Fryedai looked at Ann, her face pale as she smiled and said knowingly:

"You go."

The navigator felt tears stream down his face and his lips start to quiver, and at that moment, Fryedai could have sworn that his heart would have broken for a second time in the many long hours that he had spent upon the shores of Ale Town Island.

"But what about your friend?" He cried and Ann looked down at her bleeding side and the blood that had gathered in her hand through the fabric of her jacket.

She smiled at him sweetly and told him that her friend, Wen, was much like her so she probably had little to worry for, but inwardly Ann felt her heart began to tear at the thought of not being able to help her closest friend. Her visage was pale and lily-white, a stark and deathly contrast from her flowing crimson hair and tearful emerald eyes. Fryedai saw that the ribbon the girl wore was also stained with blood, and that it had become frayed in all her fighting. His eyes softened as he looked at her from side to side and head to tail. He would never forget her. Someone who was brave and courageous, who did what was right despite the odds against her, who stood up for the best ideals his organisation had. She was in a sense; a true hero and it was because of her that the island had been saved. Now only one threat remained - The Kraken that peered from the depths as its tentacles surrounded them. Suddenly Polly gave out another cry as more of the monster's tiny appendages slivered from the water to paw at their feet and he leaned in to give Ann a hug as he realised their time was coming to an end.

But as he came to let her go, Fryedai bent to Ann's ear. He couldn't bear to lose anyone else, a mentor, a crewmate, a friend.

"Forgive me." He whispered, and as he did, he lifted the teenager up by her waist, handing her to Nelson on the back of Polly.

"What are you doing?" Croaked Ann, her voice growing weak as the Kraken roared and the final segment of the ship they were standing on started to sink, descending into the beast's jaws.

"I'm only returning a favour." He spoke softly, and he urged them to go and fly towards *The Spectre*.

As they flew into the air, Fryedai watched the black Wraith beat its heavy wings. He was the only person left standing on the corpse of *The Ymir's Extinction*, yet he had plenty of reminders that he was not alone as tentacles rose and wormed like leeches about his ankles. In a single swipe of the axe, Fryedai chopped off a fat tentacle as he gripped the railing to the side before the cold sea, causing the sea beast to roar in rage as its appendage collapsed, falling like a tree. The monster continued to shake the splintered segment of the fallen galleon with the rest of its body. The creature's green tentacles began smashing into the windows of the cabins; the thick glass-paned sheets of the stern that he, Nelson and Ann came through were shattered into even more pieces than before and enormous tentacles, as thick as tree trunks, snaked into what was left of the brothers' cabin.

Inside, the creature wrapped itself around a cannon, pulling it into its clutches, but the massive ornament came free of its mooring, rolling across the room taking much of the giant bone interior with it. Wherever the creature's horned and vile suckers touched, was soon ripped into nothingness and the captain's cabin was destroyed and the resulting explosion caused Fryedai to fall into the freezing embrace of the sea. For a moment, he churned and spun in the glowing green substance of the Kraken's blood, before surprisingly gaining his footing on what he thought was the splintered planks of massive pieces of driftwood, however, the navigator soon realised he was actually standing on the massive creature itself! Slippery and slimy it was, like standing on a frozen lake that had just started to melt. The skin of the animal was gritty and freezing cold to the touch. Crawling forward, Fryedai splashed in the salty water until he came to the eye. Seen so close, it was huge, a vast pink hole in the bright green expanse. Fryedai still had the axe in his hand and did not hesitate. He swung the weapon high above his head, burying it in the sticky curved white of the iris.

The axe struck deep in the dome, seeping a now familiar gooey-green blood.

A geyser of clear water spurted upward like an erupting volcano, and the sea turned a milky white. His footing on his bad leg lost again as the creature sank away, leaving him drifting next to the wreck of the sinking pirate ship that was half eaten.

Was it gone? Had the creature been vanquished? He wondered with a slight relief, or had it just simply vanished as it had before. Suddenly, a rope twisted through the air as *The Spectre* sailed by, and Fryedai grabbed it as quickly as he could, his frozen hands wrapping around frayed and sea-soaked bindings. Just as he pulled himself aboard, the monster surfaced again.

"Fire!" Jackson roared, and Tom and Luke along with Arabella and Nelson set to work.

The cannons plunged their projectiles deep into the body of the creature. Columns of greenish blood spiked into the air, and then the Kraken was gone, leaving only the unique blade of Hacksaw Gill, floating in the drift.

"Thanks." Gasped Fryedai as Tom and Luke pulled him to the deck, but the Navy navigator was more concerned about the ailing girl that now lay in the Doctor's cabin, than his own safety, and he quickly ran to see if Napoleon, Nelson's strangely weird talking pet could do anything for her. As he entered the cabin with a small knock, Fryedai saw that Ann had been laid on the bed that she had once occupied for the entire duration of their outward voyage. She gave him a pale but weary smile as he entered.

"You utter bastard." She whispered softly to him amid the mounds of texts, research documents and mountains of books that adorned Doctor Rudolf's cabin as Napoleon looked her over. "How dare you steal all my thunder."

She smiled, and Fryedai embraced her in a long hug. Nobody would have been happy if he'd just let her die!

"Oi! Don't kill her!" Napoleon complained as he ironed out some bandages with his snout, patting Fryedai on the back with his trotters to release Ann. "She's only gone and lost a bit of blood so needs some rest, a few shattered ribs too. I had master remove the shot and sow her up before we came for you as you paddled in the water. You need to warm up too by the way. That explosion the Kraken caused helped us get free of its tentacles, but it also slowed us down. It's going to be a long journey back to harbour." Rattled the pig, but Fryedai didn't care, he was simply happy his friend hadn't died.

Still, the pig had been right, as Fryedai held her grinning, and the blonde began to feel the sting of the seawater that had seeped into his bones and made him gasp. Napoleon quickly ushered him to the galley where there was a fire, and he was soon warmed as Jackson turned them around to head towards the island. Something still needed to be done about Orion, and surely Commander Rockwell and the others were egger for news as they waited for them. Even more so, Fryedai was overjoyed to see in the distance a Navy ship was sailing over the early morning horizon as he looked out over the porthole window. Finally, all was calm. No more whispers, no more obsessions. The road to darkness had been cleared by light.

Act 5:
The Truth is Plagued by Whispers

37

Seen from a distance over the sea, the ship of Commodore Chesterfield, *The Sweeping Monkey*, presented a pretty and most welcome sight. Ann turned her head on the pillow as the wind from the broken window brushed through her hair and she breathed a sigh of relief. It seemed as if she'd been asleep for hours as she went to rub her eyes, and to her surprise, Nelson and Jackson were sitting in the room with her whilst Napoleon checked over her bandages with the tip of his trotters.

They smiled at her warmly as she turned to look out over the same window that she had yesterday morning, when the whole adventure had started with a stormy squall at sea.

"How long have I been out?" She asked groggily, seeing that the sky was blue and light with white fluffy clouds dotted about its canvas.

"It's mid-morning." Said Nelson softy. "You look better."

Shit! Thought Ann as she rubbed her sore head and looked at both of them. Wen's sentence was due to be carried out at midnight and Ann still had to find a way into the Prison and deal with the corrupt officials who ran it. Aside from being her closest friend, Wen also carried critical information on certain individuals that related to her *'Secret mission'* and the N.S.T.C. Without that knowledge for her little book, Ann would never be able to return to where she belonged.

She thanked Nelson and Jackson for looking after her and she drew the covers around her back, patting the cook's familiar on the head as she got up. Nothing had been removed and she found her guns laying on the side dresser along with Atlas' stolen map, her little black book, and the amulet she had taken as a prize from the pirate captain. She picked the amulet up and pondered on it for a moment. The gem was still stained with Nelson's Alchemic blood from when Atlas had used it to open up the strange and marvellous treasure antechamber, and Ann could have sworn that something rested inside the trinket to make it shine as it once had. Since Atlas had died, the indigo light from the clouded white crystal no longer shone and she found that a thin layer of bronze trailed within its centre, like a clasp or a locket. Ann couldn't resist the nature of her constant curiosity, as she softy pressed a fingernail into the bronze lining, and with the help of her left hand she opened it up, the opaque, white crystal being nothing more than an outer shell. Both Jackson and Nelson looked at her in amazement as her eyes widened.

"What is it?" They asked.

"An Amethyst." Ann replied, gazing at the deep purple stone she held before her.

Yet it was oddly shaped for a stone and its surface was perfectly round and cylindrical with a dark centre as its iris.

"It looks like an eye." She muttered as she passed it to Nelson for both the men to have a look. "Did Atlas know about this?"

Nelson shrugged. He had never seen anything like it before and neither had Jackson. It was so perfectly formed and yet so ancient looking that it couldn't possibly be another treasure that couldn't have and shouldn't have existed, but here it was.

"We should ask Tom." The drunk said decisively.

Ann could hear the fear in his voice as he spoke the words and they felt heavy. They had all seen what Atlas' treasure had done first hand to the people of Ale Town and the surrounding area. Anything that came from that crazed pirate captain should have been treated with care, especially if it had anything to do with his Great Storm.

Out through the window, they could all hear Fryedai and Luke on the deck yelling in surprise as they saw the Navy ship approach, and now that Ann was feeling well enough, the three of them went up to see what was going on as Fryedai steered them into the port harbour. Their message had gotten through, and Ann was glad someone had come to deal with their less than willing prisoner. They were all in need of dire rest to lick their wounds and bruises, and Orion Vain had apparently been more than a handful according to Jackson, when he had come around in the vault of *The Spectre*, bound in chains. It had been a hard battle against the pirates, but they had finally won.

As they docked, Jackson tied the moorings to the harbour-groin and Fryedai ordered to Tom to run the capstan, releasing the anchor. Then Orion Vain was brought up from the hold by Luke and Nelson, and Arabella stared at the pirate as she and Ann waited port-side for the Navy to arrive. Polly didn't join them. Arabella had decided that the creature had spent too much time locked away by the brothers in the pit of their own ship, and she had let the animal roam the skies around the island's bay for a time to stretch her wings.

"You're going away for a long time." Ann told Orion as he grumbled to himself over the way he had been handled.

There was likely going to be a big reward for the remaining Vain sibling and what little was left of his pirate group. Orion smirked as if he was going to say something, a smile creeping upon his lips like a crocodile, but before he could, Arie kicked him to the ground and the chains holding him rattled as he rolled in the sand.

"How do you like it?" The barmaid almost screamed, and at first Ann did nothing, watching as her friend worked through the emotions that she had been holding back from all the manipulation she had been through over the last month. "Does this seem like a fairly and justly earned reward?"

Orion laughed maniacally as he rolled around in the sand and Arabella pulled him to his knees.

"Ha-ha, you have more fire in you than your father, little bird. My brother should have chosen you to partner with instead. No matter, Atlas will come for me soon and we shall be away as we always have been. With the money and power that we have gathered we can fend the Trolls off till the time is right! My brother has a plan, he always has!"

"What are you talking about?" Ann interrupted. "You're going to the Navy and we're claiming the bounty."

Orion's face turned sour.

"No!" He hissed. "Atlas would never – They'll surely find me! He would never...He promised me he would never-"

"Can I tell him, or do you want to?" Arie asked looking over to Ann and stopping the pirate mid-sentence.

"Go ahead." The redhead nodded, and Orion looked up at her and scowled.

"Tell me what!" He demanded, and Arabella bent down to hold his grey bandaged hand that peered out from the chains as she delivered the news, whispering it into his ear as his face twisted in horror and misery.

* * *

On board *The Sweeping Monkey*, the commodore unpacked his spyglass from his brown-cuffed Navy coat and gazed at the chained man on the beach, along with the two women watching over him as he began to wonder what in all the Hells had been going on. They had received a message in the dead of night via a cable line transmission using an emergency frequency, telling them that the notorious Vain Siblings had taken over an island and that Navy personnel on the shore needed help. However, from the looks of things, the pirate ship had already been taken care of and all they had to do was haul the villains off and allow the island to return to normal.

It should be an easy enough job to tidy up that Captain Robbinson's mess, he thought. He was familiar with the old Captain of Outpost 42 but gave no regard to his over-the-top scepticism involving Mermaids, sea monsters and creatures in general that roamed the earth. Robbinson had also been particularly afraid of pirates, and had by reputation alone, only received a captainship because of his administration skills and statecraft. His number two, Rockwell, wasn't particularly well liked in the upper echelons of the command either as the man was brash and reckless when it came to dealing with Trolls.

Eventually the ship slowed to a halt. Next to him stood Admiral Greenbowe, who towered over the Commodore as if he were a sturdy oak.

"And why did you feel you had to bring me along with you, Sullivan?" Sighed the Admiral.

"Nothing special, just an old fool getting tricked and a pirate who took advantage. Thought you might have fun if you stretched your gills. You brood too much."

"And here I thought you'd be glad to have these thugs arrested?" Greenbowe huffed as he shook his head.

"I'm just concerned with what the Lords have planned. These particular pirates killed quite a few giants. The government wants to let it slide because their destroyed lands provided homes for us, yet we can't fulfil the mandate given to us to clean up the seas. So, what do you want to do?" Chesterfield asked.

"I don't know yet, I haven't decided what I am going to do. If you look at it from my perspective, if these runts hadn't started killing giants, I wouldn't have a job. I got all my promotions in that war, and now I'm not going anywhere."

"And this doesn't anger you? Gods! That's why you're so moody."

Greenbowe sighed.

"Of course, it does. I want to be Sea-lord someday."

Chesterfield stared at him as they walked off the ship and into the harbour.

"Really? You? Run the Navy? Why would you want to do that?"

"It is not important." The Admiral said evenly.

Chesterfield stood quietly for some moments.

"I have heard." He began. "That you want more power so you can bring the Navy more territory in the lawless areas of the Doorstep. The five won't be so happy about that, you know. But what do you care? You're a moody little government lapdog, aren't you? You bend to their every word."

Greenbowe didn't answer for some time as they continued walking up the harbour. He did not take lightly to being called a lapdog, even if Chesterfield was one of his closest underlings.

"That is the story?" He responded, finally.

"And do you want it?" Asked Chesterfield. "The job?"

"Yes."

Chesterfield scanned his face.

"You crafty Half-Nereridian! I didn't think you had it in you."

"There is a vote coming up soon concerning our position on The Guild joining The Parliament of Lords within the World Republic, I'll be needing your support." Replied the Admiral.

Sullivan Chesterfield paused once more.

"The Alchemists? But don't they already work for Parliament and The Company?"

Greenbowe offered him a rare smile from his green and blue speckled face.

"Some do, but not all. A new leader has risen up in a group called The Spider's Tea Party. Countering this, the Company propose to finally give the Alchemists a voice and streamline the production and distribution of Ash."

Chesterfield's eyes widened and he tapped his chin, nothing like this had ever happened in the history of the world as far as he was aware, and it was a move that could be extremely dangerous. Could this new leader really unite the estranged Alchemic factions? He thought.

"And Lord Duval signed off on this?" He asked.

The ministerial Lord for Trade was a tricky and dangerous individual at the best of times and the Commodore knew that if he signed off on the proposal then there must have been something lucrative consigned within the political binding of The Guild.

"He has." Greenbowe stated.

"Ha! That won't end well."

Suddenly, an enormous black beast with antenna and wings roared over their heads. The two men ducked for cover as their men continued to pour out of *The Sweeping Monkey* and stared at the beast passing over them as it flew towards the beach.

"What in the world is that thing?" Shouted the Commodore.

"Well." Greenbowe huffed as he got up, dusting himself down with his webbed hands. "I suppose we should go see what all the fuss is about, a hundred Threds says it has something to do with the pirates."

38

Soon after the Navy arrived, the mid-morning sun was high over the sea, glistening in orange light and cutting a swift, hissing path through the clear blue water, signalling that a brand new day had well and truly begun. For Ann, however, this meant she had truly little time to implement her plan and before they had moored, she had told Jackson and Nelson to move the ship to a more secluded part of the island which was nearby to where the Navy expected them. Once Luke, Fryedai and Tom had disembarked, the two hid *The Spectre* near to the south beach as the others ventured into town to check on the rest of the Navy and the Townspeople they had left behind, which left Ann and Arabella to wait with Orion.

As they reached the edge of town, Fryedai was surprised to find the Navy was already waiting for them, and they led the group down to where the girls were waiting as Jackson and Nelson caught them up. Where had they gotten to? The Navy navigator wondered, but he ultimately paid it no mind as he was just as happy in the company of his own crew and those who had just arrived.

Ann noted the newcomers wore the pristine white Navy coats across their shoulders as Orion whimpered on the ground, still devastated by the news Arie had given him. One coat had brown cuffs, signalling a commodore, and the other, belonging to a Nereridian, having light green cuffs, which told the redhead she was in the presence of an Admiral. In the crowd of people behind the Navy, Ann saw the jovial, smiling faces of all the townspeople they had rescued from the pirates, and they happily joined along to see what had become of their oppressors.

The two men in coats approached. Ann assumed that the human one of them was the Commodore Chesterfield that Fryedai had mentioned.

"Did you do this?" The Commodore asked, pointing to Orion Vain who whimpered on the sand and rambled endlessly.

"Yeah." Ann nodded as the Commodore looked at her and raised an eyebrow. "I helped, but it was Fryedai who knocked him out. I got Atlas though."

Just as she was about to continue, the Nereridian interrupted.

"Then where is he? Atlas is worth fifty thousand Threds, and Orion here is half that. We have orders from the Sea-lord to capture all the Atlas Vain pirates for crimes of mass genocide, and this is only one of them. Where are the other three?"

"Dead." Said Ann plainly.

"Have you the proof?" Chesterfield asked, and he bent down to check Orion's chains, taking him off Arabella's hands.

"Atlas was turned to ash." Ann responded, crossing her arms. "So, no."

"What about Gillian Mayers?"

"Fell from the mast of his ship." Arie piped up, raising her finger as Polly landed behind her and barked in reply as though she had just been for a walk, although Ann did not realise that Wraiths could bark.

"Silvers Kent?"

"Crushed to death in a tunnel, we think." Said Jackson.

Commodore Chesterfield looked astounded.

"So, they're all dead apart from Orion? How... convenient."

"Yup, and now that vice-captain sing-along here knows that he'll be rather pissed." Replied Ann with a smile. "Now, could we please have our bounty money, because I really need to get going."

Commodore Chesterfield stopped in his place.

"Do I know you?" He questioned her, and she shook her head as she tried to walk away but found that Polly sat in the way.

She turned around frowning, then looked at the Commodore, his face stern.

"Nope, I don't think so. You must have me confused with someone else. I've never seen you before, so why should you recognise my face?" She rambled nervously, flicking her hair behind her ear and curling it around her finger.

"Then where are you going? Don't you want to claim the bounty? Even Navy personnel can claim them if someone above a commodore allows it, and I'm sure that the admiral here would be more than happy to help out. After all, if you've done everything you say you have, then you should be able to claim the bounty for the whole crew, despite this group being a low level one at that."

"Low level, that guy was low level?" Gawped Nelson, in surprise.

"Yes." Responded Chesterfield. "There are pirates out there far more dangerous than Atlas and Orion Vain. Killing the giants, any idiot could have done. In fact, they did the government a favour. History notes dragons were far more troublesome."

Ann gulped.

"Ann?" Jackson whispered in her ear. "What's going on, we still have a deal right, so let's go."

"Ah." Chesterfield smiled suddenly, and everybody else in Ann's group apart from Nelson looked confused. "I would wait a moment, Mister Jackson, if I were you. I know who you are. I've just remembered where I've seen your friend before. Didn't she tell you, she's a wanted pirate…"

39

Jackson was astonished. Both Fryedai and Arabella had frozen in place. Only Nelson didn't seem surprised by the revelation which had just befallen them, and all that echoed through the air was the piercing laughter of Orion Vain.

How in all the five seas did they not figure out Ann was actually a pirate? Jackson thought. There must have been plenty of clues, and the clothes were a dead giveaway for one. He could not believe he had been that stupid, and his fists clenched with rage! Atlas had held the island for a month! After all the lying, the suffering, the misdirection, Ann was actually who she said she wasn't!

"Ann Reaper, wanted for crimes of Theft, Murder, attacks on a government prison ship, and now I suppose you can add the impersonation of a Navy officer to that list. You're wanted for a measly thousand Threds, however after this mess you can be sure your bounty is going to rise." Assured Commodore Chesterfield. "Congratulations."

"What are you doing on this island? The last I heard; you were going to prison?"

"Still am." Said Ann, levelling with his eyes in a cold stare. "Although not in the way you'd expect. Are you going to arrest me?"

Both the Commodore and Admiral smirked.

"No." The Commodore replied. "You're way too low key for the likes of us, and we have plenty of work to tidy up here. We must have just missed you, but only by the skin of our teeth. We'll let one of the lower down captains have the chance to catch you."

Ann was shocked, and so was everyone else, most of all Fryedai.

"You're letting me go?" She asked, just to be sure they weren't pulling her leg.

"Think of it as a well done for doing our jobs for us, now go before we change our minds. We wanted Vain, not you."

"Ann, we need to talk -" Began Jackson as he felt his anger rising, and Nelson had to calm him down.

"Not now." Ann uttered. "Now we need to run."

Together with Polly, she grabbed Nelson and Jackson by the hand and ran towards where they had hidden The Spectre. Arie had no choice but to follow as the townspeople also stared at her menacingly. The barmaid wasn't going to be left alone on the island now her father was dead. Everybody had hated him for what he had done, and she would be ruined, if not dead when the Navy finally took their leave.

"Rockwell, I'm promoting you officially to captain. Your next assignment is to follow them, see what they are up to. I don't trust what that girl said about going to prison."

Rockwell saluted as he came up behind the Commodore.

"Thank you, sir, but I have no ship to do that with. The Inspectre was taken by the Pirates when we first arrived." He explained.

Admiral Greenbowe looked toward Fryedai, pointing at him with a webbed finger.

"I'm sure this one will be able to tell you where your ship is, captain. If that pirate takes it, we'll just send for a new one, you better hurry though."

"But sir, won't they be gone by then?" Questioned Rockwell.

The Admiral turned his attention to Fryedai.

"Not if you know where they are going, Captain. Now go, chase your prize."

The admiral turned his yellow eyes towards Orion Vain.

* * *

Jackson sat stubbornly with his arms crossed at the back of the Wraith as they flew away. They had run a little further down the beach and towards the cove before jumping on the back of Polly and he shifted uneasily as her wings flapped.

"So, when were you going to tell us?" He demanded, as they raced towards *The Spectre*'s hiding place.

Nelson raised his hand in the middle, the dividing wall between the redhead and the drunk as Arie sat at the front.

"Actually, this works out well for me, because now I have the freedom to go look for Molly!" He shouted excitedly over the wind being created by the creature.

"Shut it, Nelly! Ann lied to us from the start. How are we meant to trust someone who lied to our faces?" Snapped Jackson. "Now we have to run, and we left Tom back at Looty and Booty!"

"Tom wanted to stay." Argued Nelson. "He said he had to make sure he did a better job if anyone ever came back there looking for trouble because of the treasure."

"A fine job he did the first time too!" The drunk retorted.

Ann gave Jackson a false smile as they neared the hiding place. He was lying too, of course. She knew the drunk hadn't fully explained his wife's disappearance to Nelson, and she kept that quiet as they neared the ship. In the grey cove, *The*

Spectre lay in wait, and Arabella set Polly down to where Napoleon waited for them on the edge of the sand.

"I only lied so I could keep you all safe." Said Ann as she got off Polly and walked towards the familiar, her boots crunching against the wet golden sand.

They all followed her, all arguing different points for varied reasons as they went. Jackson and Arie felt betrayed but both of them followed the red-headed pirate still – neither of them had anywhere else to go, nowhere to belong to except with each other and with Ann. Nelson, she knew, just wanted to find his sister and looked forward to the new adventures it would bring. Ann also wanted to find the people she cared for. The friends around her had become her family in a way, Fryedai too after all they had been through together, and they began to climb aboard *The Spectre*, ready for the next unbelievable adventure to unknown shores. The sails of the ship started to billow in the wind and the breeze felt warm as it brushed against her skin.

"Why didn't you at least tell me in the tavern when we met?" Asked Arabella as Ann faced towards the sun on the prow of the ship. "I could tell you weren't like the others, and Black Ridge, come on? No pirate is insane enough to go there."

All the while, Jackson and Nelson worked to get the ship ready to depart, arguing as they went; neither of them wanted to be captured by the Navy.

"If you'd known." Explained Ann. "You would have never helped me, and we'd all be dead. Now, can we work this out later? We've got a friend to save from a fate she doesn't deserve, and only have two more days to do it in."

Obsessions? Wantings? To which road do they truly lead?

-End-

Acknowledgements

When I started to write this book, I had no idea what to write or how to even get started. So, I would like to thank all the people who have supported me along the way, through all the revisions and changes that has helped me to build this world.

When I began to think of the adventure I wanted to write – something whimsical, fun that had serious moments too - I was on holiday in 2016; it was raining at the time and everything fun to do in the hotel was closed, thanks to the weather, as I really wanted to go swimming. However, since that was not the case: I started to browse the internet for the latest chapter of the manga I was reading, One piece. The internet was slow. After a while, and since I could not find the chapter, I started to think of my own adventure I could go on, a world I could create that was just as dangerous and fantastical as the one I loved and was so desperate to read about week after week.

I knew that this world had to be made my own. I wanted it to be human in nature, exploring light and dark, good and evil. In short, this book is about friends and family coming together, despite all the odds, and finding one another so they can overcome their issues. So, I started in May of 2017, writing through university, covid lockdowns, and in between other pursuits In the end, I decided on this; and I hope you like the result.

About The Author

Born in 1997, Benjamin Rees is a former International
Swimmer with Cerebral Palsy. Having competed at two
CPISRA World Championships for England, he has won six
international medals, as well as having competed at the British
2016 Rio Paralympic Trails. After having studied at Derby
University, graduating with a BA(hons) in 2018, Ben works as
a Cover Teacher. As well as writing, he enjoys jewellery
making and working out. "On Seas of Reapers" is his first
novel, and the first in the series. You can see what he gets up
to on Instagram @ ben.rees.758

Milton Keynes UK
Ingram Content Group UK Ltd.
UKHW010710041123
431884UK00001B/65